The Mobius Door

Andrew Najberg

WICKED
HOUSE
PUBLISHING

The Mobius Door
By Andrew Najberg

Wicked House Publishing

Cover design by Christian Bentulan
Interior Formatting by Joshua Marsella

Contents

Chapter One

The Boy Who Discovered The Door

STUART

It was midafternoon in late July. Back in town, most of the kids swam in the Millwood community pool, roamed the corridors of the Pine Grove Mall, or attempted to consume the eight to twelve scoops of a medium Hayward's Ice Cream cone before it became a puddle for the ants. More so than any other time of the year, parents were content to remain in their air-conditioned offices and retail jobs. A fact poorly recognized outside the Northeast is that humidity during a New England summer easily exceeds 100%.

In the woods, a boy named Stuart sweated through his t-shirt from shoulder to shoulder and down to his shorts. He huffed and puffed, wiping his forehead with damp forearms, swapping forearm sweat for forehead sweat and vice versa, smearing dirt all over. To anyone devoted to cleanliness, his condition would be abject misery.

As Stuart was far from devoted to cleanliness, he was quite happy. He gathered fallen branches from a recent storm to add to his fort, while in the company of no fewer than three of his best imaginary friends. Other imaginary friends came and went, but these were the bedrocks with whom he played many on-going stories that made time alone more adventuresome.

So it was that this squad arrived with a bundle of sticks at what the boy thought of as The Clearing, which was really just a spot without much undergrowth. At the edge of The Clearing stood the fort that, to the boy, served as a besieged jungle outpost, a medieval keep, or a colony in the Proxima Centauri system.

Because Stuart lacked a hammer, nails, or any other relevant tools, the fort was a sorry affair, little more than branches heaped in a rectangle, though its southern side did possess a decent view of a babbling brook that housed frogs and crawfish. It took imagination to see the fort as the rampart he did. It was certainly a fixer upper, but Stuart, like most boys in summer, had plenty of time for fixing and upping.

Moreover, what mattered most to Stuart was that the fort was his and his alone. He'd ventured deep into the woods to ensure that none of the jerks from the high school could batter it down when they took stolen six packs onto the trails. No matter how much he begged, Stuart's little brother wasn't allowed more than three blocks from home, and Stuart's mom wouldn't come this deep to meet the Virgin Mary. While not a marvel of engineering, the fort was well designed to give the boy a place of his own, at least until the next big storm.

Stuart set his burden down as his imaginary friends settled into their duties. One propped his foot on a stump and surveyed the trees with camouflage binoculars, while another checked the breach of his weapon before inspecting his barrel. The third crouched down and unslung the radio pack to establish comms with HQ. Their hike from where Stuart chained his bike at the trailhead had been quiet, but the partisans could have laid their ambushes anywhere.

With the perimeter set, construction naturally fell to Stuart as the only soldier capable of manipulating physical reality. From the bundle of branches, he dragged the fattest and longest branch, one that would make a good crossbar, and raised it into place. The structure shuddered, and a couple of smaller branches clattered to the ground. An acorn fell from its little acorn hat, bounced off a rock and tumbled to a stop against the boy's foot.

His attention caught between the trunks of two voluminous pines. There stood a door. A simple door. Oak maybe. Pine? He didn't know the different kinds of wood.

He also didn't know how he'd missed the door before, though no one could say for certain that the door had actually been there before he saw it or that, despite looking every bit like a door once consciously registered, it looked like a door at all before that moment. Perhaps the door only resembled a door after it was recognized as such. Humans have never been good at identifying effects that precede their causes. In the end, who's to say how and when unexplained doors arrive?

The door so intrigued the boy that he scarcely noticed that the crossbar had slipped and clattered to the dirt. He stepped around the stick heaps towards the two intervening pines, and then skirted around them too. The soldiers ceased to be because Stuart forgot to keep imagining them. His feet no longer needed conscious instruction to carry him forward until he stood within reach of the knob. His tongue slipped from his mouth and tasted sweat from the peach fuzz below his nose.

The door stood in the wood and so did the boy, the boy staring at the door, the door doing nothing other than being a door and being shut because that's about the extent of what doors do when not being opened. If the boy pondered for a moment what lay beyond a door that seemingly opened to the forest beyond, then one might also entertain whether the door wondered what lay beyond the boy.

Then, the boy did what one would expect of a boy of middle school age confronted with an unexplained, free-standing door in the middle of the woods.

He turned the knob and opened the door.

Back in Millwood, a man named Percy Weaver pushed open the door to Collin's Old-Fashioned Cuts and waved to Collin who was giving a woman a sharp line of bangs. Officer Douglas McCorville closed and locked the cell door in the station, incarcerating a drifter he'd picked up behind the Denny's. At the Exxon on the corner of Shelley and Capra, Heather Bradley, Stuart's mother, opened the door of her vehicle, then popped the gas tank door of her hail battered Hyundai Sonata.

In each case, the door involved did what doors do in the way that doors do them.

The door in the woods opened to nothing but blackness.

Stuart's hand fell from the knob. A few birds sang their afternoon song. A squirrel leapt from a stout branch on one tree to a thin and pliant branch on another. A trio of leaves puffed off the vibrating branch and drifted groundward.

Stuart took a single step back and grunted a simple, "Huh."

He ran one hand across his forehead and down his cheek, leaving a long streak of grime.

"Huh," the boy grunted again.

As he gazed into the blackness within the frame, nothing rational or conscious passed through his thoughts. His eyes shifted like someone in REM sleep, tackling different pinpoints across the utterly smooth surface before him. It was almost impossible to process just how black the darkness was. A YouTube video had taught Stuart about artists fighting over who had made the blackest black, but they had nothing on this. Like peering into a Pacific trench, one had the sense that the depth would never end. It bears noting that this darkness never did.

Stuart certainly had no idea what to make of it. He rubbed his eyes and shook his head. He flexed one knee than the other. Unsure what to do next, the boy reached for the edge of the door to pull it shut. His hand hesitated halfway when he realized there was no knob on the inside, not even a screwed-on plate or recessed bolt. Then, he grabbed the door and swung it shut.

The door slowed right before it banged home, easing into place with the softest of clicks. While perhaps an adult might have treated the door and the darkness within with considerable alarm, Stuart's apprehensions were counterbalanced by curiosity. He felt like he'd witnessed a magic trick.

Stuart reached for the knob again, never having seen anything like that darkness. Donning his best imaginary scientist hat, he figured himself on a distant planet studying an alien artifact. He needed to gather data and observations before he could draw a meaningful hypothesis. His mind conjured up his biology teacher, and he smiled as if to say Mr. Wexler would be proud.

The boy brushed his palms on his pants to wipe off the sweat, only slightly registering that his skin was bone dry. Despite how humid the day had been, despite how much he'd sweated, every bit of moisture was gone from the exterior of his body. Even the inside of his cheeks and throat felt a bit parched. He considered jogging to his bicycle to retrieve the water bottle from the frame-mounted holster, maybe even the fig bars from the little pouch underneath the seat, but he had a different thirst to sate first.

Stuart decided to observe the door from all angles, so he

began to circle the frame, eyes running up and down the surfaces. He took in all the expected curves and swirls of wood grain, the periodic knot. It struck him that he couldn't identify seams where pieces of wood came together. Apparently, the whole frame had been carved from a single source.

A quarter into his intended circuit, he froze. He chewed his lip and knitted his eyebrows.

There was a knob on the back side of the door.

"What the hell?" Stuart asked.

Not only was there a knob, but there were hinges as well. It was indeed notable about this door that, when closed, one side was literally indistinguishable from the other. Were he truly a scientist rather than a boy pretending to be one, he might've noticed that the wood grain was itself identical on both faces. It never occurred to him to take it another step further and wonder if both sides of the door were actually the same side. He might have then considered which side of the door, were it opened, would be considered indoors or outdoors; perhaps the whole of the world was one or the other.

Nevertheless, Stuart was faced with two mutually exclusive observations; when the door was opened, there was a knob on only one side, but when it was shut there were knobs on both. In an effort to confirm the paradox, he opened the door a second time and discovered, again, that when opened the knob was only on one side.

He closed the door again and walked back to where he'd begun. There it was, saying clear as day, "*Hey, I'm a knob on this side of the door.*"

For his part, the boy summed it up in the way that only a child could.

"Neat!"

Having established through repeated experimentation this initial observation, it naturally became time to study the darkness itself. The door was fascinating, but it was not the most striking phenomenon present.

Something primal guided his hand back to the knob.

HEATHER

Heather Bradley pulled her car into the driveway, reached up and pressed the button on the garage door opener clipped to the visor. On the stereo, almost too low to distinguish, played Screamin' Jay Hawkins, "I Put a Spell on You." What was the DJ thinking playing such a garish song? She turned the stereo off as she watched her garage door trundle up its rails.

Heather pulled forward between the family bikes and shelving buried in overflowing boxes. An unfurled child's party favor dangled limply over the edge of a cobwebbed bag of pointed hats and Skylander napkins. The floor to ceiling collection in the Bradley garage might imply that Heather was a hoarder, but she would rebut that she didn't hoard; she simply held on. After all, the rest of the house was near spotless.

She put the car into park, turned off the AC, and killed the engine. When she exited the vehicle, she didn't notice the spot in the bike tangle where her oldest son's black mountain bike with the lightning bolt reflectors should have been. If anything, a tiny part of her mind buzzed that there might be a little more space to hold on to something else.

She smoothed her palms on the pleats of her skirt and flexed her fingers before she slipped the keys into her purse and entered the "mud room," a three-foot nook at the back of the kitchen where the door resided along with a bristly brown mat and a line of shoes. Like the missing bike, she also failed to register that the shoe-line should have hosted an additional pair by this hour, less than an hour before the family's official dinner time.

She set her work shoes beside her casual sneakers and hung her purse on the back of a chair at the kitchen table. She removed her earrings and adjusted the cuffs of her blouse before unclasping a thin-banded watch with a silver face and set the adornments in a China bowl on the counter. Her steps carried her to the foyer and the base of the stairs where she rested her hand on the banister post and called up the stairs, "Stu! Mica!"

Now, were her home in proper order, the thumping of two pairs of feet should have followed. Two doors should have shut at approximately the same time, and then both of her children should have broken into view.

This afternoon only one pair of feet hit the floor. Only one door shut. Only one face, the face of her younger son Mica, appeared past the edge of the second story hall at the stair top.

Heather's smile slipped at the edges but didn't fade completely. She hadn't reached a threshold of serious concern. Stuart was occasionally out biking upon her return. The conditions for alarm had not yet been met. However, the combination of absences, the bike, the shoes, and the boy, nettled a little spot of her thoughts.

Perhaps this is why the next words she spoke towards the face tilted down the stairs were "Heeeello dear, where is your brother?"

STUART

The boy, the brother in question, Stuart his given name, pondered a question of a different sort. With the door open, he found himself unable to walk in a circle around it. His feet would move. The gyroscopic feedback system of his inner ears told him he was moving, but the door seemed fixed in place and the landscape around it didn't move with him. It felt more like the distance he travelled was distance travelled from himself, and his head started to swim and buzz like it was full of drowning bees.

Normally, he would sooner pull a muscle than give up on a physical task, but this was light years different, and all he had wanted was to see how the hinges worked on the far side when the door was already open.

Stopping brought instant relief so complete that he entirely forgot what had bothered him and resumed his gaze into the blackness. From the boy's perspective, it looked both as thin as surface tension, and as endless as the space between the dimmest stars.

It occurred to him that maybe he'd discovered something important. For the second time, he considered returning to his bicycle, but this time to ride home and call someone. NASA maybe, or the President. Did they even have phone numbers? Maybe he should call his science teacher or the police chief? Of all the people he could think of, they seemed most likely to have the heft to get ahold of NASA or the President. He even considered telling his parents.

In fact, the thought of the boy's parents almost caused him to throw the door shut and run from the woods. If he left that instant, he would definitely make it back for dinner and avoid the grounding that would result from tardiness. Had the boy closed the door, it would be conceivable that nothing further would have come of it. The boy may not have returned, or the door might not have been there if he did. Perhaps left with no one to establish its door-ness, the door would cease being a door. Perhaps this story would simply be told: a boy found a mysterious door in the woods. He opened it and found darkness, so he shut it, told no one, and lived an uneventful life until he passed in his sleep of old age.

Unfortunately for Stuart, human beings are peculiar in that

what is definite doesn't always seem as likely as what is possible. Poor people shell out scrounged cash for lotteries to possibly pay all their bills rather than definitely pay some of them. Workers the world over procrastinate paid projects because they can probably finish them in less than the designated time. A couple in our very own Millwood devoted all their extra resources into building a 2,000 square foot underground shelter because of maybe nukes, meteors, or super volcanos. To the mind of this particular boy, even if he stayed a few more minutes, he could probably hustle back in time.

This boy did not die in his sleep of old age.

Dinner approached. The door examination needed to accelerate to experimentation.

Stuart bent over at the waist and looked about his feet until he found a nice, palm sized rock. He tossed the rock in the air about six inches, the quartz trapped within it catching the light, and he caught it with the same hand that tossed it. That arm then cocked back and snapped forward. The rock departed from the boy's palm. No overcoming oppositional force acted on it to divert its path. One could assert that this was the last moment that the laws of physics could be said to truly apply to the universe.

The rock disappeared into the darkness without the slightest disturbance to its surface.

The boy listened and did not hear the stone crash into the bushes on the far side.

For just a moment, nothing seemed to happen at all as the result of the rock missile.

For just a moment.

MICA

For just a moment, Mica stared down the steps at his mother, his mother up the steps at her son. Picture this moment in time slowing down: the infinitesimal flux of muscle fibers in Heather Bradley's hand on the head of the banister post, the quiver at the corners of Mica's lips as his mouth prepared to articulate something. The little boy's honest answer would be harmless, given that dinner was not yet set and thus laying no fault on his brother. However, it still felt like tattling.

Picture a single pore on Mica's neck widening and closing, working like a gasping bellows. The skin stretched and contracted. To a microbe, it would resemble Charybdis, pulsing, swallowing, until a bead of liquid, salt, grease, and innumerable toxins in miniscule quantities bulged from the gap. Then picture a thousand pores doing so in concert all over this little brother's body. It's been postulated that the rancidness of human sweat is a vestigial, primitive defense mechanism in which fear caused us to stink like we were diseased.

Mica feared his mother's wrath, so he squeaked, "Is Stuart going to get into trouble?"

Heather gave her little boy her best sympathetic smile and climbed the steps. She sat on the top stair and patted the runner beside her. Mica swallowed and took a seat. Of course, any child with a sibling knows he was about to be invited to betray his brother. Doing so would score mommy points that would be forgotten the moment he made a mistake himself and cost him brother points that would take weeks to rebuild. However, outside exceptional circumstances, mommy points maintained a superior exchange rate. It was chocolate cake with sprinkles to vanilla ice cream.

"Well, that depends, honey," Heather said, "if he's late. But, if he told you where he went, we can pick him up in time."

It was tempting reasoning, a well-laid mommy-trap. It was like being asked to admit he'd been lying about having homework. She would tell him if he came clean, he wouldn't get to watch TV but would still get dessert, and that he'd get neither if she searched his bookbag and room. For the latter, there was always the chance he'd get away with it—just like it was possible that Stuart could still get home on time. If they went and found him, he'd be in trouble regardless.

Heather rested a hand on Mica's shoulder.

"If you know where your brother is," she said, "you need to tell me."

Mica nodded. Things had escalated. It was lie or fess up—and he'd be on the hook if Stuart ratted him out to lessen his own punishment. All it would take was for Stuart to plead, 'but I told Mica to tell you where I was'—and the shackles of a grounding would clamp down.

Mica took a long breath.

"He rode his bike to the woods."

Heather Bradley, for her part, rolled her eyes.

"Christ on a school bus," she said. "One of these days he's going to break an ankle in those woods, and I'm sure as Spring rain that he forgot his watch. You get yourself ready. I'm going to put together the lasagna, then we'll go pick his little butt up."

STUART

The boy had, of course, forgotten his watch; not at home, but that thing on his wrist might have been built by aliens for angels for all the awareness he held towards it.

His eyes fixated on where the rock had vanished.

The stillness of the moment, the same moment his brother sold him out, was so brief that Stuart's heart managed no more than a single *lub-*...

Then, at the exact spot where the rock vanished into the darkness, the tiniest, circular ripple spread. No more than a couple millimeters high, the ring swept across the surface in a flash until one of its edges reached the frame. With the instant of contact with the wood, the whole ring ceased moving. At this point, '*...-dub.*'

Darkness poured from the door like sand from a bucket with a hole in the side. The stream began exactly as wide in diameter as the rock, and the darkness struck the ground and accumulated—not quite like sand or liquid, but growing in volume. The base of the pile rose over exposed roots, swallowed leaves and other debris. The bore widened to the width of a softball.

All this while the boy was doing something that, given the uncertainty of whether it was possible to close the door at this point, was quite understandable; he was backing away. However, with most of his attention fixed on the door and the darkness, he failed to notice the crook between stones into which his foot slipped, causing the subsequent fracture of his ankle.

Were the boy much older and accustomed to pain, his situation might not have become definitively catastrophic. Adrenaline and determination may have propelled him as he crawled over tree trunks and around rocks even as he vomited and wept from agony.

The boy, however, dealt with his pain in a young boy's manner—he grabbed hold of his leg and screamed. His eyes clenched tight against tears and his ankle throbbed far worse than anything he'd ever felt. The world had become white pulsing light.

When he did finally get hold of the pain, the darkness was pouring into the world with increasing rapidity as if under great pressure, the way a bore in an earthen dam widens as the torrent sluices through. It was nearly upon the boy when his eyes reopened, already barreling over him when his vision cleared enough to register the wall of darkness. The word "Mommy" died on his lips.

For a moment, he saw his imaginary friends standing in a semicircle behind him. They reached out, their non-existent hands offering the last reassurance the boy would ever receive. Then, their faces thinned and withered. Their lips peeled back from their teeth, and their eyes sunk into their skulls. Their flesh shriveled and blotched, rolling back like burning parchment.

Instinct took control of the boy's body, and he lurched to his feet to turn and run. This was not the right thing to do. His ankle broke further, and, with a shriek, the boy pitched over like he'd been flung. His temple struck a pointy rock, and the boy left this world before the darkness embraced him.

Now, in the moments after his death, as the darkness engulfed the boy's body, something living within the darkness, something right at that expanding edge, something desperate to move as far from the door as it could, entered the boy's body through the heel just as the darkness rolled over the still foot.

The boy's body twitched. First in the extremities, and then the deeper muscles as its new driver learned to fire the necessary synapses. A hand lifted from the ground and opened and closed. Toes curled as far as almost outgrown shoes allowed. The new entrant into his physiology detected the damage to the ankle, multiple fractures, and surged the body's energy to repair. Bone mended and re-knitting capillaries pulled the bruise straight from the tissue. Swollen sinew shrank to normality, and the joint flexed as it should.

The heartbeat, then again, falling into rhythm.

The body sat up within the still growing darkness. Its eyes opened. Unlike the being who had steered the vessel before, The Visitor could see in the darkness, though what It saw exceeds the boundaries of our language; it wasn't until It rose the body to its feet and pulled itself free from the darkness and into the light that the blindness struck.

Thankfully for The Visitor, this blindness was being overwhelmed by new input; It had never known the world's light, but the vessel's biology was designed to process the data. Vision began as a dazzling color blur that sharpened into shapes. Shapes reconciled into foreign forms, but the information stored in the cerebral synapses of the host provided understanding. Trees. Rocks. Fallen branches. Leaves. The Fort. Somewhere fairly nearby stood a location the vessel's prior occupant had termed "home," a location categorized as important and safe.

Home would not be safe from the darkness entering the world, home would be a shelter from which it could search for the one who promised Sanctuary. Strange that The Promiser hadn't been waiting at the door for Its arrival, that it had been this boy who opened the door instead. Had something gone wrong? Had the offer been misunderstood?

The Visitor left the door and the darkness, any destination that could be described as "away" good enough for the moment. It had not gone far before It paused a moment to collect a sample of the sounds of the forest; chirping birds, trunks creaking in the wind, water trickling. The body's new owner was momentarily happy. It was free and moving through a whole world of new life and places to learn.

Chapter Two
Another Roadside Incident

PERCY

Percy Weaver was concerned with getting home. It was later in the afternoon than he'd planned, the haircut a luxury. He appreciated feeling good about his appearance at work, but otherwise, he was single with no prospects, something he didn't foresee changing in the near future, not as long as his mother still occupied the extra bedroom.

Now, it's also fair to note that Percy wasn't a momma's boy, though she nagged and overbore. Her dialysis left her struggling too much to stay on her own. He'd welcomed the opportunity to help, but as her medical bills grew, he doubted that she'd be self-sufficient again. Each bout of low blood pressure, every round of nausea, and every evening when he heard her kicking her legs around on the mattress seemed another nail in his own coffin. He felt like his house no longer belonged to him, and he felt like his life had ended.

That day, the day The Boy Discovered the Door, was a low blood pressure day, and he'd gotten the haircut because he could, because it stated that he was himself and that he could care for himself as he wanted. Unfortunately, that also brought on the guilt. Before he left Colin's, he lingered at the register when Colin asked, "How's your ma?"

Percy had sighed, fought the urge to run his hands through his fresh cut with the fancy barbershop product in it.

"Cranky as always," Percy said, handing over his card. Then added, "Crankier than ever."

"When my gran went through dialysis..." Colin started.

Percy finished, "...she'd say she was so weak even her blankets felt like they'd crush her."

"I know, I know," Colin said, inserting Percy's card into the dongle. "I've told you before. I ever tell you how she passed?"

Percy frowned. "Don't think that you did."

"Sepsis," Colin said. "They tell you to call if you spike a temp. Apparently, she spiked a good one. She wrote a letter to my dad at the kitchen table, opened all her windows, and then lay on her couch until she died."

"Jesus," Percy said.

Colin tapped on the store tablet to print Percy's receipt.

"She wanted the dialysis to end while she still had an estate to pass on," he said. "Guess she saw her chance and took it."

"You saying I should make the best of it 'cause she can go any time?"

"Nah," Colin laughed, tearing the receipt off the printer and extending it towards Percy. "Kill her first chance you get."

Percy chuckled as he took the receipt.

"Right-e-o, I'll get right on that."

Percy slipped his card and the receipt into his wallet. He paused at the door to look in the full-length mirror standing by the rack of hair products. He felt good about the cut. It had been too long. Colin always got it right.

"Thanks again," Percy said. "I'll be back much sooner next time."

"If I see you before Christmas," Colin said, heading back to the main floor to sweep up the cut hair, "pretty sure it's the apocalypse."

The little bell over the door rang as Percy left. The middle-aged teacher felt addled by the conversation. They'd been joking of course—but sometimes the idea of getting his life back felt like a joke. He hated that for a moment he wished she would contract sepsis or some infection and bow out, the same way he hated the impulsive flashes he would occasionally get of jerking the wheel and colliding with a bridge abutment or jumping a guardrail into a ravine at top speed. Neither was realistic within the operating constraints of his rationality, but sometimes he got so depressed they seemed the highlight of his day.

Today, the highlight of his day was without a doubt his haircut.

DOUG

Back in Millwood, Officer McCorville wrapped up the last of the paperwork concerning the day's affairs: the standard complaints between bickering neighbors about barking dogs, trespassing kids, minor vandalisms. Melanie Brightwater heard voices from her microwave again, and Sutton Wilks reported someone trying to break into his fallout shelter. Of course, Sutton called at least once a week; once again, he'd just spooked himself.

On a typical day at this hour, Connor would saunter over from the dispatch station and lend a hand with the rote part of the forms, but he'd called out with the flu. Out back, Windham washed the patrol cars with the kid serving community service for vandalizing gas station dumpsters. Windham and Doug shared a mutual dislike for each other, so during their shared shifts they generally shared the same space as little as possible, leaving Doug alone in the station.

Well, he wasn't exactly alone.

The stationhouse only had four cells, and three were empty. The fourth still held the drifter who'd said nothing that wasn't nonsense through his whole booking, not even giving his name —off putting to say the least. Chief Holler preferred a straight-forward catch and release policy with straight-forward vagrants. Normally, they sought a warm bed and meal for the night, especially when severe storms were forecast. Many of them had interesting stories. They'd cooperate, be sent on their way in the morning, and everyone at the station would feel like they'd done a good deed.

This fella, this one needed a psyche evaluation.

However, he was the last order of business before Doug drove home where a husky, a six pack of beer, and an evening of streaming shows with his girlfriend awaited.

Thinking of the latter, he pulled out his phone and punched up Sharon's number. She answered on the third ring.

"Hey babe, what's up?" she said.

"Wrapping up things at the station," Doug said, "You want me to pick up anything for tonight?"

"Yeah, about that," Sharon said. "Cindy called in. I've gotta cover her shift. I was just about to text you."

"Well shit," Doug said. "Here I thought you'd finally get to see how the show ends."

"Not in tonight's cards," Sharon said. "We'll get to it."

"She's called out a lot lately," Doug said.

There was the tiniest of pauses. Sometimes Doug wondered if Sharon forgot what he did for a living.

"Yeah," Sharon said. "I'm a bit worried about her. Been telling her to see a doctor."

"Sam needs to hire someone else so you're not the only one picking up the slack."

"Well, you know how it is, small town, small profit, pinch every penny. Listen babe," she said. "I gotta finish getting ready. Don't wait up."

With that, she hung up. Of course, Doug was pretty sure she was sleeping with Sam, the owner of the restaurant where she waited tables. She'd been "covering a lot of shifts" for Cindy in the evenings lately, and there'd been several times where Doug had seen Cindy's car in the lot during first shift while on patrol. It was possible that Cindy worked a lot of doubles, but things like the little hesitation from Sharon rankled Doug's suspicions.

At the same time, things were otherwise good between them, so he hesitated to call her out. If he were wrong, it could well end their relationship. He'd been both wrong and right before with past girlfriends. Each case had in common that digging and it never turned out well.

Regardless, now he was just headed home to a husky, TV, and beer. Still not a total loss of the evening.

Doug rose from his desk, adjusted his belt, and lumbered towards the back hallway.

HEATHER

Heather slammed the car door as she stepped out onto the roadside at the entrance to Coney Park, her vehicle blocking half the lane. Even with the lasagna assembled in the fridge, it would take ten minutes to pre-heat the oven, forty-five minutes to bake, and the drive to the park was six minutes in either direction. A guaranteed delay of over an hour.

Now, baths wouldn't happen on time, and bedtime would happen god knows when. Everyone would be tired and cranky the following day, and Heather hated when everyone was tired and cranky, especially when it was preventable. Motherhood meant preventative measures. These occasions made her wish she'd gotten Stuart a cell phone. It didn't need a touch screen or games or anything, just the ability to make phone calls. But no, Will had insisted that a boy needed nothing more than a watch, that boys had grown up like that for millennia without dying.

Heather was pretty sure that quite a significant percentage of them used to die from kidnappings, animals, and getting lost, but Will was the type of person who would want a statistic to prove it.

So, Stuart had no phone, and Heather had no way to ask him precisely where in the woods he wanted his butt reddened.

Fortunately, she knew where to begin her search. There were a couple trails Will had shown Stu on their mountain bikes, a couple of which were the same trails he and Heather had hiked when they were dating. Heather had really hoped it would be one of those and experienced considerable relief when she spotted the black handlebars just inside the edge of the woods. At least he hadn't left the bike right on the roadside like he did half the time. That was how bikes got stolen.

She leaned toward the rear car window and told Mica, "You stay right here."

Mica closed his Sonic the Hedgehog comic and nodded glumly. She couldn't help feeling a little guilty herself; Mica hadn't done anything wrong and now she was in a pissy mood. She'd been a bit brusque with him while throwing themselves out the door to come here. On the other hand, any unpleasantness was clearly Stuart's fault at the core, something she'd made sure Mica understood full well on the drive.

Heather stepped up to the trailhead, cupped her hands over her mouth and bellowed: "Stuart Bradley, you get your ass back here or I'm going to turn it red as a lobster!"

The trail mouth yawned up and over the ridge into the

depths of the park, with a mix of pine and white birch staggered across the slopes. The shrubbery, dense on the roadside, thinned on the rises across which Heather's eyes darted. The sun wasn't on the verge of setting, but it had sunk low enough for the shadows to stretch like streaked charcoal. God help the boy if she had to venture into the forest to find him. She wasn't sweating yet, but she also despised unplanned and unnecessary sweating. Such a thing led to nighttime showers, showers at hours when adults shouldn't have wet hair.

"Stuart Dexter Bradley," Heather shouted. This time though, threat left her voice. She noted in her own timber a discomfort she hadn't realized she was feeling. Stuart had been late before; she didn't have any real reason to worry, but she perspired, not from the heat, but a cold and clammy sweat. The feeling was similar to the time she'd been sorting through receipts, stood, and stalked towards Stuart's room. She'd been very pregnant at the time with Mica and had avoided any sort of exertion, but something had compelled her to move at a near run. She'd found him in his room with a bottle of Liquid Plumber he'd somehow gotten from under the master bathroom sink. There's no telling how things would have progressed from there, but the point was she'd gotten there in time to prevent whatever would have happened next.

As a result, a note of panic lilted her next call into a question: "Stu?"

The forest took on a life of its own. The shadows seemed to stretch and lengthen faster than dusk would cause. Branches creaked and groaned in the hot wind. The rustle of squirrels in branches overhead struck Heather like they were fleeing rather than gamboling. A possum poked its head from the crook between a fork of roots, its eyes shining red as they caught the light. She half expected a menagerie of animals to bolt over the ridge running in terror from—

Over that very ridge, a head then shoulders came into view. Heather placed a palm to the 'v' of her chest and released a long breath. One thousand worst case scenarios that had flooded her head all at once faded. To her eyes, he wasn't dead in a culvert somewhere or having his flesh stripped to the bone by a pack of ravenous, wild dogs.

Then, her jaw set as a patch of sun fell onto the boy. He was filthy from head to foot, his hair disheveled, his face streaked with mud. He would need a bath immediately; he couldn't sit at the dinner table like that. His clothes were grimy, and it looked like his shirt had ripped. He didn't just need a bath; punishment was in order too. Those clothes wouldn't wash themselves, but now Heather wouldn't be the one doing the washing for the next month.

"Stuart," she said. "Hurry up and get in the car."

The boy hesitated, looking at her with the strangest expression. His mouth neither smiled nor frowned, but stayed set in a straight line, lips pressed together in concentration. For half a moment, something softened in her heart, some inkling that something was wrong, not that he'd been bad but that something bad had happened in the woods, rankled the back of her mind.

That was when she turned towards her car.

That was when something screamed. Not with a voice, but more like a force—a shrill, stinking sound that cut into her ears like a violin through a megaphone.

Fiberglass exploded.

Her mind didn't know how to reconcile what she saw as her car lurched forward, spun ninety degrees, and then slid sideways. Her eyes didn't recognize that a Toyota Rav4 was bludgeoning her vehicle, swerving hard as it did until it too skidded sideways. Something about two vehicles careening laterally failed to trigger the rational part of her brain. When faced with something that defies our understanding of how things work, it is easy to see nothing at all.

Her eyes caught a piece of bright red, translucent plastic from a brake light spinning into the air among a blossoming cloud of ruby and diamond shrapnel.

A second crash jolted as the front left side of the Sonata struck a stump left by roadside maintenance crews, and the car's rear pivoted another ninety degrees until it came to a stop facing the opposite direction from where it began.

Burnt rubber and engine oil plugged Heather's nostrils. Steam hissed from a radiator. The ping of the door open bell. The clicks and clanks of an injured engine idling. A crow cawed and took flight.

Whole body trembling, Heather's hands raised to her cheeks.

At that moment, Heather Bradley was not Heather Bradley, though not in quite the same way the boy walking down the trail towards her was not her son. She was not at that moment a vessel, but more of a cage, what was her had sunken into some recess within like her mind had backed into a crevasse. Furthermore, what was her, deep within as it was, wasn't one her, but many. Heather Bradley Terrified. Heather Bradley Enraged. Heather Bradley in Despair. All of these Heather Bradley's born from one tiny detail. A small thing really, barely visible from her vantage but nonetheless the only thing in the whole world.

The rear driver's side window of her car was streaked with blood.

Her fingers were their own things too, trembling against her skin and lips like the legs of an electrified spider.

Her eyes flicked to the side at the piercing groan of a car door forcing open, a large and blurred shape that might have been blue pushing out of it.

"Oh my Hell," Heather thought someone said. "Didn't see it. Around the corner and didn't see it."

Did Heather Bradley's mouth open and close? She couldn't say for sure. The shape that had crawled out of the crashed Toyota sharpened into the shape of a man in an oversized blue t-shirt, a man Heather registered as Percy Weaver, one of the teachers at Millwood Middle. They'd spoken a few times at things like open houses and parent-teacher nights. He had a broad skeleton and a gangly build. Anything he wore looked like a bedsheet hung on a broomstick, and he was one of those people who could grow a moustache and nothing more on his face.

Heather squared to face him. She swallowed hard, tugged her shirt down to straighten out any possible wrinkles. She took a deep breath.

"You got your hair cut," she said.

Percy placed his hand on Heather's bicep.

"Ma'am, are you hurt?" He said. His eyes shifted over her shoulder to Heather's older son who was nearly to them on the trail. "Thank God you and your boy weren't in there. Thank all the Gods."

Her boy? Heather thought. Percy's gaze fell over her shoulder to the figure emerging from the tree line just feet behind her, but Heather's eyes fell back to her car. To the blood.

"My boy?" she said. "My boy? MY BOY!"

She bolted toward her car. Bits of broken plastic and other debris crunched under her heels, and she practically threw herself against the side of her vehicle, clawing at the rear door handle. Through the red smear on the glass, she saw her boy's head, mouth bloodied, roll from right to left then left to right. Her hand clawed at the rear door handle. The rear door handle. The rear door handle.

She was unaware of the irony, given the events of the day, of being faced with a door unable to do what doors do.

DOUG

Doug carried the detainee's dinner to the cell door. A time lapse of the cell would depict the expected small-town flotsam; drunken disorderlies and the just drunken, public urinators, drug possessors, petty vandals, shoplifters, and red-handed abusers. Most Friday nights, one would find James "Abe" Abernathy with flushed face and stagger he thought was swagger, and every month or so Phillis Reed was caught stealing paperclips or toothpicks or breath mints.

Inside the cell that day, the vagrant sat cross-legged on the cot with the cot's scratchy blue blanket still folded beside him. His hair was shaggy but not filthy, and the whole of him emitted a smell reminiscent of rancid olives. The man wore a wrinkled tan shirt above threadbare green slacks with mud-stained cuffs. His old and weather-beaten gray trencher was in the spare locker the station used for miscellany. All told, the clothes seemed out of some vintage second-hand store. They would have been more at home on some Hipster, which had piqued Doug's curiosity.

Both the report and arrest were also curious. Doug had found him sitting on the curb by the Denny's dumpster with his arms crossed over his knees. The folks who reported the incidents watched from the corner of the building, claiming that the vagrant had approached them as they exited their vehicles and started asking them 'strange' questions—things like 'How many muscles does a caterpillar have?' According to the manager, he'd been loitering about the better part of the afternoon.

When Doug approached, the man gave a smile, revealing yellowed and pitted teeth.

"Did you know that starfish don't have brains?" he'd asked. That continued through the whole arrest, though beyond the weird questions, the man had been compliant.

Now, Officer McCorville slid the plastic tray through the slot in the cell door, where it hooked on like a window tray at a drive-in restaurant. On the tray rested one Salisbury steak microwave meal with a mashed potato side, a twelve-ounce plastic cup filled two thirds of the way with a grape Kool-Aid knock-off, an orange plastic bowl containing a handful of gummy bears, a tri-folded napkin, and a plastic spork.

"You hungry, fella?"

The vagrant looked at Doug, then at the tray, and then back at Doug. The whites of the man's eyes were a little yellowed like they'd been stained by cigarette tar. He chewed his lip a moment.

"What side do all pigs sleep on?"

Doug rolled his eyes.

"This is gonna take a lot longer than necessary if you don't throw me a bone."

"What is the sum of copper divided by sulfur?"

Doug opened his mouth but held his tongue. He felt his blood pressure increase a tick. It struck him that it might be best to simply finish up the paperwork and let the guy be. More than likely he was high on something; Lord knows what homemade shit folks on the street were shoving into themselves, like that Krokodil that had freaking gasoline in it. Only a matter of time before people started shooting up melted Transformers. What happened to the days of crack and good old-fashioned meth?

"Alright, man," Doug said, "bon appetite."

The vagrant cocked his head.

"You got the time?" he asked.

Doug hesitated, then pointed to the rotary clock on the wall. It struck Doug as disconcerting that the guy had asked a normal question—it would have felt odd even if there hadn't been a clock in plain sight. However, the man looked at the clock blankly. Doug wondered if the guy knew how to read it.

"6:50," Doug said.

"6:49," the vagrant said.

Doug smiled. A statement rather than a question. Maybe there was hope yet.

"You got a name, fella?" Doug asked.

"Haven't worn one of those hats as long as I remember," the man said. "Ever seen two stems produce the same flower?"

Doug sighed and pinched the bridge of his nose.

"Right, right, right," Doug muttered. He planted his hands on his hips. "Look man, you gotta at least give me a name and where you're from if we're gonna continue this little pony show any longer."

"I think you should let me out of here," the vagrant said.

"Okay, I think that about covers it for tonight," Doug said. "You eat up now before it gets cold."

The vagrant rose off the cot. Doug took an involuntary step back from the bars.

"I think you should let me out of here," the vagrant said again.

Well, gotta give the guy credit, Doug figured, he was a pretty bold sort of nuts.

"Let's say I did do that," Doug said. "Where exactly would you go?"

"I can't tell you," the Vagrant said.

Nope. No, of course not, Doug thought. Big surprise there.

"Pretty convenient," Doug said, turning to leave.

"Decidedly inconvenient," the vagrant said. "Because it

would be easier to persuade you, but when you get yourself into the affairs of gods and monsters, you'd be surprised at the barriers that come up."

Doug paused halfway to the door.

"Gods and monsters," Doug said.

"Gods and monsters," the vagrant said with a shit-eating grin. Then, he grabbed the Salisbury steak and ripped nearly half of it off in a single bite. Chunks of meat fell from his mouth as he spoke. "You'll be much more inclined to believe me when we're inhabiting each other's bodies."

The vagrant's face twisted. His mouth bent into a grimace, but his upper lip also pulled up to bear his browned front teeth as his eyes narrowed with quivering lids. His ears twitched back as if trying to flatten against the sides of his head. His cheeks flushed, but his forehead and temples paled. His fingers clenched and his nails dug into his palms even as his wrists trembled. His shoulders went rigid as did his spine, but his neck flopped forward and then back as if the muscles had suddenly gone slack.

"Dude, what the fuck?" Doug said, taking several more steps back.

A shudder ran through the vagrant's entire frame, and his eyes rolled back in his head for a moment before suddenly dropping back into place. The man's body ceased all motion, and his face lost all expression.

Then, Doug's eyes happened to drop down the man's body and to the cell floor.

"Oh, hell no," Doug exclaimed.

Urine was dripping from the man's pants onto the battleship gray concrete. The dark stain of wetness had spread outward from the man's crotch to the knees and down the inseams. The puddle on the floor widened to the size of a dinner plate. The man took a step back and sat down hard on the edge of the cot.

Doug did exactly what one would expect Doug to do at this point of the conversation; as the puddle grew to the diameter of a hula-hoop, the deputy turned and walked back into the main station. There is no ideal way to deal with some situations. However, Doug figured it is reasonable and fair for one, even one in law enforcement, to decide that there are limits to what could and should be dealt with. A massive puddle of urine was not something Doug intended to deal with. That job went to the one who generated said puddle.

Doug swung open the cleaning closet door and retrieved a roll of paper towels. He removed the plastic lining from the wastebasket, tucked the towel roll under his arm, plucked up the bin, and returned to the holding room, wrinkling his nose at the smell. He then set the basket down outside the cell and squeezed the towel roll through the bars.

The vagrant paid no mind. Doug snapped, "Hey. Fire hydrant."

The vagrant didn't shift his gaze or move.

"I clean up around here most shifts, technically part of my job description, but when someone does something they're not supposed to, makes a mess that there was no call for makin', I figure they oughtta clean up after themselves best they can," Doug said. "I'm going to start shutting the station down for the night, and that mess damn well better be cleaned up by the time I'm ready to head out the door."

Then, the station phone rang. The station line only rang in one tone, that classic, monotonous *briiiiiing*. However, no one has lived with the same tone long without realizing that somehow some identical rings are different than others, that identical and different aren't always mutually exclusive. In this case, this *briiiiiing briiiiing* curdled Doug's stomach. Buxley would suffer an even longer wait in his kennel. In all likelihood, the television would sleep in darkness, the beers would stay undrunk in the fridge, and dinner would remain that thing that happened yesterday. McCorville's mind whispered that he could just slip out, turn off his phone, and pretend he'd not even known a call was coming in. The automated system would inform the caller to dial 911 for an emergency or leave a message for non-urgent issues. Windham would listen to it whenever he clocked out for the night. He could handle it. If not, he could call in Holler.

The deputy trotted to the reception desk.

As he lifted the receiver to his ear, the cord dangled a loop in its twists that cast a shadow like a noose to the station floor.

MICA

One time, Mica had learned that squirrels were stealing all the berries from the strawberry patch he'd planted in the backyard with his dad. Together, they'd staked a netting tent over the little bushes to keep the vermin away. The next morning, a squirrel had gotten tangled inside the mesh. It squealed and thrashed in all directions, a whirlwind of fight and flight. He thought about this as he watched his mom fight the car door. The hinges groaned but did not give. Each pull got her more worked up. her face looked ferocious in a way that he'd never seen before, and it scared him. Mom didn't look like mom, and that made the world feel wrong.

Unfortunately, when Mica tried to shout "Mom, I'm okay," a glut of blood spurted from his mouth. It was hot and sticky on his chin, and he realized that he was ruining the upholstery. Hot tears welled in his eyes, but he fought to hold them back as Mom's eyes widened. She released her death grip on the door handle. Of course, she was shocked that he looked like he'd thrown up blood, not about the damage to the upholstery. She didn't know he'd just bitten his cheek real good. It hurt and was bleeding, but he was pretty sure he was otherwise fine. He just needed to show her he was fine.

He unbuckled his seatbelt and shifted. His shoulder hurt and his head ached, but the burning on the inside of his cheek bothered him most.

"Don't move!" his mom yelled, muffled by the glass. "You're not supposed to move!"

Mica shook his head. He wanted to call out, but he was afraid there'd be more blood. He didn't want to freak his mom out more. He scooted to the rear passenger side and tested the door. It opened easily.

On the side of the road stood a skinny man in baggy, blue shirt and black slacks. He wore penny loafers with actual pennies stuck in them. Just a few feet behind him stood Stuart.

"Hey, Stu," Mica said. He slid out of the car, but before his brother had a chance to respond, his mother threw her arms around him. She hugged him hard, the way she did whenever she thought he'd just done something dangerous, which, in truth, was fairly often.

"Oh, my baby," Heather said.

Stuart cocked his head with an interested but puzzled expression. Mica felt a little guilty; he was pretty sure his mom wouldn't have treated Stuart with the same overwhelming concern. He hoped Stuart wouldn't be upset and be mean later because of it.

Nonetheless, the tears fell down his cheeks as the sudden lurch, crash, and spin surged into his mind. The way he'd only seen the car or an instant before it hit. The way he jerked to a stop so abruptly he didn't know he'd stopped for several seconds. He let out a sob and squeezed his mom tighter even though he knew it might get blood on her nice, white blouse.

She gave Mica a tight squeeze back. His heart leapt. Not only did he just plain need the hug, but the fact that she hugged him knowing it could ruin her shirt made it all that more special.

Heather drew back and smoothed the hair from first her face then Mica's.

"You're bleeding, honey," she said.

"I bit my cheek," Mica said. "Just my cheek."

"And your head," Heather said.

Mica reached up and touched his temple. The hair there was also warm and sticky. Mica remembered hitting his head on the door and things flashing white for a second while the car spun, but he hadn't realized he'd gotten a cut. All of a sudden, his head hurt significantly worse. He was a little nauseated too.

"Can we go home mom?" Mica asked.

"Not for a good bit, Mica," she said. "We need to wait for the police, and then we're going to get you to the hospital."

"What about dinner?" Mica said. "I'm hungry."

"Dinner's going to need to wait too," Heather said. She took Mica's hand and led him a couple car lengths further away from the vehicle. "I'm going to talk to the man in the blue shirt. Can you sit here on the curb with Stuart for a couple minutes?"

Mica nodded.

"Just holler if you need anything or if you feel any worse," Heather said.

Mica only kind of registered her steering Stuart over and ordering him to sit. However, when Stuart sat, the cheer left Mica. He turned to face who he thought was his brother.

"This is your fault you know," he said.

Stuart blinked but said nothing.

"We wouldn't have been out here if we didn't need to come get you again," Mica said.

"You did not need to come get me," Stuart said. His voice

was weird. It was flat and didn't change pitch at all. "I was already on my way back home."

"Not fast enough," Mica said. "We're probably both going to get grounded out of this when dad gets here."

"Grounded?" Stuart asked.

Mica wanted to smack his brother upside the head about as bad as he ever had in his life, but he knew that doing so would probably result in an ass kicking down the road.

"You bet we're gonna get grounded," Mica said. "Look at the car! Remember how dad reacted when you scratched it with your bike?"

Mica swung both arms wide, palms out towards the cars. Stuart kept his attention on Mica, and reached towards his face. Mica flinched away.

"What are you doing?" Mica said.

"You seem to be injured," Stuart said.

"No shit, Sherlock," Mica said, but he immediately flinched again, this time, ducking down a bit as if making himself a little smaller would make his mom not hear him swear. Then, he looked back at Stuart. His brother didn't seem to be concerned exactly. He looked rather the way he did while playing a hard level in a video game.

"What the hell is the matter with you?" Mica asked.

Stuart frowned. His eyes flicked to the trail and seemed to be searching throughout the trees.

"The sooner we leave here, the better," Stuart said. "Otherwise..."

Raised voices caused him to break off. Mica and Stuart simultaneously craned their heads to watch their mother cock her fist and punch the man in the blue shirt squarely in the jaw.

WINDHAM

Officer Alvin Windham directed Bryce to return the wash bucket and other gear to the supply closet. The officer smirked at the boy's mullet as he trudged down the hall. The kid was a mess really—mullet and ear holes big enough to cork, a dozen different stains on the front of his t-shirt which depicted a burning car and read "F'in Ass Clown." Alvin wouldn't pretend to understand kids. He'd pulled over a sixteen-year-old girl who was wearing vampire fangs—not the big Halloween chompers, but expensive looking canine fakes that could probably give someone a hell of a bite. His most recent ex's son openly talked about his porn habit at the dinner table.

Bryce closed the supply closet door.

"Am I done?" he asked.

"You gonna tag shit again?" Alvin asked.

Bryce shook his head twice.

"Damn straight," Alvin said. "Get your ass home."

The boy double timed it to the front door while Alvin took stock of the station. Doug had the nerve to radio that he was responding to a call when he could've just stuck his head out the back door like anyone else. Boy needed to grow a backbone, Alvin figured. So the fuck what if they didn't like each other?

That's how Officer 'D' was with Holler too and that two-timing girlfriend of his. Of course, Holler was without question the most formidable woman any of them had ever met, but Sharon was, simply put, a bad person. Alvin himself had brought it up one time he'd stopped at the bar for a burger while on duty, and she'd shrugged it off with "He knows who I am."

Unfortunately, Doug was one of those folks who could smell a heap of shit cupped in his palm and call it chocolate ice cream. Incidentally, that conversation at Sam's Bar had been the precise moment Alvin had lost all his remaining respect for Doug. Perhaps the worst part of it was that Doug was being cheated on with a man so unimaginative that he named his business after himself.

Alvin had been thinking of things he'd tell Doug the next time they shared a vehicle when he'd poked his head into the holding cell. The drifter was still there. *Hmm*, Alvin thought. He'd figured the fella would have his hot meal and be gone. Of course, it looked like a storm might be starting to gather outside, so maybe the feller was wanting to overnight.

"Hey bud," Alvin said as he approached the holding cell. He wrinkled his nose. Damn sure smelled like a bucket of piss. Of course, that wasn't so odd for the chronic homeless, especially the mentally ill ones, but it didn't make it pleasant. Alvin sympathized. His family had lived out of their car for six months when he was a kid, and there was nothing worse than waking up in the middle of the night in the back seat of a beaten-up Hyundai needing to take a shit.

The man said nothing. There were wadded up paper towels heaped in a trashcan. They were stained yellow. Had the man pissed himself in the cell? Doug had mentioned that the man was acting odd and might be high on something. His eyes weren't dilated, but they looked a little wild.

"You get your dinner yet?" Alvin asked.

The man nodded at the tray sitting on the edge of the cot. Most of the indigent folk who came through didn't waste much if any, but his tray looked more like a kid had been at it, food all shoved around so that it was hard to tell how much of it had actually been eaten.

"Good, good," Alvin said. "Never good to have an empty belly on a stormy night. You might not think it to look at me, but I've been there myself."

Again, the man nodded. Doug had said the initial call had

involved the fella talking nonsense, but may well be that he'd sobered up. Still though, Alvin felt himself wanting the man to talk a bit more. Most of the folks he met looking for a hot bite or a place to crash were pretty happy to pass the time with a little chat if they put themselves out into the public. If nothing else, the ones looking for handouts knew that people gave more freely to someone they were "connecting" with. The quiet ones were much harder to read.

"You got any family here in Millwood?" Alvin asked.

The man shook his head.

"Friends? An old girlfriend? A former auto mechanic?" Alvin asked, feeling himself growing frustrated. "I know you're not from around here. This ain't the kind of place you can be a complete stranger."

The man shrugged.

A bit of warmth spread up from Alvin's collar. The tips of his fingers wiggled slightly as he hooked his thumbs into his belt and adjusted his waist.

"Now, listen fella," he said. "I need you to tell me what you're doing here in Millwood. I don't like leaving folk locked in overnight who don't need to be locked in. I've a mind to give you a ride down to Father Morales at St. Edwin's. They run an overnight shelter there that'll offer you a bed at least, notably better than these bags of spring and straw we got here. Change of clothes too, no doubt; don't mean no offense."

The vagrant smiled tightly.

"Now those folk at the church, they're accustomed to dealing with folk with nowhere else to go, folk in hard times, in bad places, but I'm not gonna knowingly take them someone who might be a danger."

The vagrant nodded. Had he moved any part of his body but his head? What was his problem? Alvin fought the urge to adjust his collar, to wipe the beads of sweat he knew were on the back of his neck and forehead.

"Now listen here, mister," he said. "I'm trying to do you a solid, so how about you show a little cooperation?"

The man opened his mouth and pantomimed laughter, rocking his head back and shaking it a little like he couldn't believe what he was hearing.

Alvin found himself biting down on his lower lip, trying to will away the heat building in his temples. Part of him felt like he was outside himself watching the anger grow within him like a black cloud, but the rest of him harbored no doubt about the justice of it. Who the hell was this guy? Who was he to be so disrespectful? Disrespectful to someone trying to serve him. To protect him. The deputy's hand drifted along his belt to his expandable baton.

PERCY

Percy Weaver thumbed off his screen after talking to Deputy McCorville and pocketed his phone. His head felt like he'd opened his mouth and sucked in a thunderhead. Not only had the accident been disorienting, but the young teacher had never called the police to report something serious. He'd never been at fault in an accident before, never been in an accident save for a minor bumper clunker in the Market Basket parking lot.

Certainly, he'd never physically harmed someone before. The blood had scared the living bejesus out of Percy, but the boy got out of the car on his own and seemed okay. Fortunately, Percy knew Deputy McCorville from safety presentations at the school and a handful of student incidents. They were by no means friends, but that had settled his nerves a little even if he knew he was probably liable for the accident and the injury.

Now, there wasn't much to do but wait, so Percy inspected

his vehicle. The damage wasn't terrible—crushed bumper, rumpled grill, hood buckled. Steam leaked from somewhere in the engine, below the immediate surface, and the right headlight assembly had been destroyed. Maybe the car would make it home, but maybe it wouldn't. His heart sunk because his insurance carried a $1,000.00 deductible, much more than he could afford on his salary. Moreover, he shared the car with his mother, since she'd sold hers to cover her expenses without telling him. She didn't drive much, but her condition and medications left her reactive. He could hear her irritation in the back of his head already.

Fortunately, he didn't get the chance to dwell on it before Heather approached.

"Ma'am," he said.

"Heather," the mother said. "My name's Heather, Percy."

The teacher stared at her blankly as a shadow of moving branches swept across his face.

"You're going to be Stuart's teacher in the fall," Heather insisted. "We've met before, damn it."

Percy put on his best apologetic smile.

"Sorry, Heather," he said. "Not thinking straight. I've called the police. An officer is on the way."

Heather looked back over her shoulder and nodded.

"Thanks," she said. "Do you think you could kindly tell me how the fuck you drove into my car?"

Percy felt his face flush and he took a step back reflexively.

"I'm awfully sorry that all this happened," Percy said. "And I have no problem being perfectly candid about it—but I'd rather wait until the Officer is here. How about we just..."

"Yeah, you see the thing about that is you hurt my son," Heather said.

Percy held up both hands and stepped back again. He forced a smile.

"Now, now," Percy said. "Let's just take a deep breath and be grateful that it wasn't any worse."

Heather took an abrupt step forward and jabbed a pointed finger into his sternum.

"Grateful that I get to spend my evening in the hospital?" Heather said. "What if Mica has a concussion? Should I be grateful that it's going to take like a month or more to iron all this shit out with insurance and repairs?"

Percy raised his chin.

"Now ma'am," he said. "Your car was stopped in the middle of the road on a blind curve. Truth be told that was tremendously un..."

He didn't get to finish. He barely even registered Heather's fist speeding towards his face, and when it struck, he saw stars. Percy stumbled backwards and his feet went out from under him. His ass hit the dirt and grass with a thud.

"I want to be home eating my fucking lasagna," Heather growled.

"What the hell," Percy said. "You punched me?"

He rubbed his throbbing jaw. Those were bony damn knuckles; she packed a wallop.

For her part, Heather hissed sharply between her teeth and arched her back. She gripped her hand at the wrist and her whole body flexed up and down. Her breath shifted to something close to Lamaze as she tried to shake the ache from her bones.

"Christ in a helicopter," Heather said. "Your face made of bricks?"

"Bones," Percy moaned.

He pulled himself back up to his feet, wavering a little as he did so. He hadn't been punched since...9th grade? Steven Coren in the hallway on the way to the busses? What had it even been about?

Percy approached Heather. Even as she moved, he could see that her knuckle was turning red.

"You're gonna want to put ice on that," Percy said. "Or have them check it at the hospital."

"Just what I need," Heather muttered. "A second ER bill."

"You don't have to," Percy said. "It's just that a lot of people break knuckles that way."

Heather looked up at Percy. He could feel her gaze on what he already could tell was the swelling in the hollow of his cheek. Then, she sputtered out a laugh.

"God," Heather said. "I punched you in the face."

Percy was also angry at being hit, upset in other ways about it too. He wanted to glare at her, to snap how it wasn't funny. Part of him even wanted to hit her back.

Except he also heard himself laughing. The humor seemed disconnected at first, like the laughter belonged to some distant person or maybe a doll that he held close to his chest. Then, however, chuckles infected the rest of him, and he just couldn't hold on to his anger.

"Maybe it's for the best we don't put this in the report," Percy said, directing Heather to look at her children with his eyes. He didn't want her to get in trouble. Perhaps it was an unfortunate effect of being a teacher, but he just wanted to ensure the well-being of the kids, especially the one he'd played a part in injuring. "I'll say I hit my jaw in the accident and then insurance will cover the bill."

Heather nodded.

"Thank you," she said.

At that point, the police cruiser rolled around the corner and ground to a stop at the start of the debris field. Percy was kind of shocked that no other cars had come through in the last few minutes. This wasn't a busy road, but it was the fastest route between multiple point A's and B's.

The officer exited the vehicle and walked purposefully towards them, looking over the scene as he approached. He gave an appreciative whistle.

"Well, this looks like a fun night," Doug said. "Everyone here okay?"

THE VISITOR

The Visitor watched the flashing red and white lights with some fascination. This whole world was so bright, so full of all sorts of illumination. The people who lived here didn't seem to recognize what a marvel it was to be in such a presence, such fullness.

The other boy, the one who was still his mother's son, scooted against The Visitor. He didn't know the truth, of course. This species understood identity from the exterior-in, not the reverse. The Visitor had a lot to learn about how this world operated; It possessed the boy's memories, but, though they took much longer for the boy to gather them, they would take time to process. The priority was, unquestionably, to put as much distance as possible between himself and the door, but part of that involved being able to operate within this new environment. That would take understanding.

He needed to understand the constraints, and he could already tell that the understanding of the vessel he inhabited was incomplete. For example, the boy had understood that the "Police Officer" was someone to listen to, someone important, for vague, non-causal reasons based on associations like jail, guns, handcuffs, and courtrooms. Furthermore, he waivered about whose authority was higher; Police Officer or Mom. "Dad" loomed like a specter over both, though the newcomer suspected that the authority may have rested more in emotion than fact. There was a lot to learn and little time to do so.

Hopefully, a sign would come soon, but there was no telling how long it would be. The newcomer was not accustomed to inhabiting a world organized by the flow of time. That concept alone was disorienting and left him feeling blind. He hadn't known how narrow his vision would become as he approached the boundary or that linearity would impose itself upon him when he crossed. How did one make decisions without being able to see the effects? Especially when the decisions made in the next few hours would determine whether or not the coming darkness swallowed the whole of existence?

The boy who the vessel's memory said was called "Mica" tapped The Visitor on the shoulder. The Visitor, who, for the sake of expedience and discretion decided he should consider himself to be Stuart, regarded the child. The child's injuries did not appear severe; simple soft tissue damage, not as deep as the bone breaks or neural rupture Stuart had mended in himself.

"I got hit by a car today," Mica said.

"Yes," Stuart said.

"That makes my day a lot cooler than yours."

Stuart looked back at the adults. The newest arrival, the one whom Stuart's memories called "The Officer," was writing down explanations of the afternoon's events from the other two adults on a notepad. The man Stuart identified as a history teacher had fetched some additional papers from his vehicle and waited for The Officer to examine them. They all seemed quite grave about the whole thing. The procedure was most curious to observe, because the being that inhabited Stuart could hardly conceive of such matters generating concern while they in turn could scarcely conceive of the scale of matters Stuart found important. When he was still outside this reality, this reality had appeared so clear, so certain. Now that he was in it, it seemed to be anything but.

Interim 1
A Portrait Of Two Children

A year ago, the two boys fretted in the dining room. The dining room décor fit a fairly traditional aesthetic, with china cabinet and hutch, drawers that held the nicest napkins (which mom called 'The Linen') and an array of seasonal tablecloths. The walls displayed family portraits, deep blue curtains framed the window, and the always-set placemats gleamed with forks that got smaller going outward. If it was in its ideal state, in many ways, it would have been Heather's ideal room, drawn from the happiest memories of her childhood; mealtimes were family times, the one time everyone had a chance to speak.

Naturally, the condition of things had lapsed from ideal, each piece of furniture bearing its own nicks and scratches, nearly all left behind by two rambunctious boys. There, on the china cabinet by the tea service, glared the beige dint gouged by the Matchbox car Mica threw last summer. Fifty different foods hopelessly stained the cushion of the chair upon which Stuart always sat. For all the little damages, the room and everything within it had slowly become Their Family's.

Another thing that was Their Family's was the ceramic urn broken on the floor between the two boys. The Family literally soiled the floor among the shards—a mixture of ashes from William's line. Heather's kin all rested in mahogany boxes six feet under, but William brought the urn to the funeral of every family member no matter how distant and added a small scoop of their ashes. Last the boys heard, the urn contained thirty-five Bradleys.

Now, the carpet fibers did.

It's difficult to say how much time the boys stood motionless, simply staring at the ash medley. The dining room had no clock because Heather didn't want family thinking about the time at dinner, especially not the type of dinners she envisioned in the dining room. The old-fashioned kitchen clock hung far enough away that you only heard the ticking if you paid direct attention to it—and the boys fixed their attention to the ashes. As far as they were concerned, an eternity and the smallest length of time measurable passed simultaneously.

Stuart broke the silence.

"We're dead."

"Worse," Mica said. "We'll be grounded for a month."

"Dead is worse," Stuart said.

"Dead happens in an instant," Mica said. "Grounded lasts..."

"A month?" Stuart said.

Mica shrugged.

"You don't know anything," Stuart said.

"I know that you're the one who bumped into the hutch," Mica said.

Stuart's face paled a little. He looked at his feet. Unless she was running late, mom would arrive home any minute. Stuart rushed to the garage to look for an empty plastic bin or any other container that could hold the mess until a replacement urn was obtained. He'd hardly stepped into the garage when the door opened. Pure panic overtook him as instinct demanded he generate an explanation for the inevitable question of why he was in the garage.

He grabbed for the closest objects and found himself holding a baseball and a hockey stick just as the garage door lifted high enough for him to see his mom's face through the windshield. Her eyes widened for a second as she hit the brakes, startled to see a child in her path. Stuart scrambled back to the door.

The car pulled to a stop and Heather hit the button to close the garage door before exiting the vehicle with an abruptness that made her annoyance clear.

"You know better than to be standing in a parking space when I get home," she said.

Stuart stammered, feeling like he was on unstable footing, both literally and figuratively.

"I-I-I didn't realize you'd pull in," he said.

"You know what time it is," Heather said.

Stuart didn't, not exactly at least, but he knew better than to argue about that.

"So, what have you been up to?" Heather asked, pulling her briefcase off the floorboard. She took her suit jacket off the passenger seat, folded it neatly in half, and draped it over her arm.

As one might expect from a young boy who'd gotten home before his mom, there was no good, truthful answer to that question on any given day—but this day was a hundred times worse.

Which is why Stuart could not have described his utter relief when Mica came running up behind him. He didn't know if the tears in Mica's eyes were real or imagined, but his face was panicked all over.

"Mom," he said, wiping his eyes with his forearms. "I had an accident in the dining room."

Chapter Three
The Stranger Who Seeks Entrance

BARCLAY

The late afternoon air blew through the decayed roof slats of the church. An overcast crept across the sky and a waxing wind heralded the coming storm. Barclay Leonard knelt at the altar, clenching rosary beads between his hands. Simple prayers, as always. A turn in his luck. A winning scratch ticket. A week where he knew what he'd eat and how he would pay for it.

The wooden floor beneath his knees felt squishy like it always did from decades upon decades of termite infestation and rot. Various green, blue, and white funguses encrusted large swathes of the planks in a way that reminded Barclay of Monet's water lilies. The building's architecture was simple; a rectangle with a peaked roof and steeple— traditional colonial design.

Not many folks even knew the church stood there, and it wouldn't take much longer for the elements to ensure it no longer did. Its total dereliction out in the woods just outside Millwood had caused Barclay to make it more or less his permanent shelter. If it had an actual address he could put on applications, he might have called it home. Regardless, he'd slept there coming up on twelve weeks and never once had he seen a competing soul.

Plus, being able to pray in the House of God was one of the only things that could quiet his restless thoughts. Of course, he knew he was, in essence, crazy—or mentally disabled, disturbed, or whatever the most recent PC term for it was. He didn't have delusions like he could talk to dogs, or that the trees were whispering instructions, but rather, he caught himself in emotional spirals that escalated for irrational reasons. For example, he'd held a job selling concessions at a movie theater until a whole string of customers ordered Cokes even though the signs all clearly listed Pepsi products. Retrospectively, he knew it was absurd to even care, but that night, each and every mis-order had further fragmented his thoughts. He'd grown angrier and angrier, caught in cyclical thoughts that grew unhinged until he found himself yelling and flinging scoops of popcorn at the line.

The next day, he'd never felt so embarrassed in his life. It wasn't always anger—it could be depression, paranoia, even happiness or love—but one way or another it had led to him getting fired over a dozen times as well as registered as a sex offender. Now, he had a warrant out for his arrest for violating the terms of his probation when he'd abandoned the halfway house and ceased his court-mandated psychological treatment. He just couldn't drain other people that way, and the only medications that would make a difference would make him into something he wasn't sure could be considered human.

The truth was, he'd been damn near close to hanging himself or drowning himself in the Merrimack River before he found the church. He didn't know if it had a denomination or the last time it had sat a single soul in what were once its pews, but he'd found that here, if he simply never ceased praying, he could prevent intrusive thoughts.

And so, he knelt at the altar on the day that The Boy Who Discovered The Door discovered the door, and he continued to kneel as the black cloud began its expansion as The Visitor made its way to the site of the imminent car accident. Barclay prayed as Deputy McCorville took statements and insurance ID's and VIN numbers.

He only stopped praying when a shadow fell across him and something blocked the light streaming in through the church's doorless doorway.

Barclay twisted at the waist and neck. The light behind the new arrival silhouetted them, but they looked tall and wore a heavy coat despite the season. However, its edges wavered and fluctuated a bit due to the light, as though the light made it less substantial. Barclay's heart accelerated in his chest. He was already sweating because he wore his extra clothes rather than carry them, but a new, colder sweat joined what he had already perspired. He feared this stranger would take away the one place that mattered most.

The figure's voice sounded a bit gravelly, but also undeniably sonorous, with a strange lilt to it as it asked, "Am I in time for services?"

Barclay's eyebrows rose as he turned to gesture at the lack of any proper furnishings to the altar. There wasn't even a crucifix or a tabernacle. He wasn't sure how to respond. No way the man earnestly sought to attend a mass here.

"Don't think they're running a tight schedule 'round this place," he said, rising slowly to his feet. He clenched the rosary just a bit tighter in his left hand. He still couldn't make out the figure's face against the light, and something about that struck him as disquieting. If he'd been sweating in part before because of the heat, his anxiety had taken over the bellows.

"Don't think they're doing a bang-up job on the upkeep, either," the figure said. It—he— tossed a casual gesture to the few remaining fragments of pews and the holes in the floor. "Funny that a church would be in so desperate need of a carpenter."

"Best I can tell, this place isn't prolly been used for a hundred years," Barclay said. "Doubt there's been a new nail or board brought here for a decade, more 'n that."

"Then, may I ask you, what you've been doing these last weeks?" the figure said, stepping forward. Its features still didn't clarify, even though by all rights it should have. If anything, the edges of the silhouette grew even more unstable.

"Pardon me, sir?" Barclay asked. His voice trembled. The rosary beads rattled softly in his fingers.

"Man takes up residence in a church that's got no pastor, man makes that place his home," the figure said. "To my thinking that makes that man a caretaker of a house of God."

"Well, I suppose I could have..." Barclay started.

"...Could have taken care instead of treating the House of God with such contempt," the figure said, kicking a fast-food soda cup Barclay had left on its side. The cup clattered down into a pile of wrappers and crushed cans and other refuse.

"Now I fully intended..."

"Intended to clean up? Intended to better yourself? To act like a human being? Is that shit in the corner?"

Barclay's shame rose up his neck like bile. The figure strode forward, closing the distance to Barclay, raising its hand as if to deliver a backhanded strike. Barclay wailed and threw his arms up around his head.

"Please! Jesus, please," Barclay babbled. "I don't got much, and I can't do much. Please, I didn't really know, didn't think..."

The figure placed a hand on Barclay's shoulder. They loomed much, much taller than he was, he realized. They dropped to one knee and still made eye contact without looking up.

"It's okay," the figure cooed. Barclay's upper body shook with sobs. His thoughts were fragmenting, becoming a gibbering mess of apologies and humiliation. The figure placed its other hand on Barclay's other shoulder and both hands squeezed firmly but gently. The pressure seemed to create a space into which Barclay's erupting anguish became contained, constricted, and thereby reduced.

"No..." Barclay began, but the figure said, "It's okay," again and again, alternately 'shh'ing him like a parent to an upset child.

Barclay realized his accelerating heart pounded so hard his chest hurt and his vision tunneled. His breaths turned ragged and uneven.

"I can't speak for God," the figure said. "But I'm willing to give you a chance to repay your transgression."

Barclay felt tears of gratitude burst down his cheeks.

"Just tell me what I can do," Barclay said. "This place is all I have."

"I'm going to need to borrow your body," the figure said.

And then his firm but gentle grip tightened with a magnitude Barclay could never have before fathomed, in a way that took hold of the man far deeper than the physical composite of his being.

WILLIAM

William Bradley set his hand against the stacked pallets despite the fact he always ended up with splinters when he did things like that. Heat and dust stifled the loading dock, and the man in front of him, Lenny Day, the store manager, poured sweat. Sweat ran from his bald head, and his glasses had slipped down the glistening bridge of his nose. He wore a blue button-down shirt with growing pit stains. Rocking on his ankles, he fidgeted the bottom button of his shirt with his fingers.

"We'll get this sorted out," Lenny said. "Stephanie will be here in the morning; she took the delivery. I'm sure it's just an oversight in the log."

William scratched the underside of his chin.

"Why you gotta lie to me Len?" William asked. "Melissa in Nashua has her house in order. Gerry's got Manchester locked down tight. Why's Millwood gotta be my millstone?"

"I'm not lying, Will," Lenny said, his cheeks flushing. "Swear to God I'm not. Check the form; her signature's at the bottom, not mine."

William placed a hand on Lenny's shoulder and squeezed. Nothing but clavicle and scapula. The man lost a lot of weight lately. William had heard the rumors like everyone else about the man popping oxy and any other pills he could get his hands on. If he hadn't been a good manager once, Will would've had him drug tested on the spot, but that would ruin the man's record forever. Unfortunately, there wasn't room to "look the other way."

"I watched the dock cam back-up," William said. "You know the feed backs up straight to the cloud in damn near real time?"

Lenny's lower lip quivered. Loose skin under his chin wobbled. His face went pale as starlight.

"I-I-um, well, um," he sputtered. "You see...no, I don't...I don't see how that..."

William waved his hand dismissively. He glanced down towards his pocket as he did so. His phone buzzed. Third call in the last five minutes. It would have to wait.

Lenny had taken advantage of the slight pause to take a deep breath. His whole face gleamed with perspiration.

"It's Stephanie's signature," he said with a swallow. "Her delivery."

William shook his head.

"Lenny, Lenny, Lenny," William said. "Here's what's going to happen next."

The tears welled in Lenny's eyes before he'd finished the sentence. William told himself *just more sweat* because he was not about to be manipulated that way.

"You're gonna head to your office and pack your shit into a box," William said, even as Lenny lurched forward and clutched William's lapels, sobbing thickly. The sobs parsed into choking blurts of "You can't" and "Please" loud enough that William needed to raise his voice to the one he used when he had to address the front staff all at once. "And you're going to quietly carry it out to your car on your thirty-minute. You'll go 'out to eat' wherever you want. You won't come back."

William's phone started ringing again. He could feel the wet mix of Lenny's tears and sweat, maybe even some drool soaking through his shirt over his breast. It was disgusting.

William straightened the former manager forcefully and gave his shoulders a sharp shake.

"Jesus Christ, get a hold of yourself," William said. "The staff is watching."

Three of the stockers had stopped at the broad door that led from the dock to the storage hall, watching the scene through the semi-transparent flaps hung across the portal to keep some of the climate control in.

Lenny's head wobbled on his neck like a bobble head on a dashboard as he slowly looked over his shoulder and back. When he met gaze with William again, his face was snarling.

"You mother...," Lenny started, his arm swinging back to throw a haymaker.

William snapped a quick right jab that caught Lenny

between the eyes. His head snapped back then forward, his eyes coming back momentarily crossed. Dismay replaced anger and Lenny fell to his knees. His head drooped, and he buried his face in his hands.

The phone started ringing again. William cursed.

A shift in the light drew William's eyes toward the three employees who slowly trudged into the dock through the plastic curtain. Behind them, Brent Mathison, the security officer, stepped out of the surveillance room and made as if he were in a hurry to intervene.

"Bang up job," William called towards Brent as he fished his phone from his pocket. "Make more of a show of it."

Brent flushed and slowed to a normal walk.

"You know I can't even stop a shoplifter if they don't want to be stopped," Brent said.

William smiled patronizingly as he read his screen. Six calls from Heather.

"Help him find his way out," William said with a gesture to Lenny. Lenny had stopped crying and now was watching William glumly. William answered his phone and stepped out into the sun. Heather held back her upset as she explained the accident. She asked if he could stop by the house, grab everyone's rain jackets, and come meet them.

"I'm still at work, I'm afraid," William said. "Been taking care of something pretty serious."

"This is pretty serious too," his wife snapped.

William pinched the bridge of his nose.

"I know, I know," he said. "Is the car drivable?"

His wife said no and started to explain the damage. William's stomach curdled. Maybe it was the fact that he'd just fired someone or that the person he'd fired tried to hit him or that he'd hit the person he'd fired or that he'd considered that person a friend or...

"Right," William cut her off sharply. "Well, I need to head down and pick you up?"

"You don't need to sound like it's such a chore," Heather said. "I don't think that Mica's that hurt—but the officer is going to take us to the hospital to get him checked out. If you could get the car towed and meet us at the hospital..."

"Just couldn't be worse timing," William said, trying to pull the angry edge out of his voice to only marginal success.

Heather started to tell him where they were, but William told her he knew and ended the call. And he did know. Stu had mentioned the night before that he'd been wanting to build a fort out in Coney Park, and William figured he'd be taking the trail they both used to take, because it was also the most convenient to get to from home.

He slipped the phone back into his pocket and felt the afternoon warmth. A light breeze rolled through, rustling a couple plastic bags that must've missed the trash bin. It really was a terrible time to need to leave. He had a lot to wrap up here, and now it would have to wait. At best he'd be able to come back after seeing Mica at the ER, but just as likely he'd have to leave things hanging until the next day.

"You look like your cat just shit on your carpet," a woman's voice said.

William looked over. Stephanie, the stock manager, was leaning against the fender of one of the store's semis smoking a cigarette. She wore a blue, yellow and white plaid flannel, jeans, and mid-calf boots. No name tag, but she wasn't on the clock. Most likely, she'd "happened" to stop by to see if it was her or Len who'd been fired. After all, he'd filed the loss report and put her name all over it.

William shrugged.

"Job's got its down days," he said.

Stephanie offered him a cigarette, but he waved it off.

Stephanie took a drag and said, “I’m presuming I still have mine.”

William found himself irritated with her for interrupting his thoughts, just as he found himself irritated that Mica’s injuries interrupted things that he needed to get done. Sometimes he felt like people were just obstacles. There wasn’t enough time to end someone’s career on the same day as going to the ER. He wondered in passing why being a parent couldn’t have a pause button, but then he realized he’d probably hit that button all the damn time.

“You able to do Lenny’s?” William said after a moment.

Stephanie dropped her cigarette and crushed the butt under her boot heel.

“Pretty sure mine’s already harder than his,” she said.

That would do, certainly until the next day, maybe even indefinitely. William couldn’t deny that he preferred women managers. Easier to trust them to hold down the fort. Men like Lenny liked to hold their chest out and lift their chin high until they knew they were in a fight that couldn’t be won. Women didn’t stop fighting even then.

William thought of quite a few things he could tell her he was going to do or that she needed to do, but if she said she was capable, he might as well give her the chance to prove it. She could get the store in order for the night. He had to get his family in order.

HEATHER

Millwood General Hospital differed greatly from what TV shows and movies depict when they feature hospitals. No gurneys bustled down hallways. No horde of grumbling family or moaning patients filled the waiting room trying to get someone with a stethoscope to give them the time of day. No one shouted "code blue" or "stat." Millwood General was a glorified triage center. It dealt with stomach aches, sprained ankles, and teenagers with objects inserted in uncomfortable places. Otherwise, it always stood ready to transport patients to Manchester. For real emergencies, the rooftop helipad ensured that real emergency intervention stood only a short flight away.

Of course, Heather didn't see it in those terms from the passenger seat of Officer McCorville's cruiser. She and Will almost never got more than a sniffle and never saw their GP outside annual check-ups. The only reasons she'd been to the hospital her whole marriage, other than to give birth, was when a six-year-old Stuart broke his wrist at the playground by the ballfields, and when Mica caught that awful flu a couple years back. As a result, Heather associated hospitals with child crises, so dread nettled under her skin.

The unnatural quiet of her children in the backseat exacerbated that feeling. The cut inside Mica's cheek had already stopped bleeding with no other apparent injuries other than a few burgeoning bruises, but Officer McCorville had urged Heather to get him checked out for concussion. She couldn't deny that a concussion scared the bejesus out of her. She wouldn't be sleeping tonight.

Strangely, Heather found herself a little more concerned with Stuart. He had hardly spoken at all except to say he was okay, but he'd followed all her instructions without complaint. His compliance worried her more than anything. He certainly should have dragged his feet a bit. Had witnessing the accident traumatized him? Or had something else happened out in the woods that she didn't know about? What did he do out there anyway? She would have to ask when they were away from the officer. Maybe he'd be more forthcoming.

The ER around them was nearly empty as they filed in. The lobby accommodated twenty or so, but people only occupied five seats. An elderly couple dressed in their Sunday best busily filled out forms. A middle-aged man had his head clumsily wrapped in a bandage, a plastic bag of ice held against his temple. By the cluster of potted plants nearest the TV, a young woman bobbed a three-year-old on her thigh. The weather channel sported the headline "Atmospheric Anomaly Brings Sudden Storm," and one of those colorful maps showed a red and yellow storm cell coalescing over New England.

That's great, Heather thought. She pulled out her phone and texted Will a reminder to bring rain gear if he wasn't already on his way.

The kids quietly took seats near their mother. Heather crouched in front of them as she dug her tablet from her purse and held it out. Mica reached for it immediately, but Stuart only glanced at it, disinterested. Usually, the mere mention of the tablet got both kids bickering over having a turn.

"Take turns quietly," she said. "I've got to get us checked-in."

Officer McCorville tapped Heather on the shoulder. "I'm going to check on Mr. Weaver," he said. "You mind if I talk a couple minutes with your kids when I get back?"

"Not at all," Heather said. The officer sauntered out to the drop-off circle as Heather approached the nurse's station where she received a clipboard, pen, and an uncertainty about whether or not she'd brought their insurance card. Just past reception and to the left stood doors that led deeper into the hospital. They only opened on the public side with a card swipe or a button from the nurse's station.

While the nurse flipped through and monotonously explained the forms on the clipboard, indicating signature lines as she went, the doors opened and a man in a sharp black suit sauntered out. The suit itself was damn near nice enough to get married in, the type of garment at home in the closets of the big houses off Eldridge Street. William didn't even have anything that nice.

However, the newcomer certainly didn't look like someone who lived on Eldridge Street. He looked like someone the residents would've called the police about. His eyes were pink, puffy, and glazed, and his skin was blotchy and flaked. Wiry hair stuck to his sweaty forehead, and Heather could practically smell him just looking at him. A nervousness clung to every part of his demeanor from his trembling fingers to a twitch of his crow's feet.

The nurse noticed the man too. She said, "I'm sorry, can I help you?" in a tone that wasn't so much a question as a statement that actually said, "You can't be back there."

The newcomer stopped just inside the reception area. He stood stock still a moment then craned his head towards the nurse. A bubble of yellowish green snot dangled from the man's deviated septum. He reached up with his fingers and wiped it away, a thick string pulling out of his nostril. Heather felt bile rise a bit in her throat.

"But I was already back there," the man said. He gave his hand a sharp snap and something flew across the room.

"Oh God," Heather said, and she cupped a hand to her mouth as she gagged.

The man's eyes locked onto her. His hand, glistening in the dead institutional fluorescents, shifted, his index finger wagging at her. She didn't see anything slosh off towards her, but her imagination made her skin prickle like it was being spattered.

"You," the man said softly, then he shifted both his gaze and his wagging finger to her children. His eyes widened. He said again, "You."

The clipboard fell from Heather's hands and she strode over to her children. Maybe the man was just sick and addled, but

Heather couldn't be sure. She'd already let her guard down once, and look where that had left them.

The nurse stood up behind her desk with the phone to her ear.

"Sir, I'm going to have to ask you to please take a seat or step outside," she said. "I'm calling security."

The man scoffed. He cleared his throat harshly, pressed his mouth into the crook of his elbow, and spat. Heather's stomach roiled like a pot on a rolling boil. He would've been repulsive in any setting, but the fact that he stood in a hospital made it somehow vastly worse. Her hands trembled as she took two uneven steps back so that she could make sure her children couldn't make a move in that man's direction. She wished Will would arrive already or that the officer hadn't gone outside.

"Leave me and my children alone," Heather said.

The man cocked his head to the side. A yellowish fluid trickled out of his ear and onto his shoulder. Maybe it was the power of suggestion, but Heather felt certain she smelled it from where she stood. It smelled like sulfur and old pork.

"Your children?" The man said. "Have you asked them who they are?"

"Security is on its way," the nurse interjected.

The man shrugged without taking his eyes off Heather.

"Don't worry," The man said. "All things happen when it is the time for them to happen."

Then he turned and walked into the men's restroom. The exit would've been dramatic if it wasn't inevitable that he would eventually have to leave, voluntarily or not. It was almost funny. Almost.

In truth, Heather wanted to grab the kids and run out the front door. She knew she should have Mica checked out, but could that man be a real danger beyond the obvious health hazard? He didn't just repulse her, he alarmed her in a way beyond anxiety. She realized that the elderly couple had in fact left the waiting room, though the man with the injury still remained, as did the mother and child. The man with the injury sat dead-still, and the mother looked as pale as fresh snow.

A bead of sweat trickled down Heather's back, and she crouched as she turned to face her children. Stuart watched the restroom door, but otherwise seemed unphased by witnessing the encounter. Concern about her son's overall unresponsiveness itched the back of Heather's mind. In contrast, however, Mica had pulled his knees to his chest. Worry lined his face in a way that made Heather think that's what he'd look like as a teenager, maybe even a young man.

"Who was that?" Mica asked, his voice uncertain.

"I don't know," Heather said.

"I don't like him," Mica said.

"Me neither," Heather answered. Just then, the door the strange man had come through and the door to the parking lot opened simultaneously. A burly security officer with deep olive skin came from the former, and Officer McCorville entered from the latter. Relief washed over Heather. She looked at Mica and brushed his hair from his sweat damp forehead. His cheek had swelled. It needed ice. The security guard followed a gesture from the nurse and headed straight to the restroom. The officer cocked an eyebrow.

"I don't think we have to worry about him now," Heather said as McCorville sauntered up to the nurse's station and spoke quietly to the nurse.

Heather scooted closer to Stuart. He sat with both feet on the floor, hands rested in his lap, the posture of church discipline—something that struck Heather as rather remarkable, since Stuart rarely achieved that in church.

"Stuart?" she asked.

He didn't react. He maintained focus on the security guard

as he entered the restroom. The officer scratched the back of his head and then trotted towards the restroom as well.

At that point, the nurse said, “Excuse me, everyone. We’re going to go ahead and bring you back to the exam rooms.”

Everyone stood immediately, except for Stuart. Mica took a couple steps and tugged on Heather’s hand. Stuart did not avert his attention.

“Stuart,” Heather said. “Honey, we’ve got to go.”

“But I want to see what’s going to happen,” Stuart said, his voice lacking the childish petulance his words normally might’ve implied.

“Stuart Dexter Bradley,” Heather whispered, taking her son by the hand.

The boy looked at his mother, and the strangest transformation occurred. He sighed, and his features all seemed to soften and become more animate.

“Okay, mom,” he said with a groan in his voice that Heather thought sounded almost a bit forced. Then, she dismissed the thought as motion began. They would be out of the room in a moment. As far as Heather was concerned, the more doors she could put between herself and the stranger, the better.

THE VISITOR

The Visitor had exerted substantial effort to prevent his vessel from exhibiting the kind of fear It felt at the arrival of the stranger in the suit. Of course, the memories stored in Stuart’s neural network would have generated apprehension on their own by recognizing that the man’s behavior was abnormal based upon the standards of human society—but The Visitor recognized something that no one else seemed to notice.

The stranger smelled of, for lack of a better term, sour light. He bore a trace of the place from which The Visitor had fled. It had found him already, which meant The Source knew too. The Visitor had feared something like this might happen. The physics of this place proved remarkably effective as a barrier to entry, but the psyches of the beings here practically reached the boundary between dimensions. They were soft spots—at least the soft ones were—especially since they didn't even know or understand the boundaries of self well enough to guard themselves.

Not that how The Source infiltrated really mattered, the bigger question was when.

The Visitor looked at Stuart's mother, then followed her and his vessel's brother into the examination room. He recognized that this species typically did not allow their young to simply wander off—but The Visitor knew It would need to break away as soon as possible to search for the beacon that had drawn It here.

From a distance, the beacon had seemed brilliant, hope made pure. The darkness had initially seemed without exit and the fear immemorial and indefinite. Then, that glimmer. It had been like air allowed into a tomb. The Visitor had felt itself pulled towards it. Unfortunately, the light of this world had been so pervasive that upon arrival, The Visitor lost the beacon within that brilliant sea. Where had it gone? Where had it come from? The only hope was sanctuary.

The Visitor found it frustrating how slowly things seemed to happen in this world, the way they seemed so unaware that the very nature of their reality was threatened. Could they not feel it? Could they not sense the encroachment?

As the door to the examination room closed, the smell of light faded, replaced by antiseptic and ammonia and cold, recirculated air.

DOUG

Doug pressed his palm against the restroom door and found it locked. He looked back over his shoulder at the nurse. Riddled with anxiety, she backed away in slow, shuffling steps towards the door through which the other patients had left. He'd approached her, as the security guard disappeared into the restroom, to ascertain the situation. Trembling like a taut string, she'd told him, "He might be a patient, I don't know." Doug now nodded with his chin, and she immediately trotted through the automatic doors, deeper into the hospital.

Doug gave the door a second nudge, making sure to do it quietly this time. It was a painted metal door. Heavy hinges, a steel plate guarding the lock. Not an easy door to kick down.

"This is Officer McCorville with the Millwood PD. Please unlock this door immediately," Doug said, finding himself wishing he'd asked the nurse for the security guard's name. The climate control kicked off. Water ran down a pipe somewhere in the ceiling.

No response came.

Doug perspired and considered radioing for back-up. He wished he knew more. Was the man armed? He stepped forward to bring his ear closer to the door, careful not to disturb it and give away his proximity.

It struck him that if something sharp suddenly pierced the door, it would travel straight into his ear canal, through his brain, and out the other side. His bowel quivered, and he wondered fleetingly why the hell that came to mind.

Voices carried through the door, but they seemed strangely unintelligible. The door's metal should have conducted sound excellently, and the restroom would be a tiled, enclosed space that should serve as an outstanding source of resonance. It almost seemed more likely that the voice wasn't speaking a language at all rather than Doug not being able to hear the words.

Then what sounded like a muffled cry cut off as fast as it began.

Doug drew his taser, took a step back and kicked at the door, his heel striking just above the lock plate. A terrific jolt burst up his leg. The door didn't budge.

He kicked again.

And again.

His ankle would break sooner than the door or its frame.

A little short on breath, the deputy wiped his forehead with his sleeve. Just as he reached for his radio, he heard the lock click. The handle jiggled, and the door swung open slowly. The lights inside were out.

A cool gust wafted from the opening, carrying a thick, copper smell.

Doug switched his taser for his gun, slipped his flashlight from his belt and clicked it on. The Maglite threw its bold halo on the green and white wall tile.

A pinched and nervous voice escaped the restroom.

"Hello?" it said. "Can someone please turn the lights back on?"

Doug raised both flashlight and gun but furrowed his brow because the voice sounded more confused than afraid.

He edged into the doorway, pivoting so that his flashlight beam swept across the little entry hall to the closest corner. He then stepped forward into another pivot that let him sweep the main space of the lavatory.

It appeared empty.

"Hello?" the pinched voice said again. "Who's there?"

Doug jerked the flashlight beam onto the handicapped stall door. A metal walker with tennis balls on the feet for traction stood there, and the officer could see diabetic-tight knee-high argyle socks jutting up from a crumple of khaki pants over top some sort of well-shined loafer.

"Sir," Doug said. "I'm going to need to ask you to please pull up your pants and step out of the stall."

"Mind if I finish wiping my ass first?"

Doug recoiled slightly as he suddenly noted the overwhelming pungency of a particularly nasty bowel movement. Paper rustling in the stall. There was a strange charge in the air that made Doug's skin itch. After all, he'd expected to step into some kind of incident.

"It might speed things along if you turn the damn light back on," the voice said. Confusion was gone from his tone—now he just sounded irritated. Doug lowered his gun.

The toilet flushed as Doug stepped back to the entry and palmed up the switch. The lights flickered on with the brief hesitation of fluorescent tubes that would need changing before long. What the hell was going on? There was no sign that the security guard or the other man had ever been there. The restroom lacked windows, there were no closets or other doors beyond the stalls, and the vents were too small for a human being to crawl into. The room was solid plaster, not drop tile. The only way out was the one through which Doug had entered.

Doug's skin twitched and itched a bit. Especially at his wrists.

The man in the stall pulled his pants up, muttering irately the whole time.

"Sir?" Doug asked. "Did two men come in here? It sounded like there may have been an altercation."

"When?" the man said. "My plumbing don't work as fast as the building's, but no one's been in here in the time I've been."

The stall opened. The man looked at least eighty, perhaps older. He wore a navy polo over a white t-shirt. An abundance of liver-spots covered his skin, and his fingers visibly trembled as he gripped the walker's hand holds. Doug discreetly holstered his weapon.

"I used to work here, you know," he said. "Long time ago. Been so long folk have had children that grew up and went to college since. Hell, I remember in '06 when they tore out every wall in this wing to completely reinstall all these pipes. Electrical too."

"Is that right, sir?" Doug asked. "And no one came in here at all? Not just a minute before I started breaking down the door?"

The old man's eyes widened, and the walker froze mid-step. His brow furrowed, and his eyes slowly shifted to the door.

"That door?"

The deputy unconsciously scratched at his wrists. It burned just a bit under the fabric of his uniform. He was suddenly very aware that the door was still entirely intact.

"Yes," Doug said.

"That door doesn't look very broken," the old man said flatly. Doug felt himself growing increasingly self-conscious.

"It's a strong door," Doug said.

"Now, my good officer," the old man said, a sad sympathy pulling his features down, "I may be old, but I think I'd notice someone pounding on the shithouse latch, pardon my language."

The man crossed over to the sink, turned on the water, and pumped soap onto his palm. Two strips of toilet paper hung from the back of his pants.

"Um, sir," Doug said carefully, not wanting to embarrass the old man. Doug gestured with a wave of his hand.

"Oh," the man said, twisting painfully to look down at himself. "Oh my."

He said something else, but Doug's attention had shifted to his wrist. His skin was red, covered in little inflamed welts.

Bites. A flea jumped off his skin. It was there and gone so fast he barely even registered that he saw it, but his dog had brought fleas in before, so he knew full well what he'd seen. He shook his wrist and several more crawled out from his shirt cuff. Where had they come from? His wrists both itched something fierce. They were biting him all to hell. He stepped up beside the old man at the other sink and ran his arms under the tap up to the forearms.

The old man whistled at his wrists.

"Better get that looked at," the old man said. Then he chuckled. "At least you're in the right place."

"Yeah," Doug said with a nod, but he wasn't paying the old man much attention. He closed the drain on the sink and stuck his elbows into the basin to try to prevent any bugs from crawling up shoulder-wards. The officer also pumped several handfuls of antibacterial soap into the water and then re-immersed.

"Course, they might not be so kind about you bringing a load of bugs into a clean place like this," the man said. "Can't say I like it much either. I've got surgery coming, and I don't fancy those little bastards getting sewed up inside me."

Doug focused on trying to drown the "little bastards" as best he could. Where had they come from? Could the homeless man have brought them in? If so, where the hell did *he* go? Was it possible that this old man was the homeless man? If so, where was the security guard? This was crazy!

Fortunately, the water was helping his arms. About a dozen fleas already floated at the top of the soapy water.

"Best you leave here, son," the old man said. "I think they may just about beat you out with a stick. If they don't, I will."

Doug shot the man an angry look. He was an officer of the law after all, and threats were simply not appropriate.

The man held up two hands. His fingers were yellow from

a lifetime of smoking, and Doug noticed that his fingernails were puffy with that fungus that was a royal pain to get rid of.

"Figuratively speaking, of course," the man said, but his voice didn't sound earnest.

"What's your name sir?" Doug asked, raising his arms out of the sink. He unplugged the basin and shook his hands over the water before wiping them off on his shirt.

"Ostrikol," the man said with a beaming smile that showed off teeth that clearly knew chewing tobacco quite well. "Mikael Ostrikol. I was a nurse back in the days when men just weren't nurses. Retired twenty-two years ago."

"I thought you said you saw them change out the pipes in '06," Doug said.

The man's smile faltered.

"Stepping down from one's job doesn't mean you never go to the hospital," he said.

"And what you doing here now?" Doug asked.

The man reached up and pulled his lips away from his gums. Large bubble-like bulges covered his gums. One of them oozed a yellowish fluid onto his finger when he brushed it. It stretched away like melted marshmallow.

"Getting these cysts drained," Mikael said. He didn't seem to notice that one of his teeth had been bent inward by the brush of a knuckle as he'd been showing the cysts. "Rare condition."

Doug wanted to ask him again about the security guard, but there was simply nowhere the guard could've gone. Doug scanned the room again to be sure.

"Anyways, I'd better get out to see if they've called my name and you'd best look to that..." Mikael paused, licked his lips, leaving a smear of pus across his upper stubble, and finished with, "infestation."

The man took several steps towards the door and then stopped. He looked over his shoulder.

"You have a safe evening, officer," Mikael said. "I hear the weather says there's an unusual storm forming—don't quite know what we're in for tonight."

"I'll keep that in mind," Doug said, watching the man warily while also trying to squeeze the water out of the sleeves of his shirt. As the door closed, leaving Doug alone, the officer couldn't help wondering if he should've arrested or detained Mikael. Multiple witnesses had seen the security guard and the other man enter the restroom, but how could the situation be written up? Two men had vanished in a room with no unmonitored exits and left no trace. Mikael had been off-putting, but there was no clear evidence that he'd done anything wrong. Still—maybe a couple questions...

Doug trotted out of the restroom. The automatic doors that led further into the hospital were closing, perhaps behind Mikael, perhaps not. Could he have moved that fast with a walker? An older, black woman now manned the reception. Perhaps the other nurse had gone on break? Doug approached the new nurse. Her name tag read "Rachel Folton, RN."

"Excuse me, miss," Doug said. "Did an older man with a walker wearing a navy polo and khakis just come through here?"

"I don't know that I've ever seen a walker wearing clothes," the nurse said, with a bit of a smile. "But maybe if you tell me what the *man* was wearing?"

Doug shook his head, "Seriously, ma'am."

The smile dropped from her face.

"Mikail?" she said. "Yeah, I sent him back."

"Mind if I go back and talk to him?" Doug asked.

Nurse Folton shrugged.

"Not going to stop you," she said. "Can't see what about though."

Doug opened his mouth to remind her of the man and the security guard, but then he remembered that a different nurse had been sitting there.

"Also," Doug said. "What was the nurse's name who was here before?"

Nurse Folton furrowed her brow and frowned.

"What nurse? I've been on shift since seven this morning. Ready to get home too, I'll tell you."

"Maybe you went on break?" Doug said. "She was here just a few minutes ago. When the security guard went into the bathroom after the other man."

The nurse's hand crept towards the phone.

"Now, officer," she said. "Deputy, I mean. You're starting to make me a bit uncomfortable. I was sitting here when you came in. You asked where the restroom was and if anyone was in there."

Doug slammed his palm onto the reception counter.

"Goddammit," Doug said. "That's not what happened. There were several people here. A mother and two children. Heather Bradley admitting Mica Bradley. Where are they?"

The nurse picked up the phone and pushed a button. Doug couldn't hear it ringing, but he knew it was and so he heard the sound of it ringing in his head. He realized his blood pressure was really high; he could feel it in his temples. His wrists itched and burned something fierce where he'd been bitten, and he caught himself tugging at his collar when it suddenly felt about to strangle him.

"I'm going to step outside and get some air," he said.

"You do that," Nurse Folton said. "Security? Can you—"

Doug didn't bother to listen to the rest. He turned around and strode out the ER doors. Though the temperature hadn't yet dropped as the day drifted towards evening, the air felt refreshing. Immediately he felt less stifled and found that each deep breath he took felt like he was waking up. Was he losing his mind? Coming down with something? Was there some weird conspiracy at the hospital? What on earth could that conceivably be about?

He sighed. He wasn't sure it was even worth pursuing. Disappearing security guards, swapping nurses who made up their own version of events. Old men and their walkers and their pus oozing cysts. He figured he could talk to Heather Bradley since he needed to talk to her kids anyway and since she had the clearest confrontation with the man. But what had actually happened?

It was turning out to be a hell of a long day. Maybe the stressful day had just burned him out. He supposed that at least he'd had a day worth sharing with Sharon.

PERCY

When the deputy stepped out of the emergency room doors, Percy had thought he'd changed his mind and was going to force him inside. When they'd spoken just a few minutes before, Percy managed to convince Doug that he couldn't afford an ER tab alongside whatever the hell the car would cost to fix. The prospect of meeting his deductible for repairs and the increase in rates he'd surely see afterwards, terrified him. Living on a teacher's pay stretched him thin enough, and anything spare helped his mom defray her expenses. Sometimes it felt like he could never win.

It had, however, felt like a small win when his engine had turned over at the accident site, and that his car made it to the hospital with little more than a pull on the wheel from something in his suspension that would need attention eventually.

He'd put it in park, locked it, and left it behind. Then, with his phone pressed to his ear on hold with his insurance company, he trailed to the ER doors behind Doug.

Now, Percy sat at the wheel of his car impotently turning the key again and again. The vehicle had attempted to turn over a couple times, but now it had ceased the slightest gasp. *Great. Just great.*

Percy stepped out of the vehicle. A cool note had entered the wind. A towering storm cloud was forming over the hills to the Northwest in the direction of Percy's house. Multiple small flocks of birds were crossing the sky away from it. For all he knew, rain might already be coming down on his roof. Hopefully it wouldn't bring hail. He didn't need roof damage too. Either way, his mom would be fretting. She hated storms.

Especially this storm, Percy thought as he gazed at the clouds. They'd looked initially like a typical thunderhead, but had strange purple and green streaks in them that illuminated with muted lightning flashes. Didn't green mean tornados or something like that? They didn't get tornados in New England, did they? He couldn't waste any more time.

Percy pressed the phone back to his ear. Time to call a cab. Another expense to make the day even better.

LARRY

Larry Hoffer dangled his wrists over the rail of the catwalk that circled the base of the water tower basin. Behind him, a sign that once boldly read "Millwood Dept. of Public Works" had been peeling for so long that only every other letter was recognizable. Around the sign, all sorts of colorful tags and stencils announced to the forested hilltop who'd been there, which gangs had claimed it and forgotten, who hearted whom, and which folk in town gave the best hand and blow jobs. It was no longer legible, but once, over thirty-five years prior, a boy named Mark Bradshaw had carved a seven-word suicide note, "Today I'm here. Tomorrow I won't be," that no one ever read.

Beside him, Stanley Burrow sat cross-legged packing a bowl with part of a dense bud kept in an old Kodak Film cannister. His girlfriend Lindsay leaned back against the tower and puffed on her vape. Larry glanced at them and then back to the empty air. The water tower stood on a bluff overlooking the bulk of the town proper, blinded only on one side by the rising contours on which Coney Park sat at the edge. Just over those rises, unseen, the world was changing in a far more fundamental way than just an approaching thunderhead.

Larry let his eyes wander across the town. Sid's Records, the Alpine Gym, the Mobile where Ricky was always willing to slip Juuls to kids who brought twice the cash they would legally cost. As the storm swelled between the town and the descending sun, the increasing darkness triggered the sensors of streetlamps and exterior lights all across the town. The clusters made it easy to pick out the high school ball fields, the mall, the courthouse. Home. They would always be his home. Forever.

In his back pocket burned the last of his rejection letters. He wanted to tell Stan and Lindsay, but it was too embarrassing. Stan was off to Durham, Lindsay to BU—they'd done it. They'd earned their ticket out. Alone of them, Larry had let the evenings drinking beer and smoking joints out on the trails, make him take too many nights off, made it too easy to make an excuse to get out of his godforsaken house with his godforsaken bickering parents. He'd been sure Durham would take him, too. Until the letter came, he'd been able to see a future where he dormed with Stan, where life didn't shatter into something he couldn't recognize.

When Larry opened his mouth, he'd intended to say that

he'd failed to get in, or that his life was over, or that he was doomed to spend his whole fucking life living five miles from his parents, but because all the thoughts crowded in at once and paralyzed his brain, his tongue decided on its own what to spout.

"You ever feel like you didn't actually exist, but that the expectations of you did? And that over time there were enough expectations about you that they made you exist just so you can fail to live up to them?"

"Jesus Christ," Stan muttered. "You haven't even hit this shit yet."

Lindsay sputtered a laugh as she blew her vape cloud out her nose.

"For God's sake hurry up and have him hit it," she said. "Maybe it'll shut him up."

Larry flipped Lindsay the bird while wearing a good-natured smile.

"I'm serious, guys," he said, suddenly feeling like he had to defend something he hadn't even planned to say in the first place. "My folks used to talk about how I could be anything, how I could be famous or an athlete."

"As parents are wont to do," Lindsay said in a fake English accent.

Stan nodded with an exaggeratedly serious clench of his jaw.

"And then I kind of realized they stopped saying that," Larry said. "I think they stopped having dreams for me and started wishing I'd grown into someone different."

Lindsay gave a sympathetic whimper, reached out and tugged briefly on Larry's fingers. When they'd met, Larry'd harbored such a huge crush on Lindsay that even a little tug like that would've set him on fire. That had since faded, and he'd long accepted that she and Stan had selected each other as high school sweethearts. Even when they'd decided to go to different schools and Stan had admitted he didn't think they'd give long distance a shot, Larry hadn't felt a renewed interest. His path couldn't take him to Boston. Hell, it couldn't seem to get him more than twenty miles out of Millwood.

"That's heavy shit," Stan said. "Pretty sure the most my parents wish for me is that I don't knock anyone up before I'm 22 and that I don't spend life in prison."

Lindsay punched Stan on the bicep.

"You ain't knocking my ass up," she said.

"You musta failed health class if you think I can knock you up that way," Stan said. "Dunno how any of us got accepted anywhere."

Lindsay punched him again, this time harder, this time three times in rapid succession. Larry gave a small, sad smirk.

Stan finished packing the bowl and extended it to Lindsay. She pointed up at Larry. "He sounds like he should get first hit."

Just as Larry reached for the pipe, a crackle of branches snapped his attention over the railing. At the base of the ladder, nothing but the expected flotsam of crushed beer and soda cans, fast food wrappers, crumpled pieces of notebook paper—the type of litter you'd expect from a place frequented by unsupervised teens. The foliage grew up to the tower's stands on the left side, and it was there that Larry saw the figure emerge.

Even as he heard Stan muttering, "Shit, shit, shit," as he tried to decide where to stash the illegals, Larry breathed a sigh of relief.

"Not a cop," he whispered.

Indeed, the man was certainly not a cop. He was tall and wore a battered top hat, like something you'd see in a thrift store window for three years running. His long coat, which mostly hid a sweatshirt and badly frayed jeans, was equally worn. Larry immediately wondered how that outfit wasn't unbearable in the summer heat.

Stan leaned forward to peek over the catwalk's edge. As he did so, the Kodak Film can fell out of his lap, thunked onto the wooden walk, and rolled out over the edge. It clattered onto the sticks and gravel right in front of the newcomer. The man looked up.

His face startled Larry a bit. The skin was ferociously sunburned, peeling in swathes across the forehead, cheek-bones, nose and chin, with little angry blisters all over. The few patches that weren't clearly burned looked unnaturally pale, almost gray.

Lindsay slowly rose, careful not to rock the catwalk too much because its old nails liked to cry.

"That's Barclay," she said.

"Who?" Stan asked.

"Barclay," Lindsay said. "He used to come into my dad's store. Used to work for some contractor in town. He'd pick up the supplies."

"Looks like he's seen better days," Stan said.

Larry shushed them. The man Lindsay had called Barclay had already taken hold of one of the rungs of the tower ladder and was raising his foot to begin his ascent.

"Hey," Larry called, leaning over the railing. The old wood groaned. "Hey, we're hanging out up here."

The man took hold of the next rung and hoisted himself up.

"Really man," Stan said getting onto his feet. "You're not welcome up here."

Stan's warning was ineffectual. Two more rungs. Larry stepped to the top of the ladder.

"Dude, I'm not kidding," he said. "I'm not letting you up here."

The man didn't stop. In his peripheral vision, Larry saw

Lindsay take a step back along the walk, tugging Stan's shirt as she did.

"I don't like this," she whispered. "Barclay was always a bit off."

"There's three of us and one of him," Stan scoffed.

"Mister, I'm not going to say it again," Larry said.

From the top of the ladder, the man looked straight into Larry's eyes. He had very broad shoulders and serious meat to his hands. Several open sores oozed on his face like he'd swam in a toxic pond.

"I didn't say that you would," Barclay said.

Larry took a deep swallow. He could simply stomp on the man's face, he thought. Stomp hard, make him fall. What if the man broke his neck? He hadn't done anything violent toward them. Would it be considered self-defense?

"S-s-stay there," Larry stammered, backing up, practically knocking over Stan in the process. The man's hand grabbed the edge of the walk, and then both his palms hoisted the rest of his body up. An odor of rancid milk, copper, and something acidic invaded Larry's mouth, nose, and tongue. "What do you want?"

The man rose to his feet. He wore heavy boots, construction worker boots with steel toes, except that the leather had worn through in several places. The laces were broken and frayed. Larry glanced over his shoulder. Lindsay and Stan had retreated several feet back.

Thanks guys, Larry thought.

"Your help, of course," the man said.

"We don't have any money," Larry said. "We're just kids."

Stan nodded and held his pipe out.

"You can have our weed," he said. "I only have a little, but..."

The man cut him off with a severe wave of his hand and a scowl.

"I have little interest in intoxicants or money," he said. "But you'll have a seat so that we can discuss my request."

The man's voice didn't sound overtly threatening, but there was a finality to the instruction that compelled Larry to take an immediate seat. Larry'd never been a fighter or an athlete. Under the ratty clothes, the man's physique appeared imposing enough that talking their way through seemed like their best bet. After all, if Lindsay recognized him, other people in town would know him too, which would make it easy to catch him if he hurt any of them. But Larry still found himself wishing that they were on the ground where it would be easier to run.

Behind him, Larry heard Stan and Lindsay follow his lead.

The stranger smiled. It looked neither happy nor humorous. A simple acknowledgement of the compliance.

Larry asked, "Who are you?"

"I believe the young woman already told you," the man said. "I'm 'Barclay,' least that's the name that belongs to the memories in this body."

Larry wished he'd already been stoned. Then, maybe what the man just said would've made more sense.

"We've got to be home really soon," Larry said. "Our parents will be looking for us if we aren't home really soon."

"Yeah," Stan chimed in. "Mine are probably already looking for me."

"If you don't help me," the man said, "your parents and everyone else will die soon."

Larry felt his jaw drop. He tried to respond, to scoff or to mock, but his mouth just dropped again. And again, he wished he was stoned, this time because whether the guy was telling the truth or was batshit crazy, Larry sensed the conversation wouldn't turn out well.

"What do you want us to do?" Larry said, trying to keep his voice from trembling.

"There is a door," the man said. "I need to find what came through it."

Larry furrowed his brow. Behind him, Lindsay whispered something to Stan, but he didn't catch what.

"Okay, so, are we talking about the door to a house? You want us to break in somewhere? Cuz, I'm not really into that kind of shit."

Barclay's face screwed up as if he smelled something vile.

"Nothing so...pedestrian," Barclay said. "The door isn't so much a door as a rent in the fabric between dimensions and what lies between dimensions."

"Okay..." Larry drawled. He glanced over his shoulder. Stan was clearly trying to stifle laughter. Lindsay punched him sharply in the lower back, causing the boy to grunt. "Right...and you expect us to..."

Barclay sighed. A great weight settled onto his features. He reached into his coat and pulled out what looked like a bundle of black and white cloths bound with twine.

"I don't so much need you," he said, untying the bundle and separating out two smaller, black bundles and one white. Barclay looked from the bundles to Larry and his friends and then back to the bundles. Then, he rose to full height and rolled up his shoulders. *Jesus,* Larry thought. He must be almost seven feet tall and built like an NFL linebacker. "Rather, I have some friends who need your *bodies*, and well, I'm afraid there's just no means for me to give them back to you when I'm done."

Larry tried to step back, but his foot came down on Stan's foot and his ankle rolled. Larry fell sideways towards the edge of the walk and struck his temple on the railing. His vision blurred and everything went all fuzzy and muffled. He heard Lindsay and Stan both speaking in unison, frantic and frightened.

"I assure you," Larry heard Barclay's voice as it pierced

through the haze of the blow to his head. "If your species ever found out your sacrifice, gratitude would be assured."

The gibbering of his friends grew to a crescendo, building into two sharp shrieks that ceased simultaneously. Then, a shadow fell over Larry as Barclay drew close. The breath came hot and moist in Larry's ear.

"I truly am sorry," Barclay whispered. "There was a time when I could have simply called for a sacrifice and as many as I would have asked for would have proffered themselves to me of their own volition."

Larry's consciousness waned. He was fairly certain that the last thing he heard was the man who killed him singing Bob Dylan's, "The Times They Are A-Changin.'"

Chapter Four
The Daytime Twilight

THE CLOUD

The sun hadn't quite set, but a night-like darkness had fallen as the massive storm spread. What began as an odd cloud formation over a rather anonymous park had expanded until, in a few short hours, it spanned all of Southern New Hampshire. Satellite feeds broadcast breaking news reports. Twitter buzzed with speculations from Boston to Toronto to Tokyo. Reddit rattled with conspiracies. It started out as conversation among people fixated with social media, but they started calling their science buds and professors. From space, the storm looked like some sort of localized hurricane that welled from its eye. The scientific community rapidly ascertained that they were looking at some messed up shit.

No reports came from beneath the storm. Local lines beeped no service. Cell signals failed. While the local news busied themselves mobilizing, they had not begun reporting. A handful of eyewitnesses placed calls demanding action about the toxic spill, the wildfire, the I-don't-know-what-it-is-but-you'd-better-get-that-fixed, rousing Councilwoman Snyder, who then roused Chief Holler. Law enforcement in neighboring counties and towns only received a warning from the National Weather Service that a unique weather event might disrupt local infrastructure.

No one human knew what was beginning.

In the daytime twilight swelled a greater darkness. Nebulous, billowing, but too dense for fog or cloud. It roiled within itself, an unceasing, driving pressure pouring into the world. It followed the topography into crooks between slopes. But it also frothed up rises, accumulating until it rose halfway up the tree trunks. Its internal currents and the weight of its body caused drifts of leaves to compress and branches to bend and waft. Some places within its reach remained entirely unscathed by its presence, but others boiled while many froze. Some did both.

Most animals fled its approach except some of the sick, the injured, the insensible. Those, it engulfed within their burrows. They breathed it in and breathed it out, the air still containing the fundamental mix of oxygen, nitrogen, carbon dioxide, and other gases, but with a thicker quality, so that their lungs had to work harder to draw and expel. They did not die, but they fractured on a cellular, temporal level.

The air inside the dark took on a fetid quality, something stale and sour overlaid on a note of unrelenting sweetness. The animals who were entrapped in culverts and gullies by its swirling and converging reaches, fractured with terror, bolting blind through the impenetrable lightlessness until they struck themselves senseless against rocks and trees. A fawn peeled down the middle like its fur had unzipped. A rabbit charged headlong into a pond and thrashed itself drowned. A stray cat shriveled into a fetus and burst like a strawberry clenched in a fist.

And at the epicenter of all that formless dark, an epicenter whose outer ring now stretched half a mile at its furthest, stood a blood-stained rock against which an ordinary boy had fallen, and just a stone's throw from that rock stood an open door. Sound muffled, like a voice shouting into a feathered pillow ten feet thick. The only movement was a steady current outward, a constant welling in every direction away from The Source.

But that Source was not the door. The door itself was the throat of an hourglass. The Source lay beyond, still well inside but inextricably closing towards the door from the other side, towards the living world. Even now, the pressure built in a smooth curve, the growth of the cloud accelerating at pace. The door strained to withstand the escalating forces.

PERCY

Percy didn't know how long he waited for the cab. Calling an Uber would have been quicker, but he'd never trusted the concept and he'd known a couple folk who'd been ripped off. Percy paced up and down the sidewalk, passing the row of ornamental fir trees in giant concrete pots and biting his nails to the quick. Occasionally, he'd pause and simply gaze out across the parking lot. The lights were coming on as the storm thickened. The light pollution lit up the thunderhead's underbelly.

Flashes of the accident kept rushing through Percy's mind, as did images of the young boy with his mouth bloodied. Percy paused and forced himself to appreciate that he hadn't taken the lives of the two boys, or more seriously injured them. It didn't matter to him that the car was parked in the middle of the road. It wouldn't have mattered if Heather Bradley had driven head-on into him. He'd played a part in the accident; if someone had died, he didn't know if he could've lived with himself.

He kept getting so wrapped up in his thoughts that he

didn't consider how menacing the storm brewing overhead appeared. He didn't notice that the hot wind contained some oddly cold threads and a fetid tinge. He didn't even notice when the cab pulled up to the curb in front of him. The driver had rolled down the window.

"You the one who called a cab?" the driver said.

Percy snapped out of his near trance and nodded.

"Ayuh," he muttered. "That's right."

Millwood being a pretty small and—by New England standards—friendly place, the driver offered him shotgun, but Percy declined, electing instead to dump himself into the back seat like a sack of broken clocks. Percy immediately realized that his feet, despite the well-worn comfort of his battered penny loafers, hurt like the dickens. He spent a lot of time standing in his classroom, but he figured that standing around waiting for the police, waiting to know how injured the child was, waiting to get ahold of insurance, etc. was just harder standing. He closed the door, buckled his seatbelt, mumbled his address, and off they went.

The cab came to a sudden stop twenty feet later, lurching Percy forward. Percy adjusted his belt and frowned as he heard a voice outside through the still open driver's window. It repeated one word, gruffly.

"Wait! Wait!"

Percy twisted in his seat until he saw an old man in a navy polo shuffling a tarnished walker with tennis ball feet towards the cab. Exertion flushed the man's face, and he stopped his awkward clomping to wipe sweat from his brow three times. The old man gasped for breath as he blundered to a stop besides the driver's door. Sweat drenched the man's shirt down the chest and under both arms. Poor man, Percy thought, having to rush in his condition.

"Sorry...to...chase...you...down," the man panted. "Can...I... share...the...ride?"

The driver thrust a thumb to the backseat.

"Up to him," he said.

The old man looked expectantly to Percy. Percy sighed. If this were Boston, it'd be perfectly polite to say no. However, Millwood didn't have many proper cabs, and if the others were busy, the wait could be long. Percy had to figure that an older fellow like that would vastly prefer not to wait.

The words that came to Percy's mind were, "Fucking hell," but his mouth said, "Yeah, that'll be fine."

He hoped his tone hadn't crossed the line into rudeness. The driver put the vehicle in park and got out to help stow the man's walker in the trunk. Percy assumed the old man would take shotgun, but instead, he plopped heavily into the back seat as well. The man smelled a bit like mothballs, liniment, hand sanitizer, and something musty that Percy couldn't quite finger.

Immediately, he reached over to Percy and offered a handshake. Though he wasn't the biggest fan of coming into contact with folks—his mom's hypochondria had rubbed off on him a little—he shook the man's hand lightly, immediately noting the roughness of his skin. He clearly used his hands a lot. As their palms parted, Percy refrained from wincing when he saw how yellowed and damaged the man's fingernails were. Was that stuff communicable? He would need to Google it.

"Which part of town you live in?" the old man said. His voice might have been strong once, but it crackled as though something were in his throat, and his breath smelled like an open trashcan.

"Out off Exit 6," Percy said, trying to face front, away from the breath, as discreetly as possible.

"Ah, Coney Park way," the old man said. "Live near thereabouts myself."

"Yup," Percy said. He felt bad about ignoring an old man's attempts at conversation. The man was probably lonely, maybe stressed by whatever brought him to the hospital, but Percy's day had been long. He also found himself off-put by the man's unexpected intrusion into what he'd hoped would be a quiet ride home. Once he got home, he'd need to focus on tending to his mom until her nighttime meds, and by then he'd probably just pass out himself.

Besides, a bit of spittle hung at the corner of the man's lips —a rather large bead of it actually. For some reason, Percy felt that even in quick glances he could see it with extraordinary clarity and resolution. Within that bead of liquid, thin little black worms floated. It was patently impossible for him to actually see it, but the idea ingrained itself. His palm felt itchy, like those same worms were burrowing into the pads of his palm where they'd brushed against the man's callouses. Silence reigned for a moment as the cab pulled out of the parking lot.

"Looks like you've had a long day," the old man said.

"Yup," Percy said, though in his exhaustion it came out sounding more like "yuh." Then, he added, "Course, anyone getting a ride out of the hospital probably had a long day."

"That'd make sense," the old man laughed. Percy noticed that both his bicuspids were brown. Then the man said, "You aren't contagious or something? Do I need to break out the sanitizer and scour my hands?"

"Not sick, had an accident," Percy said, a bit startled that the man was concerned about touching *him*. However, he let that slide and attempted to preempt the obvious follow-up question, "and I'm not the one who was hurt."

"Better them than you," the old man said. "Am I right?"

"It was a little kid," Percy said.

The old man whistled through his teeth. A bubble of what

looked like chewing tobacco juice swelled and popped in an instant.

"Brutal," the old man said. "You didn't kill him, did you?"

"Think I'd be in jail," Percy said.

"Damn straight. You'd belong there. Accident or not, you'd have ruined a family. Hell, I'd have a mind to kill you myself. Twenty years or more back, a cousin of mine up in Bangor drove right into a kid on a big silver bicycle, broke both the kid's legs and dislocated a shoulder. Me and my brother beat him within an inch of his life and left him by the curb when he told us."

"Wow," Percy said, flat as a five-hour open soda. He wanted to press himself backwards against the door. Hell, he kind of wanted to hop out of the cab at the next intersection. Unfortunately, Percy noticed they were already getting to the edge of the town center, and by the next stoplight they'd be close enough to home that it didn't matter.

"Course, it was a different era then," the old man said, scratching his upper arm. Slivers of dead skin sloughed off under his fingernails and fell to the cab's leather. "Folks didn't think too much about family beating the bejesus out of family. Bet we could'a killed the prick and had a 50/50 chance of getting off on the grounds that he simply had it coming."

"Yeah, times have changed," Percy said, no longer wanting any part of the conversation. He just wanted to sit there and stew over whether or not he was going to get sued.

"Sure have," the old man said. "They've gotten dark and they're going to get darker."

Like this conversation, Percy's inner monologue shouted. The man may have said something else, but Percy figured rudeness be damned—the man was making him seriously uncomfortable. He focused his attention out the window. The downtown gave way to birch and spruce lined roads, mailboxes and driveways that slowed in frequency like a sound wave lowering in pitch. He found himself locked onto the way the scrub grass bristled along the crumbling edge of the asphalt, the barely visible yellow line having half crumbled away with it. Winter cold had gnawed at it slow and steady. One day, left untended, the whole road would be nothing but broken and irregular black chunks intertwined with weeds and wildflowers.

The old man made several comments during this time. He never seemed bothered that Percy didn't respond, so Percy didn't intend to start. Instead, he grew increasingly focused on the approaching site of the accident. Would there be a stopped car half on the shoulder? The glittering crystal confetti of shattered reflective brake light covers? A dread grew in Percy's stomach that there would be another car stopped in the road, maybe with a baby, and the cabby would get distracted by something messed up the old man said and...

The feeling of dread in Percy's stomach crystalized into a frigid ball.

When they got to Percy's house, the old man would see exactly where Percy lived. Sure, the man looked 80 years old and had a walker, but did he have a gun? Percy knew full well he had no capability at fighting—and that someone focused on nothing but an intent to harm was terrifyingly dangerous to even a trained fighter.

Minutes later, the cab coasted to a stop with a slight brake whine. The driver said nothing, just pointed to the meter. It struck Percy for the first time that the driver hadn't spoken the whole ride—he hadn't even asked the old man for a destination.

Oh Jesus, Percy thought as he stepped out with the cab between him and his home, and dug his wallet out. The driver rolled down his window. He prayed that he'd maybe tuned out the old man saying where he was headed.

The old man opened his door and Percy felt his whole spine go like ice.

Then the trunk popped and Percy wanted to laugh at himself. Was he really afraid of a man with a walker?

The cabby seemed in quite a hurry to get that walker out though, and he was back in the cab putting it in drive in a heartbeat. The bluster of motion was so purposeful and abrupt that it wasn't until the cab was pulling away that Percy realized he was still holding out a couple twenty-dollar bills.

For a moment, for Percy, time paused. Beyond the old man and his walker, lay Percy's home—the safety it promised. Even if the man knew where it was, doors locked. Easier to keep someone out than to defend oneself in the open. He gazed desperately up the walk that cut through a yard full of overgrown grass littered with bristly weeds, between garden beds clustered with tangled bushes, and up cracked concrete steps to the front door of a Cape Cod whose siding was more peel than paint, whose windows were clouded with muck, and whose roof sported mismatched shingles because he'd had to patch leaks, but the company that made the original shingles had gone under years ago. Percy hadn't chosen the house. He had inherited it after his father passed. Percy had met the prospect with more dread than excitement, and the only reasons he went through with it was because it was "what came next," and he thought maybe he could sell the property after fixing it up a bit.

Now, he desperately wished to set foot inside it again.

The old man hawked a terrific loogie and spat into the road gutter. In the middle of the lump of discolored phlegm that struck pavement sat a pitted tooth.

It struck Percy that the old man didn't really look so old anymore. He stood behind the walker, but he wasn't actually putting any weight on it. His skin looked not so much wrinkled but rather leathery and scarred. The cab, having made a U-turn down the road, sped past back towards town. Percy turned halfway in slow motion, or at least it felt like slow motion. He wanted to holler after the cab for it to stop, for it to take him somewhere, anywhere, away from here, away from the man who stood directly between himself and home.

He didn't know how to feel when the front door of his home opened, and his mother shuffled into the frame.

The man with the walker slowly looked over his shoulder to the porch, then craned his head back to Percy. He was smiling broad enough to show several missing teeth and black gums. The width of a cab still stood between the two men, but Percy could smell the man's fetid breath.

WILLIAM

William Bradley pulled into the hospital lot. He didn't realize he'd picked the parking spot next to Percy Weaver's vehicle, not even when he walked past it's shattered bumper and chuckled to himself about the pieces of shit people drove. One couldn't really blame William for not making the link though—he had a lot on his mind. He'd fired someone, leaving a significant gap in the infrastructure of a store for which he bore significant responsibility, and he'd been forced to leave before he'd wrapped everything up. He'd destroyed a career and made life a lot more challenging for an entire staff—and he resented that he would have to apologize for believing that was a serious priority; Heather had sent him several increasingly upset texts about how long it was taking him.

The wait for the tow truck hadn't helped. Even though he'd called for the truck before he'd even put his car into drive in the supermarket parking lot, he'd waited well over half an hour on the roadside. According to the driver, people's batteries had been dying all across town, occupying every roadside service vehicle in town. The driver chocked it up to some strange electrical phenomenon caused by the storm, but also admitted he was talking out his ass.

The storm, too, was distracting—the blackish green clouds had brought an early twilight and carried a smell of ozone and something both vaguely burnt and with a trace of something that reminded William of dry rot. A rough night was ahead for anyone not hunkered down under their roofs when that storm unleashed, William figured. The animals seemed freaked out too, which actually left William feeling a bit alarmed. He'd stood by his vehicle as they streamed out of the forest in droves —squirrels, rabbits, mice, rats, chattering as they crossed asphalt as though on a mission. William had been unable to avoid running over a possum when he'd started towards the hospital.

He felt bad about that too.

Finally, at his core, he was worried all to hell about Mica. He knew he came across as callous—sometimes he even was callous in the way he chose his priorities—but he'd known from Heather that Mica's injuries appeared minor. A short delay wouldn't be the end of the world, but William didn't want to delay longer than needed.

So, now, crossing the hospital lot, he only spared a quick unknowing glance at the vehicle that had come quite close to killing his youngest boy. He worried that the evening had turned into one more stressful thing to deal with—doctors, nurses, financial paperwork. He'd need to call Helen, who ran accounts payable. She knew Victor, the CFO of William's market chain. They'd be able to work out a deal. William would surely have to set up a dinner with Victor and his husband. They'd want to bring the dogs.

William sighed. Would a nice, easy evening have been too much to ask for?

DOUG

Even discounting the events of the day, Doug found hospitals awkward. His job often brought him inside, but as neither patient nor caregiver. He'd never received training beyond basic first aid, never been injured in the line of duty, nor had he ever undergone any significant procedure. When he was six, he'd been taken to the hospital for a sprained shoulder, but his only memories were things they'd put out for children: a giant wooden cube covered in doodads, a children's book about a duck in black galoshes, and an old video game with a main character that somewhat resembled the Kool-Aid Man. Police officers could access most places in the hospital, but no one particularly wanted them there, and rarely did anything they needed to do make anyone's stay better. No one looking for the comfort of family, relief from pain, or an alleviation of fear, relished being asked, "Is it okay if I take your statement now?"

Nearly every time he entered a hospital, he couldn't wait to leave.

However, the incident in the ER waiting area left Doug burning to talk to Heather Bradley to confirm his sanity, and he still wanted to talk with the Bradley boys to conclude his investigation of the accident. Something about their demeanor while in his patrol car had struck him as off—especially the older boy. He might've been addled by the accident, but something seemed strangely wooden about the child. No two children dealt with trauma exactly the same, but still, something had Doug's guts a bit in a twist. Instinct told him that talking to the children was more important than finding out what in God's name had actually happened in the restroom.

Now, Doug kept finding himself stalling. When he first arrived at the door to their examination room, the nurse had just been leaving.

"The doctor will be with you in a minute," the nurse had said as she left.

So, Doug stood there absently scratching the bites on his wrist and figured he should wait until after the doctor had talked to them. After all, if there *was* something important he could learn from talking to them, he certainly didn't want the doctor interrupting—and the doctor was much more a priority for the Bradleys.

Unfortunately, the "minute" had turned out to be fifteen. Then, as the doctor left, he'd told the Bradley's that the nurse would take them upstairs to admit them overnight. Doug had caught the doctor's arm once the door closed, and the doctor assured him that once they were settled, it would be easier to interview them.

That was thirty minutes ago, an hour total, and Doug still hadn't quite figured out how he was going to approach any of this without sounding crazy. At least in a place like Millwood, he could be a little less on point, a little less professional.

Now, he fretted about in the hallway of the general ward. The Bradley father hadn't yet arrived, for which Doug was thankful. He had met William Bradley more than once; he'd called the police department multiple times about various incidents in the local branches of the supermarkets he oversaw, and though the circumstances were never pleasant, Mr. Bradley would be best described as less than polite in all those circumstances.

Doug peered down the corridor off of which Mica's room extended.

With his mother and Mica in their room, Stuart sat in one of the hallway chairs silently watching everything watchable. Doug observed him as he watched the nurses and orderlies pass by. Stuart watched their faces and their bodies, though not in a hormonal youth kind of way (even though Valerie was the stereotype of an attractive nurse), but rather with distinct clinical detachment. His eyes scanned the various fake plants adorning the corners, seeming to take in each individual blade, leaf, and frond. Earlier, he had spent several minutes examining the objects on the janitor's cart when Mick left it parked a few feet from the boy in order to carry a mop into the room of old Mrs. Tornabene.

Maybe the boy was just quiet and inquisitive.

Doug couldn't help but consider abuse. A major lure of the Northeast was the regional reputation for keeping to oneself, which gave fantastic privacy to well-meaning folk, but a potential shield for those who saw the shield as a cloak. It didn't help that Doug knew William Bradley to have a bad temper—though Doug also knew that context was everything. Ruthless businessmen could still be loving and sweet fathers. Lieutenant Juto of the Millwood Fire Department could feel like she held the wrath of the infernos she sought to extinguish, but if you put her with her daughter, she was pink cotton and rainbows.

Also, the older boy had been, according to Heather's report, out in the woods as well. Towns like Millwood were pretty low profile on crimes, but it wasn't uncommon for folk going out into the woods to be going there to do things they didn't want others seeing them doing—and a little boy stumbling onto them...

Doug started down the hall towards the boy. Best to talk to him alone for a minute. If this was an abuse case, the boy would be reticent in front of his parents.

The boy, in turn, shifted his systematic gaze to focus on the one approaching.

"'ey there, Stuart. I'm about to head back to the station," Doug said, putting on his best Officer Best Friend Smile, the one for kindergarten and first grade classes.

The boy nodded curtly with no change of expression or

additional body language. Despite the fact that Doug had practiced and worn his smile on some of the worst days, the smile melted away at the boy's lack of reaction. Doug was no master detective, but the boy's lack of reaction was so pronounced that it felt intentional.

"Before I left, I wanted to chat with you," Doug said, trying to keep it from being apparent that his eyes were examining the boy as closely as possible for bruises, bloodshot eyes, scratches. The boy had all those things, but nothing out of character for someone who played a lot in the woods. "Things were a bit hectic earlier. We hardly got a moment."

The boy's entire demeanor changed in a single and instantaneous shift. The boy's shoulders loosened up, and he patted his knees with his hands in a brief rhythm. The blank expression and the scanning eyes transformed, the boy now biting his lip and furrowing his brow. A moment ago, the boy could've been some misplaced piece of Disney animatronics, and in a flash he'd pulled a Pinocchio, transforming into a real boy. If the lack of reaction hadn't been a reaction itself, this transformation certainly was. It bothered Doug more than a forced smile would have. People often call significant indicators "red flags," but this was more like an aquamarine flag. It signified something, but Doug had no idea what.

The boy's jaw shifted side to side as if he were trying to pop it.

"My brother hit his head on the left temple and bit a good chunk out of the inside of his cheek," the boy said. "Mr. Weaver came around the corner a little over the speed limit and was watching the far side of the road for animals when he struck..."

"Yeah," Doug interrupted. "Hell of a thing, pardon my language. It's been a long evening for you, huh? I'm sure you're well ready to get home."

"We were headed home," Stuart said, a strange hesitation in his cadence, "But here is better than home."

"Huh," Doug said, alarm bells ringing in his head. "You don't say. Why is that?"

"Because it's farther from where my mother found me," Stuart said.

That left Doug a bit blank. Did that mean home was fine? That maybe something had indeed happened out in the woods? The accident happened at the trailhead for Widower's Winder, a path that stretched all the way through the park and deeper into the foothills. Realistically, he could take a quick check, even if distant rumbles of thunder suggested a serious storm rolling in. Doug figured the inconvenience of a short patrol sounded better than ruminating about Sharon's fidelity. If nothing else, he might find evidence of gathering places for teen shenanigans, and knowledge of shenani-spots was knowledge of the most valuable sort to small town patrolmen.

"Anyone give you trouble out in those woods?" he asked. "Some of the high school boys rough you up a bit?"

"No," Stuart said. "I saw no one."

Doug frowned and scratched his head. The kid was just a boy, but even then, Doug felt himself off-put enough by the whole encounter that his entire being was on-guard. No one thing agitated him, but everything combined to kick his intuition in the crotch, roll it in tar, and push it off a diving board. He decided to try a different approach.

"You play out in those woods a lot?"

The boy hesitated.

"No, that was the first time I'd ever been there," he said.

At that point, a throat cleared behind Doug.

The officer rose and turned to find William Bradley standing behind him holding a briefcase and a scruffy teddy bear that clearly came from the hospital gift shop. He wore a tailored button-down shirt, slacks, and a tie that likely came from a store that took your measurements before they would sell you anything. However, each article wore the day in wrinkles and folds, the way his shoulders and the heavy skin under his eyes clearly carried his stress.

"Need something, Officer?" William Bradley asked.

"About to call it a day, actually," Doug said. Acutely aware that he still hadn't talked to Heather or Mica, Doug still felt he had something to act on—and if there *was* something going on in those woods, the faster he got out there, the more likely he'd find the evidence. Especially given the way the weather looked just about ready to turn fierce. "I still need to take a formal statement from your little troopers and have a final talk with your wife about the details of the incident."

Doug made to step past Mr. Bradley, but Mr. Bradley put a staying hand on the deputy's shoulder. Doug let his eyes drop poignantly to Mr. Bradley's hand.

"We appreciate your help," Mr. Bradley said softly but firmly. "But I'd also appreciate if you left my boy alone. He's been through a lot tonight, and I'm sure at this point he wants to unwind with his parents and his brother."

For a fleeting moment, Doug wanted to read this as some sort of veiled threat, that Mr. Bradley simply wanted to end the conversation. However, Mr. Bradley offered a smile, one that struck Doug as surprisingly genuine, and added, "We'll bring them by the station in the next day or two if you think there's any need to interview them. After they've had a chance to recover. Have a good evening, Officer."

As Mr. Bradley led the way into his son's hospital room, Stuart followed behind. With his hands loosely clasped, Stuart slowly looked over his shoulder and gave a slight shake of his head. Doug didn't know how to read that. Though, one thing was for certain—something was wrong under the surface. With

Mr. Bradley now there, and clearly set on keeping Doug back, the woods offered the best hope of getting an answer as to what.

MICA

Their food had just arrived, and despite how many TV shows and movies made fun of hospital food, it smelled magnificent. Mica couldn't believe how hungry he'd gotten. He hadn't eaten since he peeled an orange and ate a small stack of honey graham crackers around the time Stuart left for the park. The chicken tenders, french fries, and green beans on his tray made his mouth water and stomach churn.

His parents both sat on the rubbery looking armchairs against the wall with their Styrofoam cafeteria containers (for some reason, they'd only delivered Mica's meal) in their laps, stuffing their mouths steadily with their hamburgers and salads and talking about adult things like hospital bills, insurance deductibles, and car repairs.

Stuart sat by the window, staring out into the evening, his food untouched. Mica knew he hadn't eaten before he left for the park, hadn't even eaten since lunch. He had to be hungry enough to eat a truck. What was Stu's deal?

Mica sighed. He picked up a chicken nugget with his fingers and took a bite. He looked up to the blank TV screen. It was dinnertime, and hospital or not, there was no TV at dinner. Dinner time was family time.

The upshot was that he couldn't complain about the bed. It was comfy. Maximized comfy. It adjusted in like four different places. Four! At home, if Mica wanted his feet up, he had to stick a pillow under them. If he wanted to lean back, he had to lean against the wall or wedge his pillow behind himself. He didn't have enough extra pillows to do both, and mom didn't like him using her decorative pillows for things like that.

Clearly, his parents had been holding out on the good furniture. Did they sell hospital beds for kids' rooms?

Mica wondered if Stuart would want to give the bed a whirl. They'd really outgrown that kind of thing, but the bed might fit them both. Besides, Mica had that weird little clip thingy on his finger monitoring his pulse. They were checking to see if he was concussed, or maybe something else. There'd been something on the x-ray. When he'd asked mom and dad about it, they said there was nothing to worry about, but then a few minutes later, they'd said he'd be staying the night. He really wished they'd explain. He really wished they'd pull their seats to the bedside and eat with him, or that Stuart would talk to him, or that Stuart would eat anything.

Mica felt the tears at the corners of his eyes, so he took a bite of his chicken and wiped his eye sockets with the back of his chicken hand. The spices and the dry breading irritated the gash he'd bitten into his cheek, and he tasted a bit of blood. At least he'd have something to tell the nurse when she came in to take away his tray.

THE VISITOR

The Visitor gazed out the window, letting its attention fall in and out of focus. It was still not accustomed to "sight" based on the visible light spectrum. It only knew two states—darkness and not darkness, void and not void. In fact, seeing something that was "not void" had been so utterly terrifying and so potently compelling that it had almost seemed as if all will had been lost. The light that had flared in the darkness had been immeasurably distant, so distant that it appeared only faint, barely a pinprick, but in the absolute blackness, it had been as painful as being pierced by knives.

Now that It had arrived in the light, despite the way in which Stuart's knowledge and memories tempered the influx of information at any given moment, the sheer number of different things within the light felt almost impossible to process. The raw data was staggering, almost hard to believe that the species of this place were able to navigate it at all. It was curious how the human mind seemed engineered for efficiency rather than capacity.

The Visitor closed Its eyes and held the image of what lay outside the window to examine its parts. In the peace of the dark that resided inside the mind of this species, The Visitor proceeded to parse what he'd seen: The gas station just past the edge of the hospital parking lot sat adjacent to a strip mall, which contained a law office, a dentist's office, and an audiologist's office. Next to that was a stand-alone building with a musical instrument repair shop that advertised free first lessons to new students above its sign. A bench sat beside its front door, a bus stop on the corner. A crumpled-up paper cup and a Milky Way wrapper were on the ground next to a trashcan, stuck to the sidewalk by something sticky. The edges of the wrapper fluttered when the wind blew or a car passed by.

Down the street, more of the same. Mostly low buildings, only a handful over five stories, more strip malls and low peaked offices than anything else—all-in-all about eight blocks by eight blocks of the same. Obstructed by a couple of the taller roofs, stood the Rutledge building, where Stuart's mom worked. Each building was its own thing, but all were part of a whole—what Stuart thought of as "downtown." The idea that something was both itself and a part of a whole was something The Visitor understood better than most things. It too was part of something and part of a whole—and It didn't want to be a part of that whole anymore.

Unfortunately, that whole didn't want to lose part of itself. The Source was coming towards the door, spreading its darkness. The Visitor knew It couldn't rest here—It needed to find either the Light that had summoned It, a light fierce enough to defend this world, or It needed to find a doorway to somewhere else so It could continue the search for sanctuary. Even though The Visitor now watched as vigilantly as possible for some sign of the Light, It was beginning to resign itself to the possibility that this world may have already been abandoned by it. Time had not existed for The Visitor as It approached through the void, so it was hard to say what changes might have occurred in this place during the transition. But if it was the case that the Light was no longer here, the remaining options were not among those The Visitor wanted to consider.

The Visitor looked outside again, took in what lay outward from the city center, and returned to its processing. Beyond the downtown, roads fanned out in all directions, disappearing among trees, houses, hills, and the more sprawled lights of supermarkets, drug stores, and the more generic consumer trappings that inevitably found a nest and dug in. The hillsides rose up around the town. Just past the movie theater rose the treeless slope half the town's kids sledded down in the good snows. A simple surface lift waited for the coming winter to help ease the trip of the young ones up the rise, the result of a district fundraiser for winter sports.

For a moment, The Visitor remembered going door to door through the neighborhood with Dad, nervously clutching a clipboard with an order sheet and a catalogue on top. It had been mid-fall, and the trees displayed a glorious bonfire of color in the afternoon sun. Dad had taken off work to shepherd his son. He took fundraising seriously, believed it taught financial motivation, organization, and salesmanship. Knocking on the first several doors made Stuart's knees quiver, but each time Dad placed a hand on his back—gently, but firmly—and gave him the smallest nudge.

Then the memory disappeared, and The Visitor felt strangely empty and lost. It was odd to live with the memories and thought channels of another sentient being. The Visitor felt almost as though the boundaries of Itself and Stuart were smudging together. It wondered if the phenomenon might bring more serious consequences down the line.

Its eyes came to the lights on cell towers that blinked above the ridge that ran towards Manchester. A swathe of forest had been cleared to accommodate a dense line of other towers and implements of infrastructure. A couple of small shacks roosted at the ridge top, and near them, an older water tower looked about ready to collapse on its legs.

The Visitor paused on the tower. Something almost phosphorescent gleamed on its edges and in a meandering path both over the ridge and down it. Was that a trace of *the* Light? Had the Light been at that place recently? Or was it just an effect of the way the light of this world seemed to be a part of every surface? Finding help in this body seemed an impossible task. Taking the boy vessel had been a matter of necessity, not convenience. When one was invited, one expected to be met by the host.

The Visitor wished night would fall faster. The darkness of this world wasn't the same as the lightlessness of the void, but if a beacon *was* out there, it would be easier to spot without competing light. It was strange how those who lived here thought about how rare and precious the kind of light they lived under was—both that of the sun and that of the First Maker. Stuart himself hadn't even thought of the sun as much more than the thing that made him wear sunglasses, the thing that meant it was okay to go outside, the thing that made him wear sunscreen.

Of course, you might not know you live in the bottom of an hourglass until you look up to see sand falling.

LINDSAY

If Lindsay could've sobbed she would've, but that which she'd considered her eyes, heart, and lungs no longer belonged to her. She no longer resided in her body, but was rather tethered to it, linked to the spirit of some *thing* that had infested her when Barclay—or whatever Barclay really was—laid hands on her. For a brief moment, she'd felt a bloom of warmth throughout her whole being, which had quickly exploded into an agonizing jolt as though she'd been struck by lightning.

Before the flash, she experienced the world through her body.

Afterwards, she experienced the world through another mind, and she could feel a slow trickle of herself draining into it. It seemed as though it had extended some sort of filament into her soul, siphoning out something more precious to her than she could imagine, something she'd never even conceived could be taken.

Before she'd met Stan, she'd dated a boy named Ryan. They'd gone to a couple of movies, a couple of coffee shops, on a couple walks. Then he'd planned a "surprise," and he'd driven her to an old shed in the woods that held a smelly, moldy couch he'd covered in a sheet. He'd pressured her hard there, his hands crossing every boundary she set. Eventually, her no's were hard enough that he'd given up, but Lindsay had left the evening feeling like each of his touches had taken a bit more from her.

That was the closest she'd felt to this. With this, she knew that whatever she was losing to that pull was finite, and when it was gone, there would be nothing left of her.

Lindsay wanted to scream. This siphoning, this theft of her *self,* felt agonizing in a way that redefined what agony could actually mean—but her throat did not belong to her anymore. All she could do was experience the filtered world through the senses that had been stolen from her, and the world she saw appeared as a warped nightmare of the one she knew.

The moment Lindsay lost stewardship of her own body, she'd immediately seen a whole different dimension of Barclay; underneath what she now saw almost as kind of a Barclay mask, the being was a massive, winged serpent with a bearlike head, and hair that looked much like hair-thin willow branches. Barbs that seemed to writhe and twitch of their own accord ran up and down its entire body. However, that wasn't all he looked like. He looked like some sort of massive conduit or tunnel, a view into some other place entirely, some place massive and vast, full of turbulent forces and milky light. Whatever Barclay was, Lindsay didn't have a word outside of demon, monster, creature, any other vague generalization one might find in a child's scary story. The thing that had taken over Lindsay's body saw him with a combination of awe, love, hatred, and horror. If she'd been able to see the real thing that was Barclay when she'd still been herself, Lindsay knew she'd have died on the spot.

Right now, however, an outside observer would see this Creature walking between the two boys, or what had been the two boys, like any other man. The boys themselves both wore black jackets, shirts and pants that the Creature had somehow given them, and they walked barefoot over the sticks and mossy rocks. Just as Lindsay saw a second form for Barclay, their faces blurred and twisted. Something inside them grew just like something grew inside herself. None of them had yet spoken, and Lindsay wondered if the thing in her body even *could* speak.

She also wondered if Larry and Stan still remained tethered to their bodies in the way that she was still tethered to hers. She wished she could see them or hear them so she wouldn't feel so alone. Literally only thirty minutes ago, she'd been wondering whether she should change majors to biochemistry, how she'd like Boston, and if seeing Stan once a month would be enough sex for the both of them. At least if she had died, she would have either been nothing or moved on to some sort of afterlife. This—she didn't even know what to call it.

The Creature dropped back, closer. It stopped in front of what was once Lindsay, reached out, and took the hand. He raised it with a half bow as though he was about to kiss it or initiate an old-fashioned dance. Lindsay noted that the hand didn't really look like her own. Though she recognized a small scar across two of her knuckles that she'd gotten when she was nine, the fingers were too long. The skin had lost some of its tone, but gained a bit of gracefulness that Lindsay never had.

The Creature looked Lindsay's body in the eyes for several long moments. Lindsay couldn't really follow the thoughts of whatever entity inhabited her mind and body, but she got the impression that whatever was looking at her, it was named Veles.

It struck Lindsay that Veles wasn't just staring at her body's eyes. He knew about her tethered connection. She felt shocked and disgusted to discover that an overwhelming sense of gratitude surged through her, but Veles's acknowledgement made her existence more real. If something, even such a monstrosity, knew she existed, maybe some way back to her world existed.

As if he knew exactly what she thought, Veles shook his head slowly.

"Make no mistake," he said, in a low, serious voice. "I killed you. You aren't you. You're more like an echo—your soul's imprint on your memories. Bodies just don't have room for more than one soul, and my guardians needed the bodies of you and your friends."

Veles paused and licked his lips. He looked down the path towards town.

"If it's any consolation, this trace of yourself might linger long enough for me to achieve the greatest victory of my existence, but somehow I doubt that's a priority to someone in your unique position."

Veles paused again as if he expected some sort of answer. Lindsay, of course, still had no control over her body and felt control of her thoughts slipping as well, the panic almost a concrete thing, like hands tearing her apart.

"Just bear in mind that if I fail," Veles said, "the Abomination will decide exactly for how many eternities and how many versions of your being it wants to desecrate."

With a blink and a brush of her forehead, Veles gave her a glimpse of exactly what that might look like.

Lindsay had no mouth, no throat, no lungs, but she did have the spiritual equivalent of shrieking in utter incoherence.

Then, the world went white as a strike of lightning unlike anything Lindsay had ever seen, bathed the world with a flash someone could've mistaken for the arrival of God.

PERCY

The lighting flash that heralded the storm looked like none that Percy had ever seen. It cut the sky to ribbons. The bolt arced in a canopy over the city like a great net coming instantly into existence. Percy saw a half dozen fingers come down to streetlamps on his street alone. There should have still been twilight, but the clouds were so thick, the lightning so searing, that the world seemed veiled in total darkness.

Percy's nerves felt similarly overwhelmed. His whole body shook where he crouched behind an ornamental wall a couple houses away from his own. His vision just started returning when the clouds burst, the downpour carrying marbles of hail on its shoulders. The whole thing hit the world in a sheet, and Percy instantly felt battered in a way he hadn't felt since he'd gotten his ass kicked in 9th grade.

The initial rush didn't let up, but Percy quickly adjusted to the deluge. He had nowhere to seek proper shelter, and he hardly dared break cover. Despite the spattering rain stinging his eyes and fragments of shattering hail striking his cheeks, he peeked over the wall. A couple streetside parked cars, trees, bushes, and, of course, the road lay between him and his home. Even as getting drenched made him shiver fiercely, his spine went cold as hail stones. The front door was wide open.

When he'd gotten out of the cab and his mother came out of the house, the old man had filled him with irrational fear. They'd stood for several seconds, just a few feet apart, his mother on the porch. Percy's thoughts had accelerated faster and faster, all sorts of flashes of violence and harm throttling his rational mind. Percy would never have claimed to be a brave man, but he'd never experienced such an invasive anxiety.

Then he'd turned and ran. He'd run full sprint until his heartrate and respirations reached some physical limit he hadn't reached in decades. He'd collapsed several hundred yards and multiple curves of the street, away. For almost two full minutes, he was the picture of vulnerability: on his hands and knees in the road, unable to stand, unable to draw enough air, veins bulging, tendons rigid.

His breath had finally slowed, and a coolness spread into his mind like he'd jumped in a pond in April. He realized he'd completely abandoned his mother. Maybe she ducked back into the house if she acted immediately, but in her condition? Feeling as sluggish of body and mind as she usually did? More likely she'd just been confused by the way he'd run.

Humiliation flooded him, and he lurched to his feet. He tried calling. Though his phone was waterproof, he couldn't get the wet screen to work. When he finally did unlock the screen and gave a voice command, his mother didn't answer. That didn't surprise him though. His mom had a habit of setting the phone anywhere but right near herself; she wasn't likely to answer it on a good day.

Halfway back, he slowed, veered off the road, and went behind the houses on the far side from his own. Either the entire threat had been part of some awful panic attack and it didn't matter how fast he got back because there was no real danger, or there was someone genuinely dangerous in front of his house, or inside it. In that case, he thought it best if his return wasn't noticed—it might be the only chance he had of helping his mom.

If she wasn't lying dead in the foyer, skull cracked, the door hanging open behind her.

Percy had almost gotten close enough to get a good view of the front of the house when the lightning struck and the storm burst, driving him behind the ornamental wall, staring numbly at his open front door.

The shades and curtains were drawn, and the foyer light wasn't on, so Percy really couldn't see anything inside. Fear tried to seize him. His hands trembled and his knees shook, but this time, Percy refused to run. He didn't know what had come over him before, but he wasn't going to act like a coward again.

The wind carried bits of leaves and branches along with the battering rain and stinging hail. His feet kicked up splashes as he jogged across the street. On either side of him, the withered remains of his mother's flowers from the prior year lined the walk. In years past, she'd cleared the beds before the cold set in, but this time, she'd decided to put it off until she was ready to plant fresh in May. Just a few years ago, she would've been ashamed of herself. Maybe she still was.

He slowed to a brisk walk as he mounted the porch steps. The door stood open, water blowing inside, the foyer empty. The storm blotted out too much daylight for him to see deeper inside, but the stairs in the foyer were clear—not that she could've gone up those.

He eased through the entry, conscious not to let his soles clomp on the creaking wood planks. His gaze darted, trying to check every corner of the darkened home.

His mother sat at the far side of the living room on her lime green easy chair, the one she sat in to do her needlework. She looked as white as a frozen pond in the dim light, her eyes wide, her shoulders, over which she'd pulled her purple, knit shawl, were drawn inward. Her fingers fretted about with each other, alternately picking at the backs of her knuckles and twisting the tips in the fabric of her dress. The wall just past her head, and the small shelf upon which she liked to set her tea, hosted a collage of portraits of Percy's late father, but all of them hung or stood somewhat askew to each other.

Percy felt a moment of relief that his mother was unharmed, but then her panicked eyes snapped from Percy to the far side of the living room towards the picture window. There, in front of the closed curtains, stood the man, his walker nowhere in sight. He had removed his shirt and seemed to be messing with different spots on his chest—pushing them with two fingers and pulling at himself with a cupped hand.

Out of instinct, Percy hit the light switch on the wall next to him, but the power was out. Lightning flashed, but because the man was between Percy and the window, he appeared as a stark silhouette.

As Percy's eyes readjusted to the dark, he realized that the man wasn't prodding at himself; there was something wrong with his body. His body would sag, then he would pull it back. It would bulge like a bubble, and he would press it back in.

He only had two hands though, and Percy watched in horror as a clump of calf muscle oozed out from his pant leg onto the carpet. One of his pectorals began to drag down his abdomen like a melting slug.

Percy looked back to his mother. She breathed fast and shallow.

"Percy," she said, her voice a worn thread, "what is happening?"

"I don't know, Mom," he said.

The man in front of the window cleared his throat. Percy was certain he was about to say something terrifying, but all that came out was "Glawr" before his throat sagged down into his chest cavity and his jaw fell lower on ropes of cheek.

"Do something, Percy," his mom said. "Please, do something."

Percy nodded and took a step towards her, extending his hand. The man seemed to regard the gesture with a strange curiosity. Part of the vitreous humor ran out of one of his eyes and down his cheeks like a stream of milky tears.

"I'm going to get you out of here," Percy said softly.

To his surprise, anger twisted his mother's features.

"I don't know what this is," she said, "but I'm not going anywhere."

"But you said..." Percy started.

"Be the man of the house," she snapped and pointed to the intruder. "Get him out."

At the window, the man's flesh continued to drip off his

body, knobs of bone—his clavicle, a couple ribs—uncovered and exposed all over. The bones themselves appeared to emit a white gas, kind of like the smoke that wafts out of a dry ice freezer. Percy wasn't sure, but he believed the man was making some sort of creaking sound, kind of like a tree swaying in a strong breeze. *What in the hell?*

Percy took his mother's arm and tried to pull her to her feet. He could feel for a moment just how light she was—she had to have lost at least forty pounds. He'd taken her by the arm many times while helping her around the house, but that had always been with her willing to move. Now she pulled back against his efforts, and he felt as if he could easily pick her up and toss her over his shoulder.

"Damn, Percy, let go of me."

"Gah," Percy snapped, flinging his hands up. His mother slumped back into her chair and crossed her arms across her chest. She gave him a withering look.

"What kind of pile of useless crap did I raise?" she said.

"But Mom..." he stammered. He was used to her moods, but he detected a vehemence in her voice he'd never heard before.

"You don't deserve the right to call me mother," she said. "I should have thrown you away and tried to raise my afterbirth. My placenta had more spine than you."

Percy felt tears spring to his eyes even as he tried to reassure himself that it must be the stress of...

He realized the man—or whatever it was—no longer stood in front of the window. A large wet spot marked the floor where it had stood, but no trail led away. *Did he freaking melt?* Percy felt his bowels quiver violently.

He must have worn his apprehension on his face, because his mother said, "Oh that's right, go ahead and shit yourself like the coward you are. Only way you could defend yourself is by stinking so bad nothing will go near you."

The light was poor, but was she baring her teeth at him? Her hands were always weak, her fingers always a bit curled, but were they curled now or arced like claws?

"Take a look at your damn self," she snarled. "Your father was right to die so he could stop being disappointed by the sight of you."

Her features quivered as lightning struck. She pushed herself out of her seat and took a shaking step towards him.

"Weakling," she said. "Burden. Millstone. Albatross. I should have drowned you as an infant. Always wanted to. Birthing you is my greatest failure."

A sob burst from Percy. She couldn't mean it. Any of it. Something was wrong. She'd suffered some sort of panic attack from fear. There was no way...

A scraping sound from above caused Percy to look up. A fresh bolt of lightning flashed. Percy gasped.

Above him, the man clung to the ceiling, the flesh of his palms seeming to melt into the plaster. The flesh had fallen from his torso in chunks. His lungs were visible between his ribs, pressing against them, oozing something thick and viscous. Most striking though was that the man's pants had disappeared, and his legs had fused together into a single, elongated limb that tapered to a point of what appeared like crushed and dangling toes. That limb was arched and tense.

That single limb struck down with a blur of speed like a scorpion's tail and drove straight into Percy's mouth. A silvery, white pain flooded his being as he felt his teeth smashed out of his gums, his lips and the corners where they met, tearing with an audible rip. He gagged and vomited as the limb forced itself into his throat, he felt muscles tearing, the bones of his jaw cracking. The pain spread to his chest as his sternum and both clavicles shattered.

His spine shattered next, and with it, in a final searing agony of fire and light, his spinal cord severed.

THE SOURCE

The storm broke over the darkness first, then radiated outward like a shockwave. The phenomenon had, up until then, been closely monitored, but the weather satellites had begun to report clear skies. A ring that signals would not cross had expanded to a radius of over fifty miles. Planes that crossed that border didn't cross out the other side. The storm was forgotten, and every branch of government turned their eyes to the invisible wall, the one that cordoned off what was being called, inter- and intra-agency, "the dead zone." The media conversation shifted. Was it some sort of cyberattack by a rogue nation? A precursor to WWIII? New experts were phoned, their dinners interrupted, their evenings put to an end, their late nights in the lab snuffed like a candle. Of course, it wasn't yet fact that anyone who crossed the line into the dead zone would not cross back out.

Inside, the torrent of rain passed into the swelling darkness, disappearing through a border that swelled high enough to cap full grown birches at its peak. That border tumbled over a fresh rise and cascaded down the far slope towards a darkened house, the first house within the path of its expansion, on the edge of the park, abandoned for years and once owned by a military man who died on deployment by an IED.

The house itself did, for its part, what houses do when left unattended for years on the outskirts of a community at the end of a dirt driveway that vanished between rises beyond sight of the main road; the house had decayed. The wood frames of its windows sagged with rot like half-shut eyes. Shingles had fallen from the roof like clumps of hair, and rot pitted the beams. Its front door had ceased doing altogether what doors do, as one of the hinges had broken and it hung half into its portal, neither closing it off nor allowing entrance.

The black cloud piled up against the siding like drifts of snow, tumbled in through the cracks and the gaps and the openings toothed by splintered glass. The darkness did not discriminate between what it poured through or over, or what it swallowed. It enveloped the ratty and roach infested couch, the coffee table whose varnish had worn off to the elements, the end table with the broken leg that spilled its brass lamp onto its side like a fallen soldier, the moldy pictures on the wall of mothers and fathers and brothers whose faces had warped and bloated. It poured down halls and into the basement through loose and broken floorboards where it embraced the silent furnace and the long cold boiler in the mildewed dark.

And all around, the invasive wet of unchecked rain battered in, softening the remaining plaster and naked beams, feeding the streaks of mold that infused every part of the structure. Like the darkness, the rain did not discriminate. It soaked the world in equal measure, knowing that there was nothing on this earth that it did not possess the power to ultimately collapse. In a way, both rain and darkness could be considered natural forces in that their own nature was inextricable and constant. They would never act against themselves or against principles that drive or design them. They are uncompromising and unrelenting in serving their function and acting exactly as they do, unlike the house that no longer sheltered the things that built it, the windows that no longer blocked the wind, or the door that neither admitted nor declined. The rain rained and the dark darkened.

As secluded as the house was, it stood hardly more than a powerful stone's throw from the next. And in that house, and in the ones that could see the lights from its windows, people lived. Families ate dinner. Children slept. Teenagers listened to music, played video games, and fretted that they couldn't access their social media. The household dogs sniffed the air, perked their ears, and laid their heads back down on their blankets. None of them could, in any way, anticipate what came for them. Like the Shadow over Egypt in the days of Moses, none of them could anticipate what came behind the cloud.

The Source, on the other hand, was full of anticipation. The world into which what It sought had fled was finite, confined by gravity to a sphere of surface, and that which populated the surface failed to utilize the vastness in which the planet sat. The Source had glimpsed that world once, when the great explosion of creation had made the boundaries between all universes transparent, and for billions of years since, It had yearned to possess that world.

Now that a door had been left open to the place The Source had been so long denied admission, the hunger to devour shook every aspect of It's being. Even though no eyes could have seen the door in the blackness of the void, The Source recognized that gateway like a blazing white light; searing, agonizing. The spreading darkness tempered the Light that infused that world so that The Source could approach, enter, but that Light would need to, in time, be expunged. It would be a necessary step, one only dubiously possible. Until then, the physical principles under which that world operated were severely restricting. The imposition of time increased incrementally as The Source drew near, and It found Its vision of events unfolding blurring, distorting. Its quarry was constrained by the same physics, and the physics of the vessel it inhabited, but It had the advantage of being more suited to that world.

The Source needed more eyes on the other side. As the cloud corrupted the landscape in preparation for the arrival, The Source's influence expanded correspondingly. The fragility of the vessels made them prone to disruption on a fundamental level, so many of their wills weak enough to be readily disintegrated. Its first scout had located the quarry briefly, but The Source's command grew too strained as the being's spirit withered into interference. Then, it had set out on its own on whatever agenda such a damaged thing might pursue.

In the end, the end itself was inevitable. The quarry would be found. The corruption of the world would continue until absolute. It was only a matter of time. They must be close, certainly no distance at all compared to where The Source had come from. In fairly absolute terms, there could be no place, by definition, further from somewhere.

Interim 2
Still Life With Butterfly

The memory was closer to a still-life. Mica couldn't say if it happened on a Tuesday, or the day after he had his first swimming lesson, or whether he had worn a diaper on that particular outing. He didn't know for sure if it was spring or fall or which playground their mother had taken them to. There might have been people jogging or cycling or pushing strollers. Sometimes he heard birds, other times a barking dog. Different times the memory surfaced, the particulars were subject to change.

The certainties were simple. His mother had been sitting on a bench some distance away, reading a magazine. He was on the top of a catwalk with stairs on one side, a fire pole midway, and a spiral slide at the far end. Stuart was playing explorer. The memory didn't cover it, but at the time the memory began, Mica knew Stuart had gone down the slide at least half a dozen times escaping an imaginary bear he'd stumbled upon.

The memory started with Stuart brushing by Mica yelling, "Run!" as he dashed to the slide and dove down it headfirst. Mica had looked at the slide and shuffled his feet. Each time Stuart had slid, Mica had tried to talk himself into following behind.

But it was so high, and he would go so fast.

He'd risen on his tiptoes to peek down the slide from as far as he could manage. Stuart wasn't afraid. How was Stuart not afraid?

The butterfly had swept right across his field of view. A white admiral with bright blue wings, white stripes, and orange spots. It alit on a rail, took off, and circled Mica's head. He'd giggled, turned.

His untied shoelace fell into one of the gridded holes in the playground equipment. The aglet caught on the lip. He felt the world swing as he tumbled towards the gap in the vertical bars of the railing that allowed kids to reach for the firepole.

His life didn't flash before his eyes. He didn't send a prayer to Heaven, thinking he was going to die. He didn't think anything at all until the world stopped.

It was just for a moment, a jolt. One moment he was falling, the next he wasn't, as simple as that.

The hands grasping the back of his shirt hadn't registered yet. Only the cessation of momentum. A blink where the world felt like a still life.

Then he heard Stuart grunt as the older brother jerked backwards on the fabric. The elastic of Mica's collar gave with an audible tear and his weight lurched. The brothers both fell down to the catwalk side by side.

A couple times over the following years Mica brought up the incident to Stuart. Stuart never voiced any recollection.

Chapter Five
Why They Go Out In The Rain

MILLIE

Rain drummed on the shed's corrugated tin roof. When lightning flashed, light gleamed off hanging shovels and hatchet heads; tools hung on brackets, covering an entire wall. The wood planks of the floor had once met flush, but they had cracked, gouged, and swollen all askew. The air reeked of wet dirt and mold. A steady flow of water rushed off the eaves and spattered to the ground on both sides of the shed.

In a corner, Millie pulled her knees to her chest on the fold out, vinyl chair and squeezed her turtle doll. A cold mist blew in through the rocking door; the door didn't latch, so the wind fought against its badly rusted hinges, opening then closing, opening then closing.

Outside, an intermittent wind whistled through the trees. When the door opened its widest, Millie could see the trees along the edge of the pond, the water reflecting the lightning streaks. The little girl shivered, the damp invading her clothes. She wished the storm would just stop, that she wasn't trapped in the little tool shed. Shelly wished it even more. She petted the plush turtle's head and shushed it, even though she was really shushing herself.

Millie gazed longingly over her shoulder at the wall that blocked her view of the house. It stood only twenty feet away, down a flagstone path to the screened-in back porch, but in a storm like this, to a girl of six, it might as well have been fifty miles. She hadn't known it was going to storm when she grabbed Shelly to run away with her. She hadn't known where she was going to run away to either. She'd only known it wasn't fair to not get dessert again, to need to eat her vegetables instead of just rolls, to get yelled at for being full after just a few bites. When they'd sent her to bed early, she'd only wanted to hide in the shed until they realized she'd snuck out. Then, she'd march right back in to hugs and relief.

Now, she wanted nothing more than for her parents to march through the shed door and give her hugs and relief. The door swung open, and she did not see them coming around the corner before it closed. The door swung open, and again she did not see them before it closed.

The door swung open, and she saw figures emerging from the woods on the far side of the pond before the door closed again. Thunder rattled the tools on their hooks.

The door swung open. There were four of them. Three in a line on the pond's edge, the fourth behind them. It was too dark for her to make out their faces, and even when the lightning illuminated them, they weren't familiar enough to try to recognize in those split seconds. Strangers. Four strangers in her backyard.

The door swung open. Of the three along the shore, the one in the middle was a girl dressed in white and the ones on either side were boys dressed in black. Millie couldn't really see the one in back at all, but as she squinted at the three, she could tell there was something wrong with them. It wasn't anything she could see. It was just that she could tell there was something ugly inside, the kind of feeling she would get if she discovered Shelly was stuffed with bugs. Millie wanted to scream for Mommy and Daddy, but she was too scared to open her mouth. She whimpered and mewled, but the storm was so loud she couldn't even hear herself.

The door swung open. The wind howled and a sheet of rain swept in. Hail stones clattered against tin like marbles shaken in an old coffee can. The three figures had fallen to their knees in the water. The trees along the shore seemed to bend away from them, but Millie hoped that was just the wind and the dark. The three reached down in perfect unison. Each scooped their cupped hands into the water and poured it down their foreheads. Millie almost chuckled. With all the rain, what was the point of doing that?

That was when two things struck the little girl: the fourth figure had disappeared, and the door had ceased swinging. It simply stood open.

Millie wanted to get out of the chair, to creep closer to the door and see if she could spot where the fourth had gone. If she could see them all, she would be safe. She told herself to get up, but she couldn't.

The lightning flashed again, one of those clusters of energy that lit parts of the sky in immediate succession, bathing the world in an almost steady strobe. The three kneelers tilted their heads back, even as hail pelted their faces. Millie squinted against the brilliance as they then drew their fingers to their mouths. She couldn't tell if they opened their mouths to let their fingers in or if their fingers pushed open their mouths.

Their hands disappeared to the second knuckle, then the third. The thumbs folded in and followed, the jaws extending impossibly wide, like snakes eating mice. Their throats bulged as their hands bludgeoned their esophagi wide.

Millie didn't want to look but couldn't stop looking. She tried to imagine doing that to herself, but only came up with cartoons. She felt glad for the dark between the lightning flashes because she couldn't make out the large objects they pulled from their throats, only that those objects seemed to be attached to themselves. *It couldn't be real,* she thought. It had to be like the shadows in her room at night, the way they moved when she slept with the window open.

The wind shrieked to a crescendo. Somehow, the door didn't even budge.

She might've seen what the three figures held in the next lightning flash if the illumination hadn't shown her that all three had fixed their eyes directly upon her. They smiled hugely, with ropes of something from inside their bodies hanging out of their mouths.

She wasn't supposed to see this. This was what was on the TV late at night. This was like the movies and news she wasn't allowed to watch.

She sucked in a breath and opened her mouth to scream. For mommy. Or daddy. She didn't know and didn't get a chance to find out which would come out of her mouth.

A figure blocked the view. Dropped to a crouch in front of her. Placed a hand over her mouth. All in a heartbeat.

"Shhhh," the man said, trailing off like a hiss.

He smelled bad. Like spoiled milk and dead flowers that have been in the vase water too long. His face was blotchy and glistened with rainwater. It drooped in strange places and appeared covered with pulsing sores.

Under his hand, Millie pressed her lips together even as she sucked in and blew out as much air as her passageways could manage. She could taste something emanating off his skin. It coated the inside of her mouth.

Again, he said, "Shhhh."

This time, something sounded almost musical to the rush of air. Her muscles, which had locked up from fear, relaxed of their own accord even though her head felt as chaotic as a jar full of shaken bees. For some reason it was difficult to think too hard about this stranger, even with him right in front of her.

"Apologies for my appearance, this is not the suit I would have chosen to wear," the man said. He withdrew his hand from Millie's face and gave his own chin a tug. It would have been a playful gesture had the skin not stretched and torn off like mozzarella. Millie gasped and her eyes widened. "But I'll be able to put one on shortly that most would find more pleasant."

"Who are you?" Millie whispered.

"My name is Veles," he said, regarding the clump of his chin like it was a gemstone. She should be horrified. She knew she should be horrified, but somehow, because it seemed he thought it was normal, she felt it was somehow normal too. "And they are the Zastitniks."

"Za-stit-nik," Millie said, pausing between each syllable. "That's a funny name."

She tried to look over Veles's shoulder to see what the three figures were doing, if they were still pulling things out of themselves. Veles shifted as she did, keeping his head and shoulders obstructing her view.

"They don't laugh much, I'm afraid," Veles said. "They face serious work."

Millie tried to look over his other shoulder, but Veles shifted again.

"W-what kind of work do they do?"

"They're messengers," Veles said. "And guardians."

"Guardians? They scare me."

"They wouldn't be very good guardians if they weren't scary, now, would they? I travelled a long way to find them so that they could help me."

"Help you with what?"

Veles shrugged. When he did so, for a split second, Millie could have sworn she saw huge wings unfolding behind his shoulders in the dark, but in the lightning that flashed right after, they were gone. Something in the back of her mind told her she should run, but the buzzing in her head made that apprehension seem distant and trivial.

"Don't mind much about that," Veles said. "Or about them. None of that is important to you. What I want to know is why someone so young and precious is out so late in the rain?"

As if to punctuate the question, a particularly deep throb of thunder vibrated the shed to its foundation.

"Daddy sent me to bed early," Millie said, her voice taking on a plaintive edge. "Without dessert, or even milk."

Veles nodded and clasped his ruined chin with one hand.

"And why would he do something like that?"

"I wouldn't eat my broccoli," Millie said. "They know I hate broccoli, and they made it anyway."

"Have you told them you hate broccoli?" Veles shifted his crouch so that his knees were splayed. He hung his elbows over his knees and clasped his hands in the middle with his index fingers extended.

"*Yes!*" she said. "All the time! They just don't listen!"

"Well, that hardly seems fair," Veles said with a sharp shake of his head. "And you decided to teach them a lesson by giving them a little scare?"

Millie nodded soberly. Veles clapped with delight.

"Good for you," he said. Millie smiled sheepishly. "People need a little chaos thrown into their lives now and again. Reminds them they're human."

Millie raised her chin.

"I wish I was an adult so they couldn't tell me what to do anymore," she said.

Something shifted in Veles's entire body. He didn't move towards her exactly, more like the intention of his entire being suddenly oriented directly at her. Millie felt her cheeks heat like she'd accidentally bragged to a teacher about how well she stole the candy out of someone's lunchbox.

"Do you now?" Veles asked softly.

Millie tried to lie, to say she was just kidding, but she found herself unable to do so. She didn't know if her silent nod was intentional or not.

Veles ran a finger under his nose as if wiping sweat off his upper lip.

"To be clear," he said with a one-sided smile, "you would choose to give up your youth so your parents couldn't tell you what to do?"

Millie opened her mouth to answer, but a man's voice from not too far away called out. "Millie," her dad called, "where the hell *are* you?"

Millie squeaked and jumped to her feet. Veles's hand shot out and grabbed her by the wrist. He squeezed gently and whispered something Millie didn't understand.

The girl's thoughts muddled as he ushered her with a scooting hand out the shed door. She vaguely registered the three figures kneeling on the shore, their heads in the water. It rained on her, maybe even hailed, but she barely noticed. Her body ached. Her muscles tightened, as though they pulled her bones in all directions. Her joints ached and shot out irregular jolts of sharp pain. The bones themselves seemed to throb from their cores.

She was more focused, however, on the whirlwind taking place in her memories even as the angle from which she viewed the world seemed wrong. It became clear that she'd already finished first grade. And second. In fact, elementary school was so far back that it had begun to fade. Middle school too. High school was fresher. She'd not been athletic enough or pretty enough to mesh with the popular crowd, and she'd not been smart enough for the honors classes. She'd not been quirky enough to be an outcast, but she'd been too plain for anyone to seek a true connection.

She remembered the ease with which she had tagged along to the party someone was throwing, and then how she faded into the background with a red cup in her hand. To settle into a couch or on the back porch. You only had to talk to a couple folks just enough so that no one would wonder why you were there. Maybe make out with a few folks here and there to make sure the invites kept coming. Of course, going a little further was fun too.

Midway between the shed and the back porch and the house with every light on, she looked down at herself. Her belly protruded so far; it didn't even register with her that she'd grown over two feet in the last ten steps. Her back hurt and her ankles ached. Her nose bled as her brain strained to accommodate an associated net that spanned twelve full years of memories. It flooded into her all at once—the boyfriend with the car and the apartment. The way they'd celebrated her turning eighteen for a couple straight weeks. How she'd almost dropped out of high school, but he'd convinced her to see it through. How she'd gotten a job at the movie theater and came home smelling like popcorn and feeling like butter every night.

Had she lived any of it? She could remember so many sensations, but they felt fragmented and uneven, like the way of all memory. She felt like she loved Holt, but she also had the feeling she'd never actually met him. Flashes of him and her watching the first ultrasound struck her. When she thought about it, she was convinced that her parents would remember a lot of it too.

She paused and looked back over her shoulder. Veles leaned

against the corner of the shed, watching her depart. His face appeared downright joyful. It should have been too dark for her to notice it, but she could see ecstasy etched into every feature. Hadn't he been practically falling apart? Now he looked like a man in his prime ready to run a marathon. What had just happened?

Veles straightened and walked to the water's edge. Standing on the far shore from where the trio knelt, he too stepped into the water. He dropped to one knee and dipped his hand towards the surface. A small and luminescent orb appeared in his palm with the gesture, the way a magician might reveal a palmed coin. Millie had a flash of watching a magic show in a night club on her third date with the father of her child.

As Veles tipped his hand sidewise and let the glowing orb fall to the pond, Millie felt the baby kick. A concentric series of ripples emanated from the spot where the ball of light hit, each ring infused with a gentle aura. It was almost white with a slight blue tinge. It made her feel unaccountably sad. She couldn't imagine why, but what she was watching was somehow connected to what was happening with her mind and body.

The light pulsed and swelled through the whole of the pond. Small fish swimming lazily near the bottom became black silhouettes, but they too began to take on its light, their scales shimmering with a rippling tourmaline hue. The water itself, the molecules of conjoined hydrogen and oxygen, saturated with the energy until they too exuded the same incandescence, and then the illumination crept up from the water into the soil, where the granules glittered like pulverized aquamarines.

Veles brushed his hands together as if to sweep off the dust of hard labor.

Then, Millie became entirely aware that she was standing in

a hail storm. Her skin stung instantly in a dozen places, her clothes drenched straight through. An overwhelming fear flooded into her like she'd suddenly become aware of something that had been there all along, and so she ran as fast as she could to the back porch. When she turned back one last time, the pond glowed like a basin of liquid light. It was the most beautiful thing she'd ever seen.

MEGAN

The night had turned ugly. Hail battered the windshield, and the wind blew visible clouds through the headlight beams. Megan leaned back in the passenger seat while Stephanie clenched the steering wheel, muttering to herself about being damn near blind. She would've appeared completely relaxed if her fingers didn't have the door's handhold in a death grip.

It was hard to believe that just twenty minutes earlier they'd been having drinks at The Barnshed to celebrate Stephanie's de facto promotion. It hadn't been expected, so the moment the GM had left in some sort of rush, she couldn't help but give Lil' Sis a ring.

"I know I've said it already," Megan said, "but I'm proud of you."

"You'd better be. The raise is gonna help cover your tuition. You'll make more than me in a few years."

Megan blushed.

"You know you don't need to do that, right?" she said. "I can get a couple loans to finish here, and I'll hopefully get an assistantship for grad school."

"Mom and dad didn't want either of us to have any debt," Stephanie said.

"I don't think they wanted to die either," Megan said.

Stephanie shot Megan the angriest look she could muster as

the Taurus leaned into a curve. The tires hydroplaned on a shallow puddle, giving them both a heartbeat of that weightless feeling that comes with a complete loss of traction. The car could've been made of cotton around them for all the heft it pressed to the asphalt.

Stephanie pumped the brakes and brought the car to a shuddering stop after it regained a grip on the road, and shoulder gravel ground under the tires as the final momentum failed.

Immediately, Megan slapped both hands on the dash.

"Jesus, Steph," she snapped. "Celebrating defeats the point of a promotion if you die before you get to do the job."

Stephanie nodded, still clenching the wheel.

"I'm sorry," she said. "Guess I..."

The broken thought hung in the air for a moment. Megan stared expectantly at her sister until she registered Stephanie's perplexed expression. Her sister leaned forward, squinting through the rain blur on the front windshield. Megan followed her gaze but saw nothing.

"What is it?" Megan asked.

Frowning deeply, Stephanie rolled her window down and stuck her head out into the pouring rain. Megan shifted impatiently. To her, it just looked like darkness from the storm.

"C'mon sis," Megan said, "you're kind of creeping me out."

Stephanie pulled her door handle and opened the car. She set one foot to the shoulder and stepped half out of the car.

"Seriously," Megan said. "Stop acting like a tweak and tell me what's up."

Stephanie pointed into the darkness.

"Don't you see it?" she said.

Megan leaned forward. Even with the windshield wipers going full tilt, she couldn't see anything through all the water rushing down the glass.

She popped her own door open and mimicked her sister, holding a hand to her forehead to shield her eyes.

She saw nothing but darkness until her eyes followed the strip of road lit by the headlights. The illumination ended abruptly at a subtly shifting line. Then a deeper type of darkness than the falling night and storm had created, took over.

"What the hell is that?" Megan asked.

Her big sister said nothing, but rather leaned into the car. With a click and a clunk, she dropped open the glove box and pulled out a Maglite . The bulb blared a sharp beam, and Stephanie started towards whatever it was that obscured the road. Megan took a few hesitant steps, reticent to move too far away from the vehicle. Nonetheless, her feet shuffled forward little by little, wanting to stay close enough to hear anything her sister said over the rain.

"It looks like some sort of cloud," Stephanie said, looking back over her shoulder.

"Clouds are white," Megan said reflexively, immediately feeling slightly foolish given that the heavy storm clouds overhead were a deep charcoal color. A growing curiosity made her want to get a better look at the cloud. It was just so darn strange.

Megan couldn't entirely make out the edges of the cloud, but her sister was surely nearing the edge.

"I'd keep back," Megan said. "It could be toxic or something."

Stephanie didn't say anything, but her steps shortened and then ceased. The line where the headlights ended sat just a couple feet in front of the toes of her boots.

"Hey," Megan said, her voice shaking slightly. "Why don't you take a step back?"

Megan took two steps toward her sister, both in the hopes that she could pull her back, but also to get a slightly better look at the cloud. What kind of cloud was it? How could it hang so low over the road like that? Why did the light stop so abruptly?

Stephanie reached out with the flashlight extended. The beam made no difference in the night, and then the bulb pierced the edge of the cloud. Something inside Megan wanted to protest, to call out, but it felt more akin to hearing a distant fire engine in the night than anything imminent. The sense of alarm receded even further as the smoke— the cloud— whatever it was, lurched forward along the body of the flashlight, over Stephanie's arm. Her sister made no move nor did her expression change as the cloud engulfed her entirely in a heartbeat. The whole border of the darkness surged, nearly closing the distance to Megan.

Should she run? She realized something felt wrong with the way she was thinking, but she couldn't put her finger on it. Her thoughts came at a very slow pace, absorbed mostly by the shifting edges of the phenomenon. A reflex deep within her kept sending signals to her legs to run, to her lungs to scream.

When the darkness reached for her with what seemed like two arms extending, she knew that it was her sister reaching for her from within the cloud. That seemed alright.

MICA

Mica sat up in his bed. The local news was on the TV, with a headline about electromagnetic disturbances across town. Mica had asked for cartoons—the hospital had more than one channel that showed nothing but cartoons, but his father had insisted that the news was more important. That it mattered. Of course, Mica wanted to say that cartoons mattered, but sometimes it didn't seem to matter what mattered to him, so he said nothing and let the news run. His parents were not in the room at the moment; they'd gone to talk to a doctor or get some air, depending on which parent you listened to.

The remote control taunted him with the promise that he could change the channel to what he wanted to watch and change it back with no one the wiser, but his hands stayed still by his side, lightly holding the blanket's edge. He wasn't going to break the rules. Mica—the good little boy who didn't get in trouble. Stuart broke the rules often.

Now, Stuart stood at the window with the blinds open. The room still smelled like dinner and antiseptic. The air conditioner hummed, and a load of machines neither boy could name buzzed softly. The storm had turned the night almost black, but the lights in the parking lot and all over the building, cast a bright yellow-orange glow. In some ways, one could argue that a hospital was one of those places to which night never truly came.

From his current angle, Mica couldn't see Stuart's face, but his brother's expressions all looked so strange since the accident. He didn't seem upset or scared or worried; he seemed distant—not distant like when he daydreamed or when he'd get worried mom was going to ground him. The only way Mica could think to describe it was it seemed like Stuart wasn't really there.

Despite his own condition—a bandage on his head, his mouth hurt, and the bruises—Mica couldn't help wondering if something had happened out in the woods.

"What are you looking at?" Mica said, his voice coming out thin, high, half-cracked.

"For," Stuart said.

Mica blinked.

"What?"

"You said 'at,'" Stuart said at a measured pace. "I'm not looking *at* anything. I'm looking *for* something."

Mica furrowed his brow and sat up a little. The horizon looked menacing with its massive cloud bellies swollen with lightning. With the landscape below them so heavily shadowed, it looked buried in obsidian.

"What are you looking for?"

"Light in the darkness," Stuart said.

Mica scratched at the insides of his forearms. So little that Stuart said actually sounded like Stuart. It sounded more like someone pretending to be Stuart, and they weren't very good at it. Had his mom and dad noticed? Were they too distracted? It was like something out of a scary movie; their parents didn't let them watch much horror, but Mica had seen *Invasion of the Body Snatchers*. He'd seen part of *The Thing* when it aired on TV. Had aliens landed in Millwood? He didn't remember hearing anything about any big meteors, but then again, movies in general often depicted government cover ups.

"So, did you hit your head in the woods or something?" Mica asked.

Stuart visibly started. He turned away from the window and cocked his head at Mica. Mica sat all the way up and shifted in the bed so that his legs dangled off the edge, careful not to knock off the pulse monitor clipped to his finger. His head throbbed a bit and his joints ached. He supposed car wrecks in movies would look a lot less exciting in the future.

After a moment's pause, Stuart asked, "What do you mean?"

"What do I mean? You're acting really weird," Mica said. "Like alternate universe episode weird."

Stuart's eyes unfocused a moment. He looked up, then to the side, and back to Mica. Then he nodded and walked over to the whiteboard where the nurses had filled in the room schedule. He reached out and took a black, dry-erase marker from the tray at the board's bottom, and turned back to Mica.

"Want me to draw a moustache on my upper lip? And a little beard?"

Mica tried his best to give his brother an "I'm serious" look, but he just burst into a chuckle with a shake of his head. Maybe everything was okay, and it was just the imagination of a boy who'd been in a car accident.

Then the marker fell out of Stuart's hand and clattered to the linoleum. At first Mica thought that his brother was staring at him like he'd smeared poop on his forehead. But Stuart's focus seemed directed on something else, somewhere behind Mica—through the windows, Mica realized, as Stuart quickly strode past him to the blinds.

"What is it?" Mica asked.

Stuart hesitated, but then pointed between the wobbling slats. With the room brighter than the outside, Mica mostly just saw reflections. However, one reflection that looked like a light-bulb glare caught Mica's eye. *That's not a reflection*, he thought, *that's something very, very bright out in the hills.* Unfortunately, he could not see anything else through the glass, so he lacked any way of telling how far it was or what it could possibly be.

Mica unclipped his heart monitor and slid off the edge of the bed. His bare feet slapped cold linoleum and he shivered. His thighs felt cool under his gown; he hadn't realized how much he'd been sweating when sitting on the bed. A moment later, the two brothers stood side by side at the window, looking out into the hills.

"You haven't even asked me how I'm doing," Mica said.

"I know how you're doing," Stuart said. "I heard the doctor say you were going to be fine."

"You still could've asked me," Mica said.

"Why?"

Mica blinked.

"To show you care?"

"But I already know the answer."

Mica leaned as close as he could to the glass, blocking as much light as he could with his body so he could see outside better. From the woods at the base of the hills, just a little down from the old water tower, an ethereal, aquamarine glow radiated.

"It's pretty," Mica said. "What is it?"

"Light," Stuart said.

"I know that, but what's making it?"

Stuart said nothing for a couple beats, then turned and placed his hands on his brother's shoulders. Mica felt extremely awkward. It was like something someone in a movie would do.

"Mica," Stuart said. "I need to get to that Light."

"Uh," Mica said, "I don't think Mom's..."

"I'm not telling her," Stuart said. "I'm leaving right now."

"Do you know how badly you'll get grounded?"

"If I don't go, everyone is going to die," he said.

"Oh yeah, mom'll believe that," Mica said.

"Why the hell do I feel like that matters?" Stuart snapped. His face reddened and he held his hands palms out, shaking them twice as if to say, "It's really okay."

Mica swallowed.

"You aren't really *you*, are you?"

But Stuart turned abruptly and walked straight out the door.

DOUG

With a thrum reminiscent of distant fireworks, rain spattered the windshield hard and fast, each drop leaving quickly vanishing pocks in the sheet of wetness that ran down the glass from the vehicle's roof. Quite hypnotic, and, for a moment, Doug simply stared at the way water seemed to erase water, the way the whole thing blurred into a single sheet of water, the way the streetlights beyond appeared distorted with halos and streaks. Normally, he didn't mind the world in the rain; the stop lights, especially the green ones, glistened off the wet asphalt like emeralds scattered on the streets. But now, he was tired and drained, regretful as he imagined his poor husky whining up a storm. He'd really hoped the rain would've held off until after he left the park, but now the smudged view through his windshield too closely reflected how he felt. His mind felt like a TV that couldn't find a channel.

Ahead, on the road, the asphalt glistened. Beyond that, the trail wound deep into the woods. It wasn't Widow's Winder, but rather a trail called Reed Bow Run, that intersected Widow's Winder not too far in. Doug hadn't really spent much time in this part of the woods, let alone at night and in a storm, but Reed Bow was a much broader and easier trail than Winder. The town had even talked about paving it. Reed Bow also had the huge advantage of having two parking spaces right at the head. After all, he didn't want his cruiser getting hit on the side of the road like the Bradley's car had, and in this weather, it was precisely the kind of bad luck he could expect.

Doug intended to search as broad a radius around the trail intersection as he could, but he had absolutely no ancient hunter tracking skills. Truth was, he really had little idea what he was looking for. Empty beer cans? Scattered cigarette butts? A meth lab in an RV, or some run down torture-cabin? What was he even doing out here? It occurred to him that it would make just as much sense to simply put the car in reverse, pull a three point, and head back to the station to close it down for the night.

Instead, he pulled out his phone and opened his text thread with Sharon.

He typed: "Cross of Reed Bow and Widow's Winder in Coney Park."

Sharon would know what it meant of course; any time he went somewhere potentially dangerous, he sent a similar message, just in case. He knew he should also send a message to Chief Holler, but in the rather likely case he turned up nothing, Doug didn't want to get shit for being the dumbass who worked after shift's end to go tramping about in the back hills in a thunderstorm. After all, Doug didn't even have an actual report to investigate, and while plenty of officers "trust their gut," "gut" doesn't come across well on paper without "results."

Doug grabbed the plastic baggy that held his yellow, Millwood PD slicker and pulled the thin vinyl over his uniform. He popped open the door, stepped out, and turned on his Maglite . In the flashlight's beam, the thick rain became bright white lines that made the whole world look like a TV broadcast in poor reception.

The officer's boots squished into the soft mud of the shoulder, every step pulling away with a sucking pop. Crinkled fast food wrappers, bits of Styrofoam, water bottles and more littered the drainage trench, thrown from vehicle windows, only to end up embedded in the scraggly grass, mud, and pebbles along the shoulder. Doug panned his light slowly through the trees and over the rises. The trail was smooth, not crisscrossed with ankle breaking roots like Winder.

Doug adjusted his belt under his slicker and started forward. The initial run ascended gradually from the road for fifty yards before it crested the first rise. The mud squished around Doug's treads and sucked as his ankles in the deepest parts. A few segments did have flat, weather worn stones, and they posed the greatest danger of slipping.

The hardest part, really, was the strange numbness that came with the constant thrum of the rain. It struck leaves and dirt and rocks, and spattered Doug's slicker with the sharpness of a dozen snare drums. As the road disappeared from sight behind him and the undergrowth grew denser, it struck Doug that with so much sound all around, someone could probably walk up inches behind him and he wouldn't hear a thing. Unconsciously, the fingers of his free hand patted the butt of his handgun through his rain gear. He couldn't ask for worse shooting conditions, but the weapon did provide a sense of security.

Thankfully, not much in the form of indigenous predators lived in the area. The occasional bear showed up deeper in the foothills, as did wildcats, even the rare wolf. If Sharon were with him, she'd probably say something about Wendigos, but her superstitious beliefs took over when it came to folklore. She linked it to her 1/32 verified Native American ancestry. Doug linked it to the fact that she was a bit kooky. Either way, Doug figured this kind of storm would drive even a Wendigo into shelter.

He muttered, "Why the hell am I out here?" And he really didn't have an answer for that, even though his feet still propelled him forward. The truth was, he came to this trail outside any good reason other than something had really bothered him about the boy, and even that wasn't really based on anything—except his gut. The boy had just given him a feeling, one of those intangible, indescribable nettles. Sharon probably would've called it the boy's aura or his chi, his essence.

Then Doug froze at a clatter from the underbrush that managed to rise above the churn of the storm. The sound of breaking branches amplified, as whatever was causing it were headed straight towards him. He swung his flashlight just in time to see three deer bursting through a dense thicket full tilt. He felt the air around him move as they blasted by him, their hooves hammering the forest floor like horses in a gallop. One of their antlers snagged his poncho and tore a vast gash in the vinyl, nearly pulling him to the ground in the process.

Doug swore loudly as he staggered to keep his balance, only managing to right himself by grabbing hold of a nearby maple sapling. The bark smarted his palm, and all his joints protested against stopping his momentum.

By the time he'd fully regained stable footing, the deer were gone, replaced by a much quieter bunch of clatters from several points around him. He swung his light about but could only see shifting scrub branches. Clearly squirrels, rabbits, rats, and the like. All going the same direction as the deer.

Doug's blood dropped a handful of degrees. If he were your average townsperson, someone who slung burgers and milkshakes at Millette's Quick Eats or a checkout clerk at Ott's Corner Store, he would've immediately obeyed the clear instinct to swing heel and follow the animals. Unfortunately, as an officer of the law, he found himself feeling the push of his responsibility to investigate why the animals were running. Normally, a forest fire would be about the only thing he could imagine driving so many animals to flee, but the current conditions rendered that impossible. Hell, for all he knew, it really could be a Wendigo.

So, he did two things before he proceeded.

First, he reached under his poncho to press the transmit button on his radio. He needed to let someone other than Sharon know his location and what he was doing.

"Manchester dispatch," the tinny voice came through.

"Manchester, this is Officer Douglas McCorville of the Millwood PD."

"What you need, Millwood?"

"I'm out on Reed Bow Trail approaching Widow's Winder in Coney Park, investigating unusual animal behavior."

"Roger, Millwood. You need us to contact the nearest back up unit?"

"Negative, Manchester. Just want someone official to know where I'm at, and my station is closed down for the night. I'll check back in twenty."

"Roger, Millwood. Please advise when ready."

The second thing he did—removed his firearm from it's holster. He kept the weapon shielded under the poncho, but really, the only thing he figured would explain the behavior of the animals was an aggressive predator. Maybe a rabid animal. Either way, there was a strange sort of security in knowing that he could most likely shoot whatever lay ahead.

Then he took a deep breath and started forward. The trail took a steep upswing for a few yards that forced Doug to dig his heels in with each step, the rain pouring rivulets down the slope that turned the path into a mucky stream. Midway up, a chunk of clay broke free, and Doug dropped sharply to one knee.

"Shit, shit, shit."

It took a few more minutes to reach the top of the rise. His pants were soaked through and covered in mud, and muddy water had run over the tops of his boots, squishing unpleasantly in his socks.

"Lovely idea, Doug," he muttered. "Let's check out the woods real quick. Yeah, freaking brilliant. Could be home drinking a damn beer right now."

He took a deep breath and slowly panned the flashlight over the decline. Trees. Bushes. Falling rain. His mind ticked at something he saw but didn't initially register as his beam continued its sweep. Then he slowly brought the light back to bear on something incongruous.

A patch without forest. No trees, no bushes, no open ground —just blackness. It was like nothing he'd ever seen. The illumination from the Maglite stopped dead on an outcropping from an amorphous, cloudlike wall that seemed to stretch further into the distance on both sides and up to the treetops. He couldn't tell how far back it went because his light failed to penetrate it in any way, and the surrounding darkness of night and storm made it impossible to see its edges anyway.

Doug reached back into his poncho and activated his receiver.

"Manchester, this is Millwood, please respond."

"Reading you, Millwood."

"Yeah, Manchester, be advised, I'm still in Coney Park and, well, I don't know what the hell I'm looking at here."

"Say again, Millwood?"

Doug paused and licked his lips. Part of him was aware that whatever he said would end up as part of the official record of the...whatever the hell this was, so he didn't want to sound like a damn lunatic. On the other hand, he realized that he somewhat lacked the words to accurately describe what he was looking at.

"I'm standing on a ridge out in the park looking at what I can only describe as an enormous black cloud at ground level."

Doug started a slow backwards walk back down the trail, stepping carefully, well aware how treacherous the footing would get on the downslope.

"And I'm fairly certain it's expanding towards me."

"Am I reading you right, Millwood? A black cloud?"

"Roger, Manchester. Like from a bad fire, only there is no apparent fire, and it seems to be sticking pretty close to the ground instead of rising up."

Static responded as Doug continued his cautious backpedal. It was hard to tell distance with the cloud because it didn't have any shadow or distinctly observable features, it was just a uniform, three-dimensional nothingness, but he was pretty sure it was moving faster than he was.

Finally, the response came:

"Millwood, please clarify. Is this some sort of prank?"

"No," Doug answered. "No prank. Completely serious. I'm getting the hell out of here, and I recommend that you send units to rendezvous at Millwood PD to plan and mount a proper investigation."

Doug made it far enough down the ridge for the rise to obscure the cloud, at which point he holstered his gun and turned to face down the trail towards the road and his car. He didn't like having his back to the cloud, but he didn't really fancy getting caught by it. Was it a product of some sort of chemical spill, perhaps? Or maybe something geothermal? He clambered down the patch of trail where he'd dropped to his knee on the way up, then quickened his step.

Even as he crested the final ridge that marked the home stretch towards his car, a strange urge to stop and turn around, to look at the cloud, washed over him. What would it feel like to stick his hand into it? Would it be cool and damp on his cheeks if he pressed his face to its border? Would it feel thick in his lungs if he breathed it in? Doug gritted his teeth and ignored the thoughts as wild fantasy, the way people sometimes have a flash impulse to jerk their steering wheel down an embankment or jump off a high ledge.

When he reached his vehicle, he tossed himself into the driver's seat, stripped off his poncho, and took several deep breaths. In the process, he pulled out his phone. Nine missed calls from Sharon. Had there been no signal in the park? He played the first message.

"Hey, Doug," her voice said with a tremble. "I'm out on Wainscott Road, and I drove into some sort of...cloud, I guess. I can't see a damn thing, and it doesn't seem to be going away. I really don't know what to do."

Doug chuckled sardonically. Wainscott Road was hardly two miles away and ran along the side of the park. It was also the road Sam lived off.

When Doug heard the second message, sent three minutes later, he didn't care.

"Um...Sweetie...," she said, her voice clearly shaking. "I'm still stuck, and I still can't see a goddamn thing. This is going to sound crazy, but my car...it's freezing. I'm scared, Doug. I need you to help me. I don't know what to do."

Doug immediately dialed her number.

Her phone went straight to voice mail.

"Son of a bitch."

He set his cell on speaker and dialed Chief Holler. Then, as it began to ring, he put the car in reverse and turned the vehicle.

HEATHER

Heather adjusted her reading glasses as she tried to keep the pages she was reading from flopping about as she walked. Little traffic busied the hospital ward hall at that hour, but she still stayed mindful enough of her path to avoid colliding with any nurses, orderlies, patients' family members, chairs, or potted plants. The financial numbers on the packet she held rattled about her head, the totals not astronomical, but high enough that she was more than grateful that Mr. Weaver's insurance would eat the lion's share of the bill. Or bills, rather. How many providers did this hospital use, anyway? Middle class meant having the ability to live comfortably. Delaying death comfortably was a privilege reserved for the rich.

Of course, that didn't prevent her husband from heading down to meet with the hospital's financial consultant.

Normally, Susan would have gone home by now, but William had gotten her sent in with a couple well placed phone calls. To Heather, since Mr. Weaver's insurance would cover it, there was no reason to worry about the overall bill or its particulars. They might have to front a fee or two, a deductible—she couldn't quite remember the machinations of the industry—but for the most part, as far as she was concerned, it was covered. William could never quite believe that such a dismissal didn't rankle the accountant in her, but the way she saw it, just like at work where she was only responsible for the books of her department, she was only interested in the books of her own household.

William saw it as a matter of deep injustice for anyone to get charged more than absolutely necessary. Therefore, he fully intended to negotiate on every point of the bill that struck him as negotiable, and he would stride into battle cloaked in the armor of indignation about what he termed, 'the gross price inflation endemic of the whole health care system'. Naturally, Heather saw this as a somewhat embarrassing campaign to be a part of or witness to. So, she contented herself to allow him to marshal and guide his argumentative forces while she relaxed with her children.

She only kind of realized that she'd actually arrived back in Mica's room. If she'd been more accustomed to the hospital, she might easily have been so engrossed in the financial data that she could've arrived, settled in, and finished the whole document before she registered her surroundings.

When she looked up, she saw her son standing at the window. One of them. The one who should be in bed.

Heather stepped further into the room, deliberately turned to face each seat, the bed, the bathroom. Still just the one.

"Mica?" Heather said. The boy started and turned. His face

went white as a lawn after a Nor'easter. "What are you doing out of bed? Where is your brother?"

The scene would've been perfect if he'd made an audible gulp, but the way his mouth opened and closed twice spoke enough in its silence. The news still prattled from the TV, but static garbled the anchor and the image pixelated and resolved, pixelated and resolved.

"Um," Mica said. He looked like a trapped cat. Heather might have assumed Stuart had gone somewhere innocuous like the vending machines, but knowledge of transgression etched her youngest's face.

"Mica Bradley," Heather said. "Where is your brother?"

Mica bit his lip. Sometimes you can look at someone and imagine the sound their mind is making internally as it operates. In this case, if Heather had thought about it, she might've considered those old stock market tickers that printed ribbons, a news teletype machine, or a dot matrix printer. Instead, she became aware that a noise grew in her own head, a bit like the TV's static, or perhaps that grit that old records picked up when they get a little too worn.

Heather closed her hands into fists. She pressed her knuckles to her hips and stood akimbo.

"If you don't tell me right now," Heather said, "car accident or not, there's gonna be hell to pay, especially if your father gets wind of this."

Mica looked at his feet. His shoulders slouched and drew inward. His hand curled like his fingers, wanting to crawl into his palms.

"He left," Mica said.

"Left? What do you mean he left?"

Mica shuffled his feet. He didn't exactly glance or point with his chin, but he sort of slightly gestured with a twitch of his neck towards the window.

Thunder rumbled outside. It had been rumbling the whole time, really, but it only now became relevant enough to notice. Immediately, her face softened and worry invaded her eyes. Horizontal creases striped her forehead. Of course, Stuart not being where he was supposed to be when he was supposed to be there was no surprise in and of itself, but Heather had a hard time imagining him wandering about somewhere other than the neighborhood or somewhere immediately attached to it. There was nowhere to go around the hospital, and it wasn't like Stuart had money or a car—and he'd left his bike in the woods. Could he have gone to retrieve his bike? Why would he even think to do something like that in the rain? What if he got struck by lightning? What if a car slid on some standing water and hit him while he walked along the side of the road?

"Where would he go on a night like this?"

Mica shrugged, but his eyes trembled in their sockets. Before, the slight little shift of his head had clearly been his attempt to point outside, even though he really didn't want to. Now, his neck twitched in a way that suggested he was fighting the impulse to turn it much further.

"You know, don't you?" Heather said.

Mica swallowed and nodded. Heather crossed over to the boy and knelt in front of him. She placed both hands on his shoulders and looked up at his face.

"Mica," she said. "It's been an awful day. I'm not mad at you. I'm not even mad at Stuart."

"You're going to be," Mica said.

"I promise I won't," Heather said. "That's a bad storm outside. If your brother is out in it, I have to find him."

Mica pointed out to the hills. The light still glowed like someone had turned on a dozen blue tinted floodlights, leaving a small patch of trees looking more like a Mediterranean bay on a clear day than a forest at the foot of granite Mountains.

"That light in the woods," Mica said.

Heather frowned. She wasn't great with distances, and the heavy storm and the poor evening light didn't help. Best she guessed, it was a good couple miles off. Stuart had walked and biked such distances more than his share, more than she liked to admit her not-even-teen son had done, but he'd never done it in conditions like this. What on earth could he be thinking? Could he have been a lot more addled by witnessing the accident than she'd realized? He'd been unusually quiet the whole evening, but Heather had chalked that up to him assuming that he'd be in deep trouble once they got back home. After all, his father was in the hospital with them and not at all happy that any of them were there. What if he was trying to run away?

Heather brought a hand to her face and rubbed each temple in firm, steady circles.

"Jesus flying through space," she said. "This is the last thing I need."

Then she re-claimed her son's gaze.

"Mica," she said. "You get back in bed."

She pointed to the TV.

"Watch some cartoons," she said. "Tell your father that I said you could, and then tell him that I'm getting Stuart something to eat. That Stuart got hungry, and I took him to get something to eat."

"You want me to lie to dad?" Mica said.

Heather sighed.

"Hopefully, I'll be back before he is," she said. "And even if I'm not, it'll be better for everyone if we don't give him any more reasons to be angry at Stuart."

"If dad finds out, he'll be really mad," Mica said.

"I know," she said. "But I don't know what else to do."

Mica nodded. Heather could tell he was extremely uncomfortable with what she asked, but hopefully he understood. If not, there was only so much she could do to help him. No matter what, the longer she waited, the further away Stuart could get. It would be a reasonable task if he was headed where Mica thought he was headed, but if he changed course, got lost, or turned around, he'd be far easier to find before he'd gotten very far. Was that officer still wandering about? Should she call him?

If she should, she would have to do it on the way. She had to get going, now.

She gave her younger son a quick, tight hug.

"I'm sorry to leave while you're still in here," she said.

"It's okay, mom," Mica said.

Heather rose to leave. Her knees wobbled a bit from her anxiety, and her hands shook so much that she jingled the keys she didn't even realize she'd already extracted from her purse.

"I'll be back soon," she said.

She was halfway to the door when Mica raised his voice just a bit.

"Mom?" he said.

Heather half turned, keys still in hand, still rattling slightly. She also hadn't realized that she'd already separated her car key from the rest and held it as if she expected to plant it into the ignition at any moment.

"Yes, dear?" Heather said.

Mica looked back down to his feet.

"I'm not so sure he's really Stuart."

SHARON

Sharon shivered violently in her seat as she wrapped herself tighter in the sweater. She felt grateful for forgetting she'd left on the passenger floor among the fast-food wrappers, empty cans of seltzer water, and Dasani bottles. It smelled a bit like something rotten, but it helped a whole hell of a lot more than the tank top and jeans she'd left Sam's in. From the moment the cloud swallowed the car, the temperature had been dropping a degree a minute, easily. Her toes in their sandals ached each time she let her feet sit on the floorboard, even with the heat blasting on high.

It was summer. It didn't take a meteorologist to know that a deep freeze in summer was absurd—even in freak conditions. Whatever the cloud was, it must be the freak of freaks, and now veins of ice crystals spanned the windshield like a massive spider web had fallen over the car. God, she wished she'd worked her full shift instead of getting Cindy to cover her for a few hours, or, even better, that she'd decided to surprise Doug at his house. She often thought to do things like that, often swore off Sam like he was cigarettes.

Either way, she'd be at work or in a nice safe house, not stuck in her beat-up Volvo on Wainscott in a black cloud her headlights wouldn't even penetrate, waiting to freeze to death.

The worst part was that even as every fiber of her being prayed that any one of her calls would actually get through to Doug, she could still feel Sam between her thighs, still feel him inside her. She could still taste him on her lips, smell him in her hair—even over the musty stench that emanated from her sweater. Part of her wished she had stayed back at his house, in his bed—but he'd be on the road again before the sun rose, and she wouldn't hear from him for at least a week. Now, she couldn't even try to call him. His phone went straight to voice mail, and the voice mail was full.

She tried to refrain from glancing at the phone, from hoping to see it light up right before Doug's ring tone, "I Shot the Sheriff," chirped from the speaker. But there was nowhere else to look. The cloud around her car was so opaque that the world beyond might as well not exist, and now spreading ice crystals were overtaking that. *Which was worse: encased in blackness or in ice?* Sure as hell—none of this had been in the weather forecast.

Sharon unlocked her phone with a thumb, swiped redial. Her whole hand shook, but the motion was practiced enough to work nonetheless. The battery gauge read 23%, but her phone was prone to die as early as 16%. She didn't make enough in tips to replace it, especially since a new phone practically required a blood oath and a second mortgage.

A few seconds passed, and the screen hadn't shifted from "dialing" to an actual attempt to contact. No ring came from the speaker. Her signal gauge had no bars.

"Damn it, damn it, damn it," Sharon sobbed, striking the steering wheel with the flat of her palm three times. She snatched up her phone and threw it into the passenger seat. She let out the rest of her air, and a cloud came out of her mouth. Immediately, she clasped both her biceps and shivered. Tentatively, she reached her left hand to the windshield and touched her fingertips to the glass.

The burn was as intense as accidentally touching a hot burner. She yelped and jerked her hand back, clasping her wrist tightly. She turned her hand under the dome light and whimpered. Her fingertips were red and bleeding. On the windshield clung the skin from her fingertips, turning white as the ice outside.

"What the fuck?" She cried. She looked around frantically, wanting to thrust her hands and feet against the frame as if she could make the confinement larger by pushing against it.

Instead, her good hand found her phone. She pressed the button to light the screen. Bracing herself for the jolt of pain she knew it would bring, she pressed her thumb to it.

The phone didn't unlock.

She tried again.

Nothing.

She didn't have her thumb print anymore. It was stuck to the goddamn windshield.

She grabbed the hair at both her temples, twisted it in her fingers, and screamed. She beat her fists against the dashboard. The radio squelched alive with static and shut off.

Sharon froze. The radio.

Not the car radio, an old CB radio Doug had given her in case of emergencies. It was in the roadside kit.

In the trunk.

There were also two blankets in the trunk. Doug had given them to her as well, in case she ever got stranded on the road in a blizzard. There were road flares, a full first aid kit, bottles of water, and even a couple MREs.

But, they were in the trunk.

Her eyes went to the door handle.

If the windshield was cold enough to freeze the skin right off, how cold was that cloud? Would she freeze to death in the time it took to traverse the length of the car, lift the lid, reach inside, grab the bag, close the trunk and run back? If she opened the door at all, would she let enough cold in that the interior would freeze? She didn't think something like that was possible, but she didn't exactly pass physics.

It occurred to her that she'd stopped hearing the rain hit her car. For a few minutes after the cloud had swallowed her vehicle, she'd still heard the storm beating on the fiberglass and the front and rear windshields. Had it stopped now?

Or was the water no longer reaching her? Was that even possible? *Jesus,* she thought, *I just want someone to tell me what is going on. I want to know that this makes sense.*

She took several deep breaths, and with each cloud of condensation she exhaled, her resolve grew. Whatever was happening around her, it seemed to be getting worse. The longer she waited, the worse her chances. If only there was a hatch that led straight...

Sharon chuckled flatly.

The back seats could lay down.

Mindful not to bang her injured hand more than absolutely necessary, she drew her feet onto the driver seat. She raised her torso, tilting her head forward through the gap between the seats, steadying herself with her good right hand by gripping the head rest. The back of her neck, as it nearly brushed the roof and the dome light, registered the cold fighting its way in.

Her body spilled into the backseat, but she managed to keep her left hand in the air as her shoulder took the brunt of her weight. Her head struck the rear passenger belt buckle, sending a bolt of pain that made her clench her teeth and her vision flash. She lay motionless just a moment, collecting her will before she slithered her shoulders further onto the seat and her legs dropped off the front armrest.

She was tempted to say a quick prayer as she reached up and grabbed the back of the rear driver's side seat.

She pulled.

Immediately, she wished she had prayed. It didn't budge.

The trunk had a latch inside. One on each side. Had she locked them both?

She could feel her heart thudding in her chest like a stomping rabbit as she reached for the other rear headrest. Even that one didn't work. At least the back seat was a couple feet closer to the trunk than the front. Except the trunk wasn't popped and the keys still dangled from the ignition.

She held her breath. The fingers of her undamaged hand closed on the second headrest. She pulled.

The seat swung down.

Eyes still closed, Sharon whispered, "Thank God."

Then the engine gave a violent shudder followed by a sharp

metallic whine that rose into a shriek. Then it all ground to a total halt. The whole car lurched along with it.

Silence.

Smoke belched into the cab from the vents.

She closed her eyes and sobbed.

MICA

The quiet in the room grew unbearable. It didn't matter how many times Mica crossed from the window to the door, then back to the window. None of those short trips brought his mother or brother back to the room. He paused to get dressed. His father had brought fresh clothes to check out in because he'd gotten blood on the others. Then he paced to the window again, to the door, to the window again.

The storm raged outside, but the glow still radiated in the hills. In the movies, light always symbolized goodness and dark symbolized evil, but what if the light was more like the bait of an angler fish? What if Stuart—or whatever Stuart was now—walked straight towards something awful and dangerous? That would also mean their mother headed there too. Mica tugged at the back of his hair with anxiety and fleetingly wondered if this was what it meant to "tear one's hair out."

With each pass from window to door, Mica also unconsciously took a step or two further each time, inching his way into the hall until he realized he was standing about six feet from his door. The nurse at the nurse's station was typing something into his computer. The room next to his was empty. An orderly stood down the hall with her phone in her hand.

Mica turned as the door marked emergency exit opened. He cocked his head sideways as Percy Weaver stepped into the ward.

For a split second, Mica began to lift his arm in a wave, to open his mouth to offer some sort of greeting.

The next instant, Mica ducked into the empty room next to his own.

What happened between one moment and the next was simple.

Rather than looking down the hall like any normal person, when Mr. Weaver walked through the door, he looked in slow circles starting from the floor tiles, up the wall, across the ceiling, then back down again. There wasn't anything wrong with the motion exactly, but it felt odd to the boy. It looked like Mr. Weaver was seeing a hallway for the first time. The second thing, as the teacher's neck craned, his skin seemed to stretch and sag with the motion like it didn't fit right, the neck itself appearing too wide.

Altogether, the figure Mica saw didn't look so much like Percy but rather like someone wearing Percy. Perhaps on a normal day Mica would've thought of this as his imagination, but on this day, given what he'd seen in Stuart, Mica's body reacted without hesitation.

Once he entered the empty room, he had no idea what to do next. He looked around. The room was set up so that when looking in through the door, virtually every part of the room was visible. The only thing he could do was hide behind the door itself, which he did.

He listened intently as he heard footsteps walking towards his room. Would the orderly or the nurse see Mr. Weaver approaching and stop him? What if it really was the teacher coming by to check on the boy he injured?

The footsteps grew close. Paused.

Mica couldn't see, but he could easily picture the teacher stopping in his room's doorway, looking in at the bed, at each chair, at his family's stuff scattered about the room. Was Mr.

Weaver disappointed that he wasn't there, or angry? Had Mr. Weaver come to hurt him? Or was he just being ridiculous, addled by the car accident, his stressed-out family, the environment?

The boy felt certain he could hear Mr. Weaver breathing, a deep sound, a little raspy like he was sick. Then he heard a slow shuffle as the teacher turned and started back down the hall towards the door he had entered through.

Mica edged around the door and peeked into the hallway. His eyes widened into full moons.

Unmistakable below Mr. Weaver's freshly trimmed hairline, two spines diverged from the base of his skull and disappeared underneath his collar.

Mica tried to stop himself from gasping. The sharp sound of that fraction of a second draw seemed to reverberate down the hall. Mr. Weaver stopped immediately. He'd hardly begun turning before Mica took off past the nurse's station towards the ward's main exit.

DOUG

The headlights stopped abruptly at the cloud's edge, the beams failing to penetrate the darkness in any sense. To an uncritical observer, it would have appeared like raising a lit candle in a pitch-black auditorium; a small enough light in a vast space illuminates nothing. However, in such conditions, one could hold their hand in front of the candle and see it lit.

When Doug stuck a branch into the edge of the cloud right where the lights hit, the branch simply vanished, like it ceased to exist, and when he pulled it back, it felt cool to the touch.

The officer tossed down the stick and hefted the old CB brick that he had stuffed under his arm. He'd long lost count of how many times he'd tried to reach Sharon. The failure meant little; it was just as likely she forgot about the radio in her trunk, that its battery was dead, or that she'd put it on the wrong frequency. However, none of that was going to stop him from trying. Hell, if his near certainty that she'd been cheating on him just before she called him for help didn't stop him, then a mysterious, impenetrable blackness wasn't going to do shit.

So, he raised the CB and thumbed transmit.

The squelch that erupted from it just before he depressed the button startled him so bad the receiver clattered from his fingers.

"Doug? Doug?" the radio spat in Sharon's voice. "Please be there."

Doug lurched forward and snatched up the receiver so abruptly he nearly dropped it again, even as he picked it up.

"Sharon?"

"Thank Go...," she said. Her voice was frightened, and her words shifted abruptly into a harsh cough.

"Sharon, are you okay?" Doug said. "What's going on?"

"Smoke," she coughed. "The engine...the cold. The vents. It's so dark..."

"Honey," Doug said. "Slow down a moment. I need to know exactly what's happening."

"I don't know," she said. "I think the cold seized up the engine. Smoke poured from the vents. It's getting colder in here, and I can barely breathe."

Doug nodded and scratched the back of his head. He stepped back up to the cloud and took a deep breath. Then, he touched his fingers to it.

They passed through its surface with relative ease. He could feel a slight resistance, kind of like putting one's hand in water, and he immediately registered how cool it was. When he withdrew his hand though, it seemed undamaged.

The deputy licked his lips. "Okay. You're going to need to vent the smoke. You're lucky it hasn't killed you already."

The panic in her voice was unmistakable.

"But that will let the cloud in!"

Doug nodded again out of habit.

"I understand that," Doug said. "But the smoke will kill you if you don't."

"The darkness froze the damn car," Sharon yelled.

Doug reached for the cloud again, this time sticking his hand a bit further into it. It almost seemed to cling to his wrist as he moved his hand in waves. How far in was she? He could try to drive it blind and hope his car held up, but the road was windy with some nasty drainage trenches. If he ran straight in, what angle would he need to reach her car? If she called out, would he be able to hear her through the cloud?

"Honey," he said into the radio. "Can you hit your horn? I need to know if I can hear you from where I'm standing."

"Okay," Sharon said.

Doug shuffled as he waited, biting his lip. He knew he was way out of his depth. That he was out of the depth of any police officer. Hell, this was probably out of scientist depth and into Superman territory.

He was about to check in with Sharon when the horn sounded, a thin, flat sound somewhere far ahead. It was difficult to pinpoint; maybe something about the cloud was distorting it, but it almost sounded like it was moving. Then, it stopped.

"Did you hear it?" Sharon said.

"I heard it," Doug said.

"Thank God," she said.

Doug decided not to tell her that it hadn't helped him at all. Panic started to rise within him. He couldn't drive to her, and either she cracked her windows and was breathing that shit in or her car was still filling with smoke. What to do? What more could he tell her? He needed more information. *Any* information.

I'm going to regret this, Dough thought.

He stuck his face into the cloud and took a deep breath.

Instantly, it felt like he'd breathed a handful of powdered mint. The whole of his chest felt cold and cavernous. He was acutely aware of the passages of his lungs in a way he'd never felt—as though he recognized individual passages for the first time. A violent shiver ran through his whole body and he coughed hard; it wasn't the way one coughed when they coughed against smoke, but rather his entire body coughed because of how alien it felt inside him.

He took a second breathe. The cold seemed to deepen, but otherwise the urge to expel it seemed to diminish. He wondered vaguely if the feeling was at all like breathing in the liquid oxygen in that movie he'd seen that time. Was that stuff real? Either way, he wasn't hacking the way fire smoke made him hack.

He pulled himself out of the cloud.

"Okay," he said. His voice felt strange in his throat and sounded a bit foreign. "I'm pretty sure it's better to breathe the cloud than the smoke. It won't be for long sweetie. I promise. Do everything you can to stay warm. We need to buy enough time for me to get to you."

Even as he said it, the words felt hollow because the truth was he had no idea how he could possibly reach her.

"You can't get to me!"

"Yes, I can," he said. "Do you remember anything about the exact spot where you stopped?"

"No, I must've driven like 30 feet into the darkness. I thought I could get through. I hit a curb," she said, coughs punctuating every fourth or fifth word.

Doug pressed his knuckles to his forehead. Everyone has faced a set of circumstances to which the only rational reaction was: damn it, damn it, damn it. Of course, it's hard to doubt that one's ability to think declines in an inverse relationship to the importance one attaches to the subject and outcome of a dilemma. In this situation, one could reasonably believe that Doug's cognitive ability had receded beyond traditional definitions of cognition into a state more akin to a pinwheel on a stick.

"Okay, okay," he said. "Here's what we're going to do. Hang on."

Doug started towards the rear of his vehicle, popping the trunk as he approached. He opened a box attached to the left trunk wall and pulled out a length of coiled rope, then he grabbed a couple flares from the roadside emergency kit. The trunk slammed shut with a sharp *click*, and he quickly returned to the front of the vehicle, deftly attaching the steel hook on one end of the rope to an eye underneath the vehicle's bumper.

"Okay. Okay," Doug said again, only vaguely aware of his repetition. Then a different awareness arose. "Sharon? Honey?"

Doug unspooled the rope and wrapped the loose end around his waist. The cloud was drawing closer to the bumper. It had expanded by maybe six feet since he'd pulled the car to a stop. He considered pulling the car further back, but he knew that if he didn't find her quicker than it took the cloud to reach his bumper, he probably wouldn't find her at all.

He froze when the radio crackled to life. The voice was barely audible over a surge of static. He didn't know if she was keeping herself hushed or if her voice was shredded by smoke inhalation.

"Doug, I think something's happening in the cloud."

"What's happening?"

"I don't know. I think I hear something moving out there. Can you hear it?"

Doug shifted his ear as close to the radio as he could, but he couldn't hear anything other than the static.

"I feel it through the seat and the floor of the car," Sharon whispered. "You can't feel that outside the cloud? It's in the air. In everything."

"I don't feel a thing, honey," Doug said, "But I'm going to come in there and find you."

There was a pause of a couple heartbeats from the other end, hardly a pause, but exactly enough to recognize it as a pause.

"Doug, if you do that," she said. "I think you're going to die. I think..."

"I'm not going to die, and neither are you," Doug said. "I'm getting you out of there. You just..."

"I think I'm already dead."

Doug tightened the rope around his waist, pulling the slack against the clasp that secured it. Then he lit a red magnesium flare. The intense glow bloomed across everything except the cloud, into which it seemed to vanish utterly. The heat washed over his hand and turned the blue of his jacket to a stark black.

"That's not how today's gonna end," Doug said into the radio. Then he lurched forward into the darkness. The flare's glow vanished entirely the instant it passed the boundary, as though its existence was nothing more than a false memory of anything that might have witnessed it.

THE SOURCE

To call the light blinding did little to describe The Source's approach to the world. Even though its presence had extended through the door substantially enough that nothing else living could've registered even the faintest iota of illumination, the minutest traces that managed to pierce the shroud were, to The Source, miniature suns. If The Source had a traditional body to blister, it would blister, burn, and blacken. If it had a traditional voice to scream, it would not be able to resist howling and shrieking.

The nature of this place was still agony, but agony tempered enough at the door that The Source could extend a bit of its presence—its real presence—through the portal.

For its part in this process, the door functioned as a conduit between places like one would expect of any other door. An opening through which something could pass.

In response, the fabric of reality in the human world began to warp.

Some parts became like the world as if filtered by a smudged lens.

Some parts looked like a piece of artwork on paper upon which a glass of water has poured.

And others were rain on a lava stream.

INTERIM 3
HAPPINESS IS A HOLE IN THE GROUND

Regarded solely in the sense of material composition, the fundamental content of all holes is essentially the same, excepting minor variations in atmospheric content such as infinitesimal fluctuations in gaseous percentages. The ubiquitous "air" trapped within our atmosphere may vary minutely due to elevation, climate, local pollution sources, and other contributors, but for all intents and purposes, a hole dug in Latvia or Kathmandu fills with the same air as one dug in New Hampshire. 78.09% nitrogen, 20.95% oxygen, 0.93% argon, 0.04% carbon dioxide, traces of neon, helium, and methane can be found in the vast majority of random samples.

However, neither the 78.09% nitrogen in Latvia nor the 20.95% argon in Kathmandu made Stuart and Mica Bradley smile the way those same concentrations did in a particular hole in the ground, built into a hillside at the edge of Coney Park. It was the first and only time that Stuart had ever brought his brother to the park while their parents both worked, and it only took an hour for both of them to end up covered head to toe in dirt.

See, they'd watched a movie on one of the cable kid channels about a pair of brothers who survived a nuclear holocaust in a fallout shelter they'd built with their father in their backyard. In the movie, the shelter had simply looked so much fun with its mini fridge and its ladder and its shelf of board games, books and coloring stuff. Though the father didn't survive the radioactive Armageddon in the movie, a major theme was how their last moments of happiness had been building the bunker together as a family.

Of course, William Bradley would not, in any way, be willing to excavate a shelter with his own bare hands, nor was he the type of person who believed in the impending apocalypse—he wasn't nearly speculative enough. He certainly would not sanction his boys digging a massive pit in the backyard.

So, the two boys had decided to excise the two most dogging variables from the equation. They hadn't really thought about how they'd move the necessary furniture and supplies to the park, but Stuart, at least, had already begun to harbor some concern that they may have been too ambitious in their vision. They'd dug for an hour already and still hadn't made the hole deep enough to reach their knees. Neither brother had anticipated the number of roots they'd need to hack through with the shovel blades, nor the number of rocks they'd find immediately beneath the surface dirt.

A little blister had formed on each of Stuart's palms, and enough sweat and filth covered Mica that people could've mistaken him for a coal miner.

Suddenly, Mica gasped and dropped to one knee.

"Look!" he said in a child's overly loud whisper.

"Oooh," Stuart said, bending at the waist.

There, only half unearthed, was the largest worm either of them had ever seen—so fat and long they might've mistaken it for a tree root were it not purple and wriggling. It was at least the length of Mica's forearm and as thick as his thumb. How could such a monster exist?

"Can you imagine the type of fish you could catch with this over in Elbott's pond?" Mica said.

Stuart smacked Mica upside the head, a little firmly, a little playfully.

"They don't have fish big enough for this baby in Elbott's pond, numbskull," Stuart said. "You'd need to take this out on Winnipesauke."

Mica nodded excitedly.

"Let's take it home," he said.

Stuart smacked him again.

"Mom'd shit liquid," he said. "She hates ladybugs and fireflies. You think she'd want to hold this monster?"

"Maybe we could hide it in her bed," Mica giggled.

Stuart laughed.

"Yeah, and be grounded until we're a hundred," he said.

"Would almost be worth it," Mica said.

Stuart placed his hand on Mica's back and patted him between the shoulder blades. Together, they carefully covered the worm back up with dirt. Then they filled in the hole they'd dug back over it. On the way home, shovels slung over their shoulders, they talked about how it wouldn't be right to have killed the worm. To have grown so large, it must've been the oldest worm in the granite mountains, perhaps some great worm king. Surely, it must've ruled some subterranean society. Perhaps the younger, smaller worms consulted it for help building tunnels, and maybe even the great pines called upon it to loosen the soil for new roots.

Yes, they agreed as they passed the stop sign at the mouth of their road, to deprive the park of the worm would likely mean to deprive the park of its life. It was something they must tell no one, lest a thousand hunters seek their fame within the soil.

In their backyard, they washed up at the garden house and did their best to shake off the dirt caked into the folds of their clothes. When they paused to make sure they'd reached an acceptable level of filthy, they met eyes, and both recognized the look that one held once they'd witnessed the Lord of Worms.

Chapter Six
All Who Are Lost, Wander

THE BOX

If left in a box, it is a statistical certainty that Christmas lights stored in anything other than their original factory packed state will tangle, even if said box is left completely undisturbed, provided a couple of basic parameters are met.

Parameter 1: the box must be small enough that storing the cord within it demands that the cord come in contact with itself a minimum of once with no maximum threshold to number of points of contact.

Parameter 2: there must be enough space in the box that motion is possible.

Parameter 3: nothing within the box, like the typical plastic lattice packaging, forcibly prevents the cord from coming into contact with itself.

Mathematically, it's a simple principal. In the confined space, whether the cord is bunched up or folded back and forth on itself, at any given moment, each of those points of contact creates a possibility for the cord to tangle at that spot. Even at total rest, the possibility exists. Even with just a single contact, a long enough timeline results in a knot. The knot creates more points of contact. Cascade follows and it's no longer a question of whether a knot forms, but rather how bad it will become.

The same for realities.

CHIEF HOLLER

Talk to enough people and you'll find some for whom the world as they know it really is ending. For the folks whose earliest memories involved headlines and radio news broadcasts of Spanish Flu and trench warfare, a world of smart phones, holograms, and self-driving cars likely appeared like the lovechild of Jules Verne and HG Wells novels sprinkled with a generous dose of Revelations. In a more practical sense, one must wonder: what absolute proof do we have that the world into which we wake is the same one from which we drifted into sleep?

Arguably, Chief Louise Holler still had one foot in the world of sleep as she sipped piping hot coffee from her stainless-steel thermos and turned the wheel of her Jeep Cherokee into the station lot. Rain battered the windshield with those fat drops so fast that even the wipers on full just seemed to leave a thick blur. Brilliant lightning lit the world and the following thunder peels shocked the fiberglass and steel body of the department-issued SUV. Most folks have the good sense to stay indoors, Holler figured, but then again, most folks had the good sense to steer clear of careers in law enforcement.

As she parked, she took a bit too large a swallow from her thermos and grimaced as the hot lump throbbed down her throat. She covered her mouth in her elbow and coughed a couple times into the fabric of her jacket before she tried to radio McCorville and Windham again.

Static squelched back, and after the third attempt to hail, Holler gave up. Where the hell were they and why weren't they answering? What was going on out there? All she had to go on was an unsettling call from McCorville where he rattled off something about a black cloud and pulling his girlfriend out of it. If she hadn't already gotten a couple direct calls on her cell from upstanding folks she knew, about the cloud blocking roads and the like, she might've thought he'd either gone crazy or been speaking in metaphors. Windham should've been manning the station, but he was completely MIA.

She squinted through her windshield as if the view of the stonework at the stationhouse would give her some insight about the evening. On her way in, she'd called Deputy Howser-Brewster, or Brewhouse as everyone called her. She'd been asleep with her wife; they'd had a couple drinks and cashed in early since she'd been scheduled to kick the lights on in the morning. Brewhouse would make all due haste, but there was only so fast Holler could expect her to move after getting woken from a dead sleep. Manchester said they'd send some people over as well, and both Nashua and Amherst were ready to come out if needed, but Holler needed someone she knew. This mysterious cloud issue was the biggest situation of Holler's tenure in Millwood, but she hadn't the faintest clue what to call it, how bad it was, or how they'd need to respond. She hoped McCorville and Windham were fine and simply unable to transmit. She'd never lost a deputy before.

The volume of the rain seemed to amplify threefold when she opened the door and hopped down onto the asphalt. A lot of nights, she loved the sound of rain; she could park anywhere and zone out to the sound of it on her roof. This night, it seemed to deaden the world. Everything felt a little further away, a little harder to understand. It only took a few seconds for the rain to start running off the brim of her hat and dripping off the cuffs of her coat.

She trotted to the door, each step splashing, and punched her code into the pad. The lock clicked open.

As she tried closing the door, a gust of wind blew the storm through the gap even as she pulled it shut; she'd need to take a mop to it in a moment. Or she could have Officer Windham do it whenever he turned up. He always tried to get out of clean up duty.

Inside, she trotted past the little cluster of hardbacked chairs that passed as their waiting/reception area, then around the reception desk, where she reached underneath. She extracted a roll of paper towels and quickly unspooled a wad that she used to mop the excess moisture off herself. If she tracked water everywhere, someone could easily slip and crack their head open. She didn't want to compound their problems with something like that.

Holler threw the sopping paper towels in the reception trashcan and checked the answering machine. Nine calls. Busy night. She'd already been thinking about coming in after Jonah Tamberlin, the owner of Tacks Carpeting, had called about a cloud across Bolton Street. He'd called Holler because they'd known each other since grade school, but if McCorville and Windham were dealing with the cloud, the rest of the folks who needed assistance were in a bind. At least one of those messages would be Sutton Wilks with his nightly "watch" report, but she had to assume they'd have their hands plenty full.

Just as she was about to play the messages, her radio squawked to life.

"Chief, Doug, this is Windham, do you copy?"

Holler took a deep breath. She could feel her heart thudding from the sudden noise.

"Hell on ice, Windham," Holler said. "Where the devil *are* you?"

"Chief, I'm here on Tennyson Avenue," he said, each word abrupt. *Christ*, the man sounded tense. "I think I've found that black cloud that everyone's talking about."

"Roger that, deputy," Holler said. "What can you tell me?"

"Um, well, not a whole lot," Windham said. "It's a black cloud, a cloud that is black. Except that it isn't up in the sky; it's across the whole road and who knows how big it is, and...well, my headlights don't even seem to get an inch into it."

Holler nodded out of habit.

"Right," she said. "What is it?"

She could almost hear Windham shrug. Then he said, "Hell if I know, Chief. I'll tell you what though, the air within about a hundred yards of it feels pretty damn strange."

"Is it dangerous?" Holler asked.

"What the hell do you think I am?" Windham said. "A meteorologist?"

Her cheeks grew hot, and she braced her palm against the corner of the reception desk. She took a deep breath, mindful that Windham was reporting in under unique circumstances.

"Keep your head; don't forget to respect The Chain," she said. She strode over to the front window as if she could see the cloud just outside on the street. "I need to know what is going on out there."

"I hear ya," Windham said, "but I've got multiple calls of people trapped inside the cloud, trapped on the other side of the cloud, shooting at the cloud..."

Holler placed a palm to the glass.

"Hold up," she said. "What?"

"You heard me," he said. "Got three separate calls about folks shooting into the cloud."

Jesus, Holler thought. Of course, if you have a crisis, you can count on the people to make it worse. She needed to make calls. Could it have come from the chemical plant? Maybe some shipping accident? Something geothermal perhaps?

"I think the best thing to do at this point would be for you to come back in and regroup with us," Holler said. "We need some sort of game plan if we're going to get ahead of this thing."

"I'd love to," Windham said, "But I can't. It's blocking the road I came in on. Car's got no exit route, so I'm gonna cut away from downtown on foot. Hope to catch a ride on the old dairy road."

Holler pressed her palm to her forehead for a moment as if a second's worth of pressure might ward off the impending headache.

"What about through it?" Holler asked. "Could you drive through it?" Part of her wondered if perhaps McCorville's stranded motorist had been in the cloud. Perhaps he'd gone into the cloud to help them?

Windham answered, "Yeah, um, that's a negative, no way in hell on that one."

"Roger," Holler said. "And don't head out on foot. Sit tight. Pull back about fifty yards and maintain eyes on the cloud."

"Be aware that it seems to be expanding in all directions," Windham said. "I think we need to get on the horn with the TV stations and get out an emergency broadcast about this on every channel we can. There's no telling how many roads are blocked, and we don't want folks trying to drive blind through that cloud."

"Roger, again," Holler said. "I'm just getting the station fired up. Going to check McCorville's log and see if we can't get a better sense of the situation. Notify me if anything changes. Holler out."

The Chief scratched the back of her head as she pulled the

reception computer out of sleep mode and opened the station log. Windham was a couple miles from where McCorville saw the cloud in the park and a bit further from where he'd said the stranded motorist had called from. How big was this cloud? How fast was it expanding? The log didn't really help —the last entry indicated that Doug had headed to the scene of an accident called in by Percy Weaver and involving Heather Bradley and her children. Holler frowned, since all involved were good people. She paused. The log also reported that there was an unidentified individual detained in the cells.

Holler sighed. It was the detainee's lucky day, she figured, that so many folks might not be having a lucky day. No sense in keeping a vagrant locked up when there was something serious afoot. Thankfully, the log at least indicated that he'd been fed. It was reasonable for a late meal delivery on a busy night, but Holler prided her department on their community and "citizens-first" image. Even someone who unquestionably deserved to get locked in a cell also deserved to be treated with dignity. The Chief adjusted her belt and headed towards the holding cells.

As Holler stepped into the doorway, the smell of piss and shit punched her in the nose.

In the cell, on the mattress— a mattress that had been stripped of its blanket and sheets and torn open so that partially uncoiled springs jutted like a cactus of corkscrews— sat the detainee, cross-legged where the pillow should have been. His head was tilted back, his mouth open, his eyes open and dead gazing. Between blue lips, and badly stained teeth, jutted a fat wad of paper towels that appeared soaked in urine and shoved down so deep that his throat bulged from jaw to sternum. The skin of his neck was purple from muscle and tissue tearing to fit the load that had been jammed into his esophagus and trachea. And his Adam's apple bloated out, fat as a prune.

His hand clenched additional wads of piss rags as if he'd died with the job somehow unfinished. The empty cardboard tube lay on the floor by an untouched dinner tray.

"What the f..." Holler began, but cut herself off as she heard the station's front door swing open. She turned to see Officer Brewhouse shaking herself off.

"Sure as hell coming down out there," Brewhouse said. "Things sure picked a peach of a day to go to shit."

Holler looked back over her shoulder. She was actually uncertain what to do other than calling out the medics. She'd never had someone die in the cells before. It had never occurred to her that someone might die in the cells. Where the hell did he get all the paper towels to begin with?

Brewhouse took off her jacket and hung it on the coat rack past her desk. Then the officer began casually leafing through some of her paperwork. "I was scanning the civilian bands on the way in," she said. "There's some weird chatter going on about town."

"I think you need to come here," Holler said.

Brewhouse looked up from a little bundle of envelopes. Even as she met eyes with Holler, the Chief could feel that her face had drained pale, and she had no doubt that her expression looked as deeply troubled as she felt.

"What's happened?" Brewhouse said. The envelope fell from her fingers as she trotted towards the Chief. "Is it Doug?"

Then Brewhouse froze in the detention block's doorway just as Holler had.

"What in God's name?" Brewhouse asked.

"I don't know," Holler said. "We're going to need to see the CCTV footage. Figure out if we're looking at a murder or a suicide."

"Um, I'm sorry," Brewhouse said. "Are you suggesting he shoved those towels down his own throat?"

Holler shrugged.

"Doesn't seem any less likely than someone with access to that cell shoving them down his throat."

Brewhouse put a hand on Holler's shoulder. She was uncertain whether or not the hand was to brace her or if it was to brace Brewhouse. It could easily be both.

"Chief," the radio squawked with Windham's voice. "Chief, you read?"

"Not now, Windham," Holler said. "We've got a pisser of a situation here."

"I got no doubt you do," Windham said. "But you ain't going to fucking believe what I'm looking at right now."

"Pretty sure we can say the same thing," Brewhouse said.

WINDHAM

Some days are just a doozy, Officer Windham thought as his fingers fell from his receiver to his sidearm. As an officer of the law, he'd witnessed many things that defied the typical, rational confines of general human behavior. When he'd started out in Lowell at the end of the 90s, he'd seen gang members find innovative and terrible ways to send each other messages. He'd stepped into and then stumbled out of— nauseated— a child trafficker's storm-shelter dungeon. His own neighbor had duct taped his wife to a chair and killed her by shocking the back of her head with a stun gun repeatedly because he was convinced she'd been cheating. Windham himself...well, he'd often used his job to reassert control over his escalating fears that the world had gone so far out of control that it couldn't be reined back in. Hell, earlier that day...

But Windham didn't know what had happened earlier that

day. He'd blacked out when he'd opened that cell to make sure the vagrant knew to never bother the good folks of Millwood again. And even now, he still couldn't pull together a coherent memory of what had transpired.

He'd been mulling the events leading up to opening the cell door over and over, concerned at how irrationally angry he remembered feeling—he couldn't even remember if he'd taken care of the security footage—as he'd been en route to investigate a call about what he now thought of as The Cloud. He never made it to the site of the report; the phenomenon had blocked the road well before then.

The thunder had subsided, and the storm had lulled for the moment as he opened the cruiser door and stepped onto the wet pavement.

It was at that point that Windham had initially contacted Holler. He didn't relish much lingering anywhere near the thing, but even so, he did his best to examine the cloud while remaining safely outside of it. He hadn't learned much, but he felt he at least needed something to offer back up when they arrived. After all, once Holler took stock of the scene, they'd without a doubt be calling in specialists. Environmental scientists, chemists; the key thing that Windham had determined was that this wasn't detective work. It was science.

For example, the cloud didn't react like any gas he'd ever seen—it was thicker, denser, more cohesive. If he swept a branch into it, it didn't disperse or swirl like smoke would under the same stimuli, but rather it pulled back into itself like it had some strange elasticity. Beyond that, Windham hesitated to interact with the cloud; he was reticent to touch it. It radiated cold, much the way a freezer left open would to those who approached. He was afraid even to breathe too close to it, lest he may inhale some particle that would later turn out to be toxic, infectious, or carcinogenic. Unfortunately, this precluded the vast majority of observational data from being collected.

So, he had ceased his examination and returned to his vehicle. The cloud only needed to advance another 10 yards until it would reach the hood of the cruiser. The vehicle's engine still hummed. The shotgun stood between the driver and passenger seat. Windham hadn't shut the door before he walked alongside the hood's edge. As he proceeded to the open door, he dragged the fingers of one hand along the hood, absorbing the tactile reassurance of its reality.

That was when it occurred.

Some events are so outside of one's experience of reality that they distort the moment leading up to the event, despite a lack of any preceding physical effect on the world. There were no witnesses present, and the extraordinarily cold conditions to which his vehicle would soon be subject would destroy the circuitry of his dash cam so no records could or would verify whether or not the bending of the physical plane within his field of vision was a real effect or simply a manifestation of his fear.

The trees seemed to arch inward as if their trunks planned to tie in knots. The ground concaved like it had been channeled by a century of river flow. Small rocks and branches and clods of dirt with grass attached, rose up and hovered six to twelve inches off the ground.

Then it emerged from the cloud.

Windham stared at it and gasped.

It had Doug's head. That was certain. Its shoulders and right arm were probably his too. It's left arm and torso belonged to a woman, the bicep narrowing sharply from a broad, rounded shoulder, but there were no seams in the flesh. The transition was seamless mid-bicep just as the larger shoulder narrowed to a woman's rib cage and breast. It wasn't wearing any clothes of course, because why would something like that wear clothes? Frostbite had turned large patches of its skin blue and black. Its exposed breasts were blackened lumps with chunks of ice clinging to their undersides. From the waist down, Windham was pretty sure it was male again, judging by the hair. But if it had once possessed genitals, they must've broken off in the deep freeze from whence it came.

Finally, it carried a woman's head in its left hand. If Windham had been asked, and he'd been able to formulate words in his current mental state, he would have been nearly certain—despite the frostbite—that the head belonged to Sharon. Lord knows Windham and everyone else in town had eaten at her restaurant enough times to know her face.

Windham fell back against the hood of his car. His fingers clawed up the front of his chest until they found the receiver attached to his shoulder.

"Chief," Windham said, his voice feeling distant as if it had come from the throat of someone about twenty steps away. "Chief, you read?"

"Not now, Windham," Holler said after a heartbeat's pause. "We've got a pisser of a situation here."

"I got no doubt you do," Windham said. "But you ain't going to fucking believe what I'm looking at right now."

Windham's other hand popped the retention strap on his holster and drew the weapon.

Doug's mouth opened. The voice that emerged was wet and raspy.

"Hey, Alvin," it said. "You think you could swing by my place and let my dog out?"

That was when Windham's jaw dropped. He wanted to raise the gun and draw aim, but his muscles wouldn't cooperate. If the Doug-thing had said it was going to kill him or that it was going to drag him to hell, but the freakish thing sounded concerned.

And then came the thing that caused Windham's bladder to release.

Its right arm reached up and removed Doug's head.

Its left arm reached up and planted Sharon's head where Doug's had been.

"And when you're on the way," Sharon said, "Please call Sam and tell him it's over between us."

Sharon looked down to Doug and added "I've come to realize Doug is simply too much a part of me, and it's time I devote all my energy to keeping us together."

The Doug-Sharon abomination returned Doug's head to the neck so that it could laugh. Its throat bulged with each chuckle like each laugh was a fat, physical thing bubbling up from its gut.

"Oh Jesus Christ," Windham said.

The Doug-Sharon thing roared. Windham scrambled over the hood and slammed his back into the sideview mirror. He grabbed for the door and thrust himself around it so that there was at least some sort of physical barrier between him and the monstrosity. Instinct caused him to begin thrusting out his arms to draw aim at the thing before him, but he faltered as he realized he no longer held his gun. Had he dropped it? How? When?

There it was though, on the pavement in front of the cruiser.

"Tsk, tsk," the Doug head said. "Dropping your gun? Holler's gonna rake your ass over the coals."

"You know what," Windham said, ducking into the driver's seat. "I don't really give a shit what Holler's got to say about anything right now."

He slammed the door and threw the car in reverse.

The Doug-Sharon thing swung its shoulder back and whipped forward. Sharon's head sailed through the air and struck the shatterproof windshield so hard the skull pulverized in an explosion of red. The windshield itself didn't exactly break, but a network of shatter lines spread through its entirety so dense that Windham could barely see through it.

The rest of the thing leapt onto the hood. It reached out to the ruined windshield and pressed its palm against it. Then its hand turned to a smoky darkness that seeped quickly through the cracks and into the vehicle.

Windham did not hesitate to kick the drivers' door open and leap out, grabbing the shotgun in the same motion. The weapon was already loaded, so all he had to do was pump a round into the chamber and fire into the thing's mass. He hesitated for half a second to marvel at its steady journey through the hairline cracks in the windshield before he depressed the trigger. In that hair of a moment, the creature seemed to become aware of what was about to happen, but appeared unable to extricate itself from its journey through the glass.

A chunk of Sharon's torso disappeared in a blast of flesh and fluid. The shot also blew out the glass, freeing the creature to fall bodily into the patrol car. Threads of black filament spread across the gunshot wound in its side and wove the skin back together as if by some invisible seamstress.

Motion from the ground beside the car drew Windham's gaze from the Frankenstein's creature in the vehicle as Sharon's head also repaired itself—except those same black filaments pulled her mouth and one of the eyes off to the side where the ear should've been.

"Oh, come on," Windham said, back pedaling quickly even as he braced the shotgun into the crook of his shoulder to fire a second time.

The shot went wild because, just before he pulled the trigger, his vision blacked out entirely. Sweat he hadn't realized he'd been perspiring suddenly froze right on his skin. All sound muffled like he'd strapped pillows over his ears, and he could've smelled more had his nose been stuffed with cotton balls. He'd backed into the cloud.

He had barely even registered entering the cloud, barely thought to take a step forward, when arms abruptly closed around him and pushed him even deeper in. He didn't need to see to know that it was the Doug-Sharon thing that embraced and propelled him. He was glad he couldn't see when he felt something dig into the skin of his abdomen and breast, over his heart, when he felt a whole new flood of sensation as his body seemed to extend out from its existing boundaries into the boundaries of its invader. He could feel it inside him blooming like a frozen nova, and he felt himself blooming inside it.

And he could feel how much it hated him. How much it hated everything bright within him.

And as that brightness was dowsed...

As every light went out...

With a devastating peel of thunder, the storm renewed.

WILLIAM

It's not entirely accurate to say that William Bradley returned to find the hospital room empty. All of the equipment was still there, the EKGs, the heart monitors, the IV pole, and everything else one would find in a hospital room. The few belongings they'd brought—a couple of Heather's magazines, a couple of Mica's books, and a few other personal items, still sat pretty much exactly where they'd been set upon arrival. To someone with no expectations of what should be in the room, it would've appeared as if whoever resided there had simply stepped out.

The room itself wasn't devoid of human presence either; it

was populated by a hospital security guard, a nurse, and Mica's doctor, Dr. Paul. The level of concern on their faces certainly fit a hospital environment, significant enough that William's body went cold with alarm.

The papers pocketed in the folder William held under his arm tumbled to the floor, spreading like flower petals as each piece caught its own lift on the air.

They hadn't yet fully settled on the linoleum before William strode into the center of the room. The security guard looked to the doctor, who held up a patient hand, and the nurse took two steps back to allow the attention fall on the other two.

"What happened?" William asked, his voice withering slightly at the end.

"Nothing medical that we know of," the doctor said.

The security guard took a step towards William.

"Mr. Bradley, my name is Harvey Felton," he said, "And I'm the security supervisor. Your children and your wife have all left the hospital."

"Not a chance," William said. "Heather didn't say a thing to me."

"This is an unusual circumstance, Mr. Bradley," Harvey said. "My office is still reviewing the security tapes, but we seem to be suffering some technical issues from the storm. However, as far as we can tell, your older son left on his own. Your wife discovered his absence and left immediately herself, and then a few minutes later your younger son left as well."

"Mica left?" William said. He checked his phone. No texts, no voicemail. "What the hell kind of place do you run here?"

Doctor Paul held up a finger. "I'd like to point out that your son was not released from the hospital and has not departed with the endorsement of medical opinion." William's shoulders spread and his spine stiffened, so Dr. Paul quickly added, "He's not in any immediate health risk, though. Again, he was only here for observational purposes."

"And you just let him walk out?"

Dr. Paul and Harvey simultaneously sighed.

"Mr. Bradley, please understand, we're a hospital, not a prison," Harvey said. "Hospitals operate under the assumption that cooperative patients will continue to cooperate unless they give us clear reason to believe they might do otherwise."

William huffed, turned, and paced to the door and back. He paced to the door and back. Paced to the door and back. He stopped, held up one finger. Then, to the door and back. Each time, his walk was purposeful, as if he were about to stride out into the night. Each return, his face turned inquisitive and scowling. His mind raced. The family's only working vehicle was in the parking lot. How far could the boys get on foot? Why had they left? Why hadn't Heather texted? Why hadn't the hospital called the instant something was wrong?

"This is unacceptable," he said.

"Be that as it may," Harvey said. "That's the way it is right now. We have our security staff searching the hospital inside and out, and we have all our personnel instructed to keep an eye out for the boys. We've even called in the day security, and they'll join the sweep as soon as they arrive."

Harvey tried to lay his hand on William's shoulder, but William swatted it away. Harvey attempted a kindly smile. "They can't have gone far, not with a storm like this."

William bit his tongue. He could sue the hospital later, but right now, they were better help than nothing. Instead, he nodded curtly and left the room, heading on the quickest path to the parking lot. The family only had one working vehicle, and while he had no idea what the living hell the boys could be up to, he knew Heather would go for the car.

When he reached the curb and the end of the awning that

sheltered drop-offs, he stopped to try and call Heather before he just aimlessly blundered out into the night. He had no idea where to go or where to begin, and that was an untenable situation for someone like William. He needed to start with something he could control. Life was like chess and war; initiative was the greatest advantage.

Heather didn't answer.

William swore under his breath at the empty space that now stood where he'd parked his car. Of course, he couldn't blame her. If Stuart had really run off, she'd want the car to find him, especially given the weather. He could even understand why she might not think to call or text. Those children were, after all, her weakness and strength. William remembered when Stuart had dislocated his elbow. She could be tense with a lot of things, but that was about the only time she'd bordered on irrational.

He turned his phone back on. The signal was intermittent, but after a couple tries, he got hold of the cab company. He told them to ask the cab driver to wait at the stand upon arrival, and he began a walk around the hospital exterior, hoping to find one or both of his sons hunkered under an eve. Their absence disappointed him.

HEATHER

The phone buzzed in Heather's lap, but she ignored it, leaning further over the steering wheel to see as much as possible through the shifting coat of rain. She chewed on a string of her hair and tried not to dig her nails into the steering wheel. In the darkness outside, neon signs lit up strip mall fronts, and bright orange exit signs were visible through their plate glass windows. Here and there an office still remained open, or a restaurant had a handful of cars in the lot, but the storm had kept most folks home.

No one was walking anywhere. No sign of a young boy. What could he have wanted so badly that he'd head out into a storm? Comic books? The jump park? What on earth made Stuart think it was okay to just run out into the night, downtown? The grounding that resulted would need to be cataclysmic; certainly, he knew that. Didn't he know how bad this was bothering Mica? As if the accident hadn't been enough, the poor boy had half-convinced himself that Stuart wasn't actually himself. Lord knows the whole family would probably end up in therapy.

Still, while she knew Stuart was certainly Stuart, Heather did believe that the boy had told Mica he was headed towards the light in the hills. Though it seemed ridiculous and absurd, sometimes there was no telling how Stuart's mind worked. He always got so obsessed with his imaginary adventures.

So, now, Heather had woven street by street through eight blocks from the hospital on her way to the glow. She couldn't see the light from the street level at this point, so she had to assume that Stuart couldn't either. Since Stuart also didn't know the streets, it was hard to say exactly what route he'd taken—and it would be all too easy for him to get turned around and exhausted. It was crucial for Heather to be thorough.

The phone buzzed again. This time, she gently hit the brakes and allowed herself one hand off the wheel. As quick as she could, she flipped the phone over. It was William. She turned the screen over again. More than likely, he'd be furious, and she didn't need an argument to distract her. He didn't have a car, so he couldn't help search—and someone needed to stay with Mica. She did, however, resolve to text him in a few minutes when she got the chance.

It was, however, about time she called the police. She'd considered doing it right as she left the hospital, but she'd been convinced that she'd find him within a block—really, she'd been convinced she wouldn't have even gotten out of the parking lot before she'd run into him coming back. Then she'd told herself she'd check one more block, then one more. Then one more—and she'd finally reached the point where "just one more" reasoning had reached a buckling point. If nothing else, she knew the radius he could've reached, storm be damned, expanded with every moment that passed.

She told herself this, but it wasn't until the end of the next block that she finally pulled to the curb and dialed the Sherriff's station. The answer came on the third ring.

"Millwood P.D., Officer Howser-Brewster speaking," the voice came, sharp and clipped. Heather had used that tone herself many times. It was meant to say, *"I don't have time for this, so this had damn well better be urgent."* Not too surprising. Storm like this probably meant a lot of calls for them.

"Um, yes," Heather said. "This is Heather Bradley, from down on Dryden Circle. I'd like to report a missing child."

The officer asked for a description of Stuart, which Heather provided, and then she said, "Do you have any reason to believe that someone intends to harm your son?"

"No, of course..." Heather started, but the officer cut her off.

"Do you have any idea where he might be?"

"He ran off from the hospital within the last hour, so he can't be more than a couple miles..."

"Wait, Heather Bradley?" the officer said.

"Yes," she said.

"Your son Mica is in the log," the deputy said. "Car accident?"

"Yes," Heather said. "That's why we were at the hospital, but I don't..."

"When was the last time you had contact with Officer McCorville?"

Heather frowned.

"Hours ago? He spoke to my husband and my son Stuart more recently than I did, but it's been a bit since then too," she said.

"I see," the officer said.

"And what about my son?" Heather asked.

There came a pause and then a sigh. During that pause Heather realized for the first time that it sounded like a lot of things were happening in the background. Alongside the conversation, Heather immediately understood that no matter what the officer was about to say, it would translate the same way: *we don't have time to look for your son right now.*

"I'm going to level with you," the officer said. "I will pass your son's description on to all officers in the area right now and hopefully they will spot him. But you need to understand that right now we have a lot of reports of people missing tonight."

"Did something happen?" Heather asked. Could it be the storm? A tornado maybe?

"Turn on a TV or your radio," the officer said. "Is the number you called from the best number to reach you on?"

"Um, yes," Heather said as she reached to turn on the radio. What station was the local news? Did William's XM even get local broadcasts?

"Thank you," the officer said. "We will call you if we find him or any information."

The other end clicked off. The rain beat the roof of the car like a crowd of fists. Heather started to Google the XM station list, but she couldn't get an internet signal. Instead, she started scrolling through the FM band. Little squelches of distant broadcasts leaked through the speakers, but otherwise, static drowned every station. She thought she heard a couple playing emergency broadcast bulletins, but she couldn't make them out beyond the impression.

Instead, she texted her friend Marcine from work, 'What in the fuck is going on tonight?'

'Turn on the news,' came the reply.

Heather mashed the horn for twelve straight seconds with her elbow and shouted, "Shit," for the first three seconds of it.

Then she sniffled for a moment, wiped her nose, smoothed her blouse, and put the car back in gear. She picked the phone back up as she pulled forward and dialed her husband. Of course, there was no signal now. No matter. She just had to get to the light in the hills. She had to get to Stuart.

MICA

The night had taken on an extraordinary chill. The ground still held warmth from the summer heat, but the rain was as cold as a November squall. The clash left a dense fog swelling in the hills that had started to roll into the downtown streets, and now Mica was no longer certain where he'd seen the light. He'd hardly made it a couple blocks with his bearings intact, and it only took a few beyond that before he lost them altogether. Stu had always been the explorer, the one with the sense of direction. Mica felt like he was always trying to keep up.

Now he was soaked to the bone and shivering, a long way from anywhere he knew. No one was out and about—it was certainly an ugly night—but Mica wasn't sure if that was comforting or terrifying. He hadn't seen a single human being since he left the hospital, and only a couple of cars. Fortunately, that also meant he hadn't seen Mr. Weaver either, or whatever the heck he was. Unfortunately, it also meant that no one could help him if something went wrong.

Not that he had any idea what he could do. Should he keep trying to get to where Stuart was going? What would he do when he got there? Sure, he might learn the truth, but if Stuart wasn't really Stuart, that could get Mica eaten, dissected, or worse. What if he stumbled onto an alien nest and they laid eggs inside him? What if he just went back to the hospital, presuming he could figure out how to get back? At best, the only thing in store for him was a whooping and grounding from dad —at worst, Mr. Weaver and his two spines.

Mica shuddered at the thought. What would have happened if he'd just been in his room watching TV? What could something with two spines want from him? Had it really had two spines? What if it was his imagination? He could have just spooked himself. It had, after all, been a really long and unpleasant afternoon and evening. For a moment, Mica scowled as he imagined hearing his brother telling him to grow a spine. Easy for him, he was the brave one. His father always said, "keep your chin up," but that was hard with the rain pouring into his eyes and the chilling air making him want to hug himself.

A rattle echoed in the alley between a place that advertised paycheck advances and a cell phone repair store. Mica gasped, and his head pivoted to the dark space. The old brick walls were slick with rain. A dead bulb in a fixture failed to illuminate a rusty door. An overflowing dumpster blocked most of his view deeper in. Beyond, he heard small splashes. Water overrunning a gutter and falling twenty feet onto something made of fabric. Something made of metal, rolling.

Mica pushed his legs harder. He wasn't short legged, but he hadn't had the same growth spurts as Stuart yet. "A late bloomer," his mom said. He didn't want to outright run because he'd get tired too quick, and God only knew how far he had to go.

The streetlight overhead went out. A neon *'Open'* sign sizzled in the window of a store that clearly wasn't open. Mica looked back towards the alley. The street between him and it was empty. For a moment, his own breathing seemed like the only sound. The next light on the street went out as well, and all the shadows lengthened.

Then, he heard something. It sounded like someone had knocked over a tall stack of empty cardboard boxes from behind the store he stood in front of. Immediately, his eyes darted ahead. The next alley between buildings intersected this street three doors down. Was someone or something going to cut him off there? His breath grew a little ragged. He could ride his bike for a while, but he'd never been good at running for more than a short sprint. Just another door and he'd pass the opening.

Just as he stepped in front of its maw an enormous clatter arose—a sharp metallic rattle, the scraping of claws on cement. A large shape came barreling out of the alley, knocking over a battered metal trashcan. The shape came straight at the boy; large, brown, shambling, only changing course at the last second. It was nearly out of sight by the time Mica realized it was a large brown mutt dragging a broken chain.

He realized he'd been holding his breath, that his whole body had locked up with fright. Now, he was so filled with relief, that he looked blankly at the figure that stepped out from behind the store (a barber shop called *Collin's Old-Fashioned Cuts*) into the alley for a good three seconds before he even registered what he was seeing.

The figure was hulking, bulky, larger than a human frame should be. It was dressed in dark clothes and had hunched shoulders, and even from here, Mica could hear it breathing—a rough sound like two swatches of course fabric rubbing together. It was hard to make out much from that distance in dim light, with so much rain and haze in the air, but the features of its profile looked over-pronounced—huge orbits for the eyes, too long a chin. *It's just my imagination*, Mica told himself.

The urge to scream built—welling in his chest. Mica took a slow breath through his nose, forcing himself not to gasp. He didn't know how he managed to resist the urge.

Then, without appearing to take note of him, whatever it was continued its slog forward, disappearing deeper into the alley. Mica slowly crept out of the line of sight of the alley's mouth. Something told him he was very lucky it had not noticed him. His whole body shook with cold and fear. The fog around him seemed to thicken, causing the light bubbles of the still lit streetlamps to appear even more pronounced.

The impulse struck him to simply head to the nearest light, sit against the pole, and wait for someone to find him. He had no idea where he could go. His legs felt pretty tired. He'd already gone the distance from his house to Coney Park and then some. No one could expect more of him.

Then a deep and resonant thud from somewhere out of sight told him *he* needed to expect more from himself.

CHIEF HOLLER

Chief Holler's hand trembled as she stepped out through the station's back door. Inside, the Medical Examiner was conducting his business with the body in the cell. It had never occurred to Holler that her own station house could one day end up a crime scene—not *this* kind of crime scene. With the need to preserve unfound evidence, she couldn't freely use her own facility. Though she could, with all precautions taken, access any gear they might need, she felt evicted, stripped of sanctuary.

It was awful. It was almost impossible to doubt that the

crime had been perpetrated by one of her own, a thought she found nearly unfathomable. Windham could be a bit full of himself and abrasive, especially with some of the kids who got themselves in trouble, but she'd been talking to him as she discovered the damn body. When he'd reported in on the cloud, he hadn't betrayed the slightest hint that he already knew about the crime. McCorville had seemed addled when he'd woken her, but the man was sweeter than that smelly mutt of his. Hell, the whole town knew about his girlfriend's affair, but his devotion to her would impress a lobster.

Of course, there were the off-duty folks, but Brewhouse had her wife to vouch for her, Collin Spruce was spending the night with family in Kittery, and Michael Bausch had been attending a concert in Boston with a gaggle of friends. It made Holler's scalp itch just thinking about it, especially since the security footage had either been tampered with or suffered a catastrophically coincidental failure.

Then again, perhaps the black cloud was causing a whole lot of electrical shit to fail.

With all this stress, Holler decided to do something she hadn't done in five years. She pulled the cellophane off a pack of cigarettes she'd taken from Deputy Bausch's bottom desk drawer (she'd left a ten-dollar bill in its place). She packed the box against her palm, pulled out a cigarette, then bent forward to shield it and the lighter from the rain. The flame popped on the first try.

Naturally, she nearly vomited during a spasm of coughing on the first drag. The taste was revolting. "Nope," she said as she threw down the cigarette and crushed it under her bootheel. She spat hard twice into a puddle. Then she retrieved the butt and threw it in the trashcan by the stationhouse door.

Just then, her eyes burned as headlights turned into the lot behind the station. A Dodge Charger marked *Nashua PD* pulled up and Officer Beto Sullivan stepped out. He had Spanish skin but Irish hair, a combination that made him immediately recognizable at law enforcement conferences.

"Louise," Beto said, extending his hand.

"Beto," Holler said. She didn't really like being called by her first name—that was something only her parents usually got away with—but now wasn't the time to get caustic.

"What's the word on the ground?" Beto said.

Holler sighed and glanced over her shoulder at the station house.

"Hell if I know, had my hands full," she said. "Only have two officers out in the town and both have gone radio silent, and both need to be considered suspects in what happened here."

Beto whistled and adjusted his belt.

"What about you?" Holler asked. "I figure you might know more than us. We've been experiencing serious electronics interference. Lot of static in the lines, can't seem to keep a connection on cell or landline. TV broadcasts are okay if you're close to the transmitter, but this storm is like a wet blanket on any kind of signal, and something is outright wrong with the cable lines. Truth be told, it doesn't make a lot of sense."

Beto nodded.

"Short answer is no one knows what the fuck is happening," he said. "But it's got a lot of folks scared shitless. News already has folks from universities with all sorts of rushed data and half-cocked speculations. State government is saying they're investigating, feds are saying there's no reason for concern yet. Currently, it's being talked about as an 'unexplained weather phenomenon.'"

"We've been calling it, 'The Cloud' in our chatter," Holler said. "Have they said anything about what it is or could be?"

"Not a clue," Beto said. "They've called it an 'extreme subcell,' a 'polar vortex'— basically just throwing science-y terms at it until something sticks."

"Fantastic," Holler said. "Guess we've been pretty unimaginative about it."

"Well, you Millwood folks don't get out much," Beto said with a half-smile that didn't reach his eyes. He looked about to say something else, but two more Nashua cruisers pulled in, and Brewhouse stepped out of the station.

Beto crossed over to greet his officers as Holler turned to Brewhouse. The officer swept the rain off her forehead and wrinkled her nose.

"Did you smoke?"

Holler shrugged.

"Tried to," she said. "Changed my mind."

"Good," Brewhouse said. "Saves me the effort of kicking your ass."

Holler smiled.

"So," Brewhouse said. "You want the good news or the bad news?"

"The good news," Holler said.

"The Staties are sending a hazard response team," Brewhouse said. "Mobile command unit, labs, full hazmat gear, the whole shebang. Should be here within the hour to—and I quote —'take over management of the situation.'"

"So, we'll be crawling with self-important assholes?"

"Looks that way," Brewhouse said.

"That's the good news?" Holler said.

Brewhouse shrugged.

"I lied," she said. "There is no good news."

Holler placed a hand on Brewhouse's shoulder and nudged her to the sidewalk that ran alongside the building and led to the front door and visitor lot. When she was sure she was out of earshot from Beto and the Nashua folks, she stopped.

"You gotten through to Windham or McCorville?" she asked.

Brewhouse shook her head.

"I'm hoping I'll hear otherwise from the ME, but I'm not holding my breath," Holler said. "But I can't think of any way what we found in there makes sense without one of them being behind it."

Brewhouse pressed her lips together. Holler could practically feel the anger in her officer churning like magma in a volcano. Anger was as understandable as the situation was hard to imagine.

"My money's on Windham," Brewhouse began. "I swear if I..."

Holler cut her off.

"Then you place him under arrest when you see him," Holler said. "You detain them both when you see them. We know one of them deserves our good faith, so that means both of them get our good faith. Honestly, there's police brutality, and then there's shoving piss-soaked paper towels down someone's throat until they choke to death and their esophagus ruptures. Whoever killed that man did it out of an anger and cruelty I just can't comprehend."

"Then why..."

Holler cut her off again.

"If you find either of them, play it quietly. We don't want mistakes on this."

"Roger," Brewhouse said. "And what about the cloud?"

Holler scratched the back of her head and it practically felt like she was digging her fingers into a drenched sponge. Her mind had failed to register just how drenched she'd gotten.

"I'll need you to take Beto and his men to set up roadblocks on all main roads leading to the cloud," Holler said. "Begin evacuating folks who live closest to the cloud, but do *not* investigate the cloud. I have to presume, given their prolonged silence, that Windham and McCorville are out of commission one way or another, and we can't risk losing any more officers tonight."

"Not gonna lie—I prefer not to lose *myself* tonight, either," Brewhouse said. "Where you going to be?"

"I'm going to wait here for the Staties," Holler said. "And once they phase me out, I'm going to use our GPS tracking to see if I can retrieve our missing officers."

"Suicide mission, check," Brewhouse said with a sardonic chuckle.

"I hope not," Holler said.

Holler then walked out the station's front, hopped into the cab of her SUV, and placed both hands on the wheel. She knew she should talk with the medical examiner, but it was hard to imagine learning anything that would make the situation better. With the station house otherwise off limits for all intents and purposes, the vehicle would serve as home base and sanctuary. It was okay, she thought, thinking back to the brief stint post-college where she'd been homeless. She'd slept in her car in Walmart parking lots and rest areas, too proud to accept help from her father. It was only for a couple months, but whenever she felt down on her luck, she thought back to that patch when she'd survived on less and climbed back up with nothing but her own will.

As overwhelmed as she felt, and as long as the night ahead looked, she knew that, somehow, they'd get things under control.

VELES

The beacon in the water cast rippling light onto the branches and slopes, and Veles crouched on a rock on the shore's edge among the cattails, reeds, and skunk cabbage. *Such curious plants*, Veles thought, reaching a finger under the steady rainfall to brush a cattail flower. Such a remarkable diversity of textures, scents, and structure. The designs were intricate and fascinating, especially when one watched the flow of gene lineages and cellular formations. There were many such things as this that he would miss about this world.

Somewhere down the slopes, he knew, The Visitor approached from wherever It had been hiding itself. Even if It were without line of sight to the beacon, It would sense the pull of the illumination, just as It had within the void from which It came. Just as Veles could sense the ripple The Visitor's presence imprinted into the fabric of the world, he could sense the ripple the expanding darkness imprinted on the world as well.

Whether or not The Visitor would reach the beacon and where precisely It was located were far less than certain. Veles was significantly off-put by that uncertainty. While no one's course was set in stone, it was not hard to filter the probable trajectories of most souls. The paths many people travelled could be charted weeks in advance with only minor fluctuations. Butterfly effects did exist, but they were exceptions rather than rules.

Except now. The town below swarmed with divergent possibilities from The Visitor, from the cloud, from the corrupting malice of The Abomination that drove it, from the curious interference in vortexes around several of the town's inhabitants. Veles hadn't foreseen all this when he'd set the first beacon, and he found himself in a rare state of distress at the dissolution of clarity. The Visitor approached, but the number of intersections that could disrupt his plans proliferated—and if The Abomination managed to retrieve The Visitor first, the disaster would be unmitigated and eternal.

It was strange, Veles thought, *to feel fretful as a God*, but such was the outcome of thrusting one's hands into the affairs of the Gods. He could've kept his eyes on the mortal plane, but where would the ambition be? Could he have dealt with an eternity in mediocrity? He knew the answer was no; that the linearity of existence was simply too restricting. Simply being, "a god" lacked substantially in greatness.

Chapter Seven
Looks Like Family

STUART

A family is one.
The parents and children are one.
Inhabitant and vessel are also one.

THE VISITOR

The Visitor sensed the approach of the first pulse before Stuart's body was able to register it tactilely. Stuart's nervous system registered the pulse as a blast of frigid cold. One moment, the air was damp and humid. The next, ice crystals glistened on everything, and the air held billions of microscopic ice flakes that immediately drifted like a shaken snow globe. The Visitor registered the pulse as an infrasonic wave, which could only mean one thing: The Source had nearly arrived at the door. A second pulse would follow, then a third, and so on, accelerating the way a hard-braking vehicle increasingly decelerated.

The collision would be cataclysmic on a scale unmatched by

anything the earth had ever experienced. Even the meteor, in Stuart's imaginative memory, that destroyed the dinosaurs was like a ripple in a pond compared to a splash. It occurred to The Visitor that it could viably shatter the surface of the earth. It would seem as though a billion years of geological life of the planet happened at once.

Which made sense, of course, given that The Source was tuning the frequencies of the planet, changing its atmosphere, altering the fabric of its reality to increase its compatibility with Its presence.

Either way, The Visitor found Itself frustrated with the limitations of the body It had chanced upon. If an adult vessel had been available, it would've been vastly simpler to traverse the town. It could feel the extreme exhaustion gnawing through Stuart's muscles. The boy had already worn himself out bicycling even before The Visitor had come, and he'd never done something so bold as to set forth across downtown on foot.

Now, The Visitor felt relieved that It seemed to have finally broken the edge of the town proper, and the winding road ahead seemed likely to reach the beacon. The side-by-side buildings had ceased and been replaced with residences and a couple of small apartment complexes, all surrounded by sparse woods.

The Visitor elected to cut straight through the terrain because It could sense one of The Source's scouts weaving in and out of the downtown streets in a variable search pattern. It seemed confused about which trail to follow—Stuart's, Mica's, or their mother's—but it was only a matter of time before It realized which one burned a little brighter. If The Visitor hadn't reached the beacon by then, It might never reach it at all.

Ahead, the road wound into the trees. The trees arched over the road, meeting in the air over its center. A fresh pulse hit, and The Visitor could hear the ice forming within the branches and leaves, a deep crackling sound. A layer of frost, like the inside of a neglected ice chest, bloomed on the asphalt. Each step felt like crystal breaking apart.

It wasn't far, now.

Around the next curve, The Visitor paused. In a streetlight about fifty yards down, steam and smoke rose from a Subaru station wagon that had slid off the road into a drainage ditch as the road took another turn. The idling deep blue vehicle's engine sputtered.

Though It knew It should proceed uninterrupted, The Visitor felt a twinge of both curiosity and sympathy within its memory. Stuart's memories said it would be wrong not to make sure everyone was okay.

He approached slowly. The taillight glow glistened like rubies on the frost. Clearly, the vehicle had slid on the ice. Strange that It hadn't heard it, but if it had crashed at the first pulse, The Visitor still would've been a decent distance away. Perhaps it hadn't been going too fast. When The Visitor reached the edge of the road, It could make out the backs of the heads of a driver and passenger. Both had silver hair, the driver's pulled back in a bun, the passenger's curly and wild.

Gradually, their profiles came into view, though It couldn't see them well. The Visitor lacked height, and the vehicle was tilted. Bracing itself, It reached for the door handle only to find it locked. The rattling of the handle startled the driver, and The Visitor heard her yelp through the cracked window. Her wide-eyed face, pleated with wrinkles, appeared briefly at the glass. Then the lock clicked manually from inside.

As hard as It tried, the vessel's arms weren't long enough to lift the door up and away. So, after two failed attempts to swing it open, The Visitor paused. The driver tried to push it open from inside, but the door simply kept lifting and dropping. The

Visitor knew immediately that she was too weak to hold the door up against gravity.

So, The Visitor took a breath and carefully stepped up onto the side of the vehicle. Now It could see the passenger better. Her eyes were closed and her neck tilted a bit limply like someone in a deep sleep on too large a pillow. The Visitor pulled the door open as far as it would go and then braced it against the vessel's shoulder so It could look in.

The driver's mouth was pulled into an awful grimace. With clenched hands and wrists oddly angled, she moved her arms about like she'd forgotten what everything in the vehicle was. As she reached for the touch screen of her radio, Stuart's memories suggested she was thinking about making a call. But she pulled back. Then she reached towards the seat belt latch, but her fingers didn't extend to press the button. For a moment, it looked like she was going to try to press the buttons with her bent wrists, but then she pulled back, whimpering. She did the same thing with the keys in the ignition. The Visitor realized that when the impact had occurred, she had been holding the steering wheel with both hands and broke both her wrists and thumbs.

The passenger had faired far worse. When the vehicle had fallen sideways, it had done so against a length of concrete rebar that had, for one reason or another, been lodged in the drainage ditch bank. The ridged carbon steel rod had pierced straight through the fiberglass exterior of the station wagon, and straight into the woman's ribcage. The Visitor found Itself severely perturbed, not so much at the passenger's death, which had likely been near-instant, but at the futile struggle and confusion of the driver.

"I can't," the driver said in a clenched whisper. The Visitor watched her eyes wander in a circuit from the keys to the radio to the seat belt, reaffirming Its distress about her state.

"If I unbuckle your belt," It said, "you will fall and hurt yourself."

"I think Linda's dead," she said, with a sad sideways glance. Her lower lip pouted out slightly, and for a moment The Visitor was struck by memories of young girls in the vessel's elementary school classrooms who'd been disappointed by something or other. Perhaps this woman felt the same.

"I think so, too," The Visitor said. How strange humans were, It surmised, that sometimes children thought like the old, and the old sometimes thought like children. It was as if no matter how much innocence they lost, it was always there just waiting around the corner. Or, in a drainage ditch.

"Can you call the police?" the driver said.

"I don't have a phone," The Visitor said.

The driver let her gaze drop down to the passenger floorboard. There, against the door, lay two white phones. They were nearly identical, but one's screen had cracked like a lightning bolt. The other seemed to have some sort of round button attached to the back.

"I don't think I can climb down there," The Visitor said. It was fairly true; doing so would either hurt the driver further or It would have to step on the passenger's body. Also, it would take considerable time, and The Visitor was becoming aware that It had already dallied (a word, the memory arose, that had been a favorite of Stuart's mom) long enough.

"Am I going to die here?" the driver said.

The Visitor considered this. Certainly so, if It didn't reach the beacon. If not, well, It suspected that within the hour Millwood's meager emergency services would be so utterly inundated that most people who needed help would simply not receive it.

"It is very possible," The Visitor said. "If it's any consolation, where I come from, everyone is already dead before they're born."

Something rippled through the driver's face. It could've been a reaction to the statement, or it could've been a reaction to something internal.

"That doesn't..." she said, pausing in a wince, "make sense."

"It did," The Visitor said. "But it doesn't really anymore."

Another cold pulse surged. A delicate lattice of ice bloomed on the woman's face and arms. Her teeth chattered audibly. The Visitor noticed, for the first time, a purple patch of skin that edged above the woman's collar on the left side. There was another on her left shoulder, almost like a shadow under her sleeve. It spoke of internal damage. Even if help was on its way right now, The Visitor suspected her body wouldn't tolerate rescue.

Either way, it was time to move on. Without further word, The Visitor climbed down from the vehicle and resumed the trek towards the beacon.

WILLIAM

In the blocks after they'd left the Millwood General parking lot, it hadn't sounded real. It hadn't sounded possible. William immediately thought that the radio broadcast had been overblown; obviously someone had seen the smoke from a brushfire or there was some strange spill. The couple of old crackpots that hung out at the barbershop could spin a global conspiracy from kids passing notes in a middle school classroom, and the media latched onto any story it could find. Lord knew the local news needed a helping hand filling a broadcast, let alone offering the constant stream of information the internet jockeys demanded.

"You believe this shit?" William had asked.

The driver, Raul, shrugged and held up his hands for a brief second.

"On a normal night, I'd say no," Raul said. "But something's wrong with the air tonight."

William looked out the window and then tried to make eye contact with Raul in the rearview.

"It is a pretty bad storm," he said. "Those frigid winds were like nothing I've ever seen."

Raul took a left. William had instructed him to drive downtown towards Coney Park in a long, snaking zigzag. Raul had hesitated at first, saying his shift was about over (which William found awfully convenient), but when William told him he was looking for his missing son, Raul had agreed even before the father had a chance to offer a generous tip.

"Not going to lie, those freezes scared the hell out of me. I just about stopped the car," Raul said. "It's not just the weather; fares have been weird tonight. Had a couple fellas share a cab—from the hospital actually—and I'll be damned if one wasn't scared to death of the other. And the other, well, I don't know what word rightly describes him, but maybe *unsavory*. Truth be told, something about him was creepy enough to chase a peanut out of a piece of shit."

"I'm sure you get odd ones all the time," William said.

Raul raised his eyebrows at the rearview mirror.

"You live in this town, right?" Raul said, signaling his next turn. "We got folks who lean a few shades from normal, but they're not anything out of the ordinary if you know what I mean. This fella was like seeing a blue tomato in your garden. I actually tried to call the police after they got out, but I couldn't get through."

William had spent enough time with cashiers, stock crews and truck drivers to meet plenty of folks with obsessions, delusions, and fetishes, but they were generally functional human beings. However, he remembered one woman who'd been a night shift supervisor in Kittery; she'd always smelled kind of like acrid dirt, and her eyes always trembled when she looked at you. A few weeks after a routine check-in, the store manager had called to inform him that she'd been arrested for attempted murder and cruelty to animals. They say, "You never can tell." But sometimes, you can.

However, William found his mind more drawn to the last thing Raul had said.

"Wait. You couldn't get the cops?"

"Yup," Raul said. "Station line and 911 both. Of course, at the time, I wondered if there might've been a tornado or something, what with that nasty hail earlier."

William shifted in his seat to return his attention out the window. He realized that for an entire block, he'd hardly spared a glance for his family. Of course, at this point, they'd driven nearly every street radiating away from the hospital, creeping as slow as they reasonably could without so much as a glimpse of Heather, Mica, or Stuart. Just empty street after empty street. No pedestrians. Hardly any cars. Even for a stormy night, it had struck William as disquieting. He needed to rethink how he was going about his search.

When William had first edged into the back seat, the night had been about him. *His* wife left him at the hospital. *His* children ran out into the night. *He* was being forced to scour the town. *He* was going to run up the meter on a cab. With the broadcast on the radio growing increasingly intermittent and filled with static, now the night was about Heather, Stuart, and Mica, and making sure they were somewhere safe. Out in the night, in the storm, they'd already been unsafe. But the bizarre cloud, the concept of it, was a threat of a different order.

However, despite the newfound re-alignment of his priorities, the cloud still hadn't truly become real in William's mind.

It was like listening to reports of a devastating hurricane that would reach into New England off the seaboard or the reports of blizzard conditions from an inbound Nor'easter. He didn't question the reality of those either, but he never feared them, even when they barreled down on Millwood. Even in the worst storms, like the blizzard of '93, he never lost certainty that even if order was threatened, it would be asserted and fully restored authoritatively. It took time for the plows to do their work, for the utility crews to follow in their wake, for the salt trucks to reduce the drifts to run off. The cars on the roadside might take days to unbury, but they would get unburied. The water mains that burst would get shut off, rerouted, and repaired. The Merrimack River and the Nashua River and the Souhegan River would all swell and surge, even as they appeared narrowed by jetties of ice along their shoulders. Each day, the sun would rise and batter down the banks a little lower.

Then the roads and roofs would be clean. The church steeples would gleam white.

People would drive and walk and go to work. Children in yards. Joggers and their dogs.

Just then, Raul pulled to a stop and announced that they could go no further.

It took William a moment to resolve what he was looking at. At first, it looked like they'd stopped on an empty road that cut through an unlit field. His mind wanted the headlights to be off, but he could see them illuminating a few particles or insects drifting through the air, an occasional raindrop of the dying storm. The light, however, simply appeared to cease moving forward. The road vanished as though it had disappeared into a wall, the way it might in some Wile E. Coyote cartoon, as did the road's shoulder and the scrubby plants that grew there.

Raul opened his door and stepped out to gain a view unmarred by the wet windshield. He didn't fully exit the vehicle, but rather kept one foot on the floorboard and put his arm over the top of the cab.

"Well, isn't that something," he said.

"More like a whole lot of *nothing*," William said.

William reached for the door handle. He couldn't really see altogether that well with the water and a bit of headlight glare, but he struggled to make sense of what he did see. There was simply no making sense of it—but he didn't want to settle for that answer. So, he popped open the door and stepped out.

In simple terms, it was a massive black cloud, but one unlike any cloud he'd ever seen. It wasn't exactly black in any way he knew. What he did know, from the faded road lines, was that it was slowly moving closer.

"Maybe it's a bad idea to stop so close?" William asked.

Raul looked at William over the roof and pointed at the darkness. "You don't see something like that unless someone fucked up to a catastrophic degree or something has gone horribly off in the natural order of things."

"And that's supposed to make *something* about this better?"

"It makes it irrelevant where I stop my cab," Raul said.

Despite a cool wind that seemed to blow alongside the cloud, perspiration stickied William's skin. He could search for his family in other directions, but the odds were the kids would've headed towards home. All the places they knew best were towards home; their friends were towards home, their school, that damn park Stuart loved so much; they might not have known the area around the hospital well enough to find their way straight home, but they'd eventually get the direction right. He had faith in them for that—Stuart especially.

No. William knew—he couldn't just turn around.

"Look, I need to keep looking for my kids," William said. "I'll try to make my way through that if I need to, but I'm totally fine if you want to head on your way."

"You a believin' fella?" Raul asked.

"As much as any, I suppose," William said.

"If that were true," he said, "you'd not bother to tell me to go, because you'd be as convinced as I was that there wasn't any place safe."

"No, come on," William said. "Don't you think..."

Raul shook his head. "I don't. At least right here, I can't forget that I'm on this side of that and not inside."

William shrugged. He had no intention of wasting his precious time arguing with a cab driver who wanted to stay put. It would leave him needing a vehicle, but anyone who wanted to stay near that cloud was someone he didn't want to stay near himself. His kids were out there, maybe on the other side of that cloud.

Still, it wasn't exactly easy to find a car during a state of emergency, and William couldn't hot-wire the nearest vehicle. Even if he had one, it occurred to him that the cloud didn't look like something he could drive through. In a lot of ways, it was like getting stuck in a blizzard. People fell into three categories in such events: 1) people who evacuated early enough that it was safe and feasible to achieve a minimum safe distance, 2) people who hunkered down to weather it out, and 3) people who tried to do one of the first two but too late. Those were the people caught in gridlock when the white out hit or who found themselves snowbound in their cars half a dozen miles from home. William normally would've mocked anyone who found themselves stranded like that, and a ping of guilt wormed through his chest.

A clatter off to the side of the road drew his attention. There, at the Sunshine Service station, a couple of folks carried boxes out of the convenience mart and were loading them onto a flatbed trailer. He immediately recognized the late middle-aged woman with burnt sienna skin and pepper grey braided hair as the station owner, and he presumed that the man with her was likely a husband or brother.

Taking one last glance at Raul, who seemed absolutely fixated on the cloud, William shook his head, stuck his hands in his pockets, and approached the couple in the parking lot at a brisk trot.

The couple stopped as they noticed William's approach. The woman set her box on the edge of the trailer, while the man set his at his feet.

"Excuse me," William said. "Have you seen either of my boys come through here? 12 and 10. Stuart was wearing jeans and a black t-shirt. Mica was probably wearing jeans and a green t-shirt, but he might still be in his hospital gown."

The woman shook her head. "I'm sorry, but we haven't seen any folks for a couple hours."

"I'm pretty sure that everyone cleared out the moment this muck turned up on the news, and if they didn't, I don't think they're going to be clearing out at this point," the man said with a frown. Then he added, "Did you say a hospital gown?"

"Yeah, my boy was in an accident earlier. He disappeared from the hospital."

"Well, that's a devil of a problem," the man said. He extended a hand. "Barlow. Barlow Mentaka."

"And I'm Lonetta," the woman said, shaking William's hand as well. As they shook, William realized that she must be at least six months pregnant. He introduced himself.

"You haven't seen a Toyota Camry either?" William asked.

"Sorry, no," Lonetta said.

William ran a finger under his collar. It was getting hard to breathe, and the air had taken on a cold, damp quality that made his chest hurt a little. He snuck a glance at Lonetta's stomach, then to the boxes.

"Pardon my bluntness," William said, "but should you

really be doing that? I mean, at all? You look pretty damn pregnant, and there's a giant black cloud about 50 yards away swallowing everything in front of it."

"We gotta save what we can," Barlow said, absently waving a hand at the cloud. "Can't count on getting anything back from that."

"Don't you have insurance?"

Lonetta rolled her eyes.

"Assuming they cover...this," she said, "we don't have enough money to stay afloat until a check comes. Don't know about you, but I'm not keen on starving while I wait for adjustors."

"Fair enough," William said. "Everything you're taking already boxed up?"

Barlow nodded. "All stacked up in front of the register."

William didn't say anything else. He went straight into the station's convenience mart and picked up the first box he saw. It was full of cans and his legs wobbled a bit under its weight. Nothing could make him feel less helpless in finding his family, but at least for the moment he felt useful, more so than he'd felt while sitting in the back of the cab, even though he'd been actively searching. On his way back, William spared a glance to Raul who was now seated cross-legged on the hood of his cab. *Crazy bastard,* William thought.

When William returned and set the box on the flatbed, he waited just a few seconds for Barlow and Lonetta to return, each carrying another box.

"You don't have to take yourself away from searching for your kids," Barlow said. "The longer you wait, the farther they might get."

"I'll never find them on foot," William said, "and I have no real clue where to search."

Before they could answer, William trotted off to get another box. He'd start looking again, after he'd helped a bit. He wasn't even entirely sure why he was doing it. Was it out of generosity? Or despair? Could those be the same thing? Moving at a brisk pace, it was pretty easy to outpace the couple, because Barlow seemed reluctant to get more than a few feet away from Lonetta. There were only a couple dozen boxes left in the station, so they finished the job quickly, and William found himself slightly out of breath and shivering from the sweat-damp on his skin in the deepening cool air.

Barlow stepped over and clapped a hand on William's back.

"I can't tell you how much Lonetta and I appreciate you," he said. "We'd have cut it real close."

"You're already cutting it way closer than you should," William said, with a bit more of a chide in his voice than he'd intended.

Barlow shrugged. "It's like with the blizzards," he said. "We barely survive those too."

Then, Barlow reached out as if to shake William's hand, but William noticed that the man had a key dangling from his fingers.

"This is the key to my bike," he said. "It's parked behind the station. Take it, look for your kids."

As he spoke though, he cocked his head sideways, turning it slowly as if tracking something.

William turned. His eyes fell first on the taxi. Raul no longer sat on the hood, and the trunk was open. The taxi driver scurried into the parking lot at a pace that would put your average Saturday morning mall power walker to shame. For a second, William thought, *a bit late there, buddy*, but then he realized that a large knife glinted in the driver's hand.

William took a sharp breath. Lonetta was shifting the boxes in the flatbed about. Barlow was already turning, pushing into motion even as Raul reached the trailer. Without even breaking stride, Raul hacked the blade into the trailer tire, grabbed the flatbed rail, and swung his legs over. The trailer's shifting weight and the rock caused by Raul's jump caused Lonetta to stagger sideways and brace herself against the boxes. She hadn't even had a chance to realize that anything was amiss before Raul swung the blade down.

Lonetta shifted just before the blade would have buried itself between her ribs, and the metal vanished into her bicep instead, jerking as it skipped off her bone. She wailed, turning away from the blade, but all the way around on instinct. At the same time, she thrust her good hand up, palm out.

The heel of her palm caught Raul on the chin. His jaw snapped shut with the clash of teeth shattering. Blood spattered, along with enamel chips, as he bit through his tongue. A chunk of pink meat fell down his chin and landed on the metal floor of the trailer. The knife flew from his hand as his arms pinwheeled while he backpedaled, his shoes clopping sharply like a tap dancer.

Almost halfway across the trailer, he regained his balance, bent over at the waist, and hissed. More blood spewed from his mouth. Lonetta shuddered violently as the glow from the parking lot lights revealed pupils that were cloudy white and rectangular. At the same moment, she gagged as she caught a powerful scent that indicated the man before her had both defecated and urinated himself.

Raul righted himself, wobbling as he straightened. He reached up and pressed two fingers of each hand to his temples like he planned to message them. He squinted, his weird, milky, goat-like eyes almost disappearing behind his lids. Thick yellow fungus covered his fingernails, and the index nails had both split down the middle. The tendons in the back of his hands stood out.

Lonetta stepped back slowly, careful not to trip over the boxes behind her.

Barlow ran straight onto the tailgate and crashed into Raul from the side, hitting his wife's assailant with the full force of his weight. Raul's body launched entirely off its feet and, even as Barlow slammed into the trailer's side rail, sailed through the air where it tumbled along the parking lot asphalt like a sack of beets.

William found himself standing beside Barlow, reaching down to help him up. Barlow groaned, turning over achily and looking a bit dazed, but when his eyes fell on William, he scowled and pushed William's hand away.

Startled, William furrowed his brow. It struck him that he didn't even remember trotting over. He'd been so absorbed in the spectacle.

"What the hell's the matter with you?" Barlow said.

William's eyes widened. Lonetta was now glancing back and forth between Raul, who was lying still in a puddle, and William.

"W-what do you mean?" William stammered, suddenly feeling quite uncomfortable with himself. He realized that the lights—the ones still burning in the station and over the lot—were exceedingly bright. He could feel sweat on his forehead, and little spots floated in his vision like he had a migraine.

"You were laughing, for god's sake," Barlow said.

William nodded absently. Barlow was right. He *had* been laughing. He remembered now. It had been really, really funny. He felt a smirk popping onto his lips and fought to suppress it. He knew that didn't seem right, and now his thoughts were a bit fuzzy at the edges.

"I'm sorry," William said with a deep breath. "I don't know what's gotten into me."

Barlow pulled himself into a crouch.

"I think you should go," he said. "You're welcome to the bike. Find your kids, get away from the cloud."

William agreed. He didn't know how or why, but he wanted to attribute the strange giddiness that he could feel himself actively suppressing, to the proximity of the cloud. It wasn't that much of a stretch—he wasn't at its edge, but if it were anything like a chemical cloud, he could still be breathing in particles of it. He'd been riding around in the back of Raul's cab for some time with the windows cracked.

"You and your wife should do the same," William said. "Forget the boxes before you find yourself sticking a knife in her belly—"

Both men became aware of Lonetta again. She now held the knife Raul had dropped. Her eyes flitted from one man to the other with hostility. She held her free hand pressed against her belly.

"Go find your son," she said.

It struck William that he couldn't decide whether he wanted to bite into the meat of her arm or shoulder, or if he wanted to drive his open mouth down on the blade, and the fact that he caught himself actively in that deliberation told him it was time to go. He needed to find his kids and get to safety, or maybe just get himself to safety.

He looked back towards the hospital. Could the kids really be between here and where he'd started? Had they simply just not crossed paths? William's gut told him he wouldn't find them that way, that they had to be closer to home. They were in the cloud, or he needed to cross through the cloud to get to them.

He ran back to the road and found a pair of long sticks. He trusted his sense of direction to keep his path straight as long as he kept his footing. He would call out for his kids every few seconds. If they *were* in the dark, they probably wouldn't be moving. Nothing much at all would be moving.

It was a bad plan, he knew, but William couldn't help feeling like he *had* to search the cloud. He owed it to them somehow. It would be an adventure they could talk about years down the line, how they'd all found each other in the darkness and been guided back into the light. Something still nagged at the back of his mind, but the growing desire quashed it.

So, he hopped down off the trailer and set himself to a brisk trot straight into the cloud.

CHIEF HOLLER

She hadn't even been fully inside the hazmat suit before Chief Holler felt like she was suffocating. She didn't like elevators and drove with her windows down in any weather except a downpour. At home, her windows usually remained open, the ceiling fans never stopped spinning, and her favorite room in the house was her screened in back porch. The necessity of the suit lay beyond question; the Devil alone knew what that cloud was made of or what it would do to her if she breathed it in. At the same time, she had a hard time convincing herself that things like zippers and seals would keep her safe. Even if she survived in the suit, what would happen in a week? A month? The worst killers were the invisible ones.

Holler opened the radio channel to Dr. Adarbi, the specialist from Manchester.

"So, you're sure this suit is going to keep that shit out?"

The response came back as devoid of emotion as it was full of certainty: "The department would not have requisitioned its purchase had it not met every current police standard for officer safety."

"Right," Sheriff Holler said. "Fantastic."

"I am obliged to inform you," the detached voice continued, "that the suit does expose you to MBT and TBBPA and can, according to some studies, contribute to cancer development through long term contact."

"Lovely." Holler turned and stepped towards her patrol car.

The larger scene did little to reassure the Chief. Brewhouse stood by their cruisers, both parked at angles across the four-way intersection to block the road that led directly to the cloud. It was a bit of a hollow gesture, of course, because at this point the cloud covered enough ground that it had stretched across segments of dozens of roads. They'd chosen this intersection because the road they blocked led directly to Windham's vehicle, which they'd located through its GPS tracker. McCorville's vehicle pinged far deeper in.

A state trooper Holler didn't recognize trotted up. His flashlight swung in his hand while he walked. The flare and vanish of the beam reminded Holler of a flipped coin shining in the sun. After he confirmed her identity through the plastic mask, he informed her that a news crew from Channel Nine would be arriving in a couple minutes, then he spun heel and strode towards some other destination.

Down one way of the street, Holler could see the blue roof lights of the two vehicles that had arrived from Manchester PD, and down the other way, the vehicle lights of the officer that had arrived up from Nashua. More officers would be in-bound from neighboring areas, and word was the governor was going to declare a state of emergency and mobilize the National Guard. It was only a matter of time before the jurisdictional arguments began or a gaggle of feds showed up and just overruled everything. Already, most decisions were being deferred to the state police, but for the moment, Holler was still a hub from which spokes ran.

She'd already been told a dozen times that she should send

one of the other officers into the cloud, but she couldn't let someone else take the risk, not with two of her own already MIA. Moreover, her gut told her that if they didn't do something about whatever the cloud was really fast, the consequences would be catastrophic on a massive level. And it wasn't just her gut. The cloud itself unsettled her, but it looked enough like smoke that her mind could categorize it. However, those cold surges rattled her in a much deeper way. She'd never experienced anything quite like that, not even in winter.

So far, of the nine law enforcement officers who'd arrived on scene, not a single one had the slightest inkling or theory about what was actually happening inside that cloud or from where it had come, at least not one they were willing to share. "Experts" would come soon from pretty much every university in the area, even from Boston, but that would happen in stages. In some government circles, no doubt briefings were underway. At the heart of them, question marks. For all those in disaster planning and emergency intervention agencies, Holler almost envied the excitement they likely felt. These were, after all, the moments they'd spent their careers preparing for. Soon enough, they'd be faced with the reality.

For Holler's part, she was scared shitless. Two of her officers were already missing in the cloud. An unknown number of civilians—a number steadily increasing—were trapped. For a while, calls came in from all over town of people acting bizarrely—reports of domestic violence and other alarming incidents in numbers she'd never seen. And then she started hearing that sections of town were losing phone service altogether, with hardline breakages and cell service outages. The power grid had failed for everything inside the cloud. She had no idea what was causing the situation and no way to predict how far it would spread. For all she knew, it would reach

Manchester and Nashua. Then, she'd just be another person who failed to contain it.

Hell, she couldn't even get all the roads blocked off that led into the cloud. She was still waiting on more officers to come help evacuate the nearby residents. Phone and news alerts had gone out and people already clogged the narrow New Hampshire highways with evacuation gridlock, but like any evacuation, there were certainly people who didn't get the message and plenty of folks who thought it wise to stay put and weather it out. Unfortunately, while Holler had no idea what the cloud was, it sure as hell wasn't a storm.

Holler tried to scratch the back of her head as she stopped next to Brewhouse, only to find that the gloved hand couldn't get within three inches of her head. She vainly tried to scratch the back of her head against the back of her helmet, but she just couldn't get the right friction. Why hadn't anyone warned her that itching would be maddening? Did Brewhouse understand just how unpleasant the suit was?

"They ready to shrink you down and inject you into someone?" Brewhouse asked with an appraising glance at the hazmat suit. Her voice sounded distant and thin.

"Once I'm in there, I can't really say what's going to happen," Holler said, probably louder than needed, but she couldn't really tell how well sound escaped the suit. "There's gonna be lots of officers here from all over, but you need to remember that you're the one here to represent the folks who live here."

"Dunno that I'm up for that, Chief," Brewhouse said. "How about you not go into the freaking void and die?"

"I might make it out just fine," Holler said.

"You always say respect The Chain. Chain needs an end."

Holler sighed and placed a thickly gloved hand on Brewhouse's shoulder.

"My gut tells me that if we don't get some sort of miracle, there's not going to be any chain left to command. In the meantime, I'm going to save who I can for as long as I can," Holler said. Then, she gestured down the road toward the cloud. "Windham's car isn't far. If there's any chance we can find him alive, that's where we'll find him, and we can't just abandon him."

Brewhouse nodded. Then she turned her attention back to the laptop on the swivel station in the cruiser. The GPS tracking system illuminated the screen.

"You don't know a damn thing about what you're heading into," Brewhouse said.

"Neither do you. We're all equals here when it comes to that," Holler said. "You can hold down the fort until the experts get here just as easily as I can. Tablet please."

Holler held her hand out, and Brewhouse passed over the tablet which displayed the same GPS map. The device was already zoomed in as much as possible to indicate Windham's vehicle and Holler's cruiser. The location tracking accurately marked where she stood. The road meandered substantially in between, but if she took it slow and nothing blocked the signal, it wouldn't be a hard walk. She knew the road well enough.

"Radio check," Holler said into her mic. She could hear her own voice come from the transmitter on Brewhouse's shoulder.

Brewhouse thumbed her walkie, and her voice came through the earpiece loud and clear.

"You read?"

"Check," Holler said.

"I don't think you're going to come back," Brewhouse said.

"Maybe not," Holler said. "Hook me up."

Brewhouse picked up a climbing hook attached to a spool of line and latched it to a plastic clip on the hazmat suit's hip. Holler turned and started her slow walk towards the cloud's edge. There'd been a hitch in Brewhouse's voice. Hopefully, she would hold it together. Holler couldn't help but appreciate Brewhouse's concern. They'd served side by side long enough for real trust to develop. They felt comfortable together. The same went for Windham and McCorville. Holler would give her life for any one of them. Probably was about to.

When she got to the edge of the cloud, she hesitated. In the scope of her career, she'd entered buildings where armed assailants held colleagues under fire. She'd engaged in high-speed chases through high traffic intersections and even entered a burning building. The difference was, those were all things that she'd trained for. Those were things that she could visualize, could anticipate how they might turn out.

One more step and she would have no idea what waited ahead. Of course, she wanted to assume that it was simply a black cloud, some insanely dense smoke perhaps or some sort of mist, but she couldn't deny that the cloud itself felt wrong. Even now, she reached out and swept her glove through the edge of the cloud. A clump of black pulled away and then drifted back into the main mass.

"What the hell am I doing?" Holler asked herself.

A quiver ran through her lower belly. She wasn't going to even try to fool herself. She was petrified. How the hell did she think she was going to come back, let alone find anyone? She closed her eyes. Once she stepped through that boundary, in all likelihood, she wouldn't be able to see anything no matter how wide she opened her eyes.

Brewhouse's voice came through the earpiece.

"You okay, Chief?"

"No," Holler said.

Then she took a deep breath and stepped into the cloud. It almost felt as if she'd stepped out of the world. Instantaneously, all light and sound cut out, except for the sound of her own breath in the helmet. She could feel her heart rate accelerate and perspiration immediately broke out on her brow. The suit had fans in the helmet to dry her skin, but it wasn't enough. Her awareness of how metallic the canned air smelled and tasted intensified. She felt like she was wearing her coffin.

She opened and closed the hands in her gloves. Her fingers felt like they were buzzing with anxiousness, but somehow the feeling of tendons pulling and relaxing eased her just a bit.

She took a step and then another and another. Did the cloud resist her walking through it? They'd told her that more than a few minutes in the suit and she'd start to lose her weight in sweat—but she now felt exceptionally cold. It was like opening a door naked and stepping out into a blizzard. Goosebumps went up all over her skin and she clenched her teeth to prevent their chattering. When she moved her arms, it reminded her of moving her arms underwater, just without the same level of pushback.

Would it get denser deeper in? Was it already getting denser?

When she was little, she used to practice walking with her eyes closed. She would walk down the sidewalk, maybe home from school, or to Cathy's or Breanna's house, and she'd try to close her eyes for as many steps as she could manage on stretches where there were no obstructions, only a straight line of travel. It was a challenge just to get ten steps, nerve wracking to make it twenty. Her record was 28 without opening her eyes at all.

This was different. Here, not being able to see, despite having her eyes open, made her bowels quiver and her spine run cold.

"Jesus Christ," Holler said. "Am I there yet? How much farther do I have to go?"

"You're less than a yard inside the cloud," Brewhouse

answered. "If you just take a couple steps backwards, you'll be back out with us."

Really, it was crazy. Even in a dense smoke cloud, some light would penetrate at least a few feet in. She took another step. Did it feel colder? Could she hear a layer of ice cracking when the joints of her suit moved? Definitely some sort of pressure compressed the hazmat's fabric. She felt something push at the inside of her elbow, then at the back of the knee. She swept her arms through the cloud, but they moved almost freely, experiencing the same resistance she'd felt as she took a step.

"Feels like I'm in a goddamn ocean trench," Holler said. "I don't like this."

"What's happening?" Brewhouse asked.

"It's cold. Feel like the suit is coated in ice. Keep imagining I'm being nudged and squeezed."

"Is it wind, maybe?"

"It's disorienting."

"No one's going to blame you if you turn back, Louise."

Holler jolted at hearing her name. No one at the station ever called her Louise. Hell, no one in town did. She was Holler or Chief to everyone that didn't birth her, and her mother hadn't called her by name directly since the dementia had set in. Instead, every visit had started with her mother asking, "Where's Louise? They told me my daughter was here," and Holler assuring her, "That's me, mother."

Now, she felt strangely uncertain where she was. Hearing her name in the dark, she felt as alone as she did whenever her mother didn't recognize her. She realized that she'd shuffled her feet a bit. Had she turned? Was she turning right now? There was something extremely disorienting about the darkness around her, more so than any darkness she'd ever been in.

"It's like being in a sensory deprivation tank," Holler said into the mic. "If you told me I was floating off like Peter Pan, I'd believe you."

Louise pressed the tablet to the visor and discovered she could barely see the screen. As tight as she pressed it to the transparent plastic, there must have been a thin film of the darkness on the plastic itself. She strained to make out the details of the screen. It didn't look quite right. It didn't look like it was showing her the right part of town at all. Were there two of her on the map? The street she was on seemed to lead into the street she was on.

"I think I'm having some sort of technical issue," she said. "GPS malfunction."

Static answered in her earpiece.

"Brewhouse?"

In the back of her helmet, or maybe just behind her, she heard a raspy whisper: "They told me my daughter was here."

The experience of trying everything she could think of to remind her mother of who she was flashed vividly in her mind. Photos hadn't helped, nor had talking about shared memories. She tried bringing familiar foods like egg rolls from Asia Fusion Buffet or souvenirs such as pieces from her collection of chipped and battered mugs purchased from damn near every gift shop across New England. She dug up a diary that her mother had kept in which she'd written about her daughter's infancy, and she read her the passages. One time, Louise had worn a perfume that had triggered a strong recall from her mom, but it worked only once.

"Brewhouse, could you activate the winch?"

Louise realized she couldn't feel the ground beneath her feet. She flexed her ankle downward, and either she rose up to tiptoe without effort or her toes simply sunk through where the ground should have been. Deprived of all frame of reference, she had no idea at all.

"I need you to tell me where I am."

More static. She could tell, however, that her skin was growing exceptionally cold and that she no longer held the tablet. She had no recollection of it falling out of her fingers. Without it though, she had no hope of finding Windham, so she slowly dropped to one knee. It vaguely occurred to her that her mind didn't seem to be working right, and she wondered in passing if whatever was wrong might be a side of effect of being inside the cloud.

Her knee kept lowering. She couldn't tell, but she felt certain that she had to have lowered it far below where it should have connected with solid ground. However, she also felt that her body had barely flexed in the way it would need to in order to kneel fully. Was her perception of time wrong? Of distance? Of her body? Was she kneeling or walking? Was that why her legs kept moving?

"Brewhouse," Louise said. "Pull me out."

There was no answer. There wasn't even static.

She was cut off. Completely alone. She tried to picture Brewhouse, but the image seemed to melt out of her mind's eye. What if there hadn't been someone named Brewhouse? What kind of name was that anyway? Had she just been walking in the darkness alone? Her heart rate accelerated, as did her breathing. She pressed a hand to her chest to try to feel her heartbeat, but she couldn't feel anything through the suit except a strange crisscross of ridges all over her torso. Something was pulling at her helmet, but she dismissed it, trying to focus on testing the ridges with her fingers.

They weren't ridges. Some sort of cord. Something wrapped around her. Some sort of rope. The line Brewhouse had attached to her.

The pull at her helmet grew more insistent, but wasn't actually pulling at her helmet, rather her neck.

Her fingers followed the cord. If she could find where it clipped to her body, she could follow back. It would mean giving up finding Windham, but she really didn't think she had much of a chance at this point.

The pressure seemed to be growing in her head. She felt like she needed to loosen her collar or something, but she couldn't do anything through the hazmat suit. The fans made her face really cold. And it occurred to her that even though just moments ago she'd been unable to make anything out in the darkness, now it was as if her eyes weren't there at all.

She'd forgotten what it was like to see?

Her fingers kept following the cord. It was wrapped around her as if she'd been spinning herself into it. She felt dizzy, and it was getting harder and harder to keep enough pressure on the cord for her to follow it. Her cheeks hurt, and her forehead felt like it was tearing open when she wrinkled it in apprehension.

Her index finger traced the cord all the way up to her helmet, where it seemed to disappear straight through the fabric and into the suit itself. At first, she felt an overwhelming impression it disappeared into her skin and up her jugular, as if it had threaded itself up into her artery like a pipe cleaner into a straw. Then, she realized that it was coiled around her neck and gradually tightening, cutting off the blood flow. Was she breathing? She tried to expand her chest, but did it obey?

Her mind was frantic, but her movements felt like slow motion as she gradually reached up to get the helmet off. Her fingers felt miles away as they fumbled against the Velcro and zippers, and it occurred to her that maybe she was already dead, having either strangled or died from blood blockage. Were her lungs even there anymore? Was that the sound of her own gasping in her ears?

Finally, her hand clawed under the rope and jerked it away from her skin. She sucked in a massive breath even as she realized that she was no longer wearing her helmet at all. The frigid air sent lances of pain through her chest, and it felt like she was turning to ice from the inside out. Despite the agony, an intense clarity swept away everything that had cluttered her mind.

Even though her skin seemed to freeze momentarily to the cord every time she let her grasp linger even a fraction of a second, she fumbled across the arctic asphalt until she was pretty sure she held the cord at a point where it led away from her body. Then, she followed it hand over hand over hand, one step at a time. Her muscles screamed with whatever damage the cold was inflicting on them, and her lungs felt like they were wet and oily on the inside. Explosive coughs wracked her torso like convulsions, and she tasted blood at the back of her throat. Violent shivers threatened to topple her from her feet, and she knew that if she stumbled, she would never again rise. How many steps had she forced herself to take? How many more did she need to manage?

Then, in her ear: "They told me my daughter was here."

Louise's knees buckled, and she pitched forward.

White light exploded as she struck the ground. Vaguely, she thought she had struck her head on the pavement, but she realized that she could smell dirt and her own blood. That she could hear shouting voices. That it was hot. So unbearably hot. Her skin felt like it was on fire. Something tightened on her wrist, and she felt her chest dragging along the ground, the fabric of the hazmat suit grinding along the pavement.

"Help, someone! I need some help over here," she heard Brewhouse calling. Everything appeared as a blur of searing brilliance. It felt like she'd been in the dark for weeks and was seeing daylight for the first time.

"What..." Louise started, her voice hoarse and broken, but Brewhouse squeezed her shoulder.

"Shhhhh," the woman said. "You're hurt bad, but it's going to be okay. It's..."

But Brewhouse broke off or Louise stopped being able to hear her voice. Louise didn't mind. She found herself trying to scream but unable to make her throat produce any more sound than a hot, forced exhalation. Was it because of the pain? Those bands of pain all over her skin? The cracking feeling inside her chest? It was good that her body seemed so disconnected from her thoughts, she figured.

She closed her eyes, even though doing so didn't seem to change the nothing that she saw. Somewhere, far, far away in her mind, she heard the whisper again and again, "They told me my daughter was here."

MICA

Mica never thought he would feel so relieved to see a school. When he broke through the tree line that ringed nearly the entirety of the middle school, it might as well have been Christmas. The lights were out, which didn't surprise him since the street and house lights had been out for some time. But a fire burned in a ring of stones in the parking lot in front of the main doors, and another glowed on the far side of the building, either in or near the playground.

Mica had seen the reddish orange flicker from quite some distance. The neighborhood was so dark compared to the densely built downtown streets that, after his eyes had adjusted, it hadn't been easy to navigate. He'd lost any real idea of how to reach the light Stuart had pointed out. He hadn't been certain the firelight was at the school until he got near enough to recognize the streets.

It was a great comfort to have a destination again. Not even an hour before, he'd been worried that whatever seemed to be chasing him would catch up to him, and he didn't want to try to find his way back to the hospital because it would be very possible that he would cross its path again. As he'd escaped the perpetual light bubble of the downtown area, he'd realized just how alone he felt. He'd not seen another human being in a long time, and he'd been starting to think that was extremely unnatural. Every sound around him had begun to grow menacing, and he just knew a pack of wild dogs or wolves or something with more eyes than teeth, was in the darkness between houses, under their porches, and behind every hedge.

When he'd found himself staring into an impenetrable black cloud, he'd initially thought it was simply his eyes playing tricks on him. Or that it was some sort of dream he was having while awake. Maybe he'd convinced himself that monsters waited around every corner so well that he'd made the world one endless corner.

He'd felt the cold blowing off it from ten yards away, yet he hadn't realized it was even there until he'd almost stepped into it. Of course, Mica turned back immediately, or maybe not so immediately. As he walked, he hadn't been quite certain. He felt like he had two distinctly different memories. He had stood there for some time, right? Thinking about reaching out, wondering if eyes and claws would suddenly come out of the darkness? Or had he felt a violent shiver all over his insides, a primal fear much like he'd felt while fleeing through the downtown, and then had backed off instantly? He'd run through both memories over and over and neither felt more unreal than the other. The one thing he did feel pretty certain about was that there'd been a patch where things had gotten extraordinarily cold.

Then he'd seen the fire glow. He'd been excited to think he wouldn't be alone. But was that how he should feel? He lingered at the tree line. It occurred to him that—though he knew kids from all around town, even on the street upon which he'd just been—most people were strangers. Maybe the fire starter was one of the teachers or the principal, but what if it wasn't? What if it was some homeless crack addict who sold babies for drugs? Mica often wondered if there really were as many bad people as the adults he encountered and the television seemed to suggest. Was it safe to approach the school? Would he walk right into his brutal murder? Would that be better than wandering alone, *maybe* to eventually figure out how to get back home?

He took a deep breath and gazed at the doors. He couldn't help feeling like he was approaching his own school. Usually, he walked in with Steven and Billy, but they rode on the 76 bus, not the 73 bus like Mica. He didn't have any friends aboard 73, so he'd just sit at one of the windows in the middle and hope nobody took enough notice to pick on him. On the days he was left alone, he'd daydream about rescuing the cute girls in class from the vile clutches of aliens. He'd never been as imaginative as Stu, but he had his moments.

Mica's breath caught as he saw a bit of motion across the lot from the fire. Someone was walking towards the flame with a few logs in his arms, looking out towards the trees. Mica peered intently, leaning forward as if a couple inches closer would suddenly bring the face out of shadow. At first, he couldn't tell if it was a man or a woman, but then the flickers of firelight finally caught on his cheeks.

Mica squawked, literally, and came running out of the trees down the short slope and onto the line-painted asphalt. It was Stuart's math teacher, Mr. DeSoto. He remembered him from the open house he'd gone to with his parents, and he'd seen him at a couple of school events. Mr. DeSoto had said that Mica was probably just as good at math as Stuart was and that maybe he'd be in his class in a couple years. At the time, Mica had been kind of scared of Mr. DeSoto and how friendly he'd acted. Now, Mica had never been so glad to recognize someone in his whole life. It wasn't until he was two thirds of the way across the parking lot that he recognized a black object hanging off Mr. DeSoto's belt. A handgun.

The boy's shoes squeaked as he stopped hard, his weight lurching forward, stopping only with a fantastic pinwheeling of arms and the raising of one foot.

Mr. Desoto held both hands in the air and tensed to catch the tottering child. As Mica's balance stabilized, a goofy grin broke onto the teacher's face.

"Woah, woah," he laughed. "Can't just hit the brakes like that, can we?"

The grin seemed so good natured that Mica could feel one itching to hop onto his own face. But his eyes locked onto the gun. Mr. Desoto gently pressed one hand to the handle of the pistol, almost as if to reassure the weapon.

"This is nothing to worry about," Mr. Desoto said. "My daddy taught me to handle one of these safely, and I've used them safely my whole life."

"Y-You're on school grounds," Mica stammered. "Zero-zero tolerance."

Desoto tilted his head back and laughed loudly, but in what seemed like genuine mirth.

"Isn't that just a hoot," he said.

Then he took a deep breath and knelt down.

"You're Stuart's brother," he said, dropping the volume of his voice a little. Mica nodded and said his name. Mr. DeSoto continued. "There is a serious emergency in Millwood tonight. A lot of people are scared, and a lot of people are on the move looking for shelter."

Mica took a couple steps closer and squatted, the way everyone did in gym class who didn't have a note asking that they be allowed to sit cross-legged. He wasn't quite an arm reach away from Mr. DeSoto, but almost.

"Like me," Mica said.

"Some are," Mr. DeSoto said. "Did you know that we're a designated storm and emergency shelter? For this whole area of town?"

"No, I didn't," Mica said. He actually did, but he figured that Mr. Desoto was a teacher and liked telling people about things.

"It is; we're built for tornados, blizzards, and the zombie apocalypse," Mr. Desoto said. "And we've got food, water, blankets, and emergency medical supplies for quite a few families. An entire room full in the basement."

Mica smiled.

"That's pretty cool, actually,"

Mr. DeSoto smiled again, this time the way a teacher smiles whenever a student gets a question right.

"It is!" he said. "But the thing is, when something goes really, really wrong, people get scared. Some people, they seek help—and that's why we're here. We're here to help them. But, Mica, some people..."

"They want to take what they want," Mica said.

The smile left Mr. DeSoto's face.

"Exactly," he said. Then, he patted the handle of the pistol again. "And that's why I carry this. I sure don't ever want to use it, but I know that those folks who want to take things will think twice if they know I have it."

"Three times when they know you know how to use it," Mica whispered.

Mr. Desoto didn't seem to hear Mica because he turned and rose as the front door of the school opened and a woman dressed like she could be on the front cover of Librarian's Weekly stepped out. Her eyes brightened when she saw Mica.

"Oh my!" she exclaimed. "What's your name? I'm so glad you found us."

Mica found her enthusiasm just a little unsettling. However, he introduced himself. After he said his name, Mr. DeSoto added, "Stuart Bradley's brother."

The woman introduced herself as Mrs. Tubble. Then, she rose on tippy toes and peered into the lot. "But, where's your family?"

Mica shook his head.

"I don't know," he said. "Stuart went out on his own, mom went after Stuart, I went after mom. I guess dad must've..."

"Gone after you," Mrs. Tubble muttered, nodding slowly with a frown. She held up a staying figure to Mica.

"Stephan," she said to Mr. DeSoto. "We had two more families, seven folks total, come in on the other side, and Ms. Kimbro is settling them down in the gym. We haven't had a chance to pull out more than a couple of cots, but we should have things up and running soon enough once we get a few more volunteers to help move stuff around."

Mr. DeSoto scratched his chin.

"Any news on the radio?"

Mrs. Tubble shot a glance to Mica.

"Do you know what's happening tonight?" she asked.

Mica shook his head.

"No, ma'am," he said.

"There's a black cloud spreading across town," she started. "It..."

"I've seen it!" Mica interjected. "I was trying to walk towards the light in the hills, but I lost sight of it and got turned around. I tried to make my way back to the hospital, but it had spread across the road."

Mr. DeSoto's hand fell to the butt of his pistol, but Mrs. Tubble took a careful step forward and patted Mr. Desoto twice on the shoulder. Mica felt the urge to take a step back, but he wasn't quite sure why.

"Did you touch it?" Mrs. Tubble said, her voice a bit pinched, like she was holding her breath.

"No, no ma'am," Mica said, wringing his hands together. He'd wanted to touch it, hadn't he? The air had gotten all cold, and he'd been certain that touching it would be as refreshing as taking an ice-cold drink of pure water. He'd stood there staring into it, even as it spread towards him. He might've stood there and let it bowl him over if he'd not been suddenly struck by a certainty: Stuart had been in that cloud and that's why he'd been acting so strangely. "It changes you, doesn't it?"

Mrs. Tubble seemed to relax just a little bit.

"That's what they're saying, yes," she said.

"How?" Mica said. "How does it change you?"

A strange look passed over Mrs. Tubble's face.

"All I know is what they're saying over the radio, and I can't say it's all clear," she said.

"Mutations, disfigurements," Mr. DeSoto said. He hesitated a moment, as if trying to figure out how to say something. Finally, he added, "Personality changes."

"Personality changes," Mica said. "Like you don't act like yourself?"

"Provided we're understanding it right," Mr. DeSoto said, "yes."

That must be what happened to Stuart. Had he seen the cloud out in the woods? He was certainly the type of boy to stick his hands into it, maybe even jump right in as part of one of his adventures. Mica couldn't help feeling a little relief. Before, he'd thought it simply wasn't Stuart—but if it really was, couldn't the change be somehow reversed?

Then, Mrs. Tubble turned to Mr. DeSoto.

"And the news isn't good," she said. "They've ordered the

evacuation to stop, at least for people within a twenty-mile radius."

"To stop? Are they crazy? What are we supposed to do?"

Mrs. Tubble glanced nervously at Mica and said, "They say it's due to the risk of spreading infection."

"Infection?" Mr. DeSoto said. "Is the cloud biological?"

Mrs. Tubble shrugged. "I don't think they've got a clue what it is," she said.

"Or they're not telling us," Mr. DeSoto said.

"Does it matter?" Mrs. Tubble said. "We should go inside."

Mr. DeSoto shook his head.

"I'm going to stay out a few more minutes," he said.

"Suit yourself," Mrs. Tubble said. She stepped over and placed a hand on Mica's back, shuffling him towards the door. "C'mon. We've got a couple kids your age inside."

Mica walked hesitantly into the school. As he passed through the doors, he looked over his shoulder in time to see Mr. DeSoto checking the magazine on his weapon. The look on his face made the young boy shiver. The teacher gritted his teeth as if angry, and his eyes were wide like he'd just been startled. Mica had seen his father look a bit like that when driving in heavy snows when some "dumbass" in an SUV would come barreling by at 65 miles an hour. No doubt his hands were probably trembling. Mica had discovered long ago that adults were most fascinating to watch when they don't know anyone's watching. Invariably they looked more primitive. Some kids in the class didn't believe in evolution, but Mica had always thought that anyone who watched someone unaware couldn't possibly *not* see an ape.

Mr. DeSoto was an ape with a gun, and Mica didn't much like that.

He turned back toward the hall so that the teacher wouldn't see him gawking. Mrs. Tubble was just ahead, and they were passing the main office. Mica had never gotten in trouble, but he'd often seen boys sitting in the office chairs by the principal's door, usually looking either anxiously into their laps or defiantly into space. Strangely, Mica had always kind of envied those kids. He'd never been brave enough to get into that much trouble.

Now, he suspected he was in far, far worse trouble, and there was nothing brave about it. The more he pushed himself forward the more he literally wanted to curl up in a ball. Was that how the heroes in movies felt? Were they always worried that if they stepped wrong they would shit themselves?

They passed the boy's restroom on the right. Mica's bladder stirred. When had he last used the restroom?

"Mica?" Mrs. Tubble said.

She stood a good twenty feet down the hall at the main intersection. Left led to sixth and seventh grades, right to eighth. Straight ahead was the cafeteria, the gym, the library, and all the other shared spaces, like the art and music room. Mica hadn't even realized he'd stopped.

"The restroom," Mica said. "I think I have to go."

Mrs. Tubble furrowed her brow and frowned, but she said, "I supposed it's best to go before you hunker down. I'm going to go to the gym to check on everyone. Straight ahead. Meet me there when you're done."

Mica nodded and stepped into the restroom. Three stalls, three sinks, two urinals. In this context, they looked exactly like every other restroom in the world. When Mica stepped up to relieve himself, it occurred to him that he could pee right on the walls if he wanted to, or in the sink or trashcan, and even if someone realized he was the one who'd done it, he could just blame it on the cloud.

He relieved himself in the urinal and flushed.

He went and pumped several globs of foamy soap onto his

palm and turned the cold knob. Nothing. Some of the foam slid off his hands as he turned the cold all the way on and immediately gave the hot a twist when nothing further happened.

Then, a deep clang from under the floor.

The pipe leading to the sink rattled. The spigot shook. A piercing whine echoed out of the drains.

Mica turned the knobs closed as fast and hard as he could. The tremors beneath the floor subsided. It was time to leave the restroom.

His shoes squeaked shrilly on the linoleum floor as he skidded back into the hallway and ran full tilt for the gym. He passed under school banners that sported the school's mascot Hawk, which really looked more like a mentally challenged cartoon eagle, and spirit slogans lettered in the school's black and green. As recently as earlier that day, such accoutrements were simply part of a world that no longer seemed quite like the one that he was in now, background noise to the static of every day for his brother and a couple hundred other kids. Now, they felt like artifacts that no longer had a functional purpose except to reflect a past culture.

He approached the gym and the families in there that Mrs. Tubble was tending to. She wasn't really a teacher at the moment, just as the gym wasn't really a gym. She'd offer no lessons and no one would play dodgeball. It was pretty astonishing really. Mica felt a bit dizzy from that thought, combined with the thunder of his heart, still accelerated from the scare in the restroom.

He slowed outside the gym and placed his hands on his knees to catch his breath. He felt like an alien that had landed on a foreign world. It looked a lot like the one he knew, but everything about it seemed fake. Like an illusion. His head throbbed just a little bit, so he pressed one of his palms to his temple and, after a moment's pressure, wiped the sweat from his brow. He realized that even as he tried to catch his breath, his breathing was still rapid and shallow.

Was he okay?

Voices on the other side of the door helped clear his head from the invading feeling of panic that threatened to overtake it. It sounded like a couple of kids talking to their mother, perhaps. Probably one of the families Mrs. Tubble had mentioned, saying something about apples and ice cream, about cold canned corned beef, and someone who wanted to play on a tablet but the battery was dead and the charger forgotten.

Mica smiled. It sounded normal. Like things that any normal family would talk about. His breathing eased and his heartbeat started to slow. The relief was palpable; he consciously felt significantly safer.

The boy reached out, grabbed the horseshoe handle, and pulled.

THE VISITOR

The storm stopped as sharp as clapped hands, the applause of rain ceasing on street, leaf, and eave. Rivulets ran in root channels and road shoulders. Stream beds overran. White fog haze drifted in banks like the antithesis of the spreading cloud, swirling in the wind. Any onlooker would struggle to tell the line between liquid and ground, air and liquid.

Similarly, The Visitor was losing Its ability to distinguish itself from Stuart. The neural system of this body operated associatively, its current state constantly building connections between the present and what was stored. Already, the density of the web had grown so that The Visitor now both remembered a reality playing wiffle ball in the backyard with his little brother and shuddering in the darkness of the void, trying to find the lock that blocked passage across the Boundary. The pattern spread like a contagion. Could the vessel try to reject The Visitor's presence? It couldn't be strong enough without an occupying consciousness, could it? It had even begun to think of *Itself* as Stuart.

The Visitor paused amid the trees at the road's edge and looked at Its fingers. They appeared as Its own fingers. They weren't just the fingers of the body It was using as a vehicle to navigate. The skin, and its light abrasions, still healing, were both The Visitor's now—they weren't just The Visitor's own, in fact, but rather they *were* The Visitor. The memories that lingered in the vessel's electrical patterns were The Visitor's too. And they were part of an existence led by another consciousness. And they had been taken from that consciousness. It should have been simple, but the residual emotions embedded in Stuart's memories were also becoming a part of this new Stuart.

The Visitor had not anticipated this. It had only sought to escape into the one place It believed that from which It fled could not follow. The Visitor had once been a part of The Source itself. It knew full well that The Source had, since the inception of all things, held designs on making a move against The Light, but the agony of even considering The Light's existence directly had been so great that incursion had seemed impossible. When The Visitor had allowed Itself to recognize the beacon in the darkness, It had felt certain that the beacon came from a place The Source could not travel to. It had never anticipated that The Source was strong enough to change this world, to drive the light back from the door enough to seek passage.

Now, The Visitor felt strong surges of guilt.

Now, The Visitor felt strong fears that It had been mistaken about Its safety. Not that It had anywhere else It could have fled to. Or any other means to flee there.

The Visitor hadn't exactly taken the vessel; technically he was dead when It had inhabited him. The original Stuart had vacated through that strange portal each of the sentient beings of this world possessed, to the beyond. According to many of Stuart's stored memories, that was for the best, but according to other memories, it was absolutely terrifying. In fact, the number of stored, mutually exclusive beliefs held simultaneously by Stuart, was staggering.

The new inhabitant found Itself wishing It had taken a different vessel or not to have needed to take a vessel at all, despite lacking another means to pursue the necessary flight. Perhaps the problem was that Stuart had died because of the door, or depending on one's point of view, the curiosity inherent in his species that the door had hooked into. It was The Visitor that had chosen the method of ingress. Therefore, The Visitor had called Stuart.

It shook Its head. There was no time for such quandaries. They were distractions. So, The Visitor redirected Its attention to the forest ahead.

A human being could hardly have seen the light from this vantage, but Stuart's eyes could see, through the added perceptions of The Visitor, the luminescence that now shone from just beyond a couple of the rolling hills that defined the landscape. It would have appeared like light pollution, like a distant house amid the trees to anyone else, but to this being, it was almost painfully brilliant. The Visitor had known the instant It had looked out the hospital window that It needed to make Its way to it. The Visitor was new to these people and their technologies, but this wasn't the type of light made by something natural or by some sort of machine. It had given The Visitor the thing It sought more than anything other than simple escape: a destination. With that destination came hope.

Now, perhaps one thousand yards away, Stuart's body

could barely take another step. The Visitor hadn't anticipated the lack of physical endurance within the vessel, and now the muscles and tendons screamed with fatigue. The Stuart part of him whined, desperate to sit down and take off Its shoes. Images of an ice-cold cola, maybe a large Haywood's ice cream, surfaced in Stuart's mind, and the Visitor found Itself strangely tempted to comply. It was a simple matter to utilize the stored memories to establish an optimal path to places that supplied the things sought.

Unfortunately, no matter what sort of interference the emotions and memories of Stuart brought, the need to find a safe refuge overrode everything. The Visitor willed the body up the hill towards the light. Twigs snapped as The Visitor's feet crushed lumps of wet leaves and smashed worms writhing from the ground to escape drowning. Water squished from the mud and drenched the feet through Stuart's shoes. The Visitor didn't care. It needed to know who had lit such a beacon. The Visitor swept Stuart's hand through droplet-frosted spider webs and pulled aside branches laden with leaves and pine needles. Step by step, It grew closer, cresting one hill, descending, and ascending the next.

It was at the top of the second slope that the shimmering water came into view. To human eyes, it would appear as bright as a floodlight, but to the thing within Stuart, it practically shone as bright as a sun. The luminescence it radiated was tinged with a soft aquamarine like a bio bay, and the light pulsated as rain dripping from the tree branches disrupted the surface. The Visitor couldn't say for certain whether the water gave off the light or perhaps was light made liquid, but what It could feel certain of was, whoever or whatever had made this place, stood the best chance of anything he'd seen in this world of forestalling the darkness.

The Visitor slowly wound Its way down, following the

natural contours of the land among the tree trunks. The air took on a strange, energized quality that caused shifting swathes of Stuarts' hair to stand on end. A warmth entered into the air, and The Visitor realized this was the first time since It had come through the doorway that It was more aware that It was approaching something warm than It was that something cold was approaching It. Even as the thought struck The Visitor, It could sense that somewhere over the hills, that well of frigid black was deepening, the affront to the light of the world spreading.

By the time The Visitor reached the water's edge, It felt sweat pouring from Stuart's entire body. The lower back and armpits felt especially damp, as did the groin. Stuart's memory of building his fort, right before approaching the door, surged to mind with a ferocity that actually jarred the inhabitant's hold on the vessel for a fraction of a second. It was not accurate to say that the inhabitant tightened its grip on the vessel, but it was close enough.

A rustle in the branches behind The Visitor caused It to spin sharply in place.

Amid the undergrowth, It spotted motion. Long, swinging appendages, some with skin darker than charcoal, some with skin as white as alabaster. The Visitor craned Stuart's neck back to follow their rise. They stood at least twenty feet tall, four limbs per body, with bodies the same color as the limbs. Three bodies in all, each nearly the size of a Volkswagen Beetle. The bodies had roughly human-shaped torsos, except they bulged in places humans didn't bulge, and concaved in places humans didn't concave. Their heads dangled down on long, distended necks, with their chins the lowest point of their body, and their mouths wide and gaping, filled with sharp teeth. Flesh seemed to drip from the bodies in clumps.

The Visitor considered what place such creatures might hold in the living network of this world.

Stuart's memories shot out images from nightmares.

The voice that came from the water startled The Visitor.

"Don't be alarmed," the voice said. "The beasts serve me."

Stuart's body gulped reflexively. The Visitor wondered absently to what gulping air could possibly be an appropriate response.

The Visitor turned and immediately recognized the looming being It faced to be like itself: a driver in a vessel. This new being's vessel could have passed for any healthy human adult, except that it was too healthy, magically so. To The Visitor, it glowed with the light of something beautiful and stolen, and The Visitor saw that the old-fashioned cloak, heavy with buckles that any human would have seen it wearing, were actually outcroppings of its flesh.

Within that vessel, however, there roosted the real being: a vast, winged serpent with scales stained with blood and soaked with fear. It writhed against the confines of its vessel, seething, twisting. It writhed against the boundaries of the dimension as well, the nature of its being not meant for simple three-dimensional instrumentality. Looking at this being, The Visitor felt a kinship with the creature. No doubt it lit the beacon. No doubt it sought its own.

"Do you know what follows me?" The Visitor asked.

That Vessel's eyes didn't quite seem to fall on The Visitor, though they seemed to clearly know where It was.

"I have a mind of it," the being said, dropping to one knee. "At least, I've heard rumors among those like me who sensed an approach."

"There are others?" The Visitor said.

"Here and there, but all watch from a distance, scared to reach beyond their place. You may think of me as Veles."

"Veles." The Visitor paused as the two black beasts moved into view in broad arcs to either side. The white one remained out of sight. Apprehension nettled under Stuart's skin. "And you're different?"

"I'm here," Veles said as the two towering creatures took position behind him, each positioned at the far side of the pond on opposing sides. The Visitor suspected they formed an equilateral triangle with Veles at the center. "And you're late."

"One needs a meeting time to be late," The Visitor said.

Veles grunted. "More accurate to say you took longer to get here than I'd hoped."

"Discreet travel is not simple for the young of this species," Stuart said.

"Curse of the physical plane," Veles said. He dipped a hand into the water and let it run from his cupped palm. It returned back to the pond noiselessly, without any type of splash. Then, Veles rose. "Let's cut to it, shall we?"

The Visitor cocked Its head.

"Can you keep me safe?" The Visitor said.

Veles sighed. "You don't understand what you really are, do you?"

Just then a woman's voice intruded, frantic and slightly short of breath.

"Stuart? Darling?"

The beasts all set in motion simultaneously with long, loping strides.

HEATHER

It's a simple fact of perception that we take what matters or what we believe to matter, and discard the rest. If you put a child in a room with a puppy, a sextant, a loom, and a dishwasher for an hour, one week later they'll only remember the puppy. Even while surrounded by those things, they may well only see the thing they know, the thing that fascinates their world and makes it whole.

The trait itself is understandable; we intake an unfathomable volume of information and, to try to make sense of every bit of it, would be both Herculean and Sisyphean. How much of our life would be spent cataloging the individual blades of grass? We'd miss the whole snowstorm trying to process the flakes. Our minds strive for efficiency because they understand intrinsically how limited our time is. It's one of our most primitive mental functions.

Heather Bradley, however, did not initially recognize just how brief her life was likely about to become. Instead, as she crested the hill, she recognized that at the foot of the slope, stood the pond. On the shore of the pond, stood her son. He appeared unharmed, and he stood facing away from her.

She felt so relieved to have found Stuart that she didn't even notice the man silhouetted against the water-light like a birch against the sun. She didn't notice the small, luminescent wisps wafting off the water like dandelion seeds, only to burst into tiny white flames about a foot off the surface. She didn't notice that light seemed to be crawling up the stems of the bushes and the trunks of the trees. She didn't notice the three towering creatures sweeping towards her like massive insects.

Heather Bradley was a parent who'd just found a missing child. She'd seen him disappear into the trees as she approached. He'd been so absorbed in whatever he sought that he didn't notice her headlights fall upon his back. A powerful feeling of déjà vu had struck her as she pulled off the road, and she'd been filled with an almost overwhelming fear that a car was about to strike her vehicle.

Now, she broke into a half-run, half-trot down the hillside, the only thing initially keeping her from breaking into a dead sprint was the awareness that between the branches and the damp ground, she might well kill herself before she had her arms around her child.

She called out, "Stuart? Darling?"

Then, she finally recognized that her boy was facing someone. He was tall, well over six feet. Handsome as a demigod out of myth, he wore a heavy cloak and stout boots, and his eyes glowed with the same brilliant aquamarine as the water. Heather's mind took a moment to register that the water was glowing, but that didn't feel as important as the fact that the stranger posed an immediate threat to her child.

She skidded to a stop as her son turned and the stranger locked its gaze onto her. The stranger extended its arms sharply. It spoke no words, but it struck Heather as if a loud command had been belted.

It was then that Heather understood there were more than just the three of them. Slowly, she raised her chin and tilted her head back, back, back. Almost straight above her, a grotesque face hovered. If it wasn't so impossible, she might have thought it human, or, perhaps based on a human. Its massive mouth stretched wide open and froze in the act of lunging down at her, its massive teeth dripping saliva like rain falling from a cluster of leaves. Strange dangling bands of flesh hung from its core mass in a way that reminded Heather of Spanish moss, at least until the smell of rot filled her nostrils.

Heather's body then urged to engage in another primitive process, this one more defensive in nature, but she didn't urinate or defecate herself. She felt the same pull towards helpless collapse that she'd experienced outside the park when her car was hit. None of this was fair, it could hardly even be real. She wanted nothing more than to turn to someone else, her husband maybe, and have the problem solved for her.

Instead, she clenched her fists and took a step towards her son.

"You get the hell away from my boy."

The stranger cocked his head and offered her a smile, simultaneously genuine and patronizing.

"I'd warn you against being too threatening," the stranger said, his voice polite and smooth. It might have sounded friendly had three insane aberrations not been looming over her. "They follow my command, but they also react with instinct."

Heather's mouth went dry. It struck her that no amount of courage could give her the upper hand in anything physical that might happen here. Other strategies would be needed. She knew how to hold her own in a room full of shitty businesspeople. She'd made the dean's list. And, she was raising two boys.

"Well, how about you kindly have them go somewhere else?" Heather said.

"If only you were the only thing out here tonight I hope they'd protect me against," the stranger said.

Heather extended a hand towards Stuart.

"Well, Mr...." she began, but broke off with a pointed look toward the stranger.

"Veles."

"Yes, Mr. Veles," she said. "I'm telling you that I'm going to collect my son, but I must admit I'd really like to know what in the hell you could possibly need those to protect your from."

Veles adjusted his cuffs and straightened his collar.

"Now, Madam, if I could give you your child back, I would," Veles said. "But you see, the issue is threefold. First, this is not your child anymore. Second, what this is isn't something you want in your household. Third, when what *was* your child allowed what now *looks like* your child into this world, it left the gate open for something else that will annihilate everything it touches in this plane of existence."

Now it was Heather's turn to patronize Veles.

"Now, Mr. Veles," she said. "Hardly anything you said makes sense. I doubt I can take on these spider-tree looking freaks, but I guarantee you that if I die, I will die trying to fuck you up, and my whole afterlife will be dedicated to haunting you."

Stuart looked to Veles.

"Please don't kill her," he said. "She is...still special to me."

Veles laid his hand on Stuart's shoulder. His fingers seemed to elongate in the motion as if, for a moment, they reached halfway down the boy's torso. The boy glanced down at the fingers but made no other reaction. A sense of revulsion rippled through Heather.

"Even if I didn't like her already," Veles said, "she's needed for too many outcomes."

"I see," The Visitor said.

"Well, I don't," Heather snapped, pointing a finger at Veles. "How about you explain?"

The Visitor cleared Its throat. "I'm sorry."

Heather frowned and furrowed her forehead. She dropped into a crouch with her hands dangling between her legs, her forearms on her knees.

"For what, sweetheart?" She asked. "The accident? Running away? I don't blame you for anything."

"Veles is right," The Visitor said, taking a seat on a rock. "I'm not your son. Your son died out in the park where you found me."

"That's impossible," Heather said. "You're right here."

A horrible knot bobbed in Heather's throat. Under any other circumstance, she would've thought what he said was downright crazy, but here she was by a glowing pond while three daddy longlegs people with enormous teeth hovered above her. Under these circumstances, if Stuart had said that he came from Alpha Centauri, she would've been open to believing.

"I can't say how long I've been outside your world trying to find my way in, away from the thing to which I was attached, because time as you understand it doesn't exist there," The Visitor said. "But I finally learned how to create a doorway, and your son is the one who found that door."

The Visitor paused a moment.

"Then?" Heather whispered.

"Even with the door open, I couldn't come through. It wasn't until your son sent something through that the boundary between our respective realms became permeable."

"Sent something through?"

The Visitor chuckled.

"He threw a rock."

Heather hung her head. "Christ taking a trolley."

The Visitor visibly recoiled. Sweat broke out on his forehead and his cheeks flushed.

"When the essence of my world poured into yours, he panicked," The Visitor said. "He broke his ankle and hit his head. When he left this vessel, then I took it."

"He died quickly?"

"Yes," Stuart said. "Terrified and in pain."

Hot tears poured from Heather's eyes even as the rest of her body felt immeasurably cold. Her hands shook. Looking at the visage of her son, it was almost impossible to process that he might not be in there. It was against the rules. It was something that couldn't possibly be real.

"And, unfortunately," Veles interjected, "our newcomer here didn't close the door behind him."

The Visitor held a finger up.

"Couldn't close the door," The Visitor said. "Just like it

couldn't be opened until something from this side passed through, it can't be closed from this side alone. Think of it like in the spy movies your son watches with his father—there must be two keys, one on each side of the door."

"And now," Veles interjected, "in a fairly real sense, all hell is breaking loose."

"I didn't know," The Visitor said. "I didn't think It could follow me here."

"It?" Heather asked.

"An abomination," Veles said. "*The* Abomination."

"Is there any point at which this stops sounding batshit crazy?" Heather asked.

"Yes," Veles said. "When The Abomination enters this world far enough to collapse the laws of physics and obliterate the boundaries of order against the void of nothingness, crazy will be the new normal. Its influence is already corrupting the people of this town. Soon it will corrupt everyone and everything. But, by then we'll be dead within the darkness, so we won't care."

Heather didn't know whether to throw her hands up in despair, drop to her knees in supplication and pray, or just punch this Veles guy in the nuts. Tears sprung to her eyes. Her mouth ran paper-dry, and she felt short of breath. It was too much to take in.

Veles reached out one of his elongated hands and laid it on Heather's shoulder.

"I understand you're upset, ma'am," Veles said. "If it's any consolation, it's well been established that your life is predominantly inconsequential until it's final moments."

Heather's eyes widened.

"Don't worry. You won't have to wait long at all for the meaningful part," Veles added. Then with a gesture toward the trees, he said, "Now, we have a door to close. Shall we?"

For a heartbeat, Heather thought Veles was speaking to her, but then, one of the enormous legs of the beasts wrapped itself around her body like a boa and hoisted her into the air.

MICA

Mica didn't know the gym the way he knew his own school's gym, but it certainly looked familiar. He'd been there a couple times for Stuart's events and seen the bleachers up and the bleachers extended. He'd seen it set up for basketball, for physical fitness testing, and the Fun-raising Fair. No matter the occasion, it always felt like a school.

It didn't differ now. Mica had expected to see families setting up camp on cots with coarse, folded-up blankets and wafer-thin sponge pillows. They'd have a box of bottled water, a few snacks, and maybe some toiletries. Some parents would be rubbing their kids' backs or maybe each other's or maybe even their own. Maybe somewhere a baby would be crying as the mother said "shhh, shhh, shhh." That was what he'd seen in those disaster relief stories his father had watched, wasn't it? Crowded cots and a roaring murmur?

Instead, the gym was mostly empty. Someone had pulled out a couple carts loaded with folding chairs, and a couple stacks of what Mica suspected were packages containing unassembled cots. It all stood beside the open double doors that led to a sizable storage room. Altogether, it looked like there were about a dozen people present, not counting himself and Ms. Tubble, and only three of them were kids.

Mica couldn't help scratch his head. He'd heard his parents' cell phones sound all sorts of alert tests and witnessed the emergency broadcast system interrupt with a test on both the TV at his grandparents' house and radio shows in the car. His dad had even complained how it was a shame that everyone expected that they should always be able to get ahold of everyone at any time. So, considering all that, had people not known? Had no one been warned?

Mica bit his lip and searched the faces for people he recognized, but he knew no one. An older man with gray hair and a bald patch on his crown sat on the edge of a cot, talking to a little girl of about 4 or 5. Mrs. Tubble gestured to or at something outside of the room as she conversed with, who Mica assumed, were the families that had just arrived. It looked like she might be telling them where things were.

All of a sudden, Mica felt terribly alone. When he'd left the hospital, he'd felt like he'd had a real purpose. He was chasing his older brother towards the light. He was going to help. He had no idea how, of course, but he was going to help. Then, he was going to find out what had happened to Stuart in the woods. Unfortunately, as well as he knew his neighborhood, and as well as he thought he knew how to get places like the grocery by looking out the window, he really hadn't understood how many roads there were in the city, and he hadn't quite realized that sometimes traveling in a straight line wasn't possible. If only he'd waited for his dad.

It struck him that maybe he'd feel better if he could join in on the conversation with the other kids, so he stepped up quietly behind the gray-haired man.

"...open up storage and get out some of the school instruments," he was saying, rubbing his palms together. "Bet we can liven things up for everyone!"

"Mom said," the girl said softly, "that it's the end of the world and we're all going to die. Do you think she meant it?"

"No, I don't," the man said. "It's easy to think the worst when you're afraid."

"She said the cloud's the work of the Devil," the girl pressed.

"I know," the man said, "but I'm not going to say left or

right about things your mom said. Not my place. It's my place to make sure you're okay until all this blows over, and that's what we're here to do."

The girl seemed strangely disappointed. Had she wanted the man, who Mica guessed was her grandfather, to tell her that her mother was crazy? Or that she was right, and the Devil really was destroying the world? A memory gnawed at a back corner of his mind from when he'd stood near the cloud. Mica cleared his throat.

He asked, "Does explaining something with science mean it's not the work of the Devil?"

The older man twisted on the cot to look over his shoulder at the new arrival.

"I wouldn't say the two relate one way or another," he said. "But I certainly find the belief that science can explain it more comforting than believing it is the work of the Devil."

"Have you seen it?" Mica asked.

The man opened his mouth but then hesitated. Mica wondered if he had expected a different response or if he wasn't sure how he wanted to answer the question.

After another moment, he said, "No. No, I haven't."

Mica looked at his feet. Memories, conflicting, swirled around in his head of his moments—or hours—in front of the cloud. The coolness on his hands—how it had felt like liquid air. It was like it had poured through his fingers as he wafted them into its body—or maybe his fingers had poured through it. Had he really done that? Or was that just something he'd imagined while he'd backed away? Hadn't he stumbled on a rock a foot from the road's edge and nearly fallen on his butt? Mica felt tears welling in his eyes. His fists were clenched at his sides tight enough so that his fingernails smarted his palms a bit. The girl was staring at him. The old man wore a look of concern.

"I didn't touch it," Mica said. "At least, I don't think I did. But I wanted to. I really, really wanted to. Like right now, if I think of it, I still want to. Part of me wants to go out right now and find it just so I can run right into it."

The old man rose slowly to his feet.

"How close did you get?"

Mica bit his lip. His blood felt cold, like liquid ice, as he'd imagined the cloud would feel.

"I dunno, maybe fifty feet?" Mica lied. Whichever memories were true, he'd gotten really close. If the cloud got within arm's reach, there was no question that he would reach out his arm.

"Are you sure?" the old man asked slowly. There was something strange in his eyes; suspicion without a doubt, but something more, something that struck Mica as frightening and probably more than a little dangerous.

Thankfully, the gym door swung open with a thud, breaking the tension between them and redirecting their attention. In stepped Mr. DeSoto, helping a man with his shoulders wrapped in a wool blanket, scoot into the gym. The man, head hanging down as if he could only walk if he watched his feet, was taking short, shuffling steps and Mr. Desoto seemed to be rubbing his biceps up and down while they walked.

The man was shivering violently as Mr. Desoto steered him to the nearest cot, his legs wobbling so bad they looked like the knees would suddenly buckle sideways. Mrs. Tubble looked over as the cot's frame creaked under the man's settling weight. She reached to a box near her feet and plucked up a clipboard that had been atop one corner. As she did so, her face flashed with both happy recognition and serious concern. Mr. Desoto held up one hand. Mrs. Tubble rocked on her ankles, and she seemed, several times in a few seconds, about to speak.

"I-I-I-"the man stammered, "I've n-n-never felt a c-c-cold

like that b-before. Even n-n-n-ow I can barely st-st-st-stand or t-t-t-talk."

Mica noticed that Mr. Desoto's hand, now that he was no longer helping support the man's weight, was resting on the butt of his gun. The teacher appeared to be looking over the new arrival closely.

"We'll get you warmed up, bud," Mr. Desoto said with a smile on his lips but not in his eyes. "You want some coffee? Tea? Hot chocolate?"

The man shook his head.

"D-d-don't think my throat c-could take it," he said. "N-n-not right n-now, anyway."

Mica scooted away from the little girl and the old man, careful not to trip over any of the cots or the various supplies and possessions folks had set down. He couldn't quite see the man's face, but he could tell that his ears were badly frostbitten; the skin had split in many places and had begun to swell. With slow steps, Mica moved towards the newcomer.

"Hang tight a moment," Mr. Desoto said, and he stepped over to Mrs. Tubble.

The man stared off into space for just a moment, clasping the blanket around himself. The shivers seemed to subside as he drew several deep breaths. Then, he took stock of the gym, his eyes wandering about over the bleachers, banners, and walls. Deep crows feet spread by his eyes as he squinted, and the brittle skin split and bled. Mica knew he should recognize the man already, but it looked almost like the swelling and cuts kept moving and shifting.

The man must have caught Mica's approach out of his peripheral vision because he turned his head and focused on the boy abruptly, his eyes widening as he did so.

Mica's eyes widened too. The purplish-black of frostbite marred the man's cheek bones and nose. In other places, the skin was blotched red and peeling like a sunburn. The damage covered enough of the man's face that Mica still couldn't place it.

The man, however, clearly recognized Mica.

"Oh my god," he said. "You? You're here?"

The boy really didn't know what to say. "Uh, yeah?"

"You know who I am, right?" The man asked. He held his hands out, letting the blanket fall off his shoulders, and Mica immediately noticed that they were even more severely frost-bitten than his face. The man noticed Mica's attention. "Looks like hell, doesn't it?"

"You've been in the cloud," Mica said.

"Me? Nah," the man said. "Folks have started looting in town. A bunch of us got held up in a restaurant, and the robbers locked us into a walk-in freezer."

"I was downtown," Mica said. "It's deserted. Hardly saw a car."

The man licked his lips. A long sliver of skin peeled off under the wet friction, and a couple beads of blood welled out on the left side.

"Guess I'm not surprised you don't recognize me," the man said. "I'm not quite looking my best, and you were in the car when it happened."

Mica twitched. Dread churned through him. Was this man claiming he was Percy Weaver? Mica tried to draw a breath but couldn't. This is what he'd been running from—it was why he'd fled the hospital. It was what he'd worked to evade downtown. It was why he'd lost his bearings.

"M-M-Mr. W-weaver?" he stammered.

Mr. Weaver tapped his index finger to his nose. As he pulled it away, skin stuck to his fingertip and peeled away, revealing a strangely frost-textured subcutaneous layer that almost looked like Styrofoam.

"Call me Percy," he said without batting an eye. "Under the circumstances, I don't think there's any call for anyone to act like strangers."

He reached out and offered a handshake. Mica stared, his stomach churning at the thought of touching the blackened skin. Didn't that hurt? The strangest part was that there was some sort of earnestness in the man's eyes—almost as though he genuinely had no idea that he'd stalked Mica for half the evening.

After a moment, Percy's fingers curled back, and his hand dropped.

"Yeah, I get it kid," he said. "I wouldn't want to shake hands with me either if I were you. For what it's worth, I'm sorry."

"Thanks," Mica said, trying to figure out how to take a step back without being obvious that he was taking a step back. He was so aware of the fact that he wanted to hide his fear that he didn't think he could possibly do so. "But, to be honest, I don't really even remember it, so I'm not exactly mad about it."

"Really? You don't remember," Percy said. "Well, that's just friggin' great."

Mica opened his mouth to respond despite having no idea what to say to that. He didn't get a chance to, however, because he felt a hand on each shoulder. He looked down at the hands first. One had dark hairs on the pads between the knuckles and all around the tendons on the back, and the other had red nail polish. To Mica's right stood Mr. Desoto, and to his left Mrs. Tubble. They gently pulled him back.

"What restaurant did you say you were at?" Mrs. Tubble said.

"I didn't," Percy said. "But if you must know, I was at Alejandros."

Mr. Desoto edged Mica back a bit further so that he was now slightly behind the two teachers.

"Alejandros isn't downtown. It's by the Market Basket," Mr. Desoto said.

"Yeah," Percy said. He messaged his wrist with a wince. "That's right. Was headed home and heard the radio say to head to my nearest storm shelter."

"Cloud's between us and there," Mr. Desoto said. His hand closed on the butt of the pistol. "Has been for some time."

Percy messaged his wrist more intently with his thumb. The tendons stood out like he was having some sort of severe cramp.

"Has it, now?" Percy said. "I took a back way, so maybe I just lucked my way around it."

Mr. Desoto shifted his grip on the pistol and eased it from the waistband, holding the piece flat against the small of his back. Percy leaned forward a little bit as though it would help increase the pressure he put on his arm. The skin, red and inflamed, bunched up around his probing thumb. If Mica hadn't been watching so intently, he wouldn't have noticed when the skin tore in the thumb's wake. The swollen surface gave way to a deep blackness as if the frostbite actually originated from inside the arm and radiated out towards the surface.

"Mr. Desoto," Mica said softly.

"Not now, Mica," Mr. Desoto said. The teacher eased the safety off.

Meanwhile, Percy rubbed a trench into the flesh of his forearm, making it longer, deeper, and wider with each pass.

"Mr. Desoto," Mica said with a tug on the hem of Mr. Desoto's shirt. "I think you should back up."

Mrs. Tubble followed Mica's gaze and gasped. Percy looked at his arm then at the boy.

"I really meant to say I'm sorry," Percy said. "I wanted to tell you that. Wanted to tell you that. Wanted..."

Mr. Desoto took two steps back, drawing the pistol forward

and aiming it at Mr. Weaver. Percy rested his hands on his knees and tilted his head back. For a moment, it looked like he was simply stretching, but then, as his mouth aligned with his throat, where one would have expected the tilt to stop, the tilt continued. Percy's neck elongated, and the back of his head slid down his back.

Mr. Desoto fired.

Mica's whole body tensed from the sheer volume of the sound, and a sharp ringing flooded his ears. He could see where the bullet struck Mr. Weaver right in the middle of the sternum. The bullet exited through the middle of the back and punched straight through the teacher's skull and out the left eye socket.

For a moment, everything seemed frozen. Mica registered how hard Mr. Desoto clenched his teeth, and he only had one eye half open. Mica was suddenly aware that there had been a lot of noise in the room around him and that it had all ceased simultaneously. Percy's body halted its...changes, and every muscle appeared to go rigid.

Then, a strange black burble of gas welled out of the different entrance and exit wounds in Percy's body.

Sharp cracks erupted from his pelvis with a sound like a tree snapping under a bulldozer. His skin and muscle bulged with lumps the size of baseballs and softballs from his diaphragm to the joints of his thighs. The bulges roiled in waves underneath his clothing as though his body had been set to boil.

With an awful tearing sound, two purplish-black arms, dripping with blood and tangled with intestines, thrust from between Percy's legs. They worked themselves back and forth, tendons straining as they pushed to widen the gap through which they'd burst. Then, between them, emerged a large head covered in a huge nest of wet clumped hair. Shoulders followed, a whole, adult body rending out of Percy until its own waist either lodged against what was still intact of Percy's pelvis or the body ceased at the waist and shared a pelvis with its birther.

What remained of Percy had folded backwards, nearly in half, his neck having elongated well beyond the point where any muscles could hope to hold it erect. The new arrival slapped its palms on the ground and tilted its head to regard those who surrounded it. A woman's face, elderly and feral, oozing black lips baring brown and pitted teeth.

Mr. Desoto pulled the trigger as fast as he could, emptying the entire clip into the center mass of what used to be Percy. The rounds punched large holes through the beast and blasted chunks out of the wooden gym floor underneath the cots behind it.

The wounds started to smoke, thick black tendrils rising up. Then, something a bit thicker started burbling out. Mica recognized it as the same stuff that the black cloud was made of.

The old woman sneered.

"If you'd told me just last night that my son would be a part of something this important," she said, "I never would've believed you."

Then, the wounds from which the cloud seeped widened, and the cloud poured forth like exhaust from a factory chimney.

Mica did the only sensible thing he could. He turned and ran, heading straight for the doors to the main part of the school.

CHIEF HOLLER

Chief Holler woke in what she recognized as the back of an ambulance. Medical debris lay everywhere, and she lay on her side with the gurney tipped halfway over her. One of the doors hung open, attached by a single hinge. It was badly bent, and the red and white flashing lights reflected off everything outside, discordant with the fluorescent white interior lights that flickered and hummed. She thought she could see a boot, maybe even a leg, lying just at the edge of what she could see out the door, but it was exceedingly difficult to focus.

She felt herself groan, but she couldn't hear it. Her ears felt plugged, like when she wore her noise-canceling ear protection at the shooting range. When she tried to swallow, she could feel lines of sharp, tearing pain radiate all the way down her esophagus, but the sensation seemed strangely distant, as though she was imagining it happening in someone else's body.

Somewhere, in the back of her mind, she heard her mother's voice say, "They told me my daughter was here."

Her hands and feet seemed to keep banging against things of their own accord. She caught flurries of motion as her elbows and knees moved in and out of her field of vision. Was she suffering convulsions? Had she lost control of her muscles? Was it some sort of intense electrical shock? She could barely recognize the different parts of her body, and none of them would listen to her. She wondered, fleetingly, if paralysis felt somewhat similar.

Indeed, it seemed as though her body was growing increasingly distant. She felt as though her thoughts were sinking into some sort of pit, a field of blackness growing between herself and the outside world. It reminded her of those geometric sketches of gravity wells and black holes, where the center of the vortex vanished off towards infinity. Would she ever stop? Where was she being pulled?

She tried to make her consciousness turn around, to view back from where it receded, but doing so filled her with a cold dread, of an intensity she never could've imagined possible. At the same time, she felt herself sinking into a deeper and deeper chill, as if it were reaching towards her with a breath that drew all warmth into itself.

There was no way her heart still beat.

There was no doubt that she was somehow getting devoured. Ripped from herself, consumed by a void.

Maybe she was headed to wherever the cloud had come from. It had to be.

She desperately clawed for her body in her mind. She was certain that if she could only find some way to grab a hold of herself, she'd be able to overcome what had taken hold of her.

In the back of her mind, she heard, "They told me my daughter was here."

Then, she felt a deluge of cold and hate and despair torrent from the bottom of the well towards the world through her consciousness, like nothing she could imagine. It was a violation, simultaneously spiritual and cellular. There was nothing left of her but a desire for what was happening to her to stop and a perfect clarity that it never would.

THE SOURCE

The Source's arrival at the door was met with an explosive shudder that radiated out into the world like a tsunami. The earth cracked in jagged lines like massive cartoon lightning bolts away from the portal, and the ground itself rolled in a heaving wave that bucked roots straight from the soil. The trunks of every tree within a thousand feet exploded in a shower of splinters. The rain, which had frozen in sheets in the frigid cold of the cloud, shattered into billions of tiny crystals.

The presence that threatened to cross the threshold was not compatible with the physical universe or the light and energy that infused its make-up. Reality strained against the will that infringed upon it like an over-inflated balloon. Time warped like a wrung towel, with pockets speeding hours into minutes, while others slowing seconds into days. Gravity waxed and waned, and the boundaries between dimensions pressed against each other like tectonic plates, threatening to buckle. The bodies within the cloud surrendered all definition, recombining in the way liquids do when poured into the same glass.

A space where no universe or dimension existed, opened up in front of the doorway as The Source made Its first attempt to reach through, and then disappeared as The Source retracted in an agony that can't be measured on any experiential scale. The Source couldn't yet break the barrier. The presence that infused everything rejected It.

But, It had discovered something interesting. The vessels within that place carried within them entire universes independent of anything. Though those universes were separated from everything else in some fundamental way The Source did not yet understand, the vessels they commanded could act on the world freely. They could bring the key, the missing piece, back to the door.

Interim 4
Still-Life With Crib

Were someone to ask him, Stuart would not recall the event, at least not in any direct way. His memory stored one piece of the event as a flash of a house he'd built out of generic Lego blocks. He remembered it because he'd figured out how to overlap bricks to make a sloped roof, held up by nothing more than itself. He stored another piece of it as a flash of his brother's purple and puffy cheeks, except that he hadn't associated the thought with the appropriate gravity. Rather, the only times he remembered that skin tone, that look of his cheeks and lips, he thought of his brother being silly, fooling around.

He didn't remember because the primary experience was recorded in very simple terms: this was the day his mother slapped him across the face hard enough to spin him.

He didn't remember that it was a Saturday morning. He was four and Mica was two. His father had been out of town overnight in Summerset, Massachusetts as part of a reorganization of a cluster of stores. Coincidentally, it was one of three times William Bradley slept with one of his co-workers in upper management, occasions he saw as bearing no relevance to his family or anything regarding his emotions.

Regardless of what his father was up to that morning, mom was throwing together a special breakfast, since she knew her children would miss their father. She didn't make breakfast often; she was a cut-up-some-fruit-and-pour-some-cereal sort of woman in the mornings. As a result, she'd gotten rather absorbed in cooking, because she wasn't used to trying to tell whether the bacon was done, or if the yolk was just runny enough.

Stuart had woken early, and Mica had slept in. Stu knew well enough to keep clear of mom on a cooking morning, so he'd stuck to the living room, enjoying Saturday morning cartoons, the one time of the week where the TV and its programming were the exclusive province of the Bradley children. After about an hour, he'd found himself restless on the couch, tossing himself from one end to the other, laying against the throw pillow, laying on the throw pillow, laying under the throw pillow.

In the grand scheme of things, there would never be any reckoning of what precisely had caused Stuart to head up to his room in search of the Lego house he'd built the evening before, but he did, and there you have it.

If he'd stopped at his brother's door on his way to his room, he might not have looked in on his way back, and he certainly would not have been carrying the plastic brick house when he did.

He ambled to his room. Maybe he yawned, scratched the back of his head a little bit. He might've stopped and looked at his bookshelf while considering sitting on his floor and reading a minute; he often derailed his course to do so. Of course, had he done so that time, his brother would've been dead, but it's quite possible that the pause could've been instrumental in bringing him to the door at exactly the right time.

Instead of stopping for a book, he traversed the floor to his bed and reached underneath it. There, his hand found the house. He slid it out and picked it up. He left the room.

Mica's door was right at the top of the stairs. One reached the landing, turned right to face the hall, and immediately, the boy's bedroom was there on the right. Stuart's room was just past it, across from their parents' room.

Perhaps Stuart heard something, perhaps not. Either way, he paused in the open doorway; their parents both refused to allow closed doors in the house, even their own. The blackout curtains kept the room much darker than the rest of the house because Mica was a light sleeper.

It wasn't really like Stu to look into Mica's room while he slept. At that age, he thought very infrequently of his brother unless his brother was in the same room. This time though, he didn't just glance in and walk on—the attention he could've been expected to pay.

Perhaps it was the odd motion of Mica's feet kicking that caused the stop.

Stuart cocked his head and squinted towards the daybed, which had been recently converted from a crib. It was a rich reddish-brown wood with a vivid lacquer. The mattress, of course, was only three inches thick and less than six inches off the ground. Mica had learned to climb out of the crib; it was deemed better to risk him wandering about unmonitored than to risk him taking a bad fall.

He hadn't fallen, nor had he wandered about.

It was difficult for Stuart to make it out, to put it together though, so he stepped slowly into Mica's room. His brother was wiggling his legs around in sort of an up and down walking motion, then they jerked a bit from side to side like he was trying to rub something off his ankles. Stu reached up and flicked the light switch, and that was when the purple cheeks were emblazoned into his memory, even though they somehow lost their context.

Mica's whole face was purple. His eyes bulged and his tongue was sticking out. Stuart couldn't tell right away, but his brother had managed to twist his blanket around his neck and snag it on a screwhead that had worked itself loose.

The house had fallen from Stuart's hands and shattered. Even at his age, he knew something was wrong, so he ran straight to his brother. His hands grappled with the blanket, and it quickly gave, so easily that it was as though it had been waiting for him to try and make it give.

He listened for his brother to breathe. He'd expected a huge gasp, but the huge gasp didn't come. He leaned forward, so focused he didn't hear his mother (who'd heard the Lego's crash), come jogging up the stairs. But he did hear the slightest rasping of breath.

To be fair to her, the scene was distressing. Her baby, her sweet, little boy's face was still vivid purple, though it had slightly more pink in it. He'd all but stopped moving. His neck was angry and swollen.

And there, over him, stood her four-year old with a twisted blanket clenched in both hands.

She crossed the room in three steps. Her hand reached out like a claw and spun Stuart sharply by his right shoulder as her hip pivoted and swung her other arm in a sharp arc.

The slap shocked through the air like a miniature thunderclap.

It had taken some time before he managed to find the words and the will to explain what had happened.

Her apologies and tears poured over him for days after.

The truth was, she'd never trusted him again.

Chapter Eight
The End Has Always Been

THE VISITOR

The Visitor rode atop one of the black beasts. The other black one clutched a Heather Bradley that was too terrified to scream as it loped with its three free legs. Veles rode atop the white. The Visitor thought it was a decidedly unusual way to travel. It was a shame Veles couldn't make doorways of his own. Being bound to physical linearity sucked.

Veles looked back at the creatures and their passengers.

"The journey will not take long," he said.

The Visitor nodded. The vessel's memories held several recollections from old films of characters riding atop steeds, and The Visitor couldn't help feeling a bit of the thrill Stuart would've felt at such a scene. Stuart had been fond of creating things with his mind. He just hadn't mastered the ability to bring his creations into a shared reality the way The Visitor had done with the door, but he'd been quite proficient for a member so relatively young in his species' lifespan. Of course, in The Visitor's frame of reference, the door had taken hundreds of millions of years to craft.

Really, it was difficult to reconcile this new identity. The Visitor had believed that once the prior occupant had left the vessel, it would be a fresh start. It hadn't understood this species' identity involved an intermingling of soul and the electrical networks of the brain. At times, The Visitor found Itself slipping almost entirely into Stuart's thought patterns. In a way, It almost wished that would occur. It couldn't help feeling guilty; It hadn't wanted to take a life, but It had been planning Its escape from the void since the beginning of the universe. It couldn't let the loss of just one life cause those plans to unravel.

It took a moment to regard Its guide.

"What's your stake in this?"

Veles visibly bristled his shoulders.

"Beyond preventing the cessation of earthly existence?" he said. "Maybe I just like the air here."

"You knew I was coming."

Veles eased the freakish beast he rode to a stop. His eyes were narrowed. The Visitor didn't like what It saw; the expression held something reminiscent of The Source, The Abomination, as Veles had called it. Stuart lacked a word for the emotion it reflected, but it was something akin to loathing.

"I did," Veles said.

"You steered me here," The Visitor said.

Veles sighed.

"You could have broken through anywhere in the universe," Veles said. "From outside of time, I watched near infinite permutations of your arrival. So many ended in us all consumed within The Abomination. Of the few that ended otherwise, the largest proportion begin in this place, especially the ones in which you succeed in your escape."

"It matters to you if I succeed?"

"It doesn't," Veles said. "Only that I help you succeed."

"That Which Is won't care," The Visitor said.

"No," Veles said. "My die is cast."

"Then, why?"

Veles smirked.

"What other motive does anything possess?" Veles said. "Survival."

The Visitor hesitated and looked back at Stuart's mother. She wasn't hurt exactly, but her fear addled her beyond the ability to reason. It was hard to believe that Veles could not have found a gentler way. She was headstrong, but caring. At least her other boy should be safe on the other side of the cloud. It had been oddly difficult not to bring him when they'd watched the light from the hospital windows, but it had been for the best. The father figured in too, but Stuart had felt as troubled by the man as he'd been enraptured. Having feelings for a family troubled The Visitor greatly. Even though the fate of the Universal literally rested on shutting the door before the Source broke through, somehow not lying to Mica and making sure he was okay, vied to supersede all other competing priorities.

When It had approached this world through the endless dark of the void, Light had drawn it, but It had sensed something bright in a much more precise spot. The Light was stronger in that place. Love resided there, and the promise of protection. Thus, The Visitor had expected some sort of avatar of the Nature and the Light. So far, It had found a world of advanced animals and then, this Veles.

Veles didn't strike The Visitor as what It had expected; any added variables could be the end of everything. Something had gone wrong somewhere. Had The Visitor understood the reality, it would've come at a different time, in a different place. At the same time, The Visitor couldn't help but consider that its own judgment was clouded by Stuart's invasive memories. Could it just be a human child's irrational love for his mother preventing clearer vision? Maybe all this apprehension was the manifestation of irrational anxieties. The young of this species were prone to such.

The Visitor's thoughts were interrupted by a whimper from Heather.

"Must you scare her so badly?" The Visitor asked.

Veles grit his teeth.

"Let me tell you something," he said. "I've seen a billion futures and each depends on a billion factors. Every choice I make leads to the most possible way existence doesn't end. If the means are ugly, it is because the ends are hideous. Some are utterly unspeakable."

Then, Veles let out a long sigh.

"But, I've lived among humans long enough to find no challenge in ignoring the suffering caused by their weakness," he said. "You'll adapt."

The Visitor felt the urge to depart. To hop off the monster upon which it rode and make its own way as far as possible from this place. There had to be better help here.

As if following the same train of thought, Veles said, "There are better elsewhere, but you came to follow my call and now there's no time to seek out another."

The Visitor locked eyes with Veles.

"If I believe the path on which you lead us will destroy the world," he said, "I will go back to where I came."

Veles cocked his head. His expression read with nothing but calculation.

"There is no scenario in which you do that where I don't tear this woman and her other child to pieces," Veles said. "I've waited for you since the dawn of time."

With a sharp motion of his hand, Veles called his beasts into motion. None of this sat well with The Visitor. Veles could not be trusted, and his goals were unknown. The Visitor could not say that Veles's assistance would cause things to end badly, but It doubted that they'd end in what would traditionally be considered "well."

MICA

Mica stood panting for breath at the T-intersection and looked first left and then right. He'd only stood planted in indecision for a few seconds, and it had only taken a few seconds to run this far down the hallway from the gym, but given what he'd fled from, it might as well have been an eternity.

The screams and clamor still echoed strongly. They wouldn't for long.

He had to choose now.

To the left, all manner of artwork hung on the walls, collages from each class on whatever theme they'd had for the session. Ducks on a pond was one of them. To the right, there were orange and white striped barricades and caution tape, heaps of unmixed cement, a pallet of tile. The floor was torn up with cordoned off holes all the way to the basement in some places. The drop tiles were missing in swathes from the ceiling and bundles of wires dangled from amid the pipes and rafters. One day, it would offer cutting edge STEM education. Now, it offered the possibilities of salvation, broken ankles, and painful falls.

At the end of both hallways, doors led to the outside world, but Mica already suspected he'd find them locked. Even if they weren't, Mica realized he had no idea how close to the cloud he'd emerge out of either one at this point. What if it had already reached the school? What if the school were entirely immersed within it?

If so, was he already doomed?

That was the moment that the main lights blinked out and scattered emergency lights popped on.

Mica rocked back and forth on his heels, still no closer to deciding. He wanted to run, but he felt like every direction was the wrong direction. He tried to imagine which side of the school the cloud would reach first, but he really didn't understand the layout of the neighborhood or the school at all. The roads were all so meandering.

He did understand that down the hall from which he'd come, hardly a hundred feet behind him, stood two shut double doors. On the other side of those double doors, Percy Weaver had turned into some monstrosity that Mica couldn't comprehend. He'd run before he really knew what was going to happen in the gymnasium, but he couldn't imagine it turning out in any way that he wanted to see. For all he knew, whatever Percy had become could burst through those double doors at any second.

Thus, the matter at hand: left, or right?

He started left at a soft-stepping trot towards the art rooms. At least if he had to hide, the lack of lighting would give him a fighting chance.

Halfway down the hall, a door burst open and Mrs. Tubble rushed through. The side of her blouse was drenched in blood, and she had both hands pressed against her lower ribs on the right side. She shuffled with a limp, sobbing between breathless gasps.

Mica instinctually looked for some place to hide, but her panicked gaze found him before he had a chance. Her lips quivered, but she raised her chin. She kept one hand pressed to her wound, but the other seemed, for a moment, to try to straighten out her disheveled appearance.

She shuffled closer.

"Turn around," she snapped in a sharp whisper punctuated by her gasping breaths. She threw a helter-skelter gesture towards the far end of the hall. "I think it's going around to those doors. Can't go this way. The new wing. The new wing's outside doors. A bus. A bus is waiting."

"What happened? Are the others okay?" Mica asked as he turned.

"No," Mrs. Tubble said. "Maybe. I don't know."

She patted the boy on the back and pointed.

"The new wing is an 'L,'" she said. "Doors are at the end."

"Is it safe to go outside?" Mica asked as he ducked underneath the caution tape. Bits of construction debris crunched under his feet.

"Can't be worse than in here," she said.

Mica almost said he wasn't so sure. He'd seen the cloud. He'd felt its pull, and he had a nasty feeling that as hideous as Percy Weaver had become, the darkness was capable of producing far worse.

Mrs. Tubble gasped, and her hand clamped hard on Mica's shoulder. He craned his neck and looked back.

A flashlight beam shone out of the door through which Mrs. Tubble had come. Footsteps echoed like hammers, whoever they belonged to calling, "I don't care if you hear that I'm here." Mica immediately understood that either it was someone who had no idea what was happening or the cause of what was happening.

Unfortunately, as the light panned towards the STEM wing, and the figure emerged from the door, Mica couldn't even make out a full silhouette. The bulb was like a brilliant star. The best the boy could manage was that he felt kind of certain the feet were in boots, which, after what Percy had turned into, was in itself somehow a mild relief.

"Who's there?" a stern and crisp voice called out. The beam fell squarely on Mica and Mrs. Tubble. "I'm with the Millwood Police Department."

Mica smiled and rose. Mrs. Tubble whimpered, and a tension visibly fled her shoulders and neck. Her hand even loosened on her side, and in the light, Mica could see that her blouse was torn, and even in the brief moment of reduced tension, a gush of blood welled from the gash.

The figure lowered the light and stepped closer. He was indeed wearing a Millwood Police Department uniform, and the sight couldn't have been more welcoming if it had turned out to be Santa Claus ready to fight evil with Christmas magic and nuclear flamethrowers. Mica wished the man's drawn firearm was equally comforting, but a gun hadn't done much good for Mr. Desoto.

"Who are you? What's happening?" the officer asked. "I heard gunshots."

"I'm Mrs. Tubble, and this is Mica. I'm a teacher here," Mrs. Tubble said. She pointed in the direction of the gym. "Mr. Desoto fired the weapon. He and I and some others were attacked in the gymnasium, and he tried to defend us."

The officer took another step, and the glow of one of the emergency lights caught his face. He looked a little exhausted and dirty, like he'd been clambering around in the woods, but more importantly, he looked really familiar.

"I'm Officer McCorville," he said. "Are there other people okay in the building?"

"I-I don't know, every-everyone..." Mrs. Tubble said, and then she stumbled a little. More blood welled out between her fingers.

"She's hurt really bad," Mica said.

Officer McCorville looked at Mica and then at Mrs. Tubble's side. His brow furrowed and worry splashed across his features.

"Shit," he said. "You need a doctor. Radio and phones are all down."

"I'll b-b-be all right," Mrs. Tubble said, clenching her teeth. "I can walk for a little longer."

"Ma'am," Officer McCorville said. "We need to get you to my cruiser. I at least have a first aid kit, unless you think it would be safe enough to get to the nurse's office."

Mrs. Tubble laughed once, and a glop of blood dribbled down her chin.

"I don't want..." she said. She swallowed and took a deep breath. "I don't want to spend another second in this place."

Then, she fell over sideways. Her head struck one of the bags of cement with a dull thwack. Her hand fell away from her side, but now the blood pumped out weakly, even though it was uninhibited. Mica sobbed.

"Son of a bitch," McCorville said, dropping to one knee. He set the flashlight down, the light shining on Mrs. Tubble's face. In its light, her skin looked tremendously pale. Her eyes were wide open, and she kept trying to swallow. Her throat was making a sound that was a combination of a click and gurgle. Her fingers were shaking.

McCorville looked Mica square in the face.

"There's nothing I can do to help her," he said. "We need to get you out of here."

Suddenly, Mica realized how he knew the officer. He probably would have realized it before were it not for the circumstances.

"You talked to me in the hospital," Mica said.

McCorville nodded.

"Wasn't sure if you recognized me," McCorville said quickly, giving Mica a quick pat on the back. "Didn't want to bring it up since I'm pretty sure it's not a great memory, and your night's not gotten any better."

Somewhere in the school, fresh gunshots rang out and sent

McCorville back on his feet, flashlight and pistol in hand. He pointed into the construction.

"Quick," he said. "Door's all the way at the end. My cruiser is on the other side of the bus."

Mica lurched forward. His feet made progress. His left arm did not. His shoulder jerked hard, his feet kicked out from underneath him, and he hit the ground on his side. Something hard bit into the skin just under the ball of his thumb and painfully pressed into his wrist bone.

He rolled over and looked up his arm. Handcuffs glinted in the flashlight beam. The other end of the cuffs was attached to Mrs. Tubble's ankle.

"What the hell?" Mica said. He pulled against the restraint. Mrs. Tubble's body shifted a bit against his weight, but he had no hope of pulling her. Her face seemed to register the faintest shifts of expression at being disturbed, but nothing more.

Officer McCorville looked down. His face was wrought with pity.

"I was really worried about you and your brother," he said. "But, I must admit, I was worried more about Stuart than about you."

"What's going on, Mr. Officer?" Mica asked.

"I didn't actually get to see the Nexus myself," McCorville said. "My eyes weren't ready for the cloud yet, I'm afraid. Now, they don't do so well with the light. But we have your brother to thank for that."

Then, McCorville turned the flashlight off.

"And soon," he said, "we'll have you to thank for so much more."

Mica screamed and thrashed against the cuffs. The metal against his wrist was blindingly painful, and no matter how hard he dug in with his heels and threw his weight back, he could barely budge the teacher an inch.

Then, McCorville started to shake. He grabbed his collar and ripped his shirt open, buttons popping off and clattering in the dark. He reached up with both hands and plunged them through his own chest. Ribs cracked. The flesh squelched with a sound like sticking one's head into a vat full of shredded, raw chicken.

He jerked his hands to opposing sides and an avalanche of body parts fell out—arms, legs, shoulders, feet, fingers, heads.

They must have belonged to many people. It should've been impossible for them to all fit in his chest cavity. McCorville grabbed one of the heads by the hair, tore his own off, and smashed the new head against the stump.

The new head sucked in a massive breath and rolled its neck as if to make itself more comfortable in its new seat.

Mica screamed repeatedly, short shrill bursts, one after another.

It wasn't enough to release his terror. What he'd just witnessed and what he now stared at drove him "out of his mind."

The new head belonged to his father.

HEATHER

Though the rain had stopped and patches of sky had begun to let bits of moonlight through, enough droplets still fell from the branches to the forest floor that the sound of rain continued almost unabated. Hanging upside down, Heather clasped her biceps because it felt better than letting her limbs dangle. She was cold and damp, and her knuckles, knees, and elbows ached. Her shoes chaffed her ankles; she hadn't noticed it until she fought to keep them from falling off her feet into the darkness below. She flittingly regretted that this night did not end like so many others, with her drinking chamomile tea at her kitchen table while arranging photos in her albums.

She wished that she'd waited for William before trying to find Stuart. It wasn't that she expected some magic husband solution, but she knew it had been foolish rushing out into the storm, even if she'd known precisely where Stuart was heading. Even with the warning Mica gave her, finding him had been her only consideration. She'd failed to anticipate beasts and beings and doppelgangers. She hadn't anticipated an enormous black cloud swallowing her town. Where were the police? Where were the helicopters and the tanks and the men in white suits and massive bag outfits designed by Ziploc? She'd seen hundreds of emergency broadcast tests since she was born. Why wasn't she hearing that buzzy tone everywhere she looked? If they weren't bringing order, shouldn't they at least be maintaining the appearance of order?

Instead, the world seemed to be coming apart at the seams, and her with it. Was she really being carried like a ragdoll by some towering aberration? Maybe she'd tripped and hit her head, or maybe she'd still been in the car when the accident happened. Stuart had disappeared so many times before, for so many different reasons. The constant had always been that upon his return, order was restored to the House of Bradley, even if that restoration involved groundings, spankings, or the forced donations of toys. It would be better to wake up to *that* order, even if it was in a hospital bed.

But, she'd already lost Stuart (though that was a tremendously confusing concept, since she'd also, in a sense, just spoken with him). Now, she felt like she'd lost her husband and Mica too. Hopefully, they were still in the hospital, unaware of what was happening, or being evacuated far, far away. She hated not knowing where they were.

On the other hand, better to have them anywhere other

than waiting on the outskirts of a grove for her imposter son and some sort of God to finish preparing a journey into the cloud of darkness to fight a demon from another dimension.

For the thousandth time of the evening, Heather wondered if she'd gone insane, just checked out of Hotel Reality. If she could run in any direction, she would, but the thing that held her was so strong she might as well have been encased in stone. Its black skin felt cold and dry, like an insect, but it seemed unexpectedly flexible—it seemed to mold to her contours rather than crushing awkwardly against them. The creatures made no sound as they moved, no creaking of joints, and despite their size, they somehow didn't crash through the bushes. She wondered if they could listen to her thoughts. Nothing seemed impossible anymore.

The air took on a strange resonance, kind of like the Helmholtz frequency in a car with one rear window open. She let herself look at what was no longer supposed to be her son. He—it?—glanced over at her. His eyes trembled and his lips quivered. His cheeks seemed to forecast the path of tears. Heather's heart twinged. Part of her saw her son distraught, but part of her saw that whatever wore his expression was far too advanced in experience to be considered her son.

She wanted to demand It tell her what It wanted, but It spoke first.

"Your boy's memories are becoming my memories," The Visitor said.

"Should that mean something to me?" Heather asked.

"They were like looking at photos in an album at first," The Visitor said. "But the more I've walked with them, the more they're like *'a well-worn coat'*—to borrow a way he might have explained it."

Heather felt something stir inside her. It was both desperate longing and burning anger—like oil and water swirling in a jar.

"It's hard to carry something so intimate in such an intimate way," The Visitor said. "I don't feel I have a right to it. Do you want me to pass them on to you?"

"Gah," Heather blurted out a massive sob she didn't know was coming.

The bridge of Stuart's nose crinkled. His eyebrows drew together. He reached out as if to take Heather's immobile hand. Even if she weren't hanging the way she was, she wasn't sure she wanted to touch it.

"You're in almost all of the ones that seem to matter, you and his brother," The Visitor said. "I think he'd want you to have them."

Heather stared at Stuart's hand in horror for a moment. Could this *thing* do that? Was that even possible? Then, fury wrenched her.

"How dare you," Heather hissed. "Bad enough that you took all that he was—the things that were his alone—but then you presume to give them to someone else? What the hell *are* you?"

Tears welled in Stuart's eyes. Heather wondered if they were real or an act. Could the thing inside Stuart really cry? Did it feel like Stuart had—like people do? What in God's name was she even talking to?

"I'm sorry," The Visitor said. "The only understanding I have of emotion comes from your boy's memories. If I offended, I didn't mean to."

There was something quite earnest in the voice that spoke to her—a confusion that she didn't know could really be faked. "And you might want to know—the more time I spend in this body with these memories, the more they become a part of me. There will come a point when I can no longer recognize the division between my mind and his."

"So..." Heather asked hesitantly. "Is it possible that you go away, and he takes back over?"

The Visitor sighed. "No," he said. "If I left this body or receded too far, the body would simply die, as would all the memories within. His soul is no longer here."

It was then that she realized that Veles had dropped back and rode the white beast on the other side of her from Stuart. Stuart wiped away his tears.

Veles smirked. "Are those yours? Or the child's?"

The Visitor's upper lip snarled in a way that might have looked truly menacing on an older face.

"Let's end this," The Visitor said.

"And see who gets to watch who die," Veles tacked on with a laugh.

Heather grit her teeth, knowing exactly who among them she would like to watch die.

BREWHOUSE

The rearview mirror shook badly with each lurch of the police cruiser, making the image vibrate and distort. The road behind was empty, which left a pit in Brewhouse's gut. She clenched the wheel so hard her knuckles ached and the pads of her palm hurt. The leather seat and her uniform were wet with her lower back sweat.

After they'd pulled Holler from the cloud and loaded her, non-responsive, into the ambulance, Brewhouse had set out in the cruiser to escort her boss and friend to the hospital. She knew she could've stayed to take over the coordination, but she was too distraught by this newest blow. She hadn't seen herself as out of the fight, just in need of a pause between bouts. So, the drive to and from the hospital had seemed wise.

Then the shockwave, or whatever that had been, hit. The ambulance had swerved or slid—Brewhouse had been too focused on controlling her own vehicle to tell—and rolled. At the same time, something had seized up in the cruiser's suspension with an awful grinding of metal. That same grinding now shuddered through the vehicle, and it limped forward in an erratic, jerking kind of way, as though it had a flat.

Again, she looked in the rearview. She both hoped she'd imagined the whole thing and that she wouldn't see the cloud behind her. After the first jolt, she'd been about to exit her own vehicle to see if she could help Holler and the medics when a second shockwave blasted through, and a smaller version of the cloud had bloomed from the ambulance, swallowing it whole. Of course, for all Brewhouse knew, the ambulance was still there—but there was no way in hell she was going to take the chance of touching that awful black shit.

Instead, she'd hit the gas. The vehicle could only travel a little faster than she could've jogged, but now she was hoping to make a much longer drive. She had a suspicion that everyone who'd been near the cloud's edge when the shockwaves began, was dead, or whatever happened to people inside the cloud. That meant there would be no one to report what had just happened.

Brewhouse tried the radio again. So far, she'd picked up no signals and received no response on any channel, official or civilian. Ahead, her headlights lit up the trees. The bushes were wrought with shadow under their leaves, and everything looked sinister and menacing. It wouldn't take more than a few minutes before she'd drive past roads that led to Amherst or Milford, but Brewhouse felt like the world itself had turned against her and that there might be no "far enough away" for her to feel safe ever again.

Then, a new shockwave hit that spun the vehicle into a screeching, sideways stop. As slow as she'd been going, Brewhouse lurched against the belt and whacked her head against the window as if she'd been going thirty miles an hour. A tingling weakness swept through her entire body. As she recovered from the shift in momentum, she checked herself in the rearview mirror. Her hair had turned white, and her skin held a shriveled, waxy quality. A bit of blood smeared her temple.

She noticed a bit of blood on the glass too, at the epicenter of a spiderweb crack.

She gasped, though not at the blood—rather at what she saw through the side window.

The road—the air itself—ahead had, for lack of a better word, fragmented. A band of nothingness full of floating somethingness stretched across the road and off to the sides as far as her headlights lit. She could see a chunk of earth topped with black asphalt and one of the golden road reflectors hanging, as if by wires, several feet above ground level. A bit of sparking powerline wafted like a charmed cobra. All around it were chunks of road, dirt, grassy clods, parts of trees and stones— all floating like they'd exploded and then been frozen in time just as they started to expand.

However, they didn't really float in the air—her mind simply tried to fill in its understanding of what it was looking at by connecting it to a familiar concept. Instead, the space between them simply didn't exist. On the far side of the phenomenon, the road resumed, but Brewhouse wasn't sure it was really there—it somehow struck her more like the two-dimensional storefronts in an old western movie. The difference was that, despite how limited a stretch the paltry high beams of her vehicle lit up, she had no doubt that this façade formed a ring to prevent escape in all directions. Something like this didn't just happen. It was there to prevent her, prevent everything, perhaps, from crossing, or maybe it was just everything falling apart down to a level she couldn't even comprehend.

Either way, she couldn't see any options for herself.

Instead, she picked up the receiver, tuned to an open channel she hoped might connect to somewhere, and pressed the send button.

"To anyone listening out there, this is Officer Brewhouse of the Millwood PD," she said. "I'm sending this transmission because I have reason to believe that all roads leading out of town, at a distance of perhaps a twenty-mile radius from the epicenter of the black cloud phenomenon, may no longer be accessible. Any operative law enforcement and first line responder units in the area should maintain order. Keep people in their homes. They won't be safe there either, but they're less likely to hurt each other. Tell them to lock their windows. To block their vents. Do not let the cloud in."

She set down the receiver. The broadcast had been oddly draining. There was so much more she could say, but it was hard to feel like it mattered, especially since she didn't even know if anyone had heard. The engine sputtered when she turned the key, and then it failed.

Even as it did so, the radio burst with a static crackle. Then, she heard her own voice broadcasting over it. Every other word squelched out, but there was no doubt it was what she'd just transmitted. She felt like it was mocking her. Looking out into the void, she felt like she could make out a police cruiser on the other side, facing her. Like the world beyond was a mirror, and as she leaned forward, putting a palm to the glass, she could swear she saw herself in that far driver's seat. She didn't know what was happening. Couldn't even guess.

What she did know was that her partner was home without her. If she'd heard any of the emergency broadcasts that *had* gone out, then she'd be worried sick.

So, she opened the door, and stepped out. It would be a couple hours walk to get home, but maybe she could get there before everything died.

HEATHER

When they came to a stop, Heather's body trembled with the exhaustion of being at such an intense level of fear for so long. Her body felt sticky and oily in bands where that thing had held her—and trickles of blood seeped from her skin. Whatever they were, their skin had latched onto hers through her clothes in a deeper way than just surface contact. Now, she burned like she'd been splashed with scalding water.

The beast laid her down in a stretch of muddy grass. She shivered as her weight settled, but the cold moisture soothed her seared flesh. Ahead, Veles slid from his beast and Stuart—what was supposed to be Stuart—reached the ground with assistance from the beast who bore him. Beyond him, blackness, a massive roiling wall of blackness. It was like a towering thunderhead at ground level, and she could feel frigid air cascading off of it.

The Visitor looked back at Heather.

"What is it?" she asked.

"It's like its breath," The Visitor said, "cooling the heat off this world so it can eat it."

"Shouldn't we be going in a direction where that isn't?" Heather asked with a sardonic, spent chuckle.

Now Veles looked back with condescending sympathy in his eyes. "Our destination is at its center," he said.

"How?" Heather asked. "I don't know what the hell is going on here, but going into that looks like death."

Veles closed his eyes and reached inside his coat. He pulled out what looked like an old lantern.

"I brought light," he said without looking back.

Heather raised her eyebrows. She realized that as scared as she'd been just moments before, she felt completely calm now. It reminded her of her father's death. He'd passed a little after

Stuart was born, from skin cancer. It had started in his left temple just past his crow's feet, but by the time they'd diagnosed it, it had metastasized. None of the surgeries had taken, and they'd wrecked so much damage on his face and body. She'd cried so hard and so long from diagnosis to death, it had been months before she'd been able to cry again. It felt the same now, with fear.

"I wouldn't bring that camping," she said.

Though Veles smirked slightly at her comment, Heather could tell from the lines on the side of his face that something was bothering him. He gazed completely motionless for several moments. Heather could hear the wind rustling through branches and in hollows between houses. Drops blew and fell from leaves and eaves and everything except the cloud, spattering erratically in all directions. From the cloud, no sound came. Nothing. Was Veles listening for something? Did he see something she couldn't?

Veles gave a precise flick of his wrist and the three beasts lumbered forward into the cloud. When they vanished from her sight, Heather immediately felt a magnitude of relief she didn't know was possible.

"Where are they going?" Heather asked.

"Our adversary has its own avatars," Veles said. "Mine go to intercept."

Veles pressed his lips together and clenched his jaw. Spikes of darkness jutted out from the cloud like stalactites and drew back in, and an undulating ripple buckled from left to right. Heather's mind fought to give the movements sound; the silence made it feel even more unreal.

"It will take the weak," Veles said. "Those with holes inside that allow it entrance. It will take the dead too, though for them the uses are far more limited."

"Why?"

"Because it can't just enter our world," Veles said. "The Light will not permit it."

"So, then why are we even worried?"

"There are loopholes. There always are," Veles said. "The darkness is already here, in the hearts and minds of people. Until it corrupts and bends our world enough for its presence to fully enter, it will hunt for its quarry, lest it escape again."

"You mean, Stuart?"

"Yes," Veles nodded.

"What happens if it finds him?"

Veles shrugged.

"Then it will be able to enter this place unobstructed," Veles said. "And every light will go out."

"And this 'Light' that won't let it in won't stop it?"

"In its own way, it already has," Veles said. "It's broken this town, and the rest of the area within the influence of the cloud, off from the real."

"What the fuck does that mean?" Heather asked.

Veles raised the lantern up over his head. When his arm fully extended, the lantern ignited a creamy, bluish-green light, much like the illumination at the pond. The light rose up like a firefly caught in an updraft, swirling on air currents, illuminating the winds themselves. Along the ascent, Heather could make out the towering edge of the cloud of darkness rising like some obsidian thunderhead. It struck Heather that the light should have diminished, grown smaller, but it was like she—or part of herself—was rising up along with it.

Then, the cloud tapered off like the slope of a dome of unfathomable size. It quickly blended into the regular nighttime darkness, but the light kept rising. Like it was on its way to become a new star—

Until the sky ceased, in something that registered in Heather's mind as something akin to television static. That didn't get it right, of course. Really, it was more like the blind spots she got in the hours before a migraine, except that it canopied the whole world. She could still see the stars beyond, but the best way she could describe them was that they looked irrelevant in a way that she'd never seen before.

Then, the light vanished, as did Heather's motion with it.

She found herself back on the ground. A moment of vertigo wobbled her. For half a second, she wasn't sure she was in control of her body enough to keep herself upright, but she managed it, while feeling like a kite in a storm. Her hands pressed to her chest; she was breathless, and it took a single enormous gasp to force her lungs to expand. As she took several deep breaths, she looked at her companion.

"Was that the darkness too?" She asked.

"No," Veles said. "In simple terms, we've been quarantined. Or perhaps, more accurately, amputated. Either we shut the door and stop the darkness, or the darkness will fill every bit of this corner of the universe."

"That's just great."

Veles smiled broadly, a deep smile, one that reached his eyes and forehead.

"Isn't it, though?"

Veles's hands moved in a way that reminded her of a puppeteer controlling a marionette, and his focus intensified until he seemed wholly absorbed in his thoughts. Heather suspected he was still directing his creatures, even though she couldn't see a thing beyond that barrier. What was happening in the darkness? She pictured those old Japanese monster movies with Godzilla and Gidorah and Mothra—titanic beasts flinging each other about, biting with cavernous maws, shredding with enormous claws. If those monsters were real, the terror would be—but that was the thing about those movies. There was no way anyone watching could believe they were real. Likewise, now, something about the whole situation struck her as absurd. If she hadn't experienced such relentless fear and pain, she would have thought none of it was real.

She was about to say something about it to Veles, or Stuart, or maybe just herself, when her attention snagged, like a hang-nail on a shirt sleeve, on something off to the side. She turned. A rectangle of the air seemed to shimmer and wobble like a heat mirage over a road in peak summer sun. She stepped slowly towards it. Maybe it was a bad idea to approach it, maybe not, but frankly, there was nothing she could or couldn't do that seemed like a good idea at this point. In fact, it seemed pretty likely that any course of action she could possibly follow would in some way result in her horrible death.

So, why not check out the pretty shimmer? It reminded her a bit of the light Veles had made, but somehow cleaner. More desirable. It pulled at her, gently at first like a thread coming loose from a collar. Then, a bit more insistently. She realized that her body wasn't moving towards it, but rather her mind through a vast space around her consciousness she hadn't known was there until just this moment. When she'd been younger, she'd periodically undergone sensory deprivation therapies to relax and reset her anxieties, and this struck her as remarkably similar to the way the mind started to feel more real than the body in those exercises.

Then, when her mind reached the shimmering plane, the transition through it like passing through a thin plastic sheet that left her enveloped in a bubble. Part of her felt entirely stifled by it, as though it really was plastic and would suffocate her, but part of her felt shielded and protected.

Beyond it, however, was something that caught her next breath in her throat. Heather couldn't say exactly whether she actually saw what lay before her, or whether it was real in terms of shared experiential reality, but the place conveyed the impression of a shore beside a wavering pond with luminescent water. Bolts of lightning spit up from the surface like the electric tendrils off a tesla coil. There was something crystalline and pristine in the blue light they gave off, like it was some sort of perfect aquamarine stone converted into an effervescent form.

Across the pond on the far shore, towered an oak as massive as a redwood. The leaves were dense enough so that they seemed to form a shell around the whole oasis. Its branches thrust out in all directions from the trunk, the largest branches thicker than a man. The trunk itself was wide enough to drive a car through, and its roots bulged great rises in the soil all about the shore. Through the water, all along the pond bed, the same roots twisted and gnarled like great arthritic knuckles, looking strangely naked among all that light.

Beyond the roots, in the place where shadows should have been if everything wasn't glowing, vanished many deep holes that disappeared beyond their own bending paths. Heather had the immediate impression that she should see some sort of serpent or eel weaving in and out among the roots, snapping up pale fish and watching the branches above every chance it got. She felt she should step forward into the pool and wade out deep enough to swim into those passages. No doubt she would drown, ensnared perhaps in some tangled roots or simply lost among twists and turns, but somehow it seemed that wouldn't be so bad. It struck her as thrilling, as taking a chance for something big.

It was almost as though something physically took hold of her gaze, pulled it up from the water to the trunk of the tree and dragged it slowly skyward. Her eyes saw the grooves and ridges of the bark in intense detail. It looked as though she were standing right at its base with her nose just inches away, and somehow getting closer and closer until the grain of the bark itself seemed to enlarge, and as it enlarged it clarified into symbols, each one a hexagon with three lines traversing the center that bisected each angle.

Then, the number of lines increased, tinting blue and orange, becoming more like the streaks in a cornea than anything geometric, except that there was no pupil in the middle. Heather realized, too, that she felt with absolute certainly that they were watching her. She reached out automatically, her fingers extended, the desire to place her palm on the tree of eyes undeniable.

Just before she made contact, the tree blinked.

It wasn't that the eyes blinked—though they did. Heather couldn't quite fathom what had actually transpired, but the closest way she could process it was that the tree blinked. Its nature closed, the light of the water snuffed, and then the tree opened, and the light returned. In the process, Heather and everything around her ceased to exist, and then returned. Heather wasn't even sure how she knew that much.

In her mind came something akin to a burst of static, and then another. Heather pressed her palms to her ears, but the third burst came unimpeded. The sound seemed to originate from within her mind, which Heather thought made sense, since she was pretty sure she wasn't any place real to begin with. She'd watched enough sci-fi and horror to figure she'd taken what might be best considered a detour.

The static squelched again. Did she hear something in it? Was it really white noise? As Heather listened, she found static rising out of the air around her, not a burst now, but a steady drone. It sounded kind of like the way the static of the TV would fade into her dreams when she'd fallen asleep in front of old-school TV channels as a kid. The static seemed to fill everything, she even thought she could see that black, white, and gray grain of a dead channel in the air around herself.

In the distance, she felt like she heard something. A gravelly sound, regular but not rhythmic. She began to understand it as words among the hiss.

You are not meant to be here.

"Well, hello there," Heather thought. "Can't say I wanted to be here. Or that I know where here is."

You are in sanctuary.

Though Heather still saw the static, she also simultaneously saw the pond and tree again. Through both, she felt an impression of an eagle in the top of the tree.

"So, you're an eagle, huh?"

I am Perun. This world chose the eagle as my face.

"Alright," Heather said with a sigh. She hesitated a moment as she realized that she might not actually have a physical body to sigh with. "So, what's the score here? Am I alive or dead?"

Here, that which was and will be, is and is not.

"Oh, that's just wonderful," Heather said, or thought, or whatever it was she was actually doing. "So, you able to tell me what on God's green earth is happening out there?"

I offered sanctuary to the Refugee, but Veles led It to another door.

Heather frowned.

"With all those eyes, you didn't see that coming?"

I did. But it was the Refugee who chose to whom to listen. Now the Abomination has arrived.

"What is The Abomination?"

The creation of the enemy.

"Which enemy?"

The only enemy.

"What does it want?"

For all to be It.

"That doesn't sound like it's made of roses."

Its nature is frigid suffering.

"Okay, so can you stop it?"

The Refugee made Its choice. It is no longer of my concern.

"Can I stop it?"

It is not my concern.

"But you brought me here."

No, you just found a door that was open.

"So, what the hell good are you?"

I make no attempt to understand your affairs. Why do you bother yourself with mine?

There was a pause and a rustle in the leaves.

You may stay here until you die, if you choose. My sanctuary cannot be violated.

"Oh, that sounds just phenomenal," Heather said. She couldn't believe she actually wanted to get back to where she'd just been, but there it was. She opened her mouth to ask to be returned, but before she could, she felt herself receding. She became aware of her body, of the cold, the wet of that hellish night. Her limbs were almost completely numb and felt like they were made of leaden sludge. Her consciousness slipped back through the window that had first drawn her.

THE VISITOR

The window had disappeared, and Heather stood looking off into darkness, the cloud to her right. Veles still stood staring at the cloud with rapt attention. Within the cloud, had Stuart's memories not been so invasive, so infectious, The Visitor would have been able to see every detail of the battles taking place. Instead, It had only been aware of the feeling of utter savagery within. He'd watched that impenetrable barrier and knew that a violence unlike the world had ever seen since its primordial state, was occurring, and that knowledge had given him further misgivings about his "partner."

Veles seemed capable of a darkness not unlike the nature of

their enemy, and not all enemies of your enemy can be your friends. The Visitor might've still been thinking about that, considering that maybe he might be better off on his own, had he not become aware that something singularly unexpected was occurring in regard to Stuart's mother. One moment, Veles had been showing her the fracture in reality, and the next she'd seemed to vanish entirely from his awareness.

He'd barely registered it before it was over, and she had returned, blinking vacantly. He lunged over to her and took her hand.

"Where did you just go?" The Visitor asked.

HEATHER

Heather found herself paralyzed. She tried to speak, but her body refused to listen. She felt out of sync. It seemed like her mind and body were separate, interlocking machine parts, and they'd been crafted a fraction of a millimeter out of alignment. She'd felt similarly moments before, after Veles had taken her mind into the sky, but now it was much more pronounced, more severe. No doubt it was a side effect of seemingly being pulled out of her body. No way that didn't leave a mark. Somewhere in the back of her mind, she vaguely heard one of those fast-talking voiceovers from medication commercials listing side effects.

The child who couldn't possibly not be her boy—not in the real reality—stepped forward and took Heather's hand. His skin felt cold and clammy from the wet of the night, but there was something about the contact that she could only describe as "deep." A strange sort of energy passed from his skin into hers, and she felt something intangible shift into place, like a button sliding into its hole. Her fingers wiggled, and her whole body shivered as it realized just how long she'd been out in the cold.

"Where did you just go?" Stuart said. "What did you just see?"

"A place," Heather said. "A tree, a pond. It was all bright."

"Was he there?"

Heather really had no idea if Stuart was asking about the same "he," but how could there be something different?

"Yes," Heather said.

"Is he coming?" Stuart asked.

"No."

Desperation filled his face. Heather knew that look. It was the exact look that had been on his face the day Mica had nearly died—a look of pure need. Although Heather no longer harbored the same resentment, any time she'd consciously thought about it, the aching wound had been there. This was the first time she felt like it was a scar, instead. A light seemed to go out in Stuart's eyes. His shoulders shrunk inwards, but he nodded.

"Then we continue on," he said, with a glance to Veles.

"Is there no other way?" Heather asked. She hated the thought of spending another moment in the company of Veles and his beasts.

"Not now," Stuart said, "Not since we've been broken off."

"Before, then?" Heather said.

Stuart shrugged limply. "Don't know," he said. "But I do not believe I chose our help well."

Heather reached out and placed a hand on Stuart's shoulder. With her other hand, she reached up and brushed his wet hair out of his eyes and off his forehead. She knew it wasn't her son, but she felt like she was forgiving him. Tears rolled down Stuart's cheeks.

"I think," The Visitor said, "I may have killed us."

"It's okay," Heather said. Heather wiped one of the streams with her thumb.

"You didn't know."

"I should have," The Visitor said. "Before I fled, The Source and I existed outside of time. We could see the general path of every different future. I didn't know that when I got here I'd be trapped in the linearity of your reality. I didn't realize I was that blind, and I think I have been deceived—but I can't tell anymore."

"What are you, really?" Heather asked.

The boy took her hands in his.

"Your son's memories," The Visitor said. "I am so much them that I can barely remember what I was before."

"But you're not him," Heather said. Her heart dropped at the words as she realized just how much she didn't want them to be true. "And you never can be."

"No," The Visitor said. "I can't."

Heather took a deep breath. A thousand questions fought for control of her tongue, but she also knew that understanding it didn't matter. What mattered was that her son was dead and gone. She'd followed this thing out into the night and left her other son alone. And she had a strong suspicion there was no way back.

"I guess I don't have much of a choice..." she stared to say.

"Wrong. Absolutely wrong," The Visitor said, shaking Its head vehemently. "Choice is all you ever have. About anything. It's the only reason a conclusion in our loss isn't forgone."

The Visitor pulled away from Heather. A mist hung in the air around them, barely visible in the dim light. The cloud was nearly upon them, still expanding, still undulating. He looked squarely at Veles, "Meet me Outside."

Then, The Visitor stepped into the cloud, vanishing as abruptly as if he'd passed through a curtain. Heather gasped.

Veles looked back at her over his shoulder.

"Not to worry," he said. "There without the grace of God goes us."

"You can go to hell," Heather said.

"Great lengths," Veles said, holding up a single finger. "Great lengths I've gone to avoid that, and they will not be undone."

Veles reached into his coat and removed another copper lantern. This one, he set on the ground beside Heather. It was about the size of a softball, round, with an arced, wire handle. An old, tarnished knob protruded from its base.

"Catch up if you wish," he said, "and you will have no problem finding the way."

Then, he raised his own lantern and started forward. Unlike the way the cloud had simply seemed to swallow Stuart, it parted around Veles and his lantern. It bucked and thrust into the edges of the light bubble like it was angry at being repulsed.

A few steps later, it closed behind Veles, and Heather was alone at the edge of nothing.

She swallowed hard. Behind her, she could see a backyard through the trees. There was a chest high picket fence. Beyond it, an illuminated house. Heather figured it must be running a generator, because the neighboring houses were too dark to even be seen. Its windows were lit up, and she thought she saw silhouettes of adults and children through the curtains, moving from one room to the next. A back-porch floodlight threw its beams into the backyard, and Heather could see a glinting jungle gym, and a closed sandbox shaped like a turtle. An old-fashioned rotary push-mower was tilted against the house by the air conditioning unit and a coiled-up garden hose.

Across the distance, she felt certain she heard someone laugh. That someone cued up music on the stereo, soft bass and an upbeat horn section lit up the silence.

She could be there in less than a minute, knocking on the

door. They were a family. They sounded like they were having a good time. It would be safe. With the electricity out, she doubted they would have a working phone, but if they had a generator, maybe they had some sort of radio. Maybe one of them could even drive her back to the hospital so she could try to find Mica and Will. How could she not do everything in her power to spend her final moments with them?

Or, maybe she could just join this family for a late-night dinner and a drink and weather the whole thing out. They'd laugh and eat finger foods and dance. It would be an island against the end of time. When that island finally failed, they could fall upon each other, ripping and tearing, blending their bodies and minds, becoming one another...

Heather bit her lip hard and the pain snapped her to focus. She looked back to the cloud. It was inches in front of her. Spires of itself lurched like spears from its mass. Though they appeared to miss her physically, she felt them reaching into her heart and mind, piercing them from all angles. Each thrust felt like it left a stain within her, a seed that promised to burst. She remembered seeing some nature show about things like botfly larva and those wasps that laid eggs in a host so the babies could eat them from the inside out. She felt infested.

So, she knelt and picked up the lantern Veles had left. It was light, almost weightless, and it emanated a most unusual smell —sweet, but acrid, like a perfume gone wrong. She turned the knob until it gave a soft click, and a tiny blue flame leapt onto the wick inside the glass. The whole lantern seemed alight with it, and she felt a strange tingling in her fingers that spread through her hand and down her arm.

Immediately, the things she'd felt burgeoning inside her were driven out, and she realized that she was giving off a faint glow. The cloud buckled away from her, from the glow. The light reminded her of the glow that had infused Perun's grove, just a little bit...sickly. Nonetheless, it made her feel a great deal calmer. It was time to get to the end of things one way or another. There would be no running back towards town, no hiding in warm, lit houses.

So, she strode forward, hoping she would be able to find Stuart and Veles in the Cloud. The darkness gave way before her light, but only slightly, leaving her with a radius only a few feet in diameter, just enough to see the grass, leaves, and branches beneath her feet. She didn't know how she would find Stuart and Veles in the emptiness, but somehow, she knew there was only one path they could travel. The world swallowed by the darkness didn't work the same way it had before. All paths would lead to The Source.

Momentarily alone in the darkness, headed inextricably towards what she felt could only be her death, she immediately felt a surge of regrets. How many times had she turned Stuart and Mica down when they'd asked her to read a book or play a board game? How many games of pretend had she sidelined herself for, or even worse, ignored for chores or work? Throwing balls around and bike riding was what fathers did with their kids. Now, as far as she knew, neither of her children had any time left, and that made it feel like she had all the time in the world. She was jealous of any houses nearby, of parents who sat within with their children, even if all they did was watch the windows in the hopes that they'd suddenly be able to see something out of at least one of them again.

Heather kicked up her step and tried not to look back. She was essentially following the corpse of her dead son into darkness because what else was there? It was only a matter of moments before all she could think about was that the stars that had been overhead had never been there at all, and that the darkness towered over her like a mountain.

Though she couldn't tell from where she stood, she knew

the cloud still grew, faster now than before, and in a moment, even faster still. Soon, it would cover the entire town. Then, it would fill the bubble of existence that had been amputated from the rest until it burst like an overfilled balloon. Nothing could stop it. Its spread to the whole of the universe was inevitable and any measure against it was nothing but delay. Why was she even trying? What could she possibly do to stop it? She was so small, so insignificant. Nothing she'd ever done, nor ever would do, could possibly matter. It would be better if she just stopped. If she just sat and gave up. Maybe turned off the light altogether.

She looked down at the branches and leaves upon which she walked. She'd been vaguely aware of them crunching under her shoes, but now she realized that they weren't branches and leaves at all. She was walking on tiny, white bones, sheets of peeled skin and desiccated fur. Shards and fragments of femurs and ribs of all sizes lay littered over everything, most stripped bare, some still with sinew hanging off them like loose threads, bits of muscle and pulps pulsating like they still sought to contract.

At first, she thought they looked like they belonged to animals—birds, raccoons, deer—but then she started to note the unmistakable jaw bones and eye sockets of human beings. The ground itself, somehow, seemed dead, dried out, used up. What remained of bushes and tufts of grass were browned with an oily sickness, oozing an inky sludge as they visibly decayed. The rocks themselves looked as though they were rotting, bubbling and evaporating.

How could she possibly fight against such ruin? *It would corrupt the planet to its core*, Heather thought. *Eventually it would reach Will and Mica.* It was that thought that gave her the strength to resist against despair. If they had been taken, maybe she could've given up, but that was why she was here. That was why she trotted through the darkness holding, what she could only think of as, a magic lamp. The only hope she had to protect her family was to go forward. Veles had said her presence mattered, and if there was any hope, that was a flame worth keeping alit. She couldn't help laughing at the thought though. At first it was a chuckle, but then the laughs shook her belly. Then, she was almost doubled over with it.

She practically walked straight into Veles, and colliding with Veles was like walking into a wall. Stuart now walked beside him. The bubble around Veles and Stuart was much larger than the one created by her own lantern. Veles now held what looked like a shepherd's crook, from which dangled a lantern larger than her own, his ornate and wrought with all manner of symbols and pictograms. Within the lantern burned not one, but three flames, and Heather realized that they were vaguely in the shape of people. Them.

"We can't stop here," The Visitor said.

Heather laughed harder.

"What the hell's the matter with you?" Veles said.

"It's just...so...damn funny," Heather howled. "Who the hell am I to be doing this? What am I even doing here?"

"A chain of a thousand miles can be broken by removing just one link," The Visitor said. "Every fifth link is you."

That made Heather laugh even harder.

"And listen to you," she cackled. "Are you a freaking monk? Did you spend your free time in the other dimension pondering metaphors you might use when you actually went somewhere people existed?"

"Be silent," Veles said.

He held up his hand palm out and Heather's jaw locked. She could still hear herself laughing, but the volume dropped instantly as well as the urge to laugh any longer. Veles lowered his hand.

"You gonna kill me? Make me cease to exist?" Heather said, though she didn't feel like she meant to. The words seemed to pour from her mouth on their own. "Feed me to his monsters? Rip me to pieces? Annihilate me?"

"Maybe," Veles said. "Or maybe I'll just have my servants cease defending us against the things that live in the darkness."

The Visitor cleared his throat. It shouldn't have been a loud sound, or even a particularly noticeable one, but it seemed very loud in Heather's ears.

"It's The Abomination making her say those things," The Visitor said. "It knows exactly where we are, and it has now realized that I am here. It's coming at her because it knows she's the weakest link among us."

For the first time, Heather noticed a droning groan rising around them, a sound like steel girders bending. The air had taken on a thick, syrupy feel as though compressed by the soundwave. It had arisen so gradually that she hadn't even realized it was happening. Everything felt sour, like something one might feel in a tomb that water had seeped into for a millennium. The momentary hysteria was entirely gone now, replaced by a cold dread.

"What's happening?" she asked.

"How deep do you think a beetle could crawl into your mouth before you get tired of it being there?" Veles answered.

Veles raised his lantern higher, and its light intensified, further pushing back the darkness. However, the bubble of light ceased its expansion around twenty feet in all directions. Heather knew immediately that this new barrier wasn't quite the same as the fringe of the cloud that had just been pushed back. Though its behavior defied anything she might understand, the cloud she knew was still, in essence, just a cloud. However, within it, was a darker, more physical thing, something that walked the line between liquid and gas. It seemed more like water hidden underneath a film of oil, or perhaps the way the bottom of a pond stayed liquid during deep freezes.

Veles pointed to the canopy the light had generated that protected them. It undulated and bulged in places, like hands pressing against a taut sheet. Open and gnashing jaws pressed against it too, appearing ephemerally at random like demons. Heather saw clusters of eyes opening and closing, a sea of faces twisted in torment and anger. She could see their teeth and their tongues sticking out of their mouths. Welts and boils covered their cheeks, lacerations an inch deep, protrusions of shattered bone. They were the faces of teenagers and children, and she could hear them whimpering and moaning as the boundaries between one and the next melted, their features bleeding into one another.

Beyond that, a wave of pressing dread surged down in pulses, giving Heather the impression that some massive being hovered over them, reaching to grasp them in an enormous palm. Even as she watched, the fluctuations grew more urgent, more intrusive on their space. The end result was clear: it was only a matter of time before the light collapsed under the assault.

Already, she felt their infestation, despite the light of her and Veles's lanterns, as corkscrews of spiraling darkness lanced through the protective boundary. She felt as though she were standing in a slowly closing iron maiden.

Heather reached out and found herself almost able to touch the mass of victims. She wanted to comfort them, to tell them it was going to be okay, to tell them it was a mistake. That they must not have known they were doing something wrong to bring themselves there. That everyone makes mistakes, but they needed to accept the punishments for those mistakes, that it was only just for them to be punished, that everyone deserved punishment. That punishment was the price for existing. She needed to pay that price too. She stretched her arm out even further. *Bite*, she thought to the mouths. *Bite the muscles. Bite through the bone. I must be erased.*

The groan suddenly grew so loud and so present that it morphed into a physical thing—a bright red, barreling force. Her scream couldn't quite match its pitch, even if it seemed to go on forever. There were hands upon her. Some were pulling her away from the throat she had fallen into, and others were simply trying to pull her apart. She felt a searing pain as her muscles pulled against their sinew and tendons, trying to rip themselves free from her. She could feel the desire of every different part of her to join something out in the darkness. There was something there that she belonged to. That she had always belonged to.

Her husband was there, and her sons were there. She needed to join them. To be one with her family.

She had already lost. There was no more reason to fight.

Then, the white light came with such an agonizing force that it seemed to level everything around her like a nuclear detonation.

Heather's vision reeled. The light had been unlike anything she'd ever seen. It had come so fast. She couldn't say how long she'd been blind, but it had been some time. She hadn't been in darkness, but rather, she'd been seeing something more kaleidoscopic. Blotches and swirls of color overwhelmed her vision. They were thinning, and she felt like she was becoming aware of space beyond them.

Had she been consumed by the darkness? By the light? Had Veles done something? Stuart? Something else?

She felt the need to move. Her brain didn't send any messages to her legs or arms. It wasn't her body that needed to travel, but rather her soul or spirit. She felt like the motion wouldn't move her in space as she knew it, but that the travel would occur along a pathway outside that space, through a void she'd never fully understood was there but now recognized.

As she grappled with this new desire, some sort of path made itself known to her memories. She wasn't able to "see" it or understand it through her senses, but rather something more instinctual. The path itself felt as narrow as a balance beam, or perhaps more like threading oneself through the eye of a needle. In all directions, chaos loomed. It wasn't the chaos she'd seen in horror movies where people suffered elaborate tortures or shrieked in mad gibberish. There were no monsters or nightmarish tentacles attached to the monsters of her psyche. There were no teeth or claws or snapping, spined tails. It was chaos on a quantum level, a place where the rules of reality ceased to impose order.

She had the sense that if she strayed in the slightest, she would be annihilated in every possible sense.

The hardest part was that she wasn't travelling in the traditional sense. She wanted to step carefully, but the concept of feet felt irrelevant to moving forward. She felt the impulse to extend her arms a bit to increase her balance, but her arms felt like pointless mental constructs. She wanted so badly to rely on her body and her five senses.

Then, came the whisper. It wasn't a whisper, really—rather, more like an understanding in her mind. It wanted her to slide off the path. It promised that she wouldn't believe the kind of pleasures she could find there. Bliss like the most powerful drugs awaited, except that it never had to end. She could be herself, nothing but herself in perfect ecstasy. All she had to do was slide off the path. She'd be able to get right back on. Just a little bit off. It would be effortless, and it would so quickly ease her worry. She worried so much; she must be tired of worrying. The whisper promised she would be free of worry. That she would be in a place where she could just remain quiet. Quiet was all she'd really need, after all. It was something she obviously deserved. Was it fair that she had to fight so hard for it?

The thoughts felt oddly soothing. Heather could easily step back and rationally understand it as a temptation tactic—but it wasn't that easy.

She could feel the things it offered—though distant, diffused, and filtered. She could feel rushes of joy and bliss—if she turned her thoughts towards them in the slightest, they heightened instantly. Massively. When she looked away, it pained her, as if she'd never feel like that again. It was an agony of absence.

The absence grew, like a well overflowing inside her. She could feel it consuming more of herself, ceaselessly swallowing more and more of her being.

She was still on the path. She had to stay on the path. It couldn't consume her entirely if she stayed on the path, could it?

It couldn't destroy her so utterly if she did exactly what she was supposed to do, what she needed to do, could it?

What if she just couldn't get there fast enough? What if there simply was no winning? Maybe the path itself never existed in the first place, and what she thought was her following an instinctual trail, was just her pretending she knew her way in the endless dark. Her eternity could be simply pressing on into the void as bit by bit of herself was destroyed in increments, but only enough to feel something had been lost, leaving a proportion of what was left but never all of it. Eventually, losing herself more and more would be all she would know.

How could there have been hope.

Even without hope, her time in the woods had always taught her to follow the path, so she would keep following the path.

It didn't matter. She would burn with a cold the likes of which she couldn't imagine for a length that defied any comprehension, even in a geological scale. She would feel the agony of the components of her soul getting obliterated. All traces from her existence would be taken out of time to deprive her of any solace of the times she'd spent outside of utter torment. All-

All-All-

Then, a door.

In a field of ash, she stood facing the door. It was a simple, wooden door like any other door she'd seen, and it stood open to some sort of non-existence on the other side.

To the right, a towering oak so withered it looked made of paper had grown from a hollow riddled with desiccated cattails and disintegrating lily pads. The oak's massive roots clutched at the ground like hands in agony. A human body lay in the fetal position underneath one of its arches.

To the left, a tower of flesh; bodies merged and twisted and melded into each other in mimicry of the shape of the dead tree. The faces within remained silent, but half of each mouth moved as if to scream and howl while the other half appeared to cackle and grin. Tendons strained and muscles visibly ripped as they fought against the intertwinement. At the foot of the tower, the three beasts of Veles lay decimated, their bodies rent, torn, and dismembered.

In the middle, a door. Free standing. Emptiness in front and behind.

Ash drifted down from the sky. There was no wind, so the ash fell almost perfectly straight down.

Veles stepped up beside her.

"I'm going to need to ask you to hold on a moment while we confer," he said.

He rested his hand on her shoulder. She felt a massive jolt

like an electric shock lurch through her body. She collapsed, barely able to breathe, her heart barely beating. Her ears filled with a burbling sound like rushing water.

STUART

This Stuart knelt by his mother. The Visitor was a technicality, It told himself. Mother, *Mommy*, lay in the ash, her heart barely beating, her breaths shallow. She had fought her way there for him. For everyone. A human who'd brought herself so far beyond anything her species was meant to see, The Abomination attacking her mind the whole way. Amazing she'd come so far, that her heart held so much power. He loved her so much.

Stuart knew he really wasn't exactly himself—that he was just his memories in his body, but he could no longer recognize another part of himself to define himself by. The Visitor had gathered the last bit of Itself and lashed out against the encroaching darkness just before Veles's protection had failed.

Now, all that remained was, in essence, a facsimile of Stuart, like a minted coin, an imprint of the original. It wasn't quite the same as giving Heather back her son, but it was the closest The Visitor could come. It seemed strange, in a way, how the child valued its mother's life so much more than his own. Even as It felt it, The Visitor had been unable to understand, but the power of that love had caused the release of energy that now held the darkness back, that now gave them one last chance to reach the door.

Stuart rose. He took in the tree made of people, and the dying tree, but did not know what to do with the information. It might as well have been some sculpture in a Halloween garden. The Visitor might have understood better, but its memories had extinguished almost entirely when the shockwave erupted, and the scattered fragments that remained made about as much sense as an unassembled jigsaw puzzle in a pile without a picture to work from.

Stuart met eyes with Veles, who lifted his hands in a "What do you expect me to do?" way.

"You brought her this far," Stuart said.

Veles grinned. His teeth were nasty and yellowed, pitted at the edges. His breath smelled rank and fetid.

"I've not traveled a thousand miles with coins in my pocket," Veles said, "only to dump them in a fountain, or in some poor neophyte's bowl."

"My mother is not an alm to give," Stuart said.

Veles sighed.

"She's not your mother," Veles said. He seemed to rise in height as anger loaded into his words. "And you are not a child. You are not a human, nor are you something that belongs in this world."

"And yet, here I am," Stuart said.

"Here *we* are," Veles snarled. "And I'm not going to let the fact that you've forgotten yourself get in the way of me getting what I came for."

Veles pointed to the door. Stuart looked at it, really looked at it for the first time, and a part of his mind fell into place. He remembered standing in the woods, marveled by it, how he'd opened it and been baffled by the paradox of its handles. He remembered throwing the rock through and how he'd fallen when the cloud began its egress from the void. He supposed it made sense that he'd end up where he'd begun—except that, as he considered the door, he also knew it was no longer the door he'd left. The Source had reached the door and established a foothold in this universe. They were out of time.

Stuart blinked, and when his eyes opened, what Stuart had

thought was an open door now looked, to him, exactly like his brother. Behind his brother stood his father.

Veles took a step forward and knelt to address Mica.

"You have been expected," he said.

Mica looked at him.

Stuart wondered what part of his brother was still there. The Visitor had thought Stuart was lost, but It had underestimated how much of him had been contained in his memories. Perhaps The Source had made the same mistake, and Mica's essence still waited at the edge of consciousness. The Visitor had not understood something very basic about Stuart's nature —It had not been capable, and Stuart suspected The Source had erred in the same way.

Their father glanced dismissively at Veles and then focused on Stuart, Mica's eyes shifting to Stuart as well. It wasn't their father, of course. Their father had become a mouthpiece for The Source. Stuart could see the will of The Source woven all around him, binding him. Annoyance flitted across Veles's features. Father's mouth opened, but the words came out of Mica.

"You failed," he said. "The door is wide. The Light will fail, and I will devour this universe like I have the others."

Stuart shuddered. He could feel something like shackles reaching towards him from his brother and father.

"You can have this world," Veles said. "I brought yourself back to you. All I ask is that you allow me to pass from this world to the place from which you came."

Mica looked about slowly. At the tree. At the tree of flesh. At the bodies of the beasts, at Heather, at Stuart. Heather's breath quickened, even though she did not awaken. Her hands spasmed. Above them, the tree of flesh clawed at invisible things in the sky.

Mica's gaze lingered alternately between Stuart and Heather, but then Veles stepped forward, shoulder's back, his crook and lantern gripped firmly like a wizard's staff. Mica met Veles' gaze with the air of a trainer looking at a dog that had shamed itself.

"You come to bargain empty handed?" Mica said.

"The essence is within the vessel behind me," Veles said, gesturing towards Stuart, without looking.

"The essence never ceased being mine," Mica said. "It is a part of me, even if it denies its own nature. If you think you possess it sufficiently to use it as your bargain, then you come before me as a thief."

"I'm not here to bandy words," Veles said. He lowered his shepherd's crook between Stuart and Mica, the dangling lantern flaring sharply, the flame crackling with anger.

Then, the crook fell from Veles's hands. The lantern shattered on the ground. Its flame sunk into the ash and extinguished. Veles's eyes widened. His mouth drew into an 'o.'

Something invisible, a spasm of will made into a scorpion's tail of force, lashed out from Mica and impaled Veles. It snapped him up into the air. His arms and legs kicked weakly, futilely. His shape distorted and blurred, and then it tore into pieces that tore themselves into pieces that tore themselves into more pieces. There was nothing left by the time he should have hit the ground.

"Lesser gods," Mica smirked.

Then, it regarded Stuart.

"Are you ready to return to me?" Mica said. "We look like brothers now, but we should be whole. One."

Stuart couldn't deny the temptation, the pull he felt. It promised to suck in all the fear, all the uncertainty, until everything became nothingness, perfection. Looking at the form of his brother, Stuart knew there was nothing he wanted more than to be with his sibling. They'd been there for each other their whole lives, even when protecting the other meant damaging themselves. That was why The Source had chosen the form. It sought to use that bond as something of an olive branch.

For the first time, however, the veil of The Source's power seemed to be pulled back, and Stuart recognized something else underneath. As unstoppable as It seemed, It was also in Its final moments of despair.

It needed Stuart to reach out.

Stuart's father and Mica both reached out.

"Come," they said. "Be family."

The Source needed The Visitor to return to It. To *choose* to return to It.

"Be one, again."

Stuart shook his head. He didn't want that.

"Stuart, listen to your father," they said.

"No," Stuart said.

"Listen, or there will be consequences."

"My father loved me too," Stuart said.

Then, he looked back to his mother.

The smirk faded from Mica's face. Its focus, too, returned to Heather as she groaned and rolled onto her back. Her arm flopped over her eyes, her cheeks and lips coated with ash.

Then, she sat up, and looked straight into the face of her son.

"Mica?" she said. "Baby?"

She took in her husband behind her son. The larger tableau.

"It has you both?" she said.

Then, she drew her knees to her chest, buried her face in them, and let out a monumental sob that lurched her whole body like an electric jolt.

Fear and concern etched across Mica's features. Stuart had been right—The Source did not understand how strong the memories of its vessel still were. And Mica had been purer, more innocent, more of The Light. Discord emanated from the doorway as Mica's memories fought The Source for control of the being.

"Stu," Mica said. "I can't hold It here much longer."

In that moment, Stuart knew what he must do. The only way to defeat The Source was with the one thing it could never truly foresee, could never conceive of as possible. He would uncreate the door.

In truth, that door, the real door, was within Stuart himself, just as The Source had found the doorway in so many others. Stuart, The Visitor, indistinguishable from one another now, receded back into themself. The world fell away from them as though they were falling backwards through a window into an abyss.

The well of self is deep and nearly infinite, except that it is defined as being itself.

When this Stuart reached the boundary of who he was, he saw a door there, the same door, in fact, but from the other side. Open. With himself standing in it. Stuart remembered vaguely how he'd attempted to circumnavigate the door when it was open and found it overwhelmingly difficult. How foolish he'd been to mistake his reality for the proper path.

It was so simple.

He reached through the portal, his arm stretched as far as he could, careful not to touch Mica or his father. If the Source realized too soon that he'd come to be there, they might, in their fear, find a way to interrupt. All would be undone.

There was no knob on the inside, but the door wasn't a physical door anyway, and his arm wasn't actually reaching for it. He took hold of it with his will.

The Source recognized what Stuart intended.

Its shriek pierced through every reality, every dimension.

Stuart unmade the door. The door was a part of him—just

as Stuart's memories were a part of him. It was a conduit that linked his body and soul. As The Visitor, he'd never been able to fully understand what made humans the universes they were. How they came into themselves like a Big Bang and departed like a whisper. Now, he understood that this door was his and his alone, and that always he'd been on both sides.

In unmaking the door, he unfortunately also unmade himself.

That was also the moment that Stuart Dexter Bradley not only ceased to exist; now, he had never existed at all.

MICA

It was another lonely summer for Mica. His mom was at work. His dad was at work. He'd spent hours watching television and playing video games, and he was getting too old for his toys. His parents had talked about a babysitter, but they'd decided he was too old for a full-time sitter. They only asked Ms. Krenshaw over on the nights they'd need to work late.

Of course, it would've helped if he had friends, but he just never found himself able to get along with other kids. He spent almost all his time immersed in his own thoughts. It wasn't that he didn't want to have friends, it's just that he somehow found himself unable to respond to anything they might say that he didn't expect them to say. He would simply freeze up.

As a result, he'd spent most of his life talking with his imaginary friend, Stuart. He liked to think that Stuart was his older brother, braver, bolder, always ready for an adventure. They settled the farthest moons in the galaxy, the deepest jungles. They built wilderness ramparts and mighty castles. They rode on dinosaurs and on giant spiders. One theme united all their quests, however; they always sought to keep some great, nebulous darkness at bay.

In the dark at night, Mica felt it clawing, there, inside his closet and under his bed, in the hall, severing his room from that of his parents. It waited in caves and abandoned buildings, in the shadowed places of the world. He thought sometimes he'd invented Stuart so that he wouldn't be so scared that something evil in the universe sought after him, and him alone.

Of course, Mica's parents hated Stuart. They'd beat the point to death that Stuart wasn't real, even sending Mica to therapists to "deal with it" or "fix him." They'd banished any talk of Stuart from the house, and if they thought Mica was "playing a Stuart game," grounding was guaranteed. Stuart games, after all, tended to get Mica in the most trouble because they made him late for dinner, left him filthy head to toe, or got him the most scrapes and bruises.

Sometimes, when she caught him playing Stuart games, Mica's mom would head off to the home office or the front porch of the garage. She'd find some place to sit and get all quiet, staring off like she was trying to remember something. Mica would creep close enough to watch. Sometimes, she'd weep softly but would say she had no idea why she was so sad if asked.

For the imaginary Stuart's part, Stuart hated when Mica played out in the woods around Coney Park, especially Widow's Winder trail. Mica thought it often seemed like his own imagination would argue with him, like it had a will of its own. Mica always tried to explain to his parents that Stuart was the one in the games who kept him safe. Who talked him back. It didn't matter. They never listened.

But on the days when Mica found himself really bored and neither his screens nor Stuart could slake his restlessness, he always found himself biking down to the trail head. Recently, he'd begun heading further and further in, and he'd gotten the idea to build a secret fort, a sanctuary from the world and all the people he could never quite talk to.

On this summer day, he'd left his bike at the trailhead, just off the road behind a thick cluster of bushes, and he'd begun collecting branches in search of just the right place to build.

And so it was that he stepped between two large trunks and found himself in a sort of a clearing.

In that clearing, stood a door.

He felt, in that moment, that something he'd been missing all his life was just on the other side.

End

Thanks

Thank you to everyone who has contributed to the process of the composition of this book. Thank you, Amber, my dear wife, for putting up with me during the writing process and for helping as my most valued reader.

Of course, a huge thanks goes to Patrick Reuman and Wicked House Publishing for taking the chance on bringing this book out to the world. Thanks as well to Christian Bentulan for the incredible cover art. Thanks to Renee S. DeCamillis and Guy Medley for helping polish the manuscript to where it needed to be. Thanks to everyone else behind the scenes who has helped with all the details of this long process!

In addition, thank you to my former teachers, Michael Knight, the late Allen Wier, Dale Bailey, Marilyn Kallet, the late Arthur Smith, Elizabeth Gilbert, Kathleen Driskell, Greg Pape, Molly Peacock, and Debra Kang Dean. So many folk have helped me on this journey, some directly, some indirectly, but I value each and every person who has lent me their time.

Another thanks as well to the folk at the Meacham Writers Workshop, *Symposeum*, *The Dread Machine*, and *The Showbear Family Circus*, as well as all the other editors and staff with whom I've worked. I've been long privileged to work alongside incredible folk in various organizational, editorial, and assisting capacities that have helped me grow as a writer and literary citizen.

Finally, thank you to all the other friends and family who've helped along the way: the kids (Gillian, Elliott, Alex, Ashton),

Tiffany Najberg, Mom and Dad, Curt Allday, Matt Urmy, Michael Allen, Travis Payne, Tyler Kraha, Richard Jackson, Earl Braggs, Mike Jaynes, Alex Quinlan, Katy Yocom, Christian Collier, Elissa and John Anticev, Autumn Watts, Caleb Jordan, Vanessa Gonzales, and John Compton. I know I'm forgetting folk right this moment, but I think of the people whose lives intersect with mine all the time.

CPSIA information can be obtained
at www.ICGtesting.com
Printed in the USA
LVHW041726300423
745689LV00004B/193

9 781959 798088